Prais
Then Like The Blind Man: ORBIE'S STORY

Reminiscent of To Kill a Mockingbird, *this sensitive and gripping coming-of-age story evokes backcountry Kentucky in the troubled 1950's in prose that's spare yet lyrical—a special novel worthy of joining the ranks of an illustrious Southern literary tradition.*

—Kindle Nation

With much of faith and learning, Then Like the Blind Man: ORBIE'S STORY is a strong addition to general fiction collections with a focus on coming of age tales.

—Midwest Book Review

Debut author, Freddie Owens, swings for the fences and hits a home run with his excellent coming-of-age story set primarily in Kentucky. If you're a fan of novels like The Adventures of Tom Sawyer, Huckleberry Finn *and* To Kill a Mockingbird, *Freddie Owens's Then Like the Blind Man: ORBIE'S STORY is a Must Read!*

—Douglas R. Cobb / Bestsellersworld.com

This is an exceptional book. The first thing that hits me when I begin a novel is the 'voice'. Who is talking to me? How do I feel about this person? Well, I can tell you I fell in love with Orbie—a nine-year-old who is utterly convincing—real, authentic and unique. Owens has created a character you will never forget.

—Ned Leavitt / Literary Agent

You can almost feel like you are there with Orbie at his Granny's and Granpaw's in Harlan's Crossroads. The writing is so very "real", with such conviction and description. Overall, I could read and read and read this type of writing. This author has nailed it!

—ABNA Reviewer

I love to read and a good storyteller and writer is valuable to me. I grew up in Texas where story telling is an art. Freddie Owens is a word artist. I very much enjoyed the simplicity of the story much like The Old Man and the Sea *by Ernest Hemingway. A great story is about the character of the individuals as they surmount the obstacles to achieve a purpose. As a best selling author myself I doubly appreciate a masterpiece of artistic creation. This is such a creation. Loved it! Thank you Freddie for the entertainment!*
   —*Tony Miller / Author of "I'll See You In Your Dreams"*

Freddie Owens...has an acute sense of the language and does a masterful job with dialect. I don't know Kentucky well, but I find his characters believable and that's what counts. The plot is both scary and affirming. I cannot say enough good about this book.
   —Poet Karen Douglass / Author of *Red Goddess Poems*

Gripping! A roller-coaster ride of emotions. Superb ending! Author Freddie Owens skillfully puts together a heart-wrenching plot, exceptional characters, and awesome dialogue and 'descriptions' to deliver an unforgettable story. The Kentucky setting in the late '50's is a perfect stage for this 'mind movie'. The heart, love, and determination of Orbie, the 9-year-old main character, will instantly grab your affection. .
   —Lee Carey / Author of *Sandbridge*

From the very first page I felt drawn into Orbie's world as if I were seeing it freshly, vividly, through his nine-year-old eyes. I confess I loved every minute of it! To me, this is the miracle of good writing.
   —Shoshanna Cooper / Tea Master, Painter

Then Like The Blind Man:

ORBIE'S STORY

A Novel

Freddie Owens

(aka Fredrick O. Wegela)

Blind Sight Publications

ISBN: 978-0-9829269-7-0

Library of Congress Control Number: 2012905405

Acknowledgements

It should first be noted that this book is a work of fiction. Names, characters, places and incidents are wholly imaginary and are used fictitiously. Any resemblances (of which there may be a few) to actual events or locales or persons, living or dead, is entirely coincidental.

That said, two memories served as starting points for a short story I wrote that eventually became this novel. One was of my Kentucky grandmother as she emerged from a shed with a white chicken held upside down in one of her strong bony hands. I, a boy of nine and a "city slicker" from Detroit, looked on in wonderment and horror as she summarily wrung the poor creature's neck. It ran about the yard frantically, yes incredibly, as if trying to locate something it had misplaced, as if the known world could be set right again, recreated, if only that one thing could be found. And then, of course, it died. The second memory was of lantern light reflected off stones that lay on either side of a path to a storm cellar my grandparents and I were headed for one stormy night beneath a tornado's approaching din. There was wonderment there too, along with a vast and looming sense of impending doom. For these and many others of my childhood memories I must thank my grandparents. Had I not been exposed to their homespun, wizened and sometimes carping ways I would not have been able to begin my short story much less this novel. The same goes for my dear, good-hearted parents who survived the bad times to enjoy the good.

I also want to thank Judith Guest (*Ordinary People*) and especially Rebecca Hill (*Among Birches*) for early and crucial writing guidance. Without their unsparing feedback and mentorship I might not have dealt adequately with the "false and unlikely" as it was wont to manifest in the early drafts of the manuscript.

Literary agents Ned Leavitt and Robin Mizell deserve special thanks for their deft editorial comments and for the considerable time and energy they invested in making them. I must extend kudos to Dave King as well for a thoroughly professional editing of the manuscript. (Google Dave King Editorial Services and his book *Self-Editing For Writers*.) No writer I feel would manage long without such editorial guidance as Dave King provides.

Much appreciation goes to editors Tom Jenks and Winn Blevins (*Stone Song*), painter and tea master Shoshanna Cooper, writer Rabbi David Cooper (*God Is A Verb*) and Boulder psychologist Ina Robbins for support and guidance. I wish also to convey gratitude to all those good friends and writing workshop attendees who gave this work their studied and undivided attention. Their inspiration was invaluable.

Inspiration came also from my work as a psychotherapist and from a life of spiritual seeking, which led to encounters with Native American Shamanism, Advaita Vedanta and Tibetan Buddhism, the latter two conveyed in the teachings of Chogyam Trungpa Rinpoche and Sri Nisargadatta Maharaj.

Finally and most importantly, this book would not have been possible at all without the help and unflagging support of my loving wife and lifelong helpmate, author and psychologist Karen Kissel Wegela (*The Courage To Be Present*).

In memory of Charley and Clara Kissel
And to Albert and Vela Wegela
And to Karen;

Were it not for them not a word
Would I have written.

Granny raised her eyebrows. "You know, you just about the smartest little boy I ever laid eyes on. Folks is funny down here, Orbie. They say they love the Lord, but then again they won't abide His people. You know what I'm talking about?"

"Uh huh," I said. "Like Momma. She says she loves Jesus too, but she won't let Missy marry no coloreds."

"Lord!" Granny laughed. "How did you get to be so smart?"

PROLOGUE

You could say what happened to me happened to all of us. It happened to Victor, to Momma and Missy, Granpaw and Granny, to Moses Mashbone, to Willis, to Nealy Harlan and that old cousin of his, Bird Pruitt—to all the folks that lived and worked around Harlan's Crossroads, white and black. And I suppose you would be right in putting it that way, though you would be wrong too, dead wrong, for what happened was also altogether particular to my person alone; particular and so elusive, so hard to get hold of that few in this world, least of all myself—though I had been given a glimpse to last a lifetime—would dare say it had happened at all.

Some said it was magic. Some said no. Some said what destroyed the barn and tore the wheels off Reverend Pennycall's police car was just a late summer storm, though of unusual magnitude, which at the time seemed a reasonable enough explanation. But the thing that put the slice of worry permanently between Momma's eyes and pointed out the path I was to take—the thing that sent the Devil to his grave—that was more than just a storm.

Part One

1

EVERYBODY ON EDGE

Thursday, June 6th 1959

Momma and even Victor said I'd be coming to St. Petersburg with them. They'd been saying it for weeks. Then Victor changed his mind. He was my stepdaddy, Victor was. It would be easier on everybody, he said, if I stayed with Granny and Granpaw in Kentucky. Him and Momma had enough Florida business to take care of without on top of everything else having to take care of me too. I was a handful, Victor said. I kept everybody on edge. If you asked me, the only edge everybody was kept on was Victor's. As far as I was concerned, him and Momma could both go to hell. Missy too. I was fed up trying to be good. Saying everything was okay when it wasn't. Pretending I understood when I didn't.

Momma's car was a 1950 model. Daddy said it was the first Ford car to come automatic. I didn't know what 'automatic' was but it sure had silver ashtrays, two of them on the back of the front seats. They were all popped open with gum wrappers and cigarette butts and boy did they smell.

One butt fell on top a bunch of comic books I had me in a pile. The pile leaned cockeyed against my dump truck. Heat came up from there; little whiffs of tail pipe smoke, warm and stuffy like the insides of my tennis shoes.

It rattled too—the Ford car did. The glove box. The mirrors. The windows. The knobs on the radio. The muffler under the floorboard. Everything rattled.

We'd been traveling hard all day, barreling down Road 3 from Detroit to Kentucky. Down to Harlan's Crossroads. I sat on the edge of the back seat, watching the fence posts zoom by. Missy stood up next to the side window, sucking her thumb. The fingers of her other hand were jammed between her legs. She was five years old. I was nine.

I'd seen pictures of Florida in a magazine. It had palm trees and alligators and oranges. It had long white beaches and pelicans that could dive-bomb the water. Kentucky was just old lonesome farmhouses and broke back barns. Gravel roads and chickens in the yard.

Road 3 took us down big places like Fort Wayne and Muncie. It took us down a whole bunch of little places too, places with funny names like Zaneville and Deputy and Speed.

Missy couldn't read.

"Piss with care," I said.

"Oh Orbie, you said a bad word."

"No. Piss with care, Missy. That sign back there. That's what it said."

Missy's eyes went wide. "It did not. Momma'll whip you."

Later on we got where there was a curve in the road and another sign. "Look Missy. Do not piss."

"It don't say that."

"Yes it does. See. When the road goes curvy like that you're not supposed to pee. But when it's straight, it's okay; but you have to do it careful cause that's what the sign says. Piss with care!"

"It don't say that."

"Does too."

We crossed a big pile of water on a bridge with towers and giant ropey things looping down. On the other side was Louisville, Kentucky. After that was just small towns and little white stores with red gas-pumps, farm houses and big barns and fields, empty fields and fields of corn and fields where there were cows and horses and pigs and long rows of tobacco plants Momma said cigarettes was made of.

I had me a war on all the towns going down.

Tat Tat Tat Tat! Blam! There goes Cox Creek!

Bombs away over Nazareth!

Blam! Blam! Boom! Hodgekinsville never had a chance!

"Let's keep it down back there!" Victor hollered.

"A grenade rolled into Victor's lap!" I whispered. "BlamOOO! Blowed him to smithereens!"

I wished Momma had left him back there in Toledo like she said she would. She was always threatening around like that, but then she would get to feeling sorry and forget all about it. She'd been mad ever since Victor spilled the beans about Daddy. Victor was mad too, drinking his beer and driving Momma's Ford too fast. After Louisville he started throwing his empties out the window.

I liked to watch them bust on the road.

"Pretty country, Kentucky," Victor said.

———

It was the end of daytime and a big orangey-gold sun ball hung way off over the hills, almost touching the trees. The Ford jerked over a ditch at the foot of a patchy burnt yard, thundering up a load of bubble noises as Victor shut it down.

"Get off me," Missy said.

"I ain't bothering you."

"Yes you are."

"But Missy, look!"

A big boned woman in a housedress had come to stand in the yard down by the well. She was looking into the sun— orange light in her face—standing upright, sharp edged and stiff, like an electrical tower, one arm bent like a triangle, the other raised with the elbow so the hand went flat out over her eyes like a cap. She stared out of wrinkles and scribbles

3

and red leather cheekbones. Her nose was sunburned, long but snubbed off at the end, sticking out above a mouth that had no lips, a crack that squirmed and changed itself from long to short and back to long again.

Missy's eyes widened. "Who is that?"

"Granny," I said. "Don't you remember?"

I saw Granpaw too, sitting squat-legged against Granny's little Jesus Tree. He was turning in one big hand a piece of wood, shaving it, whittling it outward with a jackknife. The brim of a dusty Panama shadowed his eyes. In back of him stood the house, balanced on little piles of creek rock. You could see jars and cans and other old junk scattered underneath. It was the same dirty white color as before, the house was, but the sun ball had baked it orange, and now I could see at one end where somebody had started to paint.

As we got out of the car, the big boned figure in the housedress let out with a whoop, hollering, "Good God A Mighty! If it tain't Ruby and them younguns of hers! Come all the way down here from Dee-troit!" Blue-green veins bulged and tree-limbed down the length of her arms.

Victor stayed out by the Ford, the round top of my ball cap hanging out his pocket. A gas station man had given it to me on the way down. It was gray and had a red winged horse with the word 'Mobilgas' printed across the front. Victor had swiped it away, said I shouldn't be accepting gifts from strangers. I should have asked him about it first. Now it was in his back pocket, crushed against the Ford's front fender where he leaned with an unlit cigar, rolling between his lips. The sun was in back of him, halfway swallowed up by a distant curvy line of hilltop trees.

"Hidy Victor!" Granny called. "Ya'll have a good trip?"

Victor put on a smooth voice. "Fine Mrs. Wood. Real fine. You can't beat blue grass for beauty, can you?" A long shadow stretched out on the ground in front of him.

Granny laughed. "Ain't been no farther than Lexington to know!"

4

Granpaw changed his position against the tree, leaned forward a little bit and spat a brown gob, grunting out the word 'shit' as he did. Then he dragged the back of his knife hand sandpaper-like over the gap of his mouth.

"I want you just to looky here!" Granny said. "If tain't Missy-Two-Shoes and that baby doll of hers!"

Missy backed away.

"Aw, Missy now," Momma said. "That's Granny."

Missy smiled then and let Granny grab her up. Her legs went around Granny's waist. She had on a pink Sunday dress with limp white bows dangling off its bottom. The back of it was all squashed and wadded, like a used hankie.

"How's my little towhead?" Granny said.

"Good." Missy held out her baby doll. "This is Mattie, Granny. She got the same name as you."

"Well ain't you the sweetest thang!" Granny grinned so big her wrinkles went out in circles like water does after a stone's dropped in. She gave Missy a wet kiss and set her down. Then her grin flashed toward Momma. "There's my other little girl!"

Momma, no taller than Granny's chin, did a little toe dance up to her, smiling all the way. She hugged Granny and Granny in turn beat the blue and red roses on the back of Momma's blouse.

"I just love it to death!" Granny said. "Let me look at you!" She held Momma away from her. Momma wiggled her hips; slim curvy hips packed up neat in a tight black skirt. She kissed the air in front of Granny.

Like Marilyn Monroe. Like in the movies.

"Jezebel!" Granny laughed. "You always was a teaser."

They talked about the trip to Florida, about Victor's prospects—his good fortune, his chance—about Armstrong and the men down there and that Pink Flamingo Hotel. They talked about Daddy too, and what a good man he'd been.

"It liked to've killed us all, what happened to Jessie," Granny said.

"I know Mamaw. If I had more time, I'd go visit him awhile." Momma looked out over the crossroads toward the graveyard. I looked too but there was nothing to see now, nothing but shadows and scrubby bushes and the boney black limbs of the cottonwood trees. I remembered what Victor had said about the nigger man, about the crane with the full ladle.

"I want you just to look what the cat's drug in Mattie!" Granpaw had walked over from his place by the tree.

"Oh Papaw!" Momma hugged Granpaw's rusty old neck and kissed him two or three times.

"Shoo! Ruby you'll get paint all over me!"

Momma laughed and rubbed at a lip mark she'd left on his jaw.

"How you been daughter?"

"All right I reckon," Momma said. She looked back toward Victor who was still up by the Ford. Victor took the cigar out of his mouth. He held it to one side, pinched between his fingers.

"How's that car running Victor?" Granpaw called.

"Not too bad, Mr. Wood," Victor answered, "considering the miles we've put on her."

Granpaw made a bunch of little spit-spit sounds, flicking them off the end of his tongue as he did. He hawked up another brown gob and let it fall to the ground; then he gave Victor a nod of welcome and walked over. He walked with a limp, like somebody stepping off in a ditch, carrying the open jackknife in one hand and that thing, whatever it was he'd been working on, in the other.

Granny's mouth got hard. "Ruby, I did get that letter of yorn. I done told you it were all right to leave that child. I told you in that other letter, 'member?"

"You sure it's not any trouble?" Momma said.

Granny's eyes widened. "Trouble? Why, tain't no trouble a-tall." She looked over my way. "I want you just to look how he's growed! A might on the skinny side though."

"He'll fill out," Momma said.

"Why yes he will. Come youngun. Come say hello to your old Granny."

"Orbie, be good now," Momma said.

I went a little closer, but I didn't say hello.

"He'll be all right," Granny said.

"I hope so Mamaw. He's been a lot of trouble over this."

Veins, blue rivers, tree roots, flooded down Granny's gray legs. More even than on her arms. And you could see white bulges and knots and little red threads wiggling out. "I'll bet you they's a lot better things going on here than they is in Floridy," she said. "I bet you, if you had a mind to, Granpaw would show you how to milk cows and hoe tobacco. I'll learn you everything there is to know about chickens. Why, you'll be a real farm hand before long!"

"I don't wanna be no damned farm hand," I said.

"Boy, I'll wear you out!" Momma said. "See what I mean, Mamaw?"

"He'll be all right," Granny said.

The sun was on its way down. Far to the east of it two stars trailed after a skinny slice of moon. I could see Old Man Harlan's Country Store across the road, closed now, but with a porch light burning by the door.

A ruckus of voices had started up by the Ford, Granpaw and Victor trying to talk at the same time. They'd propped the Ford's hood up with a stick and were standing out by the front.

Victor had again taken up his place, leaning back against the front fender, crushing my ball cap. "That's right, that's what I said! No good at all." He held the cigar shoulder level—lit now—waving it with his upraised arm one side to the other. "The Unions are ruining this country, Mr. Wood. Bunch of meddlesome, goddamned troublemakers. Agitators, if you know what I mean." He took a pull on the cigar then blew the smoke over Granpaw's head.

Granpaw was stout looking but a whole head shorter than Victor. He stood there in his coveralls, doubled up fists hanging at the end of each arm, thick as sledgehammers— one with the open jackknife, the other with that thing he'd been working on. "Son, you got a problem?"

"The rank and file," Victor said. "They're the problem!

7

They'll believe anything the goddamn Union tells them."

Granpaw leaned over and spat. "You don't know nothin'."

"*Anything*," Victor said.

"What?"

Victor took the cigar out of his mouth and smiled. "*I don't know anything* is what you mean to say. It's proper grammar."

"I know what I aim to say," Granpaw said, "I don't need no northern jackass a tellin' me." Granpaw's thumb squeezed against the jackknife blade.

Cut him Granpaw! Knock that cigar out his mouth!

"Strode!" Granny shouted. "Come away from there!"

Momma hurried over. "Victor, I told you."

"I was just sharing some of my thoughts with Mr. Wood here," Victor said. "He took it the wrong way, that's all. He doesn't understand."

"I understand plenty, City Slicker." Granpaw closed the knife blade against his coveralls and backed away.

"Ain't no need in this Strode!" Granny said. "Victor's come all the way down here from Dee-troit. He's company. And you a man of God!"

"I'll cut him a new asshole, he keeps on that a way," Granpaw said.

Momma was beside herself. "Apologize Victor. Apologize to Papaw for talking that way."

"For telling the truth?"

"For insulting him!"

Victor shook his head. "You apologize. You're good at that."

Over where the sun had gone down the sky had turned white-blue. Fireflies winked around the roof of the well, around the branches of the Jesus Tree. Victor walked around to the front of the car and slammed the hood down harder than was necessary. "Come on Orbie! Time to get your stuff!"

I couldn't believe it was about to happen, even though I had been told so many times it was going to. I started to cry.

"Get down here!" Victor yelled.

Momma met me at the car. She took out a handkerchief and

wiped at my tears. She looked good. She always looked good.

"I don't want you to go," I said.

"Oh now," Momma said. "Let's not make Victor any madder than he already is, okay?" She helped bring my things from the car. I carried my tank and my box of army men and crayons. Momma brought my dump truck, the toy cars, my comic books and drawing pad. We put them all on the porch where Missy sat playing with her doll. Momma hugged me one last time, got Missy up in her arms and headed to the car.

Victor was already behind the wheel, gunning the engine. "Come on Ruby! Let's go!"

"You just hold on a minute!" Momma put Missy in the car and turned to hug Granny. "Bye Mamaw."

"Goodbye Sweetness. I hope you find what you're looking for down there."

"Right now I'd settle for a little peace of mind," Momma said; then she hugged Granpaw. "I'm real sorry about Victor Papaw."

Granpaw nodded. "You be careful down there in Floridy."

"Bye Momma! Bye Missy!" I yelled.

Momma closed her door and Victor backed out. I hurried down to where Granny and Granpaw were standing. The Ford threw dust and gravels as it fishtailed up the road.

Granpaw tapped me on the shoulder. "This one's for you son," he said and handed down the piece he'd been working on. It was a little cross of blond wood about a foot high with a burnt snake draped lengthwise over its arms. Granpaw moved his finger over the snake's curvy body. "Scorched that in there with a hot screw driver, I did."

It was comical in a way, but strange too; I mean to make a snake there—right where Jesus was supposed to be. Like most everything else in my life, it made no sense at all. Momma's Ford had disappeared over the hill. Pale road-dust moved like a ghost over the cornfields and under the half-dark sky. It drifted back toward the skull of Granpaw's barn, back toward the yard. I stood there watching it all, listening as Momma's Ford rumbled away.

2
KENTUCKY LIGHT

Granny held up the lamp to see by. She laid clean blue jeans and a long-sleeved red-checkered shirt over the back of a straw chair. I was lying in bed. "Where we going they's pickers and thorns," she said. "Scratch ye legs up awful, you don't put something on." The attic smelled like old kerosene and Granny's Juicy Fruit gum. Big beams ran up from out the dark on both sides, little pieces of wood nailed in between.

Granny turned with the lamp held to the side. Her skin was sunburned, worn looking as old leather. A shadow cut off half her face—an eye and part of her nose. She stood like that, with half a face; chewing gum, her teeth moving inside a mouth looked like a pouch pulled together with a string.

The arms of the red-checkered shirt hung down from the chair, reaching toward the floor without hands. Momma and Victor had left a little over an hour ago.

I started to cry.

Granny raised the lamp and the shadow flew away, eyes green glowing as a cat's. "Your Momma will be back in two weeks Orbie. That ain't no time a-tall." Midget flames like

11

the one in the lamp wiggled in each of her eyes. "Blackberries child! That's what we gonna do. You and me!"

"I'm scared Granny."

"Scared? What you scared of?"

"I don't know. I don't like it dark. There might be something in here. Something under the bed. There might be a man."

"A man?"

"A black nigger man Granny. He might kidnap me!"

"They Lord Orbie, if that don't sound like your Momma, every bit." Granny loomed over me. It was like she'd opened a door to a dark room and was holding the lamp up to see. Her words came out full of spit. "I don't hold with that word youngun! I don't care where you heard it from neither. That's the sorriest, hatefullest word on God's green earth and I don't want to hear it mentioned. Not by you ner nobody else! Not in my house." She pointed a finger at the shadows overhead. "They's colored folks and they's white. But when you get down to the rock bottom truth of thangs they's just *folk* folks!"

Granny didn't know anything about niggers. Mean niggers in Detroit with knives.

"Ain't many folks these parts believes the way I do," Granny said. "Except maybe Granpaw, and folks over to Kingdom. I know your Momma don't. Your Momma used to have more respect for coloreds. Before she went off north she did."

"Still there might be somebody," I said. "I don't like it dark Granny."

Granny set the kerosene lamp on the floor by the bed. "They ain't nothin' under there now, look." She made a motion for me to climb down and look under. She was right. There wasn't anything under there except my tennis shoes and the dirty brown linoleum floor. A big wiry-legged spider crawled into the circle where the light was and stopped. "That's just old Daddy Long Legs," Granny said. "He won't hurt you none."

I heard what she said, but I didn't believe her. I grabbed up one of my tennis shoes and slammed it on the spider.

"They Lord!" Granny breathed.

I lifted the shoe away and there the spider was, a wet circle now of crushed legs. One leg had detached and was crawling sideways across the linoleum. I slammed it with the shoe. "I hate spiders Granny."

"That ain't no reason to kill one! Get back in the bed!"

I put the shoe down and climbed back in.

"I got to kill thangs too, sometimes," Granny said. "Pigs. Chickens. Cows. Even spiders sometimes. I don't do it just to be doing it though."

That you needed a reason to kill spiders had never occurred to me. I pulled the sheet up over my chin and stared back.

"It had been different it was poison," Granny said. "I'd have killed it myself it was poison."

She knew as much about spiders as she did about niggers, which was next to nothing at all. To me spiders were creepy and mean with big fangs that could suck blood. One time at the drive-in-picture-show I saw where a spider had grown so big it ate people alive and crashed through walls. You couldn't kill it either, not even with a tank.

Again Granny raised the lamp. "You know, you look just like a baby raccoon I come up on wunst in the woodshed, it's eyes all a shine. Like glass. Watching me like it thought I was crazy." She let out a laugh. "You think I'm crazy don't you?"

I didn't know what to think. I liked how she talked though, like she was having the best old time. I liked it so much I almost forgot to cry. Her face sidled in along side the lamp frame. "Sure enough. You and that rascally little raccoon look just exactly alike!" She wagged her head, laughing. I laughed too. Then her eyes went over the floor by the bed. "I don't reckon they's a man small enough could fit under there, do you?"

"No Granny," I said.

"Me and Granpaw will be right at the foot of them steps, you get scared."

"Okay, Granny."

Granny smiled. "All right then." She went with the lamp to the ladder hole. The shadow of her shoulder soared up to the ceiling, stretched out over the beams like a wing. She started backwards down the ladder hole, facing me but looking down, frowning, holding the lamp to one side whilst she felt for the steps. When her chin got even with the floor she looked back at me. "Go to sleep now hon. Everything's gonna be all right." She went on down. The shadow of the wing slid off the beams and followed after her. The light flickered in the hole and went out.

I curled up in a ball like a rabbit, hunkering down in the featherbed, warm and listening to the crickets. I thought about Momma and Missy, about Victor, barreling down and up and over the hills of Kentucky, moving on into Tennessee and Chattanooga, going on the rest of the way, on down to Florida and that Gulf of Mexico without me. I thought about my real Daddy. I thought about the fire. My tears started again; so much so, I thought they'd never end. And that's how I went to sleep.

———

My eyes wouldn't open. Blades of white stabbed in through the lashes. I saw bright red and blue circles rising, silvery spider legs growing and fading—floating in a glare. There was syrupy stuff too, up in the corners, some of it dried off hard and grainy like scabs. I rubbed until the lashes sucked loose, until I could see the beams and the tin roof overhead—light shining through the little nail holes up there—Kentucky light.

The featherbed puffed up around me like hills. Still I was able to see the top of Granny's dresser, the big round mirror leaning over the front, looking back at the room like a big glass eye. I could see my end of the attic in there, the window behind the bed. There was a window at the other end too, full of sunshine, tall like a man with a chest full of fire.

My dump truck, the one Daddy won bowling at Ford's, sat on the dresser, shiny red with chrome bumpers and black rubber mud flaps. Granpaw's cross was up there too, leaning against the mirror, blond wood with a black snake draped along its shoulders where Jesus was supposed to be.

Momma said Jesus could have called ten thousand angels to come and save him from the cross, but God said not to, which to me didn't make any sense. To me, Jesus should have called them angels right away instead of letting Himself be killed like he did. He could have saved people for real then. That's what I would have done.

"Why, Jesus had to die," Momma said. "So people could believe on him and be saved. That's how God planned it."

"Do I have to believe in Jesus?" I asked.

"You got to come to the age of accountability first," Momma said. "You got to get under conviction."

Conviction sounded bad, like a bank robber or some bad man on Dragnet, sitting behind bars in a jail. I didn't want to be under anything like that.

"You don't have to worry none," Momma said. "Jesus loves all the little children. Little children that don't know no better's already saved."

I liked it that Jesus loved the little children, but I wasn't sure if nine-years-old was still little. It didn't matter anyhow, not if Jesus didn't come when you wanted him to. Preachers at church said Jesus was coming soon. To me 'soon' meant right away like tomorrow or next week, not years and years. If 'soon' took that long, maybe a person would be better off without Jesus. At least you wouldn't all the time have to be thinking about Him, wondering around if He was going to come or not.

Far off somewhere I heard a rooster crow. The sound zigzagged way up in the sky like a train whistle then gagged off all of a sudden like somebody had choked it. I heard things moving around downstairs. Voices. A chair being pulled across the floor.

Bacon smells drifted over from the ladder hole, making me think of home, of cartoons on TV where long fingers of

15

smoke would come out from pots and pans on a stovetop. Where they would drift over to a tomcat or a man that was sleeping and start to curl in and out in front of his nose. That cat or that man would float up off the ground then, and the smoky fingers would just float him along by the nose till they got to where the food was. This morning they were doing the same thing to me.

"Orbie! Ah, Orbie!" It was Granny yelling up the ladder hole, her breath going in and out. "I got you some eggs down here! Ah, Orbie! You up yet?"

"I am Granny!"

"Come on then. Granpaw's already eatin' his." She walked away, slipper bottoms smooching across the floor.

I slid out of bed onto the cracked linoleum, cold and prickly with dirt. I tiptoed one foot to the other, rubbing at my eyes; still trying to get that syrupy stuff out.

"Orbie! Ah, Orbie! Eggs is gettin' cold!"

"Okay Granny!" I quick put on my clothes, went over to the dresser, got my dump truck, put the cross in the back end and climbed down the ladder hole—backwards like Granny— the truck tucked under my arm. When I got to the bottom, I wrapped both arms around the truck from underneath, rounded a corner in Granny and Granpaw's bedroom and went into the kitchen.

Granpaw sat at the end of a big brown table, wheezing as he sopped up his eggs with a biscuit. His head was covered with short silvery hairs. A shiny red knot went up with his ear and then down as he chewed. He slurped coffee from a thick white mug he held by the rim between his big finger and thumb.

Under a hawk brow he spied me, standing in the doorway. His words crawled out over the table. "You ever seeed a black snake, boy?" A crooked grin fixed itself up one corner of his mouth. Then his eyes and face suddenly blew out like

16

a bullfrog's throat and there he was, choking on coffee. He slammed his mug down, sloshing coffee over the rim, spat something in his hand and wiped it on the leg of his coveralls. "Sit you down, boy!" he said. "Get you some of these eggs."

In back of him by the door hung a one-day-at-a-time wall calendar. A black number '7' took up most of the page—with the month and the year printed above, and the day, Friday, printed below. I put my truck with the cross on the floor and sat down. On my plate were two fried eggs with bacon and a biscuit broke in two, covered over with thick white gravy.

"Go on, eat," Granpaw said. "Put some meat on them bones."

I picked up my fork. I wasn't hungry but I cut out a piece of egg white and put it in my mouth. On the other side of the room under a window with a fan was a woodstove for cooking. A quiet fire played peek-a-boo behind the air holes on the door.

Granny came and stood in the doorway next to Granpaw.

"Them eggs ain't cold now are they?"

"No, Granny."

She walked around Granpaw and stood next to the stove. She had a thick white mug like his in one hand and a spoon in the other. "Orbie hon, look up here to me. You got the dry eye, don't ye?"

I didn't know if I had it or not.

"No," I said.

"Yes you do." Granny dug out a spoonful of coffee and biscuit from her mug. I'd seen her do that other times I was down here. Coffee and biscuit from a mug was one of her most favorite things. She called it 'soak'. "You know what the dry eye is?"

"No," I said.

"You get the dry eye from crying and sleeping too hard," she said. "Makes a person's eyes swell out. Like yours is now. I bet they was stuck together when you woke up."

"Uh huh," I said.

"Well," Granny said, "they'll be fine after while."

I was glad there wasn't nothing the matter with my eyes.

I cut out another piece of egg white and put it in my mouth. I let it stay there.

Granpaw's words crawled out over the table. "You ever seeed a black snake, boy?"

The piece of egg white slid over my tongue.

Granny stood with the spoonful of soak. "Stop that now, Strode. Poor thang cried hisself to sleep last night."

Granpaw put a mean eye on Granny, then turned it back on me. "I *killed* me one t'other day. You know they's two kind of black snake?"

The egg white slid down my throat. "No, Granpaw."

"Well, they is!" he almost shouted. His voice then shrank to just above a whisper. "One's regular and t'other'n's a racer. One I killed come at me with its head all raised. And I killed it! Killed it deader'n four o'clock! Now. What do you think of that?" Seemed like all the holes on Granpaw's face had opened at the same time—the mouth hole, the eye holes, the nose holes—even the little blue-purply holes on his chin, the ones Granny said he got from the fever.

Out the screen door I could see the barn. I could see sunshine beating down all over the yard. "I don't know Granpaw. I don't know what to think."

"I killed it with a grubbing hoe. Chopped its head plum off, back of that barn." Granpaw jerked his head back toward the screen. "Ain't that somethin'?"

I looked down at my plate. Three long strips of bacon lay on the side, all bubbled out and swimming in grease. I picked at one with my fork. "I don't know, Granpaw. Did it bite you?"

Granny snorted. "It ought to've child! Might've learned him a thang or two!" She held the spoon over the cup just below her mouth—full of that brown spongy stuff—laughing so hard now some drops of coffee fell down the front of her dress. "Fooling with them black snakes! You know better'n that!"

"Hesh up woman! Me and Orbie's talking here." Lizard skin came down over one of Granpaw's eyes, went back up again. A wink. He was making us out to be like partners.

I didn't want to be no partner. I looked at my plate.

Granny slurped up the soak from her spoon, one eye on Granpaw. "You ain't supposed to kill'em no how. They eat rats." A brown drop found a wrinkle under her lip and slid in.

"Black snakes is good for rats but this'n—it was one of them racers I think—it come at me so quick!" Granpaw jerked back from the table, raising both hands; big gray calluses all up and down his fingers. Again his voice crawled out over the table. "With its head all raised, and a slick black tongue, spittin' and slaverin' out its mouth. That one was ugly. Slicker'n dog shit too! Why, wasn't nothin' I could do but grab up a grubbing hoe!" He popped the tabletop with both hands. "Chopped its head plum off, that's what I done! Wasn't no time to think."

He reached up around his neck and pulled a leather drawstring over his head. Attached was a small leather pouch. "Looky here boy." He tossed the pouch with the string over the table, landing it a little ways from my plate. "There's its head, in there! Open it!"

I sat back in my chair, frozen, thinking of that snake's head in there, its tongue slicking out at me, dead.

"Go on, boy. What you scared of?"

"Get that nasty thang out of here!" Granny snatched up the pouch and flung it back Granpaw's way. It hit him in the chest and thumped down on the table. "Scare that child so bad he won't never want to go outside!"

Granpaw doubled over; laughing so hard I thought he might be near to choking. Then he just stopped everything and cocked his brow. "I'll skin it back for ye, if you want me to. You can put its skull on a strang fer a necklace. What do you think of that?"

"I don't want no damned snake head Granpaw!" My fork got away from me then, clanking loudly against my plate. A strip of bacon flipped over and landed on the table, a greasy dead piece of meat.

Granpaw hee-hawed and slapped his legs. "What's the matter boy? It'd be like one of them charms, by grabs!" His gray eye fixed me where I sat. "Where'd you learn to cuss like that anyhow?"

Granny flapped at him. "Get out Strode! Go on! Go do them chores like you was aiming to! Orbie don't need you making fun of him, poor thing. All the way down here from Detroit. He don't need that kind of foolishness! Besides we going to pick blackberries this morning and I got to get this table cleared." She pointed toward the door. "Get out now!"

Granpaw, still laughing, got up from the table. He took one limping step and looked around at the kitchen. "Where's my hat, Mattie?"

With her spoon, Granny pointed toward the door. "Out there where you left it, I reckon. Get on now!"

"Cain't nobody have no fun around here." Granpaw picked up the pouch and ditch-stepped it over to me. "Looky here boy. Ain't nothin' in that but chewing tobacco." He opened the pouch and held it down for me to see. Sure enough that's all there was—just a gnarled hunk of black chewing tobacco curled in there like a snake with one end bit off.

"Now ain't that something to be scared of?" Granpaw winked and cupped the top of my head with a hand thick as a baseball mitt. I tried to jerk loose but the hand was too strong. Looking right down into my eyes, he said, "You down here with us hillbillies now son, and ain't a one of us got a lick of sense. Why, if we did, we wouldn't know what to do with it!" He threw back his head, laughing. Then a tired sound came in his voice. "I reckon you'll learn that soon enough though." He let go of my head, raised himself on one leg and let his body down on the other. He went out the screen door that way, went out and let it slam.

I watched him standing out there on the porch, looking up at the sky, the palms of his hands on his butt, the elbows stuck out in back of him. "Yep, he'll learn. He'll learn soon enough," Granpaw said to the sky. Then he walked his bum leg down the steps and was gone.

3
HARLAN'S CROSSROADS

Granny set her cup with the spoon in a big empty tub and started piling Granpaw's dirty dishes. "Pay Strode no mind, youngun. Going on about them black snakes. You wouldn't think he was a preacher the way he does. Ornery old devil."

I stared out the door Granpaw had gone. The barn sat out there with its main and two hay loft doors wide open—a black skull laughing at the day.

Who did he think he was anyhow? Scaring me like that?

Granny wiped egg yellow and brown coffee circles off the top of the table. Then she grabbed a hot kettle from the stove, brought it over to the tub and poured hot water in. A cloud of steam rushed up to the ceiling and crawled away. "We won't have to bother with him now no how, this your first day and all." She began ladling cold water into the tub from a bucket by the door. "You haven't said two words since you been down here. What you been doing up in Detroit?"

"Nothing, Granny. Playing."

"Playing at what?"

"Ball. With my friends."

Granny busied herself over the dishes. "They's kids down here too you know."

"No there ain't," I said.

"Who said they ain't?"

I looked at my plate. Two orange egg-eyes looked back. "Momma," I said.

"She don't know. She ain't been around to know." Granny stood now, toweling off her hands. "How come you so quiet? You never used to be."

"I'm thinking Granny."

"Thinking?" Granny laughed. "You too young to be thinking. You remind me of some old farmer a worrying over his crops."

I poked one of the eggs and watched the orange run out. "I can't eat these Granny. I ain't hungry."

Granny reached down and got a hold of my plate. Her white hair was pulled straight back, gathered on either side into pincushion-sized buns. One white strand floated out over her ear like a stray feather. "Go on outside then. The hogs'll eat these and be thankful." She dumped the eggs into a dented bucket and set my plate off to the side. "I'll finish these dishes and we'll go. We got a lot to do, you and me. Picking them blackberries."

I left my dump truck and Granpaw's cross under the table and went out onto the back porch. I put my hands in my back pockets and looked up at the sky like Granpaw. I couldn't see the sun but I knew it was up there—somewhere behind the blinding white clouds. Cows decorated with splotches of white on black grazed the hillside above the barn. Pigs sniffed and snuffled inside a fenced yard near the house. A few lay sleeping in the shade of a little blue and white egg-shaped trailer that squatted in the tall weeds next to the fence. There was a chicken yard too, and a foreshortened wagon road that ended at the barn, which separated the chicken yard from the pig yard, two red clay tracks with a grassy hump down the middle.

"Orbie!" Granny called. Through the screen door I could see her still picking up utensils and wiping the table, sending out her words while she worked. "You be careful about that well now! Storm blowed the roof cockeyed and I think some of them stones is loose. I don't want you falling in."

"Okay Granny," I said.

"We'd be worried to death, not knowing where you'd gone off to."

"Okay." Already I was beginning to sweat. I went down the steps and out along the side of the house. Grasshoppers were flying every which way over the patchy grass yard, bright black wings snapping like cellophane. A weather-warped rain barrel leaned under a pipe from the roof, empty and smelling of mold. I went on out to the front yard. Granny's Jesus Tree was out there, just a few feet away from the house, twisting up out of the ground like a bunch of ropes tied together; its thorny crown was no higher than the overhang that went out over the porch.

A faded picture of Jesus Granny had found at the Circle Stump flea market was wedged in between the branches. It was dented on one corner, washed out looking and stained with rainwater. It showed Jesus lying face down on a thick stone cross rising slantwise out of what looked like a stormy, though faded, yellow sea. Yellow waves lashed at Jesus' feet, and a washed out angry sky swirled overhead. His back was all bony and gashed and bleeding, and His faded hands were driven through with thick gray spikes. His face lay flat against the stone, and though I looked for it, I could see no love in his eyes anywhere, just misery and gloom. Didn't look to me like He could save himself let alone the world.

Across the gravels of Bounty Road I could see Old Man Harlan's store. Old Man Harlan's real name was Nealy. Nealy Harlan. The store looked about the size of a small garage but with a porch and a door and a window on the front, white with red trim. Up the hill stood the big house where Old Man Harlan lived with his hunchback cousin, Bird Pruitt.

Bounty Road went in front of Old Man Harlan's house and down past the store where it crossed Nub Road, also gravel. That place, where the roads came together, was called Harlan's Crossroads; called that because Old Man Harlan owned all the land around it—the store, Granny and Granpaw's place, the graveyard where Daddy was buried and the corner Granpaw had his tobacco on.

Down from the Jesus Tree and closer to the road sat Granny and Granpaw's well, above it a round roof of flowers growing out of tin cans. It was tilted backwards, the roof was, and looked a little bit like a church lady's hat that was being blown back by wind—except today there wasn't any wind. There wasn't even a breeze. All kinds of flowers were growing up there. Bloody red ones, smiling on green veins. Some with yellow hair and orange eyes. Blue flowers too, bunches of them, little trumpets turned up to the sun, Joshua's horns, Momma called them, ready to blast out, ready to make everything come tumbling down.

Suddenly the screen door on the front porch squalled open. It was Granny. She stepped out onto the noisy plank floor, holding two buckets, one in each hand, a big white bucket with a rusty lip, and a bright silver one that looked like an oversized tin can with the label peeled off.

"It's early for blackberries," she said, "but summer's early too. We get lucky, we'll find us a few."

———

We'd climbed the hill back of the barn, and now stood looking out over Harlan's Crossroads. "I'll tell you what's the truth youngun," Granny said. "We don't get rain soon, Harlan's Crossroads gonna blow away. Sure is purdy though. Look away over yonder. See that shining?"

I could see over the four corners of the crossroads, over Granpaw's field of shiny leaf tobacco.

"Look up Bounty there," Granny said. "That shining there." Light flashed back from where she was pointing.

24

"That's new tin. Storm blowed a tree over, right onto Moses Mashbone's roof. He got that tin to fix it with. We done picking, we'll go see."

Moses Mashbone was a medicine preacher who was said to have handled snakes, something Momma had told me. I looked away and out over the hazy blue hills. "Bounty goes to Circle Stump, don't it Granny?"

"Goes through Kingdom first, then Circle Stump." Granny pointed off to the left. "Kingdom Church's over that way."

"Colored people live in the Kingdom," I said.

"Your Momma tell you that?"

"Uh huh."

"It didn't have a name till they started that Nigger Kingdom business," Granny said. "That bunch over to Circle Stump. Why, coloreds is some of the best folks in the world! You know what they did when the white folks started calling their little section Nigger Kingdom?"

"Got their knives out," I said.

"Knives?"

"Yeah. To cut the Circle Stump people. For calling them names."

"Why, they wouldn't a bit more done that than nothing!" Granny said.

"What did they do then?"

"Kept the name of 'Kingdom' without that 'Nigger' part is what. So they had just 'Kingdom', you know, like the Kingdom of Heaven." Granny turned and started along another path up the hill. "Kingdom Town. Like in the Bible."

I hurried to catch up. "Oh. Like with angels and God and Jesus and all the saved people."

"That's right. Except their Kingdom is right here on earth. Ain't that a nice idea?"

I didn't know if it was nice or not. It sounded good, but you couldn't have angels and God and Jesus walking around on the ground like people.

"Church house ain't but a mile from there. Where me and Strode goes. Kingdom Church. There's a little old creek runs in behind it. Kingdom Creek. Cotton mouth all up in there. Poison."

"Moses picks 'em up, don't he Granny?"

"What? Snakes?"

"Cotton mouths."

"Yeah cotton mouths! Copperheads and rattler too. Kill you deader'n four o'clock! God protects Moses though. Even if he was to get bit, I don't reckon it would hurt him any."

————

We came up to Moses Mashbone's house from the back way, our buckets not even half full of the sorriest looking blackberries Granny said she'd ever seen. I was sweating and miserable, thinking over all what had happened, all the things I couldn't change, worried about Momma and Victor, still mad at them for leaving me.

"Moses won't be to home, more than likely," Granny said. "Miss Alma will be though."

"That his wife?" I said.

"No," Granny laughed. "She just keeps house. Got kids of her own. And a house in the Kingdom."

Moses' house was smaller than Granny and Granpaw's, covered over with brown sandy shingles. A tree had fallen across the roof at one end and had knocked the chimney sideways. "That there's a big oak," Granny said. "Mashed in the roof there and everything. Ain't that a sight?" The base of the tree had been pulled right out of the ground, a huge circle of red clay and gnarly black roots.

"Same wind blowed our well cockeyed blowed that tree cockeyed. See that tin there?" Sheets of tin were leaning up against the back of the house. "What we seen from up the hill. Moses gonna fix his roof with that."

We walked on around to the front of the house. Granny hollered at the door. "Miss Alma, you in there!"

Nobody answered.

"I ain't got all day girl!"

Still nobody answered; then came the sound of a door closing, and a voice hollering from within. "Lawd, Lawd, I comin'! Don't has to shout now!"

26

The screen door opened and out stepped the biggest, blackest colored-woman I'd ever seen. She looked like the woman on all the pancake boxes—the Aunt Jemima woman—so giant-sized she filled up the whole doorway. Her head was wrapped in a dirty orange rag, tied around in front so the ends stood up like little rabbit ears.

Granny put her hand on my shoulder. "This here's Orbie."

Miss Alma smiled a mouthful of white-white teeth. Her breasts, titties I called them then, were big as watermelons.

"Ruby's boy," Granny said.

"Well," Miss Alma said. "I sho' is pleased to meet you!"

I tried not to look at the watermelons.

"He'll be staying down here a while," Granny said. "Till his Momma gets back."

"Hmmm, hmmm. Well. Look to me like he be shy a little bit. Hmmm, hmmm. He a good lookin' boy though."

"I thank so," Granny said.

They both looked at me like it was my turn to talk, but I couldn't think of anything to say.

"Where's Moses?" Granny said.

"Oh he be off somewhere," Miss Alma said. "You know how he do."

Granny reached one of the buckets of berries up to Miss Alma. "Ain't much to look at but they'll do for jam."

"Lawd, Lawd," Miss Alma said. "Moses be pleased to get deze, sho' will. Ya'll come in now. I gots ice tea."

"No. We best be getting back, Miss Alma. Thank you kindly." Granny looked up in the sky. A few clouds drifted up there, dark little clouds with white silvery sides. "Reckon it'll rain soon?"

Miss Alma laughed. "It do, I hope dey no wind in it."

"No. We don't need no more of that. Look over there Orbie." Granny gestured toward a little hill of dirt by the fence. A big rusty door slanted up one side. "That's Moses' storm cellar. Only one around except for Nealy Harlan's. There's a bad storm we come down here."

"How come you don't use Mr. Harlan's storm cellar?" I said. "It's a long way over here, Granny."

"It ain't long if you go the road," Granny said. "Besides, Nealy won't let nobody use his cellar. Stingy old goat. He don't even use it himself, him nor Bird neither one. They's a bad storm, they come down here like the rest of us."

"Have moonshine in dat cellah of his," Miss Alma said.

"Barrels of it," Granny said.

"Hmm, hmm, sho' do."

Daddy told me once about Old Man Harlan's moonshine; how he sold it to the colored. "You know what moonshine is son? Make you sicker'n a dog!" Said Old Man Harlan had to sell his moonshine in secret because of the law. "He might hate the colored, but he don't hate their money. Never could trust a man like that."

When we got back to the crossroads, Granny stepped up a little bank and went into the graveyard. She did this so suddenly it near gave me the heebie-jeebies; still I managed to follow her in. Grave markers stuck up everywhere. Some were badly cracked and crumbling, some so dingy gray and grown over with black stuff you could hardly read the names.

"Nealy Harlan ought to be horsewhipped for letting it go like this," Granny said. Everywhere there were all kinds of weeds and picker bushes growing. Dandelion fuzz balls. Gawky dead cottonwood claws reaching down from above.

"I want you just to look!" Granny pointed along where there was a busted out place in the fence. "All the time after us and won't even fix his own fence line." On the other side of the busted out place stood a weeping willow tree, its umbrella of leaves drooped and withering in the sun.

Granny pointed again. "They're over that way, near where that break is. Your other Granny and Granpaw. Granny and Granpaw Ray."

"And Daddy," I said.

"That's right. Dead people needs to be took care of too, you know. Not left around like this." Granny motioned her hand out over the graves. "All growed over with weeds."

We made our way through picker bushes, around crosses and gravestones, toward the busted out place where a few slats of the fence still lay broken on the ground. Something inside the weeping willow tree's umbrella of leaves startled me, a dim shape of something or somebody hunched over in there, breathing and alive. It caused the hairs on my neck to stand.

"I declare!" Granny shouted. "Bird! What you doing in there?" The shape parted the leaves with a gnarled cane and waddled out in the sun. It was Bird Pruitt—Old Man Harlan's hunchback cousin—bent under a lopsided hump and wearing a thick purple dress that drooped dead to the ground.

"Ain't you hot in that?" Granny said.

"Ain't nobody's business if I am," Bird said as she waddled up closer. On her head sat a purple pillbox hat, its wiry net bent up in the air like frozen smoke, only purple colored. She reached out with the gnarled cane and poked me in the chest. "You! Ruby's boy! I never did get to whip you."

Missy and me had stayed once with Bird when Momma and Victor went off to Circle Stump with Granny—the first and only other time Victor had been down. Bird had said then that Victor ought to whip me more because my real Daddy never. Said all my real Daddy ever did was spoil me. I told her to shut her old mouth and she came at me with her cane.

"Leave him alone," Granny said.

Bird took her cane away. "You *are* Ruby's boy, ain't you?"

"His names Orbie," Granny said. "You know who he is."

Bird kept her eyes on me. "You awful skinny, Ruby's boy. Have to fatten you up." She reached out for one of my arms.

"Don't," I said, backing away.

Half her teeth were gone, and I could almost see the bone of her skull, just beneath her skin, gray bleached out skin that looked cold and watery even in the sunlight.

"Stop it Bird," Granny said. "He's just down here a little while. Ruby and that man of her's went off to Floridy."

Still not taking her eyes off me, Bird said, "Daddy's in the ground now, hain't he? You will be too, soon. It's awful to be in the ground. Awful." She grinned again and looked around at all the graves. "Awful, awful," she said, shaking her head. Then, breathing and heaving up under that hump, she began a slow spidery walk around the graves out toward the gate.

"She ain't easy to figure, that one ain't," Granny said.

I shivered at the thought of her skull. "She's crazy, ain't she Granny?"

"Some will say she is," Granny said. "Wanders all over everywhere. Nealy don't know where she is half the time."

"I didn't like what she said about Daddy. About him being in the ground."

"Your Daddy ain't in the ground, hon; he's in heaven. Look over here." Granny pointed to some graves near the fence. "They're not as bad as I thought they'd be. Grass needs trimming is all."

Crumbling white slabs of stone marked Granny and Granpaw Ray's graves — 'Louis Jefferson Ray' on Granpaw's and 'Pearl Anne Ray' on Granny's—and that was all. Daddy's gravestone looked almost new, shiny gray with a curved top. It said "Jessie Louis Ray, Born May 6th, 1931, Died August 15th, 1956. Loved By All." There were some dead roses piled at the bottom.

Granny reached down with one hand, grabbed up the roses and pitched them over the fence. She set the remaining bucket of blackberries down and stood there, looking over the graves.

A sad feeling came over me then. I remembered Daddy's bird claw hand, the one with the baby and ring fingers missing, how it moved through the air when he led singing at church. I remembered when they buried him, how it had rained—a cold misty rain you could feel all the way to the inside of your bones. How Momma had leaned against Granny, Granpaw holding an umbrella over their heads. I remembered the wet light on the stones. The Lord's Prayer. The red clay around the soles of my shoes. I got all heartbroken then and started to cry. "Some man poured fire on Daddy. A colored man."

"They Lord," breathed Granny. "They told you that?"

"Victor did," I sobbed. "It burned him alive."

Granny shook her head. "Lord A Mighty."

I had so many tears I could hardly see the gravestones.

Granny put her arm around me. "Cry all you want to, hon; Granny don't mind."

We stood in front of the graves. I cried till I couldn't cry anymore. Birds hopped and chirped in the cottonwoods overhead, happy, like to say there never was—nor ever would be—anything to be sad about.

"Did Granny and Granpaw Ray freeze to death?" I asked. "Nobody knows that for sure, hon. They had fever. I reckon it was fever and the cold both what killed them. Poor Jessie was just a baby. Now he's gone on to be with them."

It was peaceful by the weeping willow tree. Daddy was gone to be with Granny and Granpaw Ray. I wondered where that could be, if it was really heaven or if it was like Bird said, under the ground, down in some dark place where dead people walk around—like the zombie-people in my body snatcher book.

I wished Daddy could come back alive again—but not like that. I wished he could come back for real.

PART TWO

4
VICTOR

1955-1956

After I was born Momma and Daddy moved from Circle Stump north—all the way to Detroit, Michigan. That was in 1950. Daddy got a job in the steel mill there. Our house, a yellow single story Daddy got on the GI Bill, was the last one on a dead end street called Leroy. All the houses there looked alike. Pointy tops and picture windows with little front porches and forty foot yards. Some nice yards and some with just old burned up grass and weeds like ours had.

There were lots of kids in our neighborhood too. Yankee kids and kids like Missy and me who came up from the South—from places like Circle Stump and Hazard and Old Mulky—kids whose fathers had come up looking for work in the car factories and the steel mills. These were the ones we played with, not those others, not the Yankee kids. The Yankee kids spit on us and called us 'white trash' and 'pinko'. 'Pinko Commies and Hillbilly Trouble Makers,' they called us, talking all jagged-edged like their words was broke glass.

"Ain't no music in the way they talk," Daddy would say.

"They just saying that cause of the Unions anyhow. Ya'll ought to try and get along."

Course we never did.

Me, Daddy, Momma and Missy all went to the Detroit Zoo one day—I think it was in June of 1955—a year before Daddy's accident and the day I first met Victor. Momma was pushing Missy in a baby carriage. I was walking next to Daddy, keeping an eye out for colored kids.

The other day a gang of colored kids had jumped me at the schoolyard. They'd been throwing a basketball at one another, whacking each other with it, pushing, laughing and cussing at one another, and then this one big colored kid knocked into me.

"Watch out nigger!" I yelled.

They all jumped in on me then, held me on the gravels by the teeter-totters and yanked my pants down. They spat on me there and laughed and made fun of my thing. One colored boy rubbed it with the small end of a stick.

Look dat piss ant worm. You put dat in yo Momma, boy? Hey boy?

It made me feel all tingly and nice and mean and bad too, all at the same time—like the time I had poison ivy and Mrs. Profit, our baby sitter, rubbed lotion on me down there.

The kid that ran into me put a knife blade cold against my belly button.

Cut his dick off, Lawrence! Cut Whitey's dick!

I kicked and screamed but there were too many of what I thought of then as little gorilla hands, pink monkey-nails digging in. They would have cut me—I was sure they would have—but then Daddy came with his baseball bat and chased them all away.

At the zoo we were going around, looking at all the animals—the giraffes, the elephants, the zebras and baboons—when I saw this flat-nosed colored boy standing next to the water fountain, mouthing a big red Popsicle. Red

Popsicle-lips. Red inside his mouth too—pinky-red—like a baboon's butt.

I sidled in closer to Daddy.

"You can't measure everybody by the likes of a few," Daddy said.

While I owned that this was probably true, I stayed close to Daddy just the same. After while we came in front of a building with steps going up to a giant sized double door.

"Now, this here's a Cat House," Daddy said.

Momma said, "Don't be talking that way."

"Well it is," Daddy laughed. "Ought to have a sign out here a saying so. Ought to have a red light over the door."

"It's that kind of talk I don't like," Momma said. The way she said it I knew it would be trouble to ask her why. Inside, there were big cages with tigers and lions and leopards that moaned and growled so loud the floor trembled under our feet—a great big stinky-breath place with giant echoes like in a cave.

"I told you it was a cat house," Daddy said.

"Look at 'em all!" I shouted. "Goddamn!"

"Orbie!" Momma hard-whispered.

"What?"

"You know what."

"God don't care," I said.

"You just think he don't."

We came to a big cage with a white tiger that was walking around in circles. Yellow fangs, knives, hung out his mouth. He went with his head down, looking at the floor, making hot-breath sounds, going "Huh... Huh... Huh... Huh...", just walking round and round, muscles rolling over in big white shoulders.

"He looks lonesome, don't he? Sad," Momma said. She bent down to fix Missy's straps. "Maybe he's got a momma and daddy too. Maybe he's got kids."

"He'll eat you guts and all," I said.

"Hush that talk!" Momma said. She looked at Daddy. "See how he talks? That's your doing."

Daddy smiled.

"I seen it on TV, Momma," I said. "First they scare you. Then they make you so you can't move. Then they eat you. And your eyes are still open and everything!"

Missy pointed at the tiger and shouted, "Dat!" Her white hair, white as the tiger's almost, made an upside-down bowl around her head.

"Everyone of God's creatures got a family. Ain't that right, Missy-Two-Shoes?" Momma said.

Missy smiled and put all her fingers in her mouth.

"He used to work for Fords," Daddy said, all serious like. "He was a foreman there. A good foreman too. Must have run a foul of the law though. Be in a cage like that. Look at him. Why, he's even wearing stripes."

"Probably he robbed a bank!" I said.

"Probably," Daddy winked. "Probably he did."

"Ya'll make fun if you want to. I know what I'm talking about." Momma looked her usual pretty self, wearing that curvy blue dress, the one Daddy said showed off her legs.

"He *was* a foreman though," a man said in back of us. He was fine looking and tall, way taller than Daddy, dressed nicer too, with silvery pants and a short-sleeved shirt that was black with silvery diamond shapes up the front. "The foreman of the jungle." He was wearing thick black-framed eyeglasses. They slid down his nose as he talked and nodded toward the tiger. "I imagine he's worrying about production. That and the cost of living, of course." A thick new cigar, unlit, stuck out between the man's fingers. "Our Mr. Foreman here would like to balance the books, if you know what I mean. But he's in a bit of a fix." He put the cigar in his shirt pocket and looked at Momma. "It *is* sad, Ma'am. I agree."

Daddy shook hands with the man and looked at Momma. "This here's Mr. Denalsky, Ruby. From the picnic."

Momma put on a company smile. "Real nice to see you again Mr. Denalsky."

"Nice to see you as well, Ma'am." Mr. Denalsky shook Momma's hand. He gently put his other hand, the left hand, on top of hers. There was a clean tattoo on the back of the hand—a sharp red heart with a beige-colored snake coiled around it. Green letters were written across the snake's body.

"'Born To Lose'," Momma read. "You believe that Mr. Denalsky?"

Mr. Denalsky pulled his hand back a little and smiled. "I got that when I was younger. When I was in the army. Back then I was more cynical."

"You've changed your mind since then," Momma said.

"I've come to see things a little differently, yes. You see; every living thing eventually loses. Suffers and dies." His voice was like a man I heard on the radio once, all deep and smooth like. When he smiled, he glowed, and the glow made all his good looks come out at you like a friend. He kept holding Momma's hand. "That we lose is not a cause for despair. It inspires tenderness, Ma'am. Kindness."

"Why, that's so purdy," Momma said, gently pulling her hand away. "And so spiritual too."

A little curl of black hair had fallen across Mr. Denalsky's forehead. "Victor Ma'am. Call me Victor." He looked at Daddy too. "Both of you; please." He said it straight out; like there was nothing in the world he would like more. A little red mole gleamed at the side of his nose.

"Victor," Momma said and smiled.

He slapped Daddy on the shoulder. "Your husband is one hell of a worker Ma'am. I don't care if he is a *Union Man*." He said this jokingly but nobody laughed.

"Much obliged," Daddy said.

"That's so nice," Momma said. "Ain't it Jessie? Ain't it so nice?"

Victor opened his eyes at Daddy. "I'll bet the Local appreciates the work you're doing."

"I'm just a volunteer," Daddy said.

"Still it could lead to something, you know." Victor looked at Missy then, then at me, soft eyes floating over big muscled shoulders. "That your little sister?"

"Her name's Missy," I said.

Victor reached in his pants pocket, brought out a piece of caramel candy, unwrapped it and gave it to Missy. Missy put it right away inside her mouth and began to chew. Caramel colored spit bubbled at the corner of her mouth.

"She can talk when she wants to," Momma said.

"I have no doubt about that at all," Victor said, his smile somehow too smooth. Still, I wanted him to pay me some attention too.

"My name's Orbie," I said. "I like army men. My Daddy used to be in the army."

Victor reached up and touched his glasses, pushing them back along the bridge of his nose, his eyes going on Daddy. "What theater?"

"Two years in London," Daddy said. "Didn't see much action."

"A damn good thing too," Victor said. "I was at Normandy. All but three men in my platoon died."

"Lord A Mighty," Daddy said.

"Golly!" I yelled. "Was you shot?"

Victor laughed.

"He can be polite when he wants to be," Momma said.

"I'm sure he can," Victor said; still laughing.

I didn't see what was so funny though. "Did your guts hang out?"

"Orbie!" Momma shouted.

"That's enough, son," Daddy said.

"That's all right." Victor squatted down in front of me. His hair was black, shiny with hair oil and combed straight from the front to the back. "Want to see where I got hit?"

"I guess so," I said, not sure if I did or not.

Victor turned his shoulder and pulled his shirt away so I could see the back of his neck. At the bottom was an ugly white dug-out-place, a gash that looked like somebody took a knife and cut.

"That from a real bullet?"

"Shrapnel," Victor said. "A piece of mortar shell hit me there, right at the base of my neck. Any higher and it would have taken my head."

"God."

"I spent six weeks in the hospital. That was it. They sent me home after that." Victor stood up. "I used to believe in war. Anymore, I'm not so sure."

It got a quiet time between all of us there, even with the noise of all the big cats and the people walking around. Out the corner of my eye I could still see the white tiger, going from one end to the other of his cage. Victor got a faraway look about his eyes. Then his chin started to quiver.

"Lord have mercy," Momma whispered.

Victor was sad, but I wasn't sure why. To me, you had to have battles. So the good people could win. You had to have blood and guts and bombs. That was the fun part.

Victor blinked and a tear slid down the side of his face. He wiped at his eyes with a hankie. "Forgive me. I didn't expect this."

"War's a terrible thing," Momma said.

Daddy nodded. "Yes it is."

Later, when Victor was gone Momma said, "Such a sad, good person he is. And so kind too. He's got spiritual ideas, don't he? I liked what he had to say, didn't you like what he had to say, Jessie?"

"Sure did," Daddy said. "He ain't like them other foremen over there. At Ford's, I mean. Them fellers'll look at you one way and you'll think that's it, but then when they walk off, you'll see more eyes popping out the back of their heads. Staring at you in ways you didn't expect."

I wasn't sure what Daddy was talking about, but what he said about Victor was true. All I saw when he walked off was just hair, black hair—and no eyes.

"Huh... Huh... Huh... Huh...," the tiger went. Circling. Going round and round in its cage.

———

Shortly after that, Daddy started fixing things on Victor's truck. The first time was spark plugs. The second, a broken mirror. Then brakes and a door handle. Sometimes Victor would help. Other times he went in the house and talked to Momma.

"How come you're all the time fixing on his old truck?" I asked Daddy one day.

Daddy was leaning up with a can; pouring water in the radiator. "I thought you liked Victor."

I wasn't sure if I liked him or not.

Daddy set the water can down.

"You like Victor?" I said.

"Yes I do."

"You think he'd get mad if you didn't work on his truck?"

"He might be disappointed some. It don't pay to disappoint people, son."

"How come?"

Daddy banged the hood closed. "It just don't is all."

"What about the other day?" I said.

"What other day?"

"When them men came. When you was washing the car."

"You heard that?"

"Some of it. The window was down. They were from the Union," I said. "They wanted you to do something but you said 'no'."

"That's right. I thought you were coloring."

"I was," I said. "That man with the pushed in face smiled at me."

"Lord God," Daddy said.

A couple days ago I was coloring in my coloring book, sitting in the back seat of Momma's Ford. Daddy had been going around outside the car, washing it down with a hose when another car pulled up in the driveway, a shiny red Mercury with a Davy Crockett coon tail tied to the aerial.

Two men got out of the car and came up to Daddy. Daddy was holding a sponge in one hand and a hose in the other. One of the men was big as two men put together. His thick wrists stuck out the sleeves of a white sports coat that looked two sizes too small. He wore white-framed sunglasses over a face that was sunk in on one side like a balloon losing air. The other man was tiny, shorter even than Daddy. He wore a gray suit and a slantwise hat like Dick Tracy's. He even looked a little bit like Dick Tracy, all high-cheek-boned and sharp-eyed. He came up to Daddy with his hand out, wanting

42

Daddy to shake. Daddy couldn't though, because of the hose and the sponge. The Dick Tracy man saw this and grinned.

"What did they want?" I asked.

"Nothing much. Wanted me to help them." Daddy pulled a rag out of his back pocket and began to wipe his hands. "Said they was Inspectors; said they was hired by the Union. Even had badges."

"You disappointed them," I said.

Daddy looked at me straight on. "That's right son. I told them 'no'."

———

When Victor went in to talk to Momma sometimes I'd go on the floor by the table in the kitchen with my coloring books and listen. I heard Victor tell Momma how his parents had to get a divorce. How he had to live with his mother, then with his father. How his parents had come overseas from the Old Country on a boat and didn't have any money and had to work hard and stand in a bunch of soup lines. He talked about his grandparents too. How they lived on a farm in Poland where they raised pigs and cows and grew cabbages and carrots and still they almost starved.

He was obliged to live with his father, he said, because his mother did bad things. He never said what the bad things were, but every time he talked about his mother his voice would go all soft and low. Then a sad still quiet would come over the kitchen.

Momma would drink coffee, smoke cigarettes and listen. She liked Victor. I could tell. I think she liked his glow. She even let him bring his beer in, something she never allowed Daddy to do.

"There's very little alcohol in beer," Victor said.

"I reckon if you've got to have it, you've got to have it," Momma said. "My church don't allow it though."

"I don't have to drink, if it offends you."

"It don't," Momma said. "They's folks where I come from drinks moonshine. Good Christian folk, some of them. I'd rather you was honest than slipping around."

"Thank you," Victor said. "My own parents were Catholics. They both drank. Like fish, you might say. Maybe that's why Catholics and Protestants don't get along, generally speaking."

"I wouldn't know about that," Momma said. "Born again folk don't drink unless they taking Communion. Then it's just that Mogen David wine."

Victor held up his beer. "Sangre de Cristo!"

"Excuse me?" Momma said.

"Sangre de Cristo. The Blood of Christ."

"We don't believe that way," Momma said. "It's just a remembrance. That's what the Bible says. 'This do in remembrance of me.' Sometimes we'll use grape juice."

"I'd like to go with you sometime," Victor said all of a sudden. "With you and Jessie, I mean. To church."

Momma smiled. "It's just a store-front church Victor. Folks there, well, they're just like me."

"If that's the case, I definitely want to go," Victor said. He took a sip off his beer.

Momma giggled. "Oh now Victor, I told you. I didn't get no farther than the eighth grade."

"I don't care about that," Victor said. "When I talk, you listen. You understand. That's what counts." Victor took another sip. "Formal education is overrated anyway. My father, he worked hard to get me two years of college. Then there was the war and I got drafted. What I've learned since, I've learned on my own. I read. I write a little. That doesn't make me better than you, or anybody else for that matter. Farmers? Tillers of the soil? I'm from that stock too."

Momma got up to wipe the table.

Victor's eyes followed her. "Ruby? Do you remember when we first met?"

Momma wiped harder at the table. "Why yes. It was at

that picnic Fords put on."

"You were the finest looking woman there."

Momma hopped like a bird to the other side of the table. She picked up the saltshaker and set it next to the pepper. "Oh Victor, go on now. Ain't no truth in that." She went on with her work, wiping where she had already wiped before. "It's sweet of you to say so though."

"Go on yourself. I know a good looking woman when I see one." Victor emptied his beer, got up and put it down next to the sink. His good looks sparkled out at Momma. "You wouldn't happen to have a cup of coffee, would you?"

"I always got coffee. You want cream?"

"Just sugar," Victor smiled. "Just stick your finger in it." Momma knocked over the salt and looked at me, her face glowing bright red.

I looked at the floor.

———

Victor did come to church, first with us—then all by himself—though he always would sit close by to us. People at the church liked Victor. Even when he used high-sounding words they did. He was always willing to go over things again—for people who didn't understand. He was good that way.

"Why, he's just an old hillbilly in northern clothes," Momma said. "I never seen nobody with so much patience."

"I reckon," Daddy said.

"It's a shame what he went through though. I mean, with his family and all."

"He had a hard row," Daddy said.

"But look how good he turned out. Why, it's almost like he's found another home here at our little church."

"He shore got a way with people," Daddy said.

"Don't he now?"

———

One time The Lane Sisters sung a song for Victor. Mary, Elsie Mae and Loretta. They liked Victor more than anybody. Daddy said they were sweet on him; said all they wanted was to be his girlfriend. They got up one Sunday and Loretta, she was the pretty one, said her and her sisters had practiced up a song special for Brother Denalsky. 'We'll Understand It Better By and By', she called it; and it was their prayer, she said, that Brother Denalsky, and all God's beloved children would someday come to understand better the pain and sorrow of this world. She stepped back then and the piano lady played the starting in part, and then all the sisters started in singing together. When they got through the first verse they started on the chorus.

By and by, when the morning comes,
When the saints of God are gathered home,
We'll tell the story how we've overcome,
For we'll understand it better by and by.

Victor listened for a while, and then he started to cry. He wiped his eyes with a clean white handkerchief. He leaned over and put his whole face in the handkerchief. He cried and blew his nose. Preacher Hilly walked over—probably he was going to talk to him about Jesus—but before he could get there Victor got up, walked straight to the back of the church and out the door.

"Thank you Jesus," Momma said.

After church The Lane Sisters came up to Momma and Daddy. "That man's under conviction," Loretta said. She always sounded like somebody with a cold, all stuffy nosed and sniffling.

"If ever one was," Momma said.

"I hope we didn't embarrass him none," Elsie Mae said.

"I wouldn't worry about that," Daddy said.

"He's real good looking," Loretta said, smiling. "A real gentleman."

"Well," Daddy said. "You know he isn't married."

Mary and Elsie Mae giggled. They were fat girls. Loretta was slim and pretty, like Momma. She had a red dress on. Red shoes.

"Got a good high paying job too," Daddy said. "You want his phone number? I'll give it to you, if you wannit."

Mary and Elsie Mae went all bug-eyed.

"Brother Ray, you stop teasing," Loretta said.

"I'd be glad to put in a good word. I *work* for the man." Daddy looked around at Mary and Elsie Mae. "I could put in a word for the three of you, if you'd like. I could say I know three girls would like to kiss him all over."

The Lane sisters stood there now with their mouths dropped open.

"Jessie stop it," Momma said.

The Lane sisters broke out in a three-girl giggle.

"Brother Ray!" Loretta laughed. "You the sorriest thang I ever laid eyes on. And you a Christian."

"That's right, I *am* a Christian! You think I'm gonna dry up and blow away 'cause of it? Naw sir. Christians need lovin' too. Not just talk-about-it love either." Daddy smoothed the little hair left at the side of his head and twinkled his eyes at The Lane Sisters. "Ya'll better get to kissing on somebody, you don't wanna blow away."

Everybody laughed then, even Momma.

———

When I wanted, Victor would let me look at the gash on his neck. Or sit in his lap and trace a finger around the heart with the snake on the back of his hand. One time he showed Momma and me another heart, which was the medal he got from the war, purple with a gold picture of George Washington on the front.

"It's bronze, not gold," Victor said. "It's The Purple Heart. I got it because I was wounded. A consolation prize."

"You must be proud though," Momma said.

"Not really. It takes more stupidity than bravery to catch a little shrapnel."

"It took a lot more than that," Momma said. "I'll tell you what's the truth. I'm glad Jessie never had to go into battle. And I'm glad for men like you, that did."

47

———

Victor was good in a whole bunch of ways. Going to church. Bringing Missy and me presents for Christmas. A bag of army men. A new baby doll that could pee in its own diaper. Taking Missy and me to the zoo. To the picture show. The carnival at Fun Park. The Merry-Go-Round there.

He made Daddy his 'right hand man' at Fords—even with him being in the Union. Daddy would talk to Victor about what the worker-men needed. Victor bragged on Daddy. He even tried to get Daddy on Management's bowling team, but the Union wouldn't allow it. Said Daddy rolled a mean bowling ball, missing fingers and all.

They would ride home together on bowling nights, him and Daddy would. One time Daddy came in smelling like beer. Momma got mad. Later on, I heard her talking to Daddy, telling him how they should be strong and not bend to Victor's ways. Then Victor might have a chance to be saved, have a chance to find a good girl—Loretta Lane maybe—settle down and be happy in the Lord.

———

Victor wrote things on little notepads and scraps of paper. Poetry, he called it. Impressions of the day. All I knew about poetry was just nursery rhymes and the rhymes on cards at Christmas time.

"He writes in that book," Daddy said one night, as he and Momma were getting ready for bed. I was in my room with the door open unable to sleep.

"It ain't right to spy around on a person," Momma said.

"I wasn't spying around. He was sitting up in the cab of that truck, writing. He wasn't even *trying* to hide it. I climbed in; he never even looked up. We were supposed to be going bowling."

"He told me he writes. He likes words," Momma said.

"He's got a whole book full of writing," Daddy said. "I found this today."

I could hear paper rattle. Something Daddy had.

"A letter?" Momma said.

"Something come from his book."

"Jessie, you know it ain't right snooping in another person's business."

"I reckon if you find something on the ground you can read it, can't you? This was in the driveway."

"How do you know it's his?"

"Wrote in his hand, that's how. I ain't seen no handwriting finer than Victor's."

"You ought to give it back."

"Well, I reckon I will give it back," Daddy said. "In good time. You wanna hear what it says? It's kindly sad and strange at the same time."

"It ain't my business."

"Well, you ought to hear it anyhow. It tells something about him. That we didn't know about, I mean."

"Sounds like you're bound to read it no matter what I say," Momma said.

Daddy didn't answer. I heard him and Momma moving around in there, getting ready for bed. It was Momma that spoke up first. "Read it if you aim to."

"You sure?" Daddy said.

"No. But it ain't the first time I haven't been."

Daddy rattled the paper. He was a slow reader. Some words he stretched out longer than others. Words he didn't know he had to spell out loud.

"And it is through him," he read. "I bring the a-b-y-s-s. I don't know what that is."

Momma laughed. "A rotten tooth, maybe. One a dentist has to pull."

"That's abscess," Daddy said. "This is a-b-y-s-s. Abiss, I reckon. I don't know."

"Read," Momma said.

The paper rattled, then Daddy's voice came again. "And it is through him I bring the *abiss* into my own heart and ask if I am any better. And how life might become worthy, though *steeped* in this

49

barroom darkness, this gray *plastered* wall, which has cracked so p-i-t-i, pitifully. And how we might take it along with us, this death, this *alcoholic* death and its untended women and children to the final s-t-o-i-c—stoik, I reckon is what it says—stoik end of these worlds."

It got quiet in there a while. Then with tears in her voice Momma said, "I believe he's talking about his daddy there, Jessie. One killed himself."

5

SOMETHING YOU COULDN'T DO ANYTHING WITH

It was summertime when Daddy got killed. Then came fall. Dark rainy days and leaves on the ground. It was sad not having Daddy around, kissing on Momma, laughing and talking up things from the factory. I missed his big lightbulb head, his big ears, his hands on Sunday morning, all scrubbed for church, work hands like claws too big for the arms, scrubbed red but still dirty, black lines, factory grease in the knuckle cracks. And how he smelled—I missed that too—like Lava soap and gasoline and cigarettes all mixed in together.

Momma kept to herself; got that purple skin under her eyes. Blood eyes. She wouldn't put on make up, and she wouldn't fix up her hair. The house got a gray time. Even the yellow gloss on the kitchen wall had lost its shine. Some of it was 'cause of gray skies and rainy weather. The rest was just old cigarette smoke and ashtrays that never got dumped.

Momma would lie up in bed or sit in the rocking chair in the living room in front of the TV, smoking one cigarette after another. Sometimes she stayed up late and rocked herself in the rocking chair with the TV set off. It was kind of like she was waiting on Daddy to come home. I would be in the kitchen drawing or playing with my army men and hear her rocking in there with the lights all off. I'd see her cigarette glowing and the shape of her head moving with the rocking chair backlit by the living room window. I would go crawl up in her lap and lay my head against her shoulder. She would put her arm around me then, and I would just be there with her, rocking back and forth, listening to her heartbeat.

———

One day it snowed so hard they closed all the schools. I was in the living room with Momma and Missy, sitting on the floor with a blanket wrapped about my shoulders. Missy had crawled under the coffee table, and was bashing at her doll's face with one of Daddy's old shoes. We were watching one of Momma's TV programs. A man in a white chef's hat was chopping celery and talking all serious about chicken salad sandwiches. I thought it was stupid. He put the celery in a bowl with pieces of chicken and mixed in mayonnaise and spices and set it off on the side and started in talking about all the different kinds of bread you could use. I got up with the blanket still around me and went to the front window. Outside was a big man in sunglasses and an orange snowsuit, shoveling snow off the sidewalk in front of our house. The snow was higher than the man's knees—white and sparkling under a sharp blue cloudless sky.

"There's somebody out here Momma," I said. "There's somebody shoveling our walk."

"Who? Who is it?"

"I don't know. He's orange. He's got sunglasses and a big bushy hat."

When Momma looked out the window, she got all happy—then worried. "It's Victor! I didn't ask for no help."

After while he came on the porch and rang the doorbell. Momma put her coat on and opened the door. I pulled the blanket tight around my shoulders and went next to Momma. The day was so bone chilly cold the insides of my nose holes stuck together. I looked up at Victor. "Momma said she didn't ask for no help."

"Hush," Momma said. "I was just thinking how you ought not have bothered with all that, Victor."

Victor smiled. He looked at us through the dark glasses, his voice all deep and friendly-like. "Jessie was my best worker. A good friend. I'm honored to help you Ruby."

Victor's breath came out in little white rags of steam that vanished almost as soon as they appeared. Snow shovels scraped in the distance. Victor's pickup truck sat in our driveway with a plow blade straight across the front. All the snow behind Momma's Ford had been cleared away. Momma looked at it all and started to cry.

"You and the children," Victor said. "Orbie here, and Missy, well, you've become almost like family to me."

"I know, I know. I'm sorry. It's just...it's been so hard." Momma pulled a Kleenex out of her coat pocket and blew her nose. "I can't talk about it right now."

"You don't have to Ruby. I understand. You need time." Victor lifted the snow shovel onto one shoulder. "We all need time."

———

It wasn't two days Victor called again. He kept on calling too, checking was everything all right, was there anything he could do? Finally, Momma let him come and fix the basement windows. Then a whistling noise in the refrigerator wouldn't go away and he had to fix that too. He shoveled more snow. He spread salt over our icy front steps. He spread it along the sidewalk in front of our house. In the springtime he came and raked dead leaves, got Daddy's old push-mower out and cut the grass.

People in the neighborhood liked Victor, all except our baby sitter, Mrs. Profit, who was bone skinny and nervous and talked a mile a minute. She didn't like it when Victor made things simple so she could understand, when he tried to talk like a hillbilly, saying things like *You all come*, or *Fair to middlin'*.

"Why, he don't even got the accent," she said to Momma one day. "He's a broke-mouthed hillbilly you ask me."

"People over to church think it's sweet," Momma said.

"Sweet? Well, I don't. It's like he's talking down to me. Like he thinks I'm dimwitted or something."

"Oh, I think he's just trying to get along," Momma said.

Mid spring he was calling Momma every week. Then it seemed like everyday. Everyday, there Momma would be, talking to Victor on the telephone. She was still on bad times though, Momma was. She cooked and cleaned house, got Missy and me washed up and ready for bed. She was our mother, and she loved us, but I could see there was still something sad she was dragging around inside. It was like a dead cat I saw once all froze up in the back yard, something you couldn't do anything with.

Victor leaned in on Momma. He leaned in on Missy and me too, saying what a good boy I was, how Missy would grow up to be a beautiful young woman some day—just like her mother—how he wished he had a little girl like her. Said he damn sure wasn't going to spend the rest of his life working for Ford Motor Company. Breathing those factory fumes. Chasing after lazy good for nothings, just to get them to do an honest day's work. Not when he could make triple or even quadruple the money working for himself. Said if a man really wanted to get ahead, he had to have plans that were *significant*.

I liked that word *significant*, even if at the time I didn't know quite what it meant, I liked how it felt in my mouth, on the tip of my tongue, like something that if you didn't pay attention to it, it would cause you a whole heap of trouble. I liked going around the house saying it.

Significant. Significant. Significant.

I liked that Victor liked us, but I didn't like the way he was all the time trying to be on my mind. It was too close together somehow—like when Momma started talking about Jesus and wouldn't shut up. A Dark Thing would come then, so sticky hot it would gum up all my army men and tanks, making them so they couldn't move or explode or be in battles and wars like they were supposed to be.

After some time Momma started feeling better. She looked better too, started to put makeup on, not much, just a little lipstick and color for her cheeks. One day Victor asked her to go to the picture show, and she said yes. After that they started going out all the time. First to the picture shows. Then dinners. Then dancing. I think Momma liked dancing the best. Her and Victor would stay out late, come home making noise, laughing, whispering, Mrs. Profit, our baby sitter, shushing them not to wake Missy and me, smoking, clinking glasses, Mrs. Profit saying goodbye, then kissy stuff, and Momma telling Victor 'no'. Then Victor laughing, saying goodbye, going out the door, the whole place smelling like beer.

One Saturday after dinner Victor came in drunk. He got down on his knees in front of Momma, crying, wrapping his arms around her like some big cry-baby-bear. He loved Momma, he said. He loved me and he loved Missy and he wanted us all to be a family together. Momma told him she wouldn't talk to him about it until he sobered up. She made him lay down on our couch. He was there when I went to bed and he was there in the morning when I got up.

I thought Victor was all right, but I didn't want to be a family with him. I didn't care he was trying to be so nice. He didn't joke around or laugh or anything, not like my real Daddy had. I didn't like his smell in our bathroom either. Cigars and toilet shit. Daddy never smelled that way.

One time, Missy and me were playing in the living room, and for no reason he told us to keep it down. We weren't even making any noise. I got mad and told him to shut his mouth and he drew back his fist like he was going to hit me. I saw then he had something like worms, slimy red worms turning

55

over in his eyes, twisting around on sharp glass, cutting themselves in there and getting mean.

Momma said he looked like Superman in disguise. "Why, with them glasses, he looks just like that Clark Kent. Don't he look just like that Clark Kent?"

I thought he did too, a little bit maybe, especially with his hair combed back the way it was. I didn't want to say it, but really he looked better than Clark Kent. That was because of his glow. But when the glow wasn't there, he'd be just all by himself, watching things dead on. It was like he'd somehow gotten bored with everything and was waiting—for what, I didn't know.

Momma said he might make Missy and me a good Daddy— with a little practice he might. "He's got a good job. And good prospects too! And he wants so much to take care of us all!" I think that's why she left Missy and me with Mrs. Profit one day and went off with Victor to the Justice of the Peace. That was in September of 1957. That was why she married him. That and their dancing, and that smoochy stuff I heard him and Momma do on the couch late at night, Momma saying 'no' and 'no' and 'no' and then nothing. Nothing at all.

PART THREE

6
THE ALAMO

1958

"Orbie, turn that down," Momma said. "Me and Victor's talking here."

"Aw, Momma. It's Davy Crockett."

"I don't care what it is. It don't need to be that loud." Davy Crockett was pointing his gun over a wall, shooting at the Mexicans. "Aw, Momma."

"You heard your mother!" Victor said. "Turn it down, or turn it off!"

I got up and turned it down. We'd finished eating supper a while ago. The whole house smelled like fried chicken and dishwater. I could see Momma and Victor out the corner of my eye. Four empty beer bottles stood like smoke stacks on the coffee table's glass top.

"Imagine that," Victor said, "a Negro." He took a swig off his beer and pushed his eyeglasses up. He held the bottle upright on the arm of his chair. Blue Ribbon beer. He'd been drinking it all through supper. "At work. He wanted to talk to me about Jesus. Asked me if I knew Jesus." He looked at Momma like she'd be stupid not to know what he was talking about.

"Victor honey, that don't matter. Jesus loves everybody. It don't matter the color a person's skin is." A big King James Bible lay open-faced across her lap.

"Oh, you Christ-Sellers are all alike," Victor said. "Would you let Missy marry one?"

"No," Momma said.

"Why not? Your own mother would. She'd even come to the wedding."

All the air went out of Momma's chest. "I wouldn't let her do that Victor. Marry one, I mean."

"But I thought Jesus loves everybody, Momma."

"Well He does," Momma said. "He's God's only son."

"God's only son," Victor said. "You really believe that."

"Yes I do, Victor. With all my heart."

Victor took out a pad of paper and a blue ballpoint pen from his shirt pocket. He wrote something on the pad and gave it to Momma.

Momma read the letters out loud. "A-T-H-E," she began and gave Victor a sideways glance.

"Go on," Victor said. "Read it."

"A-T-H-E-I-S-T." Momma gave Victor another look. "You always coming up with something big, Victor. What is this?"

"Atheist Momma."

"Atheist?"

Victor smiled. "That's right. Means I'd no sooner believe in God than you'd let Missy marry a Negro."

This was how they argued—Momma on God's side, Victor on the Devil's.

Victor put the pad of paper back in his shirt pocket. He held onto the pen, his good looks spoiled now by the worms in his eyes.

"And here I thought you coming to our little church meant something," Momma said.

Cannon fire exploded from the television set. The Mexican army men, dressed in gray coats and white pants, stormed over the hills, some of them carrying wooden ladder-things that looked like backbones with the ribs chewed off. Black smoke boiled up over the walls of the Alamo.

Momma said, "There is a God, Victor. Even you ought to know that."

Victor took another swig of beer. He threw his head back, turning the bottle practically upside down. Bubbles and foam jumped up inside the neck. He set it on the coffee table empty. That made five. Five empty brown bottles with blue ribbons on the coffee table. He worked the push button on his pen, making it click. "Prove it to me Momma."

Momma closed the Bible. "Prove what? That they's a God? Victor honey, I never heard tell of such a thing. Prove it yourself. All you need do is look around."

"I do look around, and do you know what I see? I see a lot of pious do-gooders like yourself. Like that Negro preacher at work. I see them sticking their noses in where they don't belong."

"But Victor honey that ain't..."

"I'm not finished yet," Victor said, holding his hand up like a cop. "These people, they act so good, so pious, so 'above it all'. But when push comes to shove they're just hypocrites. Like yourself." He waited for that to sink in. Then he worked the button on the pen. *Click-click.* "If Jesus loves *negroes,* Momma, why don't you?"

Again the air went out of Momma's chest. Me, the empty beer bottles, Victor's pen, even the Battle of the Alamo—all seemed to be waiting for Momma to speak. "Can I talk now, Mr. Two-Years-of-College?" she finally said.

Victor raised his arm from the elbow up, fingers curled around the pen, thumb on the clicker. He watched Momma like that, smirking, like he knew everything there was to know and Momma would be a fool to doubt him.

"They's different people, Victor," Momma said. "Just because I don't mix with every kind don't mean I'm not trying. At least I'm *trying* to be like He was. The Lord's ways are mysterious."

"Who says?"

"Why, it says so in the Bible!"

"I'm afraid you'll have to do better than that Momma," Victor said.

"No I won't. I won't have to do no better." Momma put her hand on the Bible. "It's God's Word we're talking about here."

Victor wore silver pants and a white short-sleeved shirt, unbuttoned at the top. There were a few spots of beer on the belly. "The Bible is just a fairy tale Momma. Just a made up story you would have to be a fool to believe."

"It's God's word!" Momma said.

"Prove it to me Momma. Prove to me there's a God."

Be quiet Momma. Don't make Victor mad. Don't make The Dark Thing come.

It was nighttime outside. A picture window rose up in back of Victor framed with dark red curtains. A roar swelled from the television set. Mexican soldiers were swarming up the wall of the Alamo. Davy Crockett knocked one off with the butt end of his rifle.

"I don't have to prove you nothing," Momma said. "What did they teach you in that college? That they's no God? Well, there is one. And His word is right here." She thumped the Bible with the palm of her hand.

Click-click, went Victor's pen.

"Prove it to me Momma."

"Quit calling me that!" Momma said. "I ain't your Momma, and I don't have to prove you a *damned* thing!"

"Better watch those cuss words Momma. What will the Lord think?"

The Dark Thing was getting big now, getting heavy, mixed in with all that chicken grease from dinner—chicken grease and Pabst Blue Ribbon beer.

Momma slammed the Bible onto the coffee table, yelling now. "I said don't call me *Momma!* Your Momma's dead! Wasn't nothing but a drunk let her own kid go hungry! If it hadn't been for your Daddy you'd have been out on the street!"

"That's not the point!"

"It is too the point! You ain't had no raising is the point!"

Victor took off his glasses and tossed them on the Bible. A thousand Mexicans charged the Alamo.

"Your Daddy sent you to that college didn't learn you a thing! Bunch of fifty dollar words nobody understands!"

Victor hauled off suddenly, throwing his pen across the room. It sailed all the way past the TV set and into the dining room, smacked against the wall there and broke apart, landing on the dining room table. "You Bible-Thumping-Bitch!"

Okay Momma stop it now! Can't you see?

But Momma couldn't see. Couldn't see that pen. Couldn't see the greasy red mole next to Victor's nose, how shiny it had become. Couldn't see the worms. "Your Daddy had you working in that store of his for nothing! Wouldn't even let you out to play!"

Victor slapped the arm of the sofa chair. "Son of a bitch, Ruby!"

"Son of a bitch, yourself!" Momma yelled. "You ain't no child! I ain't your Momma neither!"

I held my breath. More cannon fire exploded from the Alamo. I could see the moon—a pale thumbnail rising in the glass of the picture window behind Victor's head—floating peacefully as if, quietly tilting over the watery half-reflection of the television set. Suddenly there was a humungous loud crack and the coffee table's glass top, Momma's Bible, Victor's horn rims and all the beer bottles dove straight toward the floor.

"Bastard!" Momma yelled. "You goddamn bastard!"

I jumped up.

Victor's hand was bleeding. I could see the heart tattoo, wrapped around with the snake's tan-colored body, 'Born To Lose' written there in green letters. Victor looked at the hand. Then he looked at Momma. Then he cocked the hand back in a tight knuckled fist and rabbit-punched her square in the face. The sound of it was like a mallet on wet meat. Brown curls of hair fell across Momma's forehead. Victor came back around with his open hand and slapped her across the back of the head. A plate of false teeth popped out bloody on the couch. Victor grabbed Momma's hair and bent her head back, his eyes all over the front of her. "You want Jesus! I'll give you some Jesus!"

Momma's mouth had dropped open. She cried out, trying to flail at Victor with both fists.

"You leave my Momma alone!" I shouted. I ran between them, pushing backwards, trying to make Momma far away. Momma wrapped an arm around me, holding her other hand over the place Victor had punched. Victor stood over us, his fist raised, trembling to come down.

"Get out of the way, you little shit!"

"No Obie!" Momma hugged me to her. "Ooo tay!" She was trying to talk without her teeth. "He ma boy!"

"You leave my Momma alone! I'll kill you, you hit her again!"

Momma grabbed up her teeth and pushed them back in with her thumb. Hugging me, dragging me along with her, she slid to the end of the couch.

Victor took a step toward us, his fist still raised.

"Victor, please! Please don't!"

Victor stood there, looking down at us, frowning, the red mole shining. It was like he didn't know what else to do. He unclenched his fist. Blood made red cracks over his fingers, over his fingernails. The snake on the tattoo looked at me sideways and slid away.

Victor's eyes began to well up, his chin to quiver. Crocodile tears began to bulge and stream down his cheeks, one then another, over the red mole and around the twitching corners of his mouth. That's what he did when he got drunk, when he was mad, when he wanted to hurt me, hurt Momma, hurt Missy, hurt the walls, the tables and chairs, anything he could get his hands on, crying like he was so sorry, like he was somebody you had to feel sorry for. His hand dropped to his side.

"I'm so sorry, Ruby," he said.

"It's too late for sorry."

Victor reached out with his bloody hand, but Momma

pulled back. "I just want to look at that eye."

"Stay away from me!" Momma's voice was trembling now.

"You're right, Ruby. My mother was a drunk, a drunk and a whore." Victor's throat swelled with a sob he tried to gulp down. He looked at the television set—at the ruin of glass, the King James version of the Bible, its gilded pages crushed against the floor, at the beer bottles pointing in every direction. Then he heaved up a sigh and let loose with a kick, the shiny brown toe of his shoe catching the empty frame of the coffee table, smashing it, flipping it up and over and upside down in front of the television set. He stood over the mess of everything, looking at nothing, his face crazy with tears.

"Victor honey? I'm so sorry," Momma said. Then she started to cry too.

The Battle of the Alamo was over.

———

I could hear them through the wall.

First Victor, blubbering and mumbling like somebody under water.

Then Momma in a smooth sad voice saying, "Victor honey, it's all right. I didn't mean to. I was just mad was all."

I lay in bed, looking up into the dark. The room was pitch black except for the window over Missy's bed, backlit by a sky of sparkling stars. Pinholes to heaven, Momma called them. She said nighttime was just a black sheet with pinholes God put over the world so people could sleep. Said He left the pinholes so no matter how dark it got, people could still see heaven's light.

A white square slipped in against the wall opposite my bed. Car lights. It slid over Missy's teddy bear, over the Indian war bonnet Momma got me for Christmas. I could hear crickets chirping outside the window, Missy sleeping in the bed across from mine.

Victor and Momma's bedsprings started to creak—soft and slow at first—then louder—then faster and louder. Then like a train, squalling, blowing clouds of lightning and dirty black wind.

"Orbie? What is that Orbie?" It was Missy, sleepy-talking from her bed. "What is that? You sleep?"

"Hush," I whispered. "Momma and Victor's making a train."

That Dark Thing would grow. It would get big.

"That ain't no train," Missy said, awake now.

The springs began to beat even louder—faster.

Faster than a speeding bullet! More powerful than a locomotive!

Momma cried out, "Oh! Oh Victor!"

Missy jumped into my bed. Her baby doll's plastic head whacked me in the face.

"Get back in your *own* bed!" I said.

"I'm scared Orbie." She pushed her back up against mine.

I was scared too, and mad at Victor. Mad at Momma. I wanted to jump up. Run in there. Save Momma. Then I heard her turn over in bed. Laughing.

———

We had a screened-in porch with jalousie windows you could angle out to let in air. That was in the summertime mostly when Momma fixed on people's hair. Momma liked to fix on people's hair. She was good at it too, and she didn't cost a bunch of money, not like a for real beauty operator would. She was going to go to beauty school some day she said, but there was no telling when that would be.

A lot of people came over to get their hair done. Jenny Dee Danielson, Opal whose husband had lung cancer, Sheri Slabodnik, Mrs. Brown, the Lane sisters from church who sang pretty. Then there'd be people in the neighborhood like Pat Nichols who was a Mormon, a great big fat lady who wore black slacks with sweaters stretched tight over big giant titties. Her and Momma would argue on the Bible. Sometimes they'd get to arguing on Joseph Smith or Jesus or if you could have more than one wife, if that was okay with God. Momma said it wasn't. Pat Nichols said it was.

All kinds of people would come over. Momma would work on them, even when her eye was puffed out, the bruised skin covered with layers of cracked makeup. Nobody said anything about it except old nosey Mrs. Profit. She came over one day to get her hair fixed. Momma had put silver clips in it and was trying to trim up the ends. Bone skinny Mrs. Profit, the skin peeling off her hands, sitting in Momma's beauty chair—smoking one cigarette after another.

I was running my dump truck along a board propped up at one end with a brick. Momma's Victrola was going like usual. And like usual she was too busy to change the records so the last one on the stack a happy Sunday song called This Little Light Of Mine played itself over and over again.

This little light of mine, I'm gonna let it shine.
This little light of mine, I'm gonna let it shine.
Everyday, everyday, everyday, everyday!
I'm gonna let my little light shine!

At first Mrs. Profit didn't say anything about Momma's eye. She started in on old man Slabodnik and his accordion instead. The music he played sang out over the neighborhood. I liked it. Kids in the neighborhood did too.

"Why, he's disturbing what little peace they is around here!" Mrs. Profit said, her voice like fingernails on a blackboard—so screechy-keen it near made my teeth hurt.

Momma tried to go along with her. "Lord, Mrs. Profit. I hope you don't mind me playing my records then?"

"Course I don't. You don't play'em all over the neighborhood like he does. I tell you what's the truth Ruby. If I had me a gun I'd shoot that thing of his. Shoot him too!"

"Now Mrs. Profit, you don't mean that."

Mrs. Profit gave Momma a dead-on look. "Where did you get that eye Ruby?" The question came so quick Momma's mouth dropped open. "That Polack hit you, didn't he?"

"Mr. Slabodnik?" Momma said.

"No, Victor!" Mrs. Profit screeched.

"Victor?" Momma touched the cracked patch of makeup next to her eye. "Why no, Mrs. Profit. I got this on the car door while I was getting the groceries."

"Groceries?"

"Why yeah. I slipped on one of Orbie's roller skates." Momma pointed a skinny black comb my way. "Isn't that so Orbie?"

What really happened was our secret. I liked having secrets with Momma. I liked having the go ahead to lie.

Momma winked. "Go on. Tell Mrs. Profit."

"Yeah, Mrs. Profit. Momma banged her head on the car door."

Mrs. Profit's splotchy hands were joined at the fingertips, pushing at one another. A spider doing push-ups on a mirror. "You got to get the hell away from him Ruby."

"Now Mrs. Profit. Don't be talking that way." Momma walked around to the back of her. With the comb she pulled up a wall of black hair and started trimming along the edge. "That's Orbie's Daddy now."

"He ain't my *real* Daddy!" I said too loud.

Momma looked at me over the top of Mrs. Profit's head. She puckered her lips like a fish and shook her head for me to shut up. "Victor's been real good. Why, he even went to prayer service the other night."

Mrs. Profit knitted her eyebrows together. "That's right Orbie. He *ain't* your real Daddy!"

"Orbie, go on outside and play hon; ain't no need of you being in here with us old women."

"Aw, Momma. I got my truck and everything in here." I knew there wasn't any use arguing though, not with Momma mad like she was. I picked up my truck and the board and the brick and went outside. I went around the porch where Momma was fixing on Mrs. Profit's hair, slammed the truck down in the yard and hit it with the board. Right away I got a bad feeling because of its being a present from Daddy.

I looked around the yard. It had holes and patches of dirt.

Toward the back of the fence sat a rusty swing-set with a broken seat. One of the legs had pulled loose from the cement. Water dripped from a spigot under the kitchen window onto a green hose that lay in a tangle next to Daddy's old push-mower. A smell of rubber and burnt grass came up from there. I could hear Momma and Mrs. Profit through the open jalousies.

Mrs. Profit's voice screeched over the happy Sunday song. "I seen him over here! Hungry like a man!"

Momma was mad. "Mrs. Profit, you don't know nothin'!"

Hide it under a bushel—NO!

I'm gonna let it shine.

"...not two weeks in the grave! Nice my ass!" It was Mrs. Profit again.

"Why we didn't start to go out, it was almost a year!"

"Yeah. But even 'fore that..."

...gonna let my little light shine!

"Yes you'd better!" Momma yelled.

The music stopped.

Mrs. Profit sounded sad. "I'm trying to help you Ruby."

"You ought to be ashamed!"

"Ruby, honey, listen to me!"

"Get out, I said! And don't come back!"

The patio door slammed.

I heard Momma say, "You old snake." Then she started to cry. I heard her in there, catching up her breath, real low and quiet like. I wanted to go in and comfort her, but then she would know I'd been listening.

I picked up the dump truck. There was a little mashed in place over the driver's window where I'd hit it with the board. I went over to the water spigot and turned it on. I put the truck under so the water would run over the mashed in part—make it all better.

7
FEELINGS

Thursday, June 6th 1959

The sun hadn't come up yet, and there were about a gazillion streetlamps. Momma's Ford went like usual, like somebody's old washer machine, rattling and clatter knocking down the big empty street. I could see its reflection, snaking in, and then out of the dark, glassy-eyed store windows. There were lighted billboards everywhere. Wanting you to buy Five-Cent White Castle Hamburgers. Velveeta Cheese. Wanting you to see the Detroit Tigers. Buy 21-inch Television Screens. Huge buildings went up in the shadows on every side—so tall they hurt my neck to see the tops, diamond stars twinkling up there in the black sheet God had spread over the world, not a bit of real daylight anywhere.

Momma said, "This ain't the way to Kentucky."

Victor looked straight ahead, both hands on the steering wheel. He was chewing the end of a dead cigar. He wore a white short-sleeved shirt, 'Ford Motor Company' wrote in red squiggly letters across the pocket. A muscled arm went out from his shirtsleeve to the steering wheel. "I've got a little business with Armstrong. Then we'll be on our way."

"It ain't even light out. I thought you was finished with all that."

Victor took the cigar out of his mouth. "This isn't about the Hotel Momma. It's about 'you know who'." He put the cigar back in.

Momma sent fast eyes back to Missy and me. Missy was curled up in the back seat with her thumb in her mouth asleep. I was up on my knees next to the side window, pretending not to listen.

"I thought all that was over with Victor," Momma said.

"So did I," Victor said. "So—did—I."

————

When Victor came out of Armstrong's, the sky was just starting to get light. An upside-down-moon sliced the skin under Victor's nose, an upside-down-moon with a dead cigar sticking out. He was carrying his green file box, the one he kept all his business papers in. He kept poems in there too. Momma had a magazine with one of his poems in it. He said poetry was a waste of time.

"How come you wrote it then?" I'd asked one day.

"I don't know. Habit, I guess. Something I got into when I was in school."

"How come you got into it?"

"Never mind how come. I got into it, that's all."

He walked up to Momma's window and handed in the box. "Put this on the floor, would you Ruby?" He came around to his side, got in and slammed the door. I could see he was mad.

"What did Armstrong have to say?" Momma said.

Victor didn't answer. He just stared out the front window, chomping his cigar.

Armstrong was Victor's lawyer friend, a big fat man with a fat man belly and a fat man face. He had a black feathery mustache and wore dark blue suits with red ties and shoes

72

that were so shiny-black I could see the kitchen table in the toes. He carried a black leather case shaped like a box with a big gold buckle and a gold lock with a little gold key. He would come in our house on Leroy Street, spy me on the floor under the kitchen table and grin a mouth full of big yellow teeth. They reminded me of old piano keys, the teeth did.

He owned the hotel Victor might be the boss of in Florida. The Pink Flamingo Hotel. If things worked out good, Victor might get to be partners with Armstrong. That's what Victor wanted. Him and Momma talked about it all the time. To be partners would cost a bunch of money. Victor had money in the bank. Momma had money from Daddy's insurance. They could put that in with the money from the house. That's how they talked. It was money, money, money, all the time—even when Disneyland was on.

Every time Armstrong would come over, him and Victor would go off in the bedroom and talk business. They didn't let anybody come in there either—not even Momma.

"You know. The Unions are ruining this country," Victor said, talking on one side of his mouth; the other was taken up with his cigar.

Momma put her hand on Victor's neck, resting it just above that shrapnel wound. "What's wrong hon?"

Victor shook his head and Momma's hand flew away. "Now the goddamn Union Steward's in on it!"

"Watch your language hon," Momma said. "In on what?"

Victor started up the engine, took the cigar out of his mouth and looked at Momma. "You said not to talk about it. Not in front of the kids you said."

"Well, can't you talk around it?"

"I don't want to talk around it!" Victor put the cigar back in his mouth and slammed his fist suddenly into the ceiling, rattling the rearview mirror. "I get enough of goddamn *talking around it* at work!"

"I'm sorry hon," Momma said. "Really I am."

"*Sorry* doesn't get it Ruby."

———

There was an office on the other side of the gas pumps with a desk and chairs and a pull-knob candy machine. Stacks of pop cases stood inside the door, stretching along the bottom half of a big plate glass window. The window was partly lit with the morning sun, revealing on its surface a layer of light blond dust. There were Venetian blinds hanging cockeyed in the window. A man stood in there in the dim office light, pulling at the cords of the blinds, trying this way and that to get them to straighten. On the other side of a narrow alleyway was a sign over a broken awning that said 'Family Restaurant', and down from there was a double door under another sign painted to look like blue frost that said, 'Cold Beer'.

Missy got up on the seat next to Momma. "Pee-pee Momma."

Victor brought out a black wallet from his butt pocket. "This is Flat Rock Momma. We've got to get gas."

Momma was busy reading her King James Bible. She was following the words along with her finger, mouthing them as she did.

"Pee-pee," Missy said.

Victor's eyes became slits. "Momma?" he whispered. "Oh, Momma?"

The Bible lay open across Momma's lap. She wore a tight black skirt and a white blouse with blue and red roses. The blouse had a V-neck you could see the soft part of her titties in.

Victor caught my eye and nodded toward Momma. "Momma, oh Momma? Are you in there, Momma?" He wanted me to see something on Momma. I didn't want to see anything on Momma—not with him.

"Ruby D.," he said. "Call for Ruby D."

"Momma," I said. "Victor wants you."

Missy beat the back of Momma's seat. "Pee-pee, Momma!"

"Shit!" Momma marked her place with a piece of paper and closed the Bible. "I can't get nowhere on this!" She

74

looked at Victor. "Gas? We'd better get us a car first! You got to have a car before you can put gas in it!"

Victor grinned. "It's your car, Momma. You said it would take us anywhere we wanted to go."

"We don't choke to death first," Momma said.

———

Momma and Missy went off to the toilet to pee. I stayed in the car. Victor stood out front with his arms crossed—Clark Kent in a Ford Motor Company dress shirt—the boss of the whole world.

The man who'd been trying to straighten the blinds came out wearing a gray ball cap with a red winged horse on the front. He wasn't a very tall man, but he was built stocky and square with orange sideburns and hair and an orange sunshiny face. He stepped up to Victor, smiling, wiping his hands on a blue rag. Victor said something to the man; then he frowned and made a gesture toward the car.

The Orange Man nodded and grinned and wiped his hands. Then he came over and raised the hood. It went straight up in front of the window, blocking my view. I crawled over the seat and opened the door on Momma's side, got out and slammed it shut. Right away the Orange Man bumped into me. I went five fingers flat into a pool of oil. The oil was warm with purple and yellow wavy lines.

"Uh oh, son!" The Orange Man said. "I didn't see you there." He had a warm friendly voice. He reached down a hand with freckles and hair, pulled me up and set me safely on my feet. His face had a million freckles. He wiped my hand with the blue rag. "You okay kiddo?"

"Yeah," I said. "I ain't hurt or anything. Where'd you get that horse at Mister?"

The Orange Man smiled. "What horse?"

"That one!" I pointed up at his ball cap.

He took it off, looked at the winged horse on the front and pretended to frown. "Well. This is a Mobil horse. It's on all our signs. We sell Mobil Gas here. See that." He pointed out the word *Mobilgas* sown in black thread under the winged horse. I liked the way he smiled, all warm and sunshiny-like. I could feel myself smiling back. He popped the ball cap back on his head. "You ever pump gasoline son?"

"No." I looked at the gas pumps; guards standing there, not saying a word. "I ain't big enough. My stepdaddy says I'm a runt."

"Well, you are pretty small."

"I'm nine years old."

"Nine?"

"Yeah."

"Well you better come on with me then," the Orange Man said.

"Orbie! Get back in the car!" Victor was still up at the front, but standing to one side now. He barked at me, "Let the man do his job!"

I could feel my heart start to pound. The Orange Man smiled. "He's all right, sir."

"Go on!" Victor said. "Get back in there! Get out of the way!" The Orange Man held onto my shoulder. "He's all right, sir. It's my fault. I was just going to show him how to pump gas."

Victor didn't even look at the Orange Man. He pointed at me and he pointed to the car. "Get in there I said!"

I looked up at the Orange Man. The smile was gone from his face. "Maybe next time, son," he said. He stepped to the door and opened it for me. I climbed in, my heart falling down a hole in the middle of my chest. The wings on the Orange Man's ball cap flew out toward Victor. "He's okay now."

"Mind your own business," Victor said.

The Orange Man stood with his mouth open.

Victor took his glasses off and started wiping them with his handkerchief. He turned and walked back to where he was before, the hood of the Ford blocking him from view. The Orange Man looked in through the open window. "We'll get that gas another time son. Here." He took off his ball cap and handed it through the window. "Go on, take it. For good luck." I took it but then I looked away, ashamed of Victor;

ashamed that I had to have a stepdaddy like him.

"Look there on the inside," the Orange Man said. There were letters stitched in blue on the inside of the cap just above the hem, a letter J and a letter C. "Stands for Jim Conlin. That's me. Friends call me J C." The Orange Man smiled his sunshiny smile.

"I said to mind your own business!" It was Victor again; he'd walked back around. "Or are you hard of hearing?"

"No sir," the Orange Man said. "I can hear just fine. Always have."

"Okay then. I'll take care of the boy, you take care of the gas."

"Of course sir," the Orange Man said. "I was just about to do that." He went off then to pump the gas. I could hear him get the nozzle in and turn the handle. The gas hummed in the tank. When he finished with the gas, he went around to the front and closed the hood. Victor stood out there again like the boss of the world, looking around at everything, checking things, wiping his glasses, frowning at the gas pumps.

I ran my hand over the gray bill of the ball cap and studied the winged horse. I looked at the blue letters on the inside. I thought how if I had a horse with wings I could fly away to Florida all by myself, be up in the sky with the seagulls and the pelicans, looking down on all the blues and the whites and the greens and the pinks. It wouldn't be anybody's business either, not Momma's, not Victor's. It would be mine.

———

"Where's Victor?" Momma said.

"I don't know Momma. He was up there." I pointed to the front where Victor had been standing.

Momma got her Bible down. "Gone off to the toilet, I reckon. Did you see him go off to the toilet?"

"No Momma."

She took a puff off a cigarette and opened the Bible. It was hot outside. I sat back on the back seat away from her;

afraid she might start in on Jesus.

"Hey there, son." It was the Orange Man again at the back window. He handed in two Coca Colas. "Thought you kids might enjoy these." I gave one of the Coca Colas to Missy and kept the other for myself.

"Awful hot out today," the Orange Man said.

Momma looked around from the front seat and smiled. She mashed her cigarette in the ashtray. "That's real nice of you, Mister. Orbie. Missy. Say thank you to the man."

"Thanks Mister," I said.

Missy just stared.

I showed Momma the gray ball cap. "He gave me this Momma. Look on the inside there. See the letters. People call him that."

"I'm sorry to say, but it's true," the Orange Man smiled. "J C," Momma said. "I like that. Just like our Lord."

The Orange Man laughed. "Hardly Ma'am. I get a fair amount of teasing about that."

"If it was me, I'd be proud." Momma said.

"I'll try and remember that Ma'am."

"Ruby," Momma said. "My name is Ruby."

"Ruby." The Orange Man smiled, his hair all shiny orange in the sunlight. He looked at me, then at Missy. Then back at Momma. "I better get back to work. Real nice to meet you Ruby. You and your kids." He winked at me and went off toward the office.

"Real nice feller," Momma said.

"Uh huh," I said.

Missy had stood up. She was leaning against the back of the back seat, hugging the Coca Cola bottle to her chest with one hand—the other hand pushed up between her legs.

"You got to pee again?" Momma said.

Missy shook her head and pointed out the window. There was Victor, standing under the 'Cold Beer' sign, watching us. He started toward the car, carrying a six-pack of beer in one hand and a bag of ice in the other. He put the ice and the beer in a cooler he got out of the trunk and set it in the front seat between him and Momma. Suddenly, he reached over the seat and yanked the gray ball cap out of my hand.

"Hey, the gas station man gave me that," I said.

"You didn't ask me about it."

"It doesn't belong to you." I looked at Momma. "Tell him it doesn't belong to him Momma."

"I'd be ashamed Victor," Momma said.

"Shame has nothing to do with it." He put the hat on his own head and adjusted the bill over his eyes. "Too big for him anyway."

———

Outside Toledo the road was so slicked over with grease you could hear the tires lick through it. The Ford slowed to a stop.

"My, my. Would you look at this traffic?" Victor pushed the bill of the ball cap up and took a sip off his beer. He looked over at Momma. "What did that guy want back there in Flat Rock anyway?"

"That gas station feller?"

"Fellow," Victor said. "Him. Yes. That *fellow*."

"Why nothing. Come over to give the kids Coke Colas."

"What did he want in exchange?"

"Exchange?"

"Tit for tat, Momma. Exchange."

"Nothing. Just passing the time of day."

"What was he smiling about then? I saw him smiling."

"Can't a man smile at me? I don't get upset when some woman smiles at you."

"Hell you don't. You know how I am, Ruby."

"Yeah," Momma said. "I know how you are." She set the Bible on the dash, reached down on the floorboard and brought up a magazine—the one Victor had his poem in—*Motor City Love* in glossy white letters written across the front. Below the title a pretty woman in a long, curvy red coat leaned back against a white Thunderbird with her arms crossed. One naked leg stuck out from where the coat came together, you could see up the side. Momma fanned herself with the magazine. "I wished it would hurry up and rain."

"It will. Don't worry." Victor looked at Momma and grinned. "That magazine will keep you cool. As long as you don't read it." Before Momma could answer him he said, "'Where Feelings Fail', by Victor Denalsky," his voice like somebody on the radio, deep and smooth, wanting you to like it even if you didn't. "She promised to me herself, and I accepted. But what is a promise, she never promised herself? What was accepted, where feelings fail."

"That's so sad," Momma said.

"An old flame," Victor said. "She broke my heart. I broke hers. My one and only publication." He took a sip off his beer.

"That's so sad," Momma said.

"It's crap," Victor said. "Don't worry about it."

Black and blue clouds bulged overhead. A light flashed inside them. Then came thunder.

Doom! Da doom doom doom!

"Been looking like rain ever since Flat Rock," Momma said.

I stood on my knees, looking over Missy's shoulder. There was a yard of junk cars out there, and behind it a long gray building like a battleship with antennas and windows. Smoke stacks pointing up in the sky like guns. A siren started and a fiery-red mouth opened inside the building. A creepy orange mist filled the dark windows, spilling out over the junk jalopies and truck cabs piled atop one another like bugs.

"Fire," Missy said.

"They're making steel in there," I said. "Remember when Daddy took us?"

"No."

"Where Daddy worked. Don't you remember?"

Missy looked again at the building. The misty light made an orange belly on the clouds. "Daddy don't work in there Orbie."

"I know that silly. This is Toledo." I punched her in the

arm, not hard, just enough so she'd remember.

"Momma," she whined.

"Hush. I'm just playing with you. Daddy did work at Fords. Remember? He worked in Detroit."

"Oh."

"This is Toledo. See?"

Missy put two fingers in her mouth and looked at me. Then she took the fingers out and smiled. "Yeah, Detroit." She climbed up with her doll, up on the back of the front seat next to where Momma was. "Momma, look at the fire. It making steel like Daddy."

Momma fanned herself with the magazine. "I declare. It is ain't it?"

"Daddy worked in Detroit didn't he Momma?"

"Yes he did, sweetheart."

Victor cleared his throat. "Your father worked at Fords Missy. You already know that."

"She's just a child Victor," Momma said.

Victor finished his beer and put the empty somewhere on the floor. "Why can't you just *say* what happened and be done with it? It's been three years."

Something in Victor's voice caused me to sit up straight.

"You're talking like a man who's had one too many Victor. I told you about that."

"Beer's got nothing to do with it, Momma."

"It wouldn't have, you didn't drink it all the time. You already half drunk!"

"Not yet, Momma. I *am* working on it though."

Missy said, "Say what, Momma?"

"Nothing sweetheart. Victor's just talking old foolishness is all." She looked at Victor. "I don't know what's eating you, but I'll tell you one thing's for sure. You keep on the way you have been and you can put me and the kids both on the next bus home!"

"Oh, come on," Victor laughed. "You wouldn't do that."

"I would too! You'd get plenty of peace and quiet then. I told you Victor. They not ready."

"They not ready! They not ready! What is that? Some kind of hick Latin?" Victor's beer-breath floated back over the seats. "How do you know they're not ready?"

"They just kids, that's how," Momma said.

At the gray building the fire mouth started to close down; it sucked away the blood color from the clouds, from the yard, the junky cars and truck cabs. Black smoke poured out from the stacks. More lightning. Thunder.

Da doom doom doom!

Victor pulled out another beer and popped off the cap. I could see the snake around the heart tattoo on the back of his hand.

Every living thing eventually loses. Suffers and dies.

Missy was on her knees; pushing herself up next to Momma. There was a bruise mark along her leg, a smoky submarine under yellow water. Victor had spanked her the other night for refusing to eat black-eyed peas.

"Not ready for what, Momma?" she asked.

Momma frowned at Victor. "See what you started?" She turned to Missy with a softer voice. "Nothing sweetheart. Victor's just talking about Daddy is all. You knew he died didn't you?"

Missy nodded, putting on a baby voice. "And I was *too* liddle."

"That's right sweetheart. You was."

"Where did Daddy die?"

Victor looked back at Missy, impatient. "You know that already, Missy."

"Victor hush," Momma said without looking at him. "You already know where, honey. Remember? He died up there in that steel mill in Detroit." She looked around at the long gray building. "Like Victor said. Like over yonder. It was an accident."

Missy looked at the building. I looked at it too. A block of lights and smoke looked back. Something bad was in there—I could feel it—something worse even than the Dark Thing. All of a sudden I got this all-over numb feeling—like I was asleep and awake at the same time—and then I was floating—floating up toward the ceiling. My whole body. Or maybe it was just my head. Anyway, I was looking down. Looking down on Momma and Missy. Looking down on Victor.

Then it was like the ceiling wasn't there anymore and I was floating a few feet above the car. Victor and Momma and Missy were still below, but sitting in theater seats now, eating popcorn, wide eyed, watching as if a scary movie, gray and white lights flickering over their faces. I could see a long line of traffic going in either direction, how it had boxed in the Ford, trapping it in just one place. Then the line started to move and I was back inside the car again, still floating along the ceiling.

"How Momma?" Missy said. "How did Daddy die?"

"Go on. Tell the girl," Victor said.

"Shut up Victor!" Momma's voice had razor blades now, razor blades and knives. She reached around and tried to smooth Missy's hair. "It was an accident, sweetheart."

There. See? It was an accident. That's all it was. Shut up now! Stupid little mouse face!

Victor slammed his hand against the steering wheel. "Accident my *ass*! Some son of a bitch, a *Negro*, poured hot steel on Jessie! That's what happened. Burned him alive!"

Something rolled over in my stomach—a mess boiling up—eggs and tears mixed with tail pipe fumes and clotted milk.

"Victor!" Momma shouted.

But Victor went on like he hadn't heard, adjusting the bill of the ball cap. "Jackson was his name. We called him Black Jack." He drove the car slow behind all the other cars. He growled at the windshield. "Had no business on that crane with a full ladle, that's all. They should've investigated it then! Not like they're doing now! After the fact! Bringing in that smart-ass Union Steward!"

Momma threw the magazine at Victor. He ducked but it hit him anyway.

"Son of a bitch, Ruby! I'm trying to drive here!"

"I'll kill you! You bastard!"

I could see my own self now—still from the ceiling—my own body, skinny bird legs, red shorts, tooth pick arms in a white Davy Crockett tee shirt, trembling like a squirrel on a cold branch. I could see my head, too big for my body, the ears sticking out lopsided like Daddy's pear halves, the cheeks stretching away from the nose holes, the mouth open, eyes steamy red with tears.

When the scream blew out of me, it was like I'd come back from a long way away. "You never said that Momma! You never said he got burned up! It was an accident you said!" Hot tears flooded down my face.

Momma looked lost. "It *was* an accident sweetheart. The man done it made a mistake was all. Sometimes things happen by mistake. Wasn't nothing anybody could do."

It came up all of a sudden, blue jam, chunks of banana and bacon and raisins—everything from this morning's breakfast— splashing in a yellow gush against the black vinyl seat.

"What's the matter now?" Victor said.

"Lord, God!" Momma said. "Orbie's puked all over the back seat!"

"Jesus H. Christ! We can't stop here!" Victor yelled. "There are some rags under the seat there. Hell!"

Da doom doom doom!

Momma found the rags. "You can just drop us off at the next bus station Victor! I mean it! I had just about all I can stand of you cussing and carrying on. Taking the Lord's name in vain. Bringing out what happened to their Daddy! If that don't beat all!" She leaned over the back seat and started in wiping at the puke. "You ought to be the one back here cleaning this!"

Missy sat in her corner with her baby doll. "You sick Orbie?" Inside my mouth a sour milk taste burned. I tried to wipe my mouth on my arm.

"Here honey, let Momma help." Momma looked at Missy while she wiped my mouth. "He'll be all right." She had me take my Davy Crockett tee shirt off. Davy Crockett had puke all over his face. Momma said she'd get me another shirt as soon as we could stop. She finished wiping the back seat and threw the rags out the window. She rolled up my shirt and put it under the front seat.

"It stinks Momma," Missy said.

"It'll clear. We can't stop here."

I was still crying but soft now. "Did that man really... burn him up Momma? Did he really do... like Victor said?"

Momma looked into my eyes, her lips dark red. "It was an accident, honey. Wasn't nothing anybody could do. Try and understand."

"I unnerstand," Missy said.

"That's good sweetheart. I know you do." Momma turned toward the front.

Fat drops of rain started to slap across the black hood of the Ford, first one then another. *Slap! Pop! Pop! Slap!* One at a time they hit. Cool air rushed in through the windows.

I looked out at the sky. The clouds had gone from black to gray, stretching out over the sky like an upside down ocean with lights flashing inside it.

"You kids roll them windows up," Momma said.

I rolled up my window, still crying.

The rain exploded so hard it looked like white dust, a mist all over the cars and the road. The gray building was behind us now. I could see it way back there behind the white dusty rain, a black battleship going down under the clouds.

"He's got nothing to cry about," Victor said.

"How you can be so smart and *stupid* at the same time is beyond me," Momma answered. "I told you not to never mention what happened to their Daddy. They got feelings Victor."

The rain drowned over the windshield wipers.

I thought about Black Jack and the fire. I thought about coloreds. Negroes. Niggers. Mean niggers in Detroit with knives. Daddy burned up alive by one.

Not no accident, not like Momma said.

I looked outside at the rain. The sky exploded like a bomb. One mountain crashed into another mountain. Thunder. Rain smashing and smoking over everything.

Victor leaned over the steering wheel trying to see.

PART FOUR

8

NOBODY TO PLAY WITH

Granny fibbed about kids being down here. There weren't even any grownups far as I could see except Bird and Nealy and that was across the road. Mostly I played by myself. I read comic books, drew sailing ships and made battles with my army men. I climbed up the chicken yard fence and watched Granny slop the hogs. I threw rocks at the barn door. I threw rocks at the dirt dobber's nests in the hayloft. I moped around until I got tired of moping around, then I beat on things with sticks. Weeds. The side of the house. The milk bucket. I put dents in one of Granpaw's hubcaps with a hammer.

Granny had fibbed about him too, saying how Granpaw and me would have fun together, how he'd take me fishing, show me how to look for worms. That never happened. He tried to teach me to hoe tobacco, but the hoe was too big and kept going the wrong way, slipping out of my hand and cutting into the tobacco stalks. Granpaw got fed up with that. "I reckon you ain't big enough to handle a hoe yet," he said. "Best you go on up to the house."

He worked all the time. Most mornings he was already gone when I came down to breakfast. At the end of the day he came in all wore out and grouchy-like. He'd sit down to supper and not even talk at all unless he was wanting something. Then it was Mattie this or Mattie that, Mattie pass the butter or Mattie, where'd you put that cornbread?

After supper he would go in the front room and sit under the light bulb that hung naked in there from a black twist of cord. Moths and other flying insects would be making circles in and out of the light, flying off other places and coming back around. Granpaw would open up his Bible under there and read, every now and then stopping to spit in a big blue Maxwell House Coffee can he kept on the floor by his chair. He read like Momma did, mouthing the words, following them along with a calloused big finger.

I'd lie in there on the floor and read my comic books. I had Superman and Flash Gordon and The Fantastic Four. I had Batman and Robin. I also had "The Body Snatchers" a book Victor gave me, all about pod creatures from outer space that took over people's bodies and walked around like zombies.

The front room was just plain. Green cracked walls. Brown linoleum on the floor. There were two windows, one that looked out on the front porch and one behind a bumpy red couch that looked out toward the barn. There were cigarette burns on the arms of the couch Granny had covered with pieces of dingy lace. Across from the couch was a table with Granny's sewing machine. There was a small day-bed beside the sewing machine with a picture of Jesus and The Last Supper hanging on the wall above. Jesus looked sad. He always looked sad. Even when he was smiling he looked sad.

On the walls and over the fireplace were pictures of Granny and Granpaw and of Momma and Daddy and of Missy and me. There were other pictures too—people I didn't know—a wall-eyed woman with a square jaw, her hair piled up on top like a box—a little colored boy on a tractor with a chicken in his arms—three happy looking colored women, standing on a porch in housedresses, all squinting and smiling in the sun.

When Granpaw read his Bible, he would rub at the knot on the side of his head. One time Granny yelled at him to stop, and he did for a while; but then he started doing it again.

"Strode you'll get that to bleed," Granny said.

"Shit," Granpaw said, closing the Bible. "Cain't a man do nothing private around here?" He set the Bible on a side table by his chair.

"You'll make it worse," Granny said.

Granpaw spat in his coffee can, set it down and wiped his mouth with the back of his hand. Then he got up from his chair and did that stepping-off-in-a-ditch kind of walk, in a circle, looking all around the room, at me, at Granny, at the pictures on the walls. His hawk eyebrow tried to pin everything down. "Ain't a thing in this world the matter with me," he said to the air in front of him. Then he did that ditch-walk back through the kitchen and went off to bed.

Granny said he was sicker than he let on. "Had that stroke last year. That's how come him to walk that way. Too much sugar."

Too much sugar was why he had to shoot himself in the butt too. Once he shot himself in front of me and Granny in the front room, dropped his coveralls right there and poked a needle in his butt. He yelled and jumped up in the air. "Good God A Mighty, that hurt!"

I thought it was for real.

"Strode," Granny said.

Granpaw looked at me and grinned. "Did you think Granpaw was hurt son? Come here and look at my needle."

"Leave him alone," Granny said.

Granpaw laughed.

I tried to stare daggers at him but all that did was make him laugh even louder.

"He ain't stout like he used to be," Granny said. "He'll kill hisself, working the way he does. Ornery old devil."

Granny worked too. She was all the time feeding the farm animals, the chickens and the hogs, hoeing out tobacco, cleaning house, washing clothes, sewing and cooking. On top of that she went to church. Granpaw was too tired to go to church so I got to stay home with him. I was glad about that.

————

The chickens belonged to Old Man Harlan, but Granny took care of them. Because of that, she got most of the eggs. They walked funny; the chickens did, like they were trying to be real careful not to step in anything messy. They would put one foot down; then look around like they were seeing if there was anything on the ground they didn't want to step in. Then they would put their other foot down. The rooster's name was Geronimo. He was a big black rooster with a red head and green and black burnt-up looking butt feathers.

The day after blackberry-picking Granny and me were out taking care of the chickens. Granny had fed them and was pouring water from a bucket into a long wooden trough. "If I had more time, I'd try to sell me a few of them eggs, but then I wouldn't have none to give away." She finished with the water and set the bucket down. "I'll take some over to Kingdom sometimes. Sometimes I'll make up a basket for Moses, if the chickens is laying good. See them little chickens yonder?" Granny pointed out two white chickens that stood next to the fence, stretching and fanning themselves in the sun. "I want you to take care of them for me. I'm thinking of entering them in a beauty contest."

"A beauty contest for chickens Granny?"

"Yeah for chickens," Granny said, "at the County Fair. They'd take first prize, they was big enough. Don't you think they would?"

They already looked pretty, standing up bright as snow in the morning sun. Snowbirds, I thought they were, showing off their snowy bright wings.

"What you want me to do Granny?" I asked.

"Feed them. Take care of them. You know. Be nice to them. So they'll grow good."

"What do you want me to feed them?"

"Corn. Or that feed there." Granny pointed to a grass sack by the fence. "Or just get you a piece of good loaf-bread and break it up. They'll like loaf-bread. Can you do that?"

I nodded that I could; glad to have something to do. I liked the chickens a whole lot. I named one 'Johnny' and the other 'Elvis'.

"Those are boy's names," Granny said.

"I don't care Granny." I pointed to Elvis. "That red thing. See how it flops over his eye?"

"Her eye," Granny said. "That's a comb. All chickens got combs."

"Elvis Presley's hair goes like that. He sings Hound Dog music."

"Hound dog music?"

"Uh huh. And Jailhouse Rock!"

Granny seemed to ponder that a second; then she said, "I believe I heard that on the radio once. Sorry old jitterbug music, if you ask me. What about that other there? She don't have hair."

The other chicken's comb went straight back like a little saw blade. "That's a flat top Granny. Like Johnny Unitas. Johnny Unitas is a quarterback. He throws the football."

"Only ball I ever seen a chicken throw was itself, and that from the top of a fence post to the ground," Granny said. "They're your chickens. I reckon you can call them anything you want to. I never heard of no boy chickens in a beauty contest though."

———

Sometimes I'd pretend Elvis and Johnny were captured by Apache Indians. The Apaches would be all the other chickens plus their big chief, Geronimo The Rooster. I'd play like I was Davy Crockett or Daniel Boone, coming to save Elvis and Johnny from the Indians.

I'd have to get me up some corncobs from the chicken yard first, which that wasn't too easy because of flies and bees and wasps zooming around, trying to get on me. I had to watch not to step in any chicken poop too or pick up any chicken-poop corncobs. I'd get an armful of corncobs and take one and hold it up from the bottom so it pointed up in the air like a sword and start marching it toward the chicken house door. I'd wait for the hot part of the day when I knew all the chickens would be in there sleeping in the dark. I'd march up on them but real quiet like, waving that one corncob in the air, trying not to make too much noise because I wanted it to be like a surprise and I'd be whispering a little battle hymn I made up along the way.

Battle Creek Michigan! Battle Creek Michigan! Battle Creek Michigan!

And when I got to the door I'd look in and there would be all the chickens in there sleeping and I'd point the corncob and draw back and yell as loud as I could. *BATTLE CREEK MICHIGAN!* Then I'd let fly with the corncob and all the chickens would wake up and look about and I'd already be throwing more corncobs, shooting my six shooters, my rifles—*Bang! Bang! Bang!*—from the doorway. A bomb would go off as the chickens would all bust loose at the same time, squawking and screaming and banging their wings, stirring up dust and shit and old spider webs and pieces of straw. Some would push through the holes where planks had busted out. Some would run along the floor and hit against the walls.

One time Geronimo flew at me with a bunch of other chickens, rushing in a wind of flapping wings, filling the doorway, their beaks flashing like orange scissors, squawking and carrying on I had to turn and run out the door where something caught me up by the arm and wouldn't let go until I was looking it direct in the eye. It was Granny. "What you up to, youngun?"

"Playing," I said.

"Playing?" Granny said. "Looks to me like you fixing to kill Nealy's chickens! Scare'em so bad they won't never want to lay! What about Elvis and Johnny? You supposed to be taking care of them."

94

"I am Granny. I'm freeing them from the Injuns."

"Injuns?"

"Uh huh. All them other chickens. Geronimo's the chief."

"Can't you find anything else better to do?"

"No," I said.

Geronimo and the chickens had scattered out across the yard. One chicken stood at the door of the chicken house, looking in. Elvis and Johnny were right near by, their heads going side to side, looking up at us as if waiting for the answer to a question nobody had asked.

"They're my friends, Granny. I've been feeding them like you said. They follow me around."

Granny seemed to relax a bit. She looked at me. "It ain't been easy down here, has it hon, what with me and Strode so busy and all—and you with nobody to play with? Things will get better though."

"You always saying that," I said.

"I know, but they will. Wait and see if they don't." She walked off toward the house. When she got to the chicken yard gate, she turned and looked back. "I catch you pestering Nealy's chickens again, I'll cut me a switch!"

9

MOSES MASHBONE

I lay with my chest flat against the ledge of the well, my elbows
sticking up on both sides. I had the thought I might be like
a cricket with big elbow legs and a head with big antennas
that could feel things in the dark. I looked over the ledge like
that—like a cricket.

*You be careful about that well. Storm blowed that roof
cockeyed and I think some of them stones is loose.*

The well was a tunnel hole of dirt and rock and tree roots
reaching out like claws. It went way down in the black part.
I could hear water dripping, and my cricket-antennas were
feeling down there, feeling the cool air—trying to see inside
the black part.

I wanted to go in there. Cool in there, cool water and rocks
and slippery things in the dark, out of the sun, the sun that
was so hot and bright it made you feel like you couldn't hide
anywhere, people's eyes, even the animals', the cows' and
the chickens' and the pigs', all of them on you, baking you,
making you hot. If I could get down in the black part wouldn't
nobody look at me, wouldn't nobody know where I was all the

time either and it would be cool and wet and it would smell like plant roots and dirt and it would be like leaves.

Why we'd be worried to death. Not knowing where you'd gone off to!

I pushed myself down from the ledge, walked around to the other side and gave the post there a kick. It staggered back, loose at the bottom. The flowered roof moaned and wobbled to where it was almost flat again. Then it went back like before, like a church lady's hat in the wind.

Daddy's dump truck sat next to the well. Granpaw's cross was there too, the burnt snake crawling along its arms. I dragged the truck to the road, filled the bed with gravels and dragged it back to the well—got the cross and stuck it in the gravels.

Spooky like a grave. Daddy's grave.

I liked it like that. I lifted the truck and everything onto the well ledge and climbed up after it. I backed the truck so the dumper part was hanging out over the well hole, and I sat next to it on the ledge, my back to the hole, mostly out of the sun except for my legs. I let my eyes move up Bounty Road, up the hill in the direction Momma and Victor had gone—to the place where the road made a way through the cornfields. Momma and Victor had so far been gone only a few days. I thought about St. Petersburg and The Pink Flamingo Hotel, what it might look like rising up out of the white sand. I thought about sailboats and the blue ocean waters of the Gulf of Mexico.

A rumbling sound came from the other side of the hill, low and far away at first, barely a grumble, then louder and louder, until it was thundering at the top. A black something-or-other—some kind of motor vehicle—shot out, smoking and rattling between the cornfields. "A car!" I thought. "Momma's Ford!" Dust exploded, boiled up behind and out the sides, spreading out wider than the road.

It could be. Yes it could be Momma's car! Maybe her and Victor changed their minds! Maybe they were coming back to get me after all!

Behind the car the dust kept opening out like a fan, a church fan, Momma's yellow fold out fan she used on hot summer days when the preacher wouldn't shut up. It flattened and spread out over the cornfields.

It could be them!

And then I was sure it was. And I waved my hands and shouted, "Momma! Momma! Momma!" I thought my heart would jump out my mouth. The rumble became a roar so loud I couldn't hear anything else—not even my own shouting—and I thought for sure it was them and I waved and I waved and I shouted "Momma!" and I'd have jumped off the well and gone to meet the car, except I saw it didn't have all its side windows. All Ford cars had side windows in the back except of course if they were trucks and Momma didn't drive no trucks.

Who it was, was somebody else, I'd have to wait to see, and I did, and it *was* a truck, an old pick-up truck, and it zoom-rattled by without even slowing down. A man with a wide cracked face—a colored man's face—a straight line for a mouth, straight blue-black hair down along his shoulders, sat up behind the wheel. A dusty black cowboy hat crouched like a duck a top his head, hind end tail feathers up in the air. He wasn't even looking at me, but he waved anyway, like he didn't have to look to know I was there, to know it was me. And he drove that truck fast, roaring on up the road with all the dust exploding, blowing out the rear end. By the time the dust cleared, he had gone all the way over the next hill.

My truck, the red dump truck—still with the dent over the driver's side window—sat on the ledge of the well piled up with gravels from the road, the cross leaning backward now like a man looking up in the sky with his arms spread wide. What had been a roar had gone back to a rumble—low and far away—and even that was almost gone. Suddenly I wanted to dump everything, throw all of it in the well, all the gravels with the cross and the creepy snake.

I hit the lever on the dump truck hard, but it wouldn't go. I hit it again harder. Still nothing. It seemed to be waiting for something or someone, maybe for some little man to come and drive it away. Then that whole part of the ledge dropped an inch and busted apart. Exploded. The cab of the dump truck, Daddy's gift, flipped back and over and into the well. If I hadn't caught hold of one of the posts I'd have gone in too. The truck bashed against a rock on the other side, fell, silver headlights, bumper, mud flaps and all, spinning over and under with the cross and the rocks and the gravels, banging against the dark wall of roots and rock all the way down—splashing inside the black part—where I couldn't see it anymore.

Granny's voice cracked like a tree limb in a storm. "Orbie! What are you doing up there!"

I jerked around so fast I almost lost my grip. Granny had slipped out onto the front porch and was standing with her fists on her hips, arms turned outward. Always she was catching me at something. I jumped down from the well. "Nothing Granny; I ain't doing nothing."

"Don't look to me like nothing! What did I tell you about that well?" Granny came down from off the porch, brushed past me and over to the well. "They Lord Orbie! Did you do this?"

"What?"

"This!" She pointed to the place where the ledge had broken away—a yard-long gash shaped like a grinning mouth.

"No Granny," I said. "I didn't do that."

"Who did then?"

"It broke off by itself. I lost my truck down there, Granny. And Granpaw's cross."

"Didn't I tell you?"

I started to cry. "I didn't know it was going to break!"

"You ought not have been up there in the first place! What if it was you that fell in?" I pictured the truck tumbling into the well and me tumbling in after. "Yeah," Granny said. "That truck don't matter."

"Daddy gave me that truck!" I shouted. "He won it... at Fords!"

Granny let me cry a while, and then she told me how sad Momma would be if I was to fall in, how even Victor would be, and Missy too. How her and Granpaw would be beside themselves with grief. How they would have to bring my dead body up on a hook. "What were you doing up there anyhow?"

100

"Looking."

"Looking? Looking at what?"

"Things Granny. Rocks. A truck."

"That dump truck of yours?"

"No, a truck Granny. A real truck. It came from up there." I pointed up to where the road went over the hill. "I thought it was Momma. It looked like her, Granny. It looked like her car."

"I thought you said it was a truck."

"It turned into one when it came down the road. A colored man was driving it. He had a big black nigger hat on too!"

Granny's eyes flashed green. "Around here you say 'colored' or 'negro' or nothing at all! I told you." We looked at each other a few seconds. "Probably old Moses you saw," Granny finally said. "Moses Mashbone, whose house fell in with that tree. Remember?"

"Uh huh," I said. "His hair's longer than Momma's."

"That it is," Granny laughed. "His own momma was pure Choctaw. Married a colored man down Mississippi way, she did."

"Momma told me he's a medicine man," I said.

"That's what they say," Granny said. "He was struck by lightning once. Blacked out three years; then come back alive."

"Does he mash bones, Granny?"

"Why no!" Granny laughed. "That's just his name. He can heal people though. I seen that part."

"He saved Granpaw," I said.

"Ruby tell you that too?"

"Yeah."

"I never will forget how he helped Strode. Him bleeding the way he was."

———

Momma had told me the story of how Moses saved Granpaw many times; how one day he gashed the calf of his leg on a plow blade.

"He liked to've bled to death," Momma said.

Granny tried to tie off the top part of his calf with a belt, but it did no good. Granpaw was hunched over on the couch, pressing his leg, trying to stop the blood. Granny was beside herself, walking up and down, grabbing first one hand then the other. Finally, Granpaw told her she'd better go get help. Said he'd be all right, that Momma was there and she could take care of him.

"Nodded over to where I was standing," Momma said. "Like I knew what to do. And me about to shit myself."

Granny got the mule from the barn and was just about to ride off when she saw Moses Mashbone come out from around the back of the house. Momma saw him too. Said it was real strange, the way he stood there with his hat and that long hair, his face black as the Bible tucked under his arm, the smoke curling up around him from a hand-rolled cigarette he held pinched between his fingers.

"Why he looked like he'd been waiting out there back of the house. Waiting especially for something bad to happen," Momma said. "Short and stout, built like a wrestler with thick legs and arms and big flat hands."

Said Granny jumped down off her mule like the world was on fire, run over to Moses and started yelling about Granpaw.

Moses just shook his head and waved Granny off, like he didn't need to hear anything about it, like he already knew. He threw his cigarette down, took a knife from his belt and cut two long pieces from Granny's clothesline without even asking if he could. Then he went inside.

Granpaw was still hunched over on the couch, hugging that gashed calf with a bloody towel.

"I never seen anything like it," Momma said. "Old Moses acted like he knew exactly what to do."

He told Granny to go get a pan of salt water hot. He undid the belt Granny had tied. Then he took the two pieces of clothesline and tied off the gash. He tied it off at the top where the belt had been, then at the bottom just above the anklebone.

He told Granpaw to take the towel away, and when he did, Momma said you could still see the blood gushing out. The blood dripped down onto some old sheets Granny had laid up under Granpaw's leg. "You'd a thought them clotheslines would have been enough to stop the blood from a lot worse, tied around the way they was," Momma said. "But they didn't."

The blood spread out like a smile, Momma said, a terrible bloody smile on Granpaw's leg. Didn't seem to bother Moses though. He just stood there looking down at Granpaw. Told him just to let the blood run. Then he opened his Bible and began to read.

"Strangest thing I ever seen," Momma said. "Granpaw sitting there, bleeding like a stuck hog and Moses reading from his Bible."

Moses read, "And when I passed by thee, and saw thee wallowing in thy blood, I said unto thee: In thy blood, live; yea, I said unto thee: In thy blood, live."

Momma said while he was reading that, the bleeding just stopped. Just like that. Said it was a miracle.

Said Moses told Granny to wash the cut with salt water, clean it out with kerosene and wrap it good. Granpaw and Granny were happy and thanked Moses for what he'd done, and Moses told how he had a church they could all come to anytime, and Granny and Granpaw were so happy they said they would, and they did.

"And that's how Mamaw and Papaw come to learn things from Moses. How we got started over to Kingdom. Kingdom Church Of God," Momma said. "I must have been every bit of twelve or thirteen."

Kingdom was where the coloreds had church. White folk went to Circle Stump. That was Baptist. People there said Kingdom Church was awful. Said Moses Mashbone was nothing but a geechee witch doctor. Said he was bad—like the Devil was bad.

"Claimed he put a spell on Mamaw and Granpaw," Momma said. "Said they wouldn't have joined no nigger church, unless they was 'put on' with some kind of spell."

Momma wanted to keep going to Circle Stump Baptist. It wasn't that she hated or even disliked the coloreds, she said. It was just everything was so wild and strange at Kingdom. "Why that Moses even brought snakes in, handing them around to everybody like they was toys!"

She didn't tell anybody how unhappy she was though. She was too afraid. Afraid Moses might put her in a spell. Mostly she just sat off by herself and didn't talk to anybody.

"One day Moses seen me, you know, sitting off by myself. He came right over and asked me what the matter was; his voice like a little old lady's, so kind and sweet natured it made me want to cry," Momma said. "I just started in boohooing right there."

She told Moses how unhappy she was, what the Circle Stump folks were all saying, and how she was afraid of him putting a spell on her.

Moses just looked at her for the longest time. Then he smiled and said there wasn't anything in the world the matter with a girl that wanted to go to her own church. Said that's where a girl ought to be.

"Mamaw and Granpaw didn't like it. They told Moses I was too young to be going off to another church all by myself. Said I'd just have to get used to things the way they were. Well, I'll tell you what's the truth, Moses threw him a fit," Momma said. "He shook his head and spat and grabbed off his hat. That same black hat he always wears, you know, that one with the rattlesnake band. He grabbed that and threw it on the floor right there in the church house in front of Mamaw and Granpaw and all the rest of the churchgoers, stomped and mashed it flat with the heel of his boot. Then he stomped off mad as a hornet. Left Mamaw and Granpaw standing there with their mouths hung open, long faced as two old billy goats. Nobody had ever seen Moses get mad that way before."

They let Momma alone after that, and she went back over to Circle Stump. Circle Stump was where she met Daddy.

"He was just a little old country boy come to church

with his uncle," Momma said. "Uncle Joe and Aunt Dolly Ray was the ones raised him. His own momma and daddy had took sick with fever one winter and died. That was your Granny and Granpaw Ray, Orbie, on your Daddy's side. Buried up there to Harlan's Crossroads. Joe found them in bed together froze to death. Said each had a poultice of lard and turpentine froze to their chests. Never would go to no doctors. Your Daddy was down in between them, down under the blankets there, still alive!

"I tell you what's the truth. If Mamaw and Papaw had got their way, if Moses hadn't a freed me, I might never have married your Daddy. You and Missy might never have been born."

10
OLD GOOSEBERRY

The sky was a white frying pan turned upside down over Kentucky. You had to put your hand over your head and look between your fingers to see the sun. That's how white it was. Everything that wasn't in the shade fried. The porch steps fried. The dirt fried. The rocks. My bomber plane left out in the yard. Everything fried.

It was Saturday. Granny's calendar said 'June' with a big number '15' underneath. Momma had been gone over a week. It rained only one time; little bitty sprinkle drops didn't even get the ground wet. I was laying out on the front porch drawing sailing ships when suddenly this stumpy longhaired colored man stomped up on the planks and leaned a stepladder by the door. It was the man I'd seen barreling by in that pickup truck. He wore a black cowboy hat with a snakeskin band. His hands hung half-open from the wrists, almost black, black fingers thick around, nails and knuckles spotted with white paint. He stood by the ladder, frowning down where I lay next to my drawing papers and colors.

Granny came to the door. "I allowed that was you, Moses. That there's Orbie. Ruby's boy."

"I see you," the colored-man said, frowning.

"Down here from Detroit," Granny said like she was proud of it. "Moses been painting our house a little to the time. Say 'hidy', Orbie."

I felt the word in my mouth but it wouldn't go.

The colored-man had a funny way of talking, making his voice go loud suddenly when he didn't have to. "Cat got yo tongue. DON'T! he boy?" Long black hair made curtains down the sides of his head. "I SEE you."

I got to my feet, the 'hidy' word still stuck in my mouth.

"Say hidy," Granny said again. "Be nice."

Moses spied his eye at my drawing papers. "I know boy draw too." His face was shiny with cracks and little dug out places, a piece of shiny black coal with eyes. "You be like PEACH tree leaves and CREAM!"

"That would be Willis," Granny said to me. "A little colored boy Moses takes care of. There's one you could play with. Gone off to Tennessee now though. Peach tree leaves and cream is good for poison ivy."

I didn't want to be no peach tree leaves and cream, not with no colored boy. Right then Granpaw came around the corner, ditch-walked to where we were and stopped. He spat, took his hat off and held it over his head like to shade his eyes with. He looked at the sky that way.

Moses stepped out in the yard and gazed up with Granpaw. Granpaw was all white and silvery, Moses black. Salt and pepper shakers. Both thick around and short, with thick-fingered hands. Both acting like there was something serious important up in the sky. Granny had said Moses was a lot older than Granpaw. To me they looked the same.

"See that?" Granpaw said. "That whorl in thar."

"Hmmm," Moses said. "Old Gooseberry."

"Reckon it is?" Granpaw said. "It is, ain't it?"

"It won't never rain then," Granny said.

108

Granpaw spied his eye on me. "There's a black snake in them clouds by grabs. Look up thar!"

I looked but it was too bright to see anything.

Granpaw suddenly hollered, "Watch out boy! It's crawling right toward you!"

I jumped backward and knocked up against the wall.

"Strode! Stop that," Granny said.

Granpaw slapped his leg and hee-hawed. Moses made a little disgusted sound with his tongue and went back looking up in the sky.

Far as it mattered to me, they could both go to hell.

"I'd be ashamed Strode," Granny said.

I got my drawing papers together and went inside. I let the screen door slam. Over the bed in the corner was the picture of Jesus and the Lord's Supper. Always sad. Always waiting. I drew back with the drawing papers and let fly. They went ever which way across the floor. I wished I was back home in Detroit, playing with my friends, baseball and football and cops and robbers, away from this ignorant old goddamn place. Bunch of old hillbillies, gawking around. I sat down at one end of Granny's couch and started to cry.

Granpaw came up to the door. He mashed his nose against the screen, one hand cupped around the side of his face. "You all right in there son?"

"Go away!"

"Aw now." Granpaw opened the door a little and looked in. "Ain't no need a crying, son. Granpaw was just funning."

Tears streamed over my cheeks. "I hate you!"

Granpaw came inside. "Aw now, son."

"I ain't your son!" I said, something catching up in my throat. "My Daddy's dead!"

Granpaw ditch-walked over to the couch. "I'm jest a sorry old sumbitch, Orbie. Only thing sparks me anymore is some old ignorant fun."

"You don't have to scare me to have it!"

"You right there, you right. I'm sorry about it too. You can see I'm sorry about it, can't you?" Granpaw set himself down on the couch next to me, his face covered with short silvery hairs. "Why, I'd hurt my own self before I'd hurt you. You my grandson."

Granpaw sat a minute, staring out the window. "You know, it's hard to learn a old sumbitch like me anything." He wagged his chin back and forth; whisker hairs throwing back the light. "I'll bet you, you could though."

"What?" I said.

"Learn me. Learn me to be nice. Couldn't I do with that?"

"Yes!" I said, still trying to be mad.

"Yes sir. Granpaw could do with that. He sure could. You could tell him when he's crossing the line. You know. Tell him so he'll know when to quit. Sometimes folks will cross a line without even knowing it."

I'd stopped crying. What Granpaw said, how he was saying it, made me feel better someway.

"Couldn't you? I mean when I cross that line, you know." Granpaw nodded his head at me and winked. A smile almost as warm and nice as Daddy's used to be suddenly spread across his face.

"I wished Momma would come back," I said. "I don't like it down here."

"Well," Granpaw said. "I haven't been much help I'm sorry to say. You can forgive old Granpaw though. Can't you?"

I sat there a long time, not saying a word. Granpaw sat too. He looked at me a while, then out the window. More time went by. The thought came to me he might could stay waiting like that a long, long time—that he meant what he said and that there was no other place he would rather be. I looked out at my drawing papers scattered over the floor. One was wedged up under Granny's sewing machine. "What's gooseberry Granpaw?"

Granpaw cleared his throat. "Why, gooseberries is gooseberries. They'll grow hereabouts some places. Sorriest fruits I ever eat. Worse than rhubarb, them is."

"What about what Moses said," I said. "When you were looking in the sky?"

Granpaw turned his head to look at the room. He looked at Granny's sewing machine, the bed, the picture of Jesus and the Lord's Supper. "You mean Old Gooseberry."

"Yeah," I said. "Old Gooseberry."

Granpaw stood up from the couch and stared out the window, stooping to look in the sky. "Like a shadow, it is. Or a shade. In and around them clouds, by grabs. A whorl."

"What's a whorl Granpaw?"

"Like in the Bible. A evil spirit. Don't come to the eye direct neither; not like other things. Have to look sideways to see it. Look and not look at the same time."

"It's the Devil, isn't it Granpaw?" I said.

Granpaw nodded. "Some say so. Why they ain't been no rain to speak of."

11

BROTHERS OF THE WATCH

Granny and Granpaw's house had three tin roofs, one over the main part, one over the back porch and one over the front—all with patches of rust and nails sticking out. Except for the places Moses had painted, it looked dirty and sun baked, stained with orange dust from the road. When it was hot outside, I'd go in the crawl space under the house and play. I'd make forts and have battles and listen to the goings on up above. One time I was there Granpaw came stomping up the back porch steps.

"Strode, that you?" Granny called from the kitchen. I could hear her through the floor.

"It's me," Granpaw said.

"You early ain't you?"

The screen door squalled opened. "Finished that south row. Yeah, I'm early. I'll start in again in the morning." Granpaw did that stepping-off-in-a-ditch walk. *Soft step, hard. Soft step, hard.* Then a chair scraped where he sat down. "Where's that Orbie?"

"Outside a playing, I reckon."

"Thought he might like to go with me over to Nealy's. I need me a twist of tobacco. And we need flour."

"Not from Nealy we don't. Costs too much."

"Have to drive in to town then."

"I'd rather do that as give Nealy our money." There was a chopping sound, *chop, chop, chop, chop*, Granny chopping up vegetables for supper. Dust and little pieces of dirt came down from the under-boards where she stood.

"Moses staying to supper?" Granpaw asked.

"Said he would, then he changed his mind. Reverend Pennycall paid him a visit t'other day, him and Nealy both. They been going around."

"Sumbitch," Granpaw said.

"Strode!"

"Well, a man can eat where he wants to, cain't he?" Granpaw said. "Hired him to paint! Nealy did. Beats all I ever seen."

"No use to holler at me," Granny said. "I don't belong to the Brothers." *Chop, chop.* More dirt drifted down. "They'll be another example made of, I bet you anything they will."

"Makes me so mad I don't know what to do," Granpaw said. "Men like Nealy and that Reverend Pennycall, lording it over folks twice as good." Granpaw got up all of a sudden and started for the door.

"Don't be stirring up no trouble," Granny said.

The screen door opened and Granpaw's boots went down the back porch steps. "Orbie! Ah Orbie!"

"Don't you buy no flour over there!" Granny yelled.

———

A white car, covered half way up with orange dust from the road, was parked in the driveway at Old Man Harlan's store. It had a red bubble light on top and a star with the word 'Sheriff' wrote across the door.

"Police," I said.

"Reverend Pennycall," Granpaw said. "It was a sorry day in hell when he became Sheriff."

114

Up the hill a little way was Old Man Harlan's house. It had a long porch with a swing and big pots of blue and red flowers up and down the front steps. Bird Pruitt was standing at the top of the steps hunched over with her cane. She wore that same purple dress and pillbox hat, its wire net twisted above her head.

"Crazy old bitch," Granpaw said; then looked at me. "I ought not have said that. Ought I?" Steep steps went up to a solid wood porch in front of Old Man Harlan's store. By the front door was a sign for RC Cola, under it another sign, a piece of cardboard on a nail that said 'Coloreds Served Around Back' with an arrow pointing the way. Granpaw shook his head. "They was another place handy, I'd go there to trade."

The store was just one room, dark and shadowy even in the daytime. A red pop cooler sat in the middle. Old Man Harlan had chewing tobacco, cigarettes, chewing gum and peppermint candy, all under glass at the counter. Shelves with a few store goods—baking soda, turpentine, linseed oil, Kellogg's Corn Flakes, matches, canned soup—went along the wall on the other side. The back door stood wide open, but Old Man Harlan was nowhere around.

Granpaw went over to the pop cooler, me following behind. The floorboards creaked under our feet. Granpaw raised the lid of the cooler and looked in. "What kind of soda you have boy? We got Orange in here, Coke and something looks like purple."

"That's Grape, Granpaw. I want Coke."

Granpaw grabbed out one Coke and one Orange. He popped the lid off the Coke in the opener on the side and gave it to me. "This Orange here's for Moses. He'll like Orange."

We went around to the back door. A colored-man was outside there; standing in the hot sun, no hat on, just a ragged pair of coveralls strapped over dingy long johns. Up the hill a little ways stood Old Man Harlan's house.

"Toad?" Granpaw said. "Where's Nealy?"

The colored-man bowed his head and backed up a step. Short gray whisker hairs went all over the top of his head.

"Up da house."

"Come inside a minute," Granpaw said. "You'll fry out there."

The colored-man stayed where he was. "Mista Halan, now, he don't 'llow dat."

"I do," Granpaw said. "Come in here." The colored-man stayed where he was.

A door opened at the house. Old Man Harlan and another man stepped out. They looked at us then started across the yard. Old Man Harlan was carrying a fruit jar full of something looked like water. His head was bald and shiny, pink from sunburn, and the skin under his eyes sagged in puffy half circles.

The other man had a great big belly and a swollen, bulgy looking head with no neck on it at all. He wore a faded straw hat and a white short-sleeved shirt that was sweated through at the armpits. A pair of black suspenders crawled over his shoulders buttoned onto a pair of official-looking gray pants. On one of the straps wobbled a silver star. He had a gun too, a big silvery cowboy gun with a white handle that stuck out at an angle from a holster on his hip.

Granpaw fixed a hawk eye on Old Man Harlan. "Toad will get sun stroke, standing out here. He's old, Nealy."

Old Man Harlan was a head taller than Granpaw; scrawny looking and beak nosed. He wore a blue shirt, the sleeves rolled up to his elbows and a black vest. A gold chain looped out the pocket of the vest. "He'll get a lot worse he steps inside my store. That right Toady?"

The colored-man chuckled. "I reckon dat so. Yessah. Sho is." The man with the police badge touched his hat to Granpaw. "Brothah Wood."

"Reverend Pennycall," Granpaw said.

An ugly grin went across Old Man Harlan's face; his voice was rough and full of spit. "A man breaks the rules is like to go without. You remember that, Toady."

The colored-man hung his head.

Old Man Harlan squeezed by us and went inside. He went behind the counter, got a paper sack and put the jar inside.

"Mighty precious water be puttin' it in a paper sack," Granpaw said.

Reverend Pennycall's nose hole's flared. "That wouldn't be any of ya'll's business, now, would it Brothah Wood?"

Old Man Harlan took the bag with the jar back to the door and handed it to the colored-man. The colored-man smiled, first at Old Man Harlan, then at the rest of us. Then he ducked his head and went away.

Old Man Harlan spat after him. "It was left up to me, they'd all be back in chains. Good for nothing sons of bitches." He looked at Granpaw and me. "What? What ya'll staring at?"

"Pawdon me, Brothah Wood," Reverend Pennycall said. "May Ah pass?"

"This way son," Granpaw said to me. We went back in front of the counter, and Reverend Pennycall stepped inside, so big he blocked out most of the light.

"Mattie still aim to horsewhip me?" Old Man Harlan said.

"Not that I know about," Granpaw said.

"Bird said she was."

"Bird's butter is like to slip off her corn too," Granpaw said.

Old Man Harlan bent his neck a little to the side. His head went with it. He reminded me of a cartoon buzzard I saw once on TV. He looked at Granpaw that way; he looked at me that way—from the side. He let out a squawk and slapped the counter. "Butter off her corn, Strode! Waw! Waw! Waw!"

Reverend Pennycall frowned at Old Man Harlan.

"I swear, I'd a never thought to say it like that, but you right!" Old Man Harlan's face had turned red. "Her butter does have a way of slippin' off!"

Granpaw didn't laugh. Neither did I.

Reverend Pennycall took his hat off, grabbed a hankie out his back pocket and wiped it around on the inside. "Come Sunday, they be dinnah on the ground, Brothah Wood. Up Circle Stump way. Brothah's Of The Watch'll be there. Talk about this here situation we got."

"What sitchi-ation is that?" Granpaw said.

"Why, the colored folk situation, Brothah Wood. Things been getting out of hand." Reverend Pennycall looked at Old Man Harlan, then back at Granpaw. "They'll be good food. And good preaching too. You and Sistah Wood welcome."

"Thank you, but I got my own church to go to," Granpaw said.

"If you call it that," Old Man Harlan said.

"I do," Granpaw said.

Reverend Pennycall put the hat back on his head and smiled. "They always room at the Cross, Brothah Wood. Ya'll just remembah that."

"Maybe I don't want that kind of room," Granpaw said.

Reverend Pennycall nodded. "We all need that kind of room, Brotha Wood. All we sinnas do." The store turned quiet. There was a clicking sound and then a hum from the pop cooler.

Old Man Harlan looked at me. "Reckon when you'll get to see your Momma again, son?"

I didn't know what to say.

"In another week," Granpaw said. "She'll be back in another week."

Old Man Harlan looked at Granpaw. A spit-filled grin hung off the side of his face. "You know that Lucy Stokes run off with a man. From Ohio I think. Ain't that right, Reverend?"

"Ah believe it is," Reverend Pennycall said. "Yessaw, that's right."

"Left all her kids and that husband of hers too," Old Man Harlan said. "She was a looker. Lookers'll do that."

"Ruby ain't Lucy Stokes," Granpaw said.

"Course she ain't," said Old Man Harlan and winked at me. "She ain't her a-tall."

The store got quiet again. Old Man Harlan grinned his hang-jawed grin. Seemed like the shadows were all leaned back in the corners, watching Granpaw and me. I thought of how pretty Momma was, how Victor liked to kiss on her. How Momma liked to kiss on him.

Granpaw looked down at the glass case. "Give me some of that chew Nealy. And a stick of that." He pointed to the

118

peppermint candy.

Old Man Harlan's white hands moved under the glass. He got the stuff in a sack and handed it out to Granpaw. "Two dollar."

"Two!" Granpaw said. "I can get this at Grinestaff's for half that!"

"Best go to Grinestaff's then," Old Man Harlan said. "I ain't running no charities here."

"You never charged this much before!"

"Never been threatened a horsewhipping before!" Reverend Pennycall put his hand on the counter and leaned toward Granpaw. He rested the palm of his other hand on the white handle of his gun.

"Horseshit," said Granpaw. He handed the paper sack back to Old Man Harlan. "How much for the sodies?"

"Fifty cent."

"Fifty!" Granpaw said, but put the money on the counter anyway. He looked Old Man Harlan in the eye. "I wasn't aimed to mention this, but now that you done showed your ass, I cain't hardly keep from it." He nodded toward Reverend Pennycall. "I reckon this goes for you too Reverend. Moses Mashbone a eating with us ain't none of your all's goddamn business!"

Reverend Pennycall's face soured over.

Granpaw took a hold of my hand. "And the way ya'll treat the coloreds around here, it wouldn't surprise me you *both* was horsewhipped one of these days!" We walked toward the door.

I could feel Old Man Harlan's eyes, his buzzard look, Reverend Pennycall, the shadows in the corners of the store, all watching us go out the door.

"I wouldn't be burning no bridges, Strode!" Old Man Harlan called. "Not if I was you I wouldn't!"

We went down the steps, got down to the end of the driveway and crossed the road. "You was going to cut Old Man Harlan, wasn't you Granpaw?" I said.

"Only thing I aimed to cut was a piece of my mind, son. Men like Nealy and the Reverend got to be told. They'll like to run all over you otherwise."

We walked on back to the house. When we got there Granpaw opened the Orange drink and took a sip.

"You said that was for Moses," I said.

"I know it. He owes me one though. After today."

PART FiVE

12

POTATO FOOT

Granny pushed open the screen door.

"Oh no! It's Hag Woman! Flash Gordon to the rescue!"

"Hag Woman?" Granny came onto the back porch.

"Here she comes Ladies and Gentleman! Hag Woman from Ugly Town! Death Ray! Death Ray! ZZZ! ZZZZ!"

"I'd be ashamed, swinging that thing at poor old Granny. Do I look like a bug?"

I drew the fly swatter back ready to blast Granny again. "Flash Gordon's coming to the rescue, Granny. This is his Death Ray Gun."

Granny let the door slap shut. "You swing that thing at me again and I'll death ray *your* gun!"

A shadow of something moved behind the screen.

Granny stepped in front of me, fists punched into her hips, elbows turned outward like wings. She spied some jars I'd knocked over at the end of the porch, one smeared with the innards of a mashed fly. "I use them jars to can with. What you doing out here?"

"Killing flies."

123

"Flies? On my jars?"

"Uh huh."

Granny's hands dropped to her sides. "I'd ruther you not mash flies on my canning jars, Orbie. Why don't you go out to the barn and play?"

I tried to look around Granny to see what the shadow was. "What's in there, Granny?"

"Tain't no *what*. It's a *who*."

"Who then?"

"Well, that's what I came out here to tell you." Granny started down the steps. "Put that fly swatter away and come out here a minute."

I hung the fly swatter on its nail by the door and followed Granny down the steps out next to the pig yard and the trailer. It was late in the afternoon, and the sun was stepping its way down a purple-white-mountain of clouds.

Granny said, "You remember t'other day when we talked?"

"No."

"Yes you do. You was throwing corn cobs at Nealy's chickens. You said they wasn't nothing else to do down here, and I told you things would get better. Remember?" She looked up to the house, then back at me. "Listen now. I got you a surprise."

"What Granny?"

"Oh Orbie, it's a boy!" She was almost whispering now. "A little colored boy. Talks funny but you'll get used to that. It ain't like you can't understand him."

Already I was getting scared.

"Stutters a little bit is all. It's Willis, back from Tennessee. Moses told him about you." Granny smiled. "I told you they was kids down here."

I got a feeling of being dizzy, like I was high up on a cliff somewhere about to fall. "I ain't playing with no goddamn coloreds Granny!"

Granny's mouth went hard. She reached out with both hands and closed my arms together. I tried to twist away. My face was so close to Granny's I could see the little coffee stained wrinkles under her lip. "Let go of me you old bitch!"

124

"Now you listen here to me!" Granny whispered. Hard puffs of chewing-gum-breath hit me square in the face. "I have had just about enough of that sorry talk!" She sent fast eyes up to the house and then back again to me. "What if he was to hear you?"

"I don't care! Let me go!"

"Shhhh! Orbie! I declare!"

Then I whispered too. "I don't care, Granny."

"Ain't no need of getting all red-faced about this! He's just a boy like you are."

I jerked away from Granny and ran over next to the fence. Granny stood up.

The screen door banged to. Out on the porch now came a little colored boy. He had a walking stick looked like a tree limb somebody'd cut to fit under his arm. He leaned on the stick, made a step, brought the stick to the front, leaned on it, made another step.

"That there's Willis," Granny said in her loud way. "Rode over here on his mule!"

The colored boy was even skinnier than me. He wore coveralls without a shirt. The coveralls were puffed out around his body. He let himself down the steps, using his stick, one foot at a time. He didn't have any socks or shoes, and I could see there was something the matter with the foot on his right leg.

I stepped back against the fence.

The colored boy hop-walked himself over to Granny. He smiled a thick row of white teeth. I could see how the rib bones curved under his skin. The foot on his bad leg had toenails but no toes—a black potato with little white potato eyes sticking out the end.

"How you been sweetheart?" Granny gave him a hug, and then she kissed him on the head. "You been a good boy, today?"

"Yessum," Willis said.

His head was shaved, and he had pretty brown eyes. His face was pretty too—like a girl's—smooth with round cheeks and dimples. When he smiled, his head hung to the side, eyes slanting in a way I thought they'd slide right off his head.

"Ha–Ha–Hidy," he said, his smile all pretty and melting-like.

"Orbie, come on now, tell Willis hidy," Granny said.

I tried to back up more but the fence wouldn't let me. "Hidy."

The colored boy smiled that girl smile again; his face sliding off to the side.

"Mind what I told you Orbie," Granny said.

I looked at the boy.

"Go on, Willis," Granny said.

The boy came over to where I was—dark chocolate all over except for the bottoms of his hands.

"Go on, Orbie," Granny said.

I remembered the time at the schoolyard when the colored boys had my pants down.

Cut his dick off, Lawrence. Cut Whitey's dick.

I hawked up a gob and spat it at the colored boy. "Get away from me, nigger!" Squeezing through the fence I ran across the chicken yard; Granny shouted after me. I ran to the chicken house and stepped over the plank threshold, waiting there a few seconds until my eyes caught up with the dark. There were chickens, sleeping in lines on railings going diagonally up and down. Some were hunkered in little boxes along the wall.

I squatted in a corner away from the door. Some of the chickens looked at me. Elvis and Johnny looked at me. *Granny could go straight to hell.* I thought about Momma and Missy and Victor. I thought about Florida and Superman and Jesus. I wished somebody like that would come, somebody strong, take me away from this chicken shit farm. I wished Daddy would come.

A stick poked itself inside the door, then a bumpy bare foot. "Orbie? You in da-da-dare?" It was the colored boy, his voice all high-pitched and sissy-sweet.

I tried to make myself small. "Go away!"

"Miss Mattie. She se-se-send me for da eggs." Willis walked in to where there were chickens sitting in boxes right above my head. He balanced on his good foot and waved the stick in front of him, trying to feel his way through the shadows.

"Watch out with that stick!" I said.

"I gots to get da eggs."

"Get them then. I ain't stopping you."

The colored boy looked down where I now sat hunched in the corner. "Day ya'll is! You want to see ha-how I does it?"

"No."

"Ha-How I gets da eggs?"

"No, I said! You can't hear so good, can you?"

He didn't answer. Then, before I could say anything else, he began to sing.

Just a closer walk with thee
Granted Jesus is my plea.

It was the same song they sung at Daddy's funeral. A sweet sad song that made me think of Daddy going up to heaven with the angels. The colored boy sang so sweetly I could feel the hairs stand up on the back of my neck. He felt his way to the boxes over my head, still singing, not stuttering now at all.

I got up from the corner.

The chickens weren't nervous or anything. They just sat there in their boxes while the colored boy reached in under and got their eggs.

Daily walking close to thee
Let it be, dear Lord. Let it be.

When he finished the song, he looked at me. "Hold deze." He gave me the eggs and turned with his walking stick toward the door. I went with him; still under the spell of his singing. The eggs felt warm and good on my arms. I walked all the way back to the house that way; still making sure to keep a little distance between him and me.

"Where did you learn to do that?" I asked.

"What you mean?"

"With them chickens. Making them be quiet like that. When Granny gets eggs they run all over."

"Mo teach me," the boy said.

"Mo?"

"Mo."

———

"Didn't I tell you they was kids down here?" Granny had a big grin on her face, standing in the doorway with the screen pushed open.

The colored boy and me came up the steps, and I gave Granny the eggs.

"That's Willis, Orbie. That's his name." Willis grinned with all his teeth.

"You better get on home," Granny said to Willis. "It'll be dark soon."

"Yessum," Willis said.

Granny and me followed him around to the front of the house where his mule was tied. The mule's name was Chester. He was old with a curvy back and no saddle, a piece of metal in his mouth with a rope on each side. Granny got one of her chairs and put it next to the mule. Willis climbed up, grabbed the hair on the mule's neck and pulled himself to where he could hike his potato foot over. Granny handed him his walking stick. He sat up there and grinned.

Granny and me watched him ride off.

Later on I said, "He sung a song Granny. He made all them chickens just be quiet."

Granny looked at me and smiled. She was busy fixing up ham and biscuits for supper. "He might come over again sometime." I watched her mix white flour and ham grease in a pan. "You don't have to play with him though. Not if you don't want to."

———

Next day I was out on the front porch, drawing airplanes dive bombing a battleship. I made the sky full of smoke and some of the airplanes on fire. There was a submarine too. I was just about to explode the ship with a torpedo when I heard something sounded like water pouring out by the well. What it was, was Chester, Willis's mule, peeing a big yellow

128

stream there. Willis sat on top of him, smiling, a red scarf tied over his head.

"Go away!" I shouted.

He didn't move or anything, just sat up there on that mule, smiling.

"I don't have to play with you!" I said.

He watched me a minute more, then turned the mule around and rode off.

The next day it happened again. I was out there drawing, and there he was by the well again, sitting on Chester. I hadn't heard him come up or anything. It kind of spooked me, but then I remembered myself and pretended he wasn't there. Without looking at him, I got up and went in the house. I sat in there in the front room on Granny's couch, pretending to be busy with my drawing. When I went back outside, he was gone.

13
THE POSTCARD

"**Y**ou ain't young no more," Granny said.

"That's a fine thing to say and us with Nealy to pay." Granpaw sat in one of the cane chairs on the front porch, his forearms resting on his thighs.

I was looking at a Superman comic book, at a picture of Superman who was lying down, dying from being next to Kryptonite. Kryptonite was green rocks from the planet Krypton—the only thing that could kill Superman.

"If you was to drop dead he *sure* wouldn't get paid," Granny said. "Then where would *I* be?"

"Ain't nobody dropped dead yet," Granpaw said.

"You already had one stroke," Granny said. "You was to ask me, you about to have another."

Granpaw spat. "See now, that there's the thing of it Mattie. Nobody asked you."

Granny sat on the other side of the door away from Granpaw. She'd stretched a pillowcase over a silver hoop and was pushing a needle trailing pink thread up from the bottom. "It would be good if you was to rest a little."

Right then a man with stick legs rode up in the yard on a skinny black bicycle. The front wheel bumped over a rock. The man had to jerk the handlebars this way and that to keep from falling.

"Morning Cecil!" Granny said.

"Mrs. Wood." Cecil got off the bicycle, put down the kickstand and went around the front to a scuffed leather bag that made a belly over the handlebars. He wore a black ball cap, the bill turned backward so that the back of his neck was under shade. He fished around inside the leather bag and brought out a handful of letters.

"I plumb forgot you was coming," Granny said.

Cecil made a face and walked over to the porch, nodded to Granpaw. His voice came out deep as a bullfrog's. "Mr. Wood."

"Cecil," Granpaw said.

"It's Friday Mrs. Wood. I always come on Friday." Cecil handed the letters to Granny.

"You skinny as a rail Cecil," Granny said. "Stay to lunch, and I'll fatten you up."

Cecil grinned a mouthful of crooked teeth. One had broken off slantwise. "I best be getting on. Thank you." He stepped back away from the porch and looked up at the sky. His bullfrog voice could well have belonged to a man twice his size. "You reckon there's rain in them clouds Mr. Wood?"

"No. I don't reckon there is," Granpaw said.

Cecil took out a handkerchief and wiped his face. His adam's apple had a way of going up the length of his throat, making a u-turn up there and dropping back down. "Shore is hot."

"Shore is," Granpaw said.

Granny looked up from the letters. "Orbie, go get Cecil a cold drink of water."

"No, now Mrs. Wood," Cecil said, "I got to get on with the mail. Much obliged though."

"Well," Granny said. "You welcome."

Cecil wiped his face. He kicked the kickstand away and pushed off. "Ya'll take care now." The front wheel jerked side to side till he got it straight. Then he rode off.

Granpaw looked in the sky at the clouds; heaps of them piled everywhere. "No. I don't reckon there's any rain in *them* clouds." He stood, took off his hat and slapped the brim against his pant leg. "Reckon I will lay down a spell, Mattie."

Granny was looking through her letters. "Go on then. Rest."

"What ya'll reading there son?" Granpaw asked me.

"Superman," I said.

"Superman? What's that?"

"A man, Granpaw. He's made out of steel. Nothing can kill him except Kryptonite."

"Crib Night?"

"Kryptonite Granpaw. It makes Superman weak."

"I never heard of such a thing." Granpaw's face looked tired. "Must be some of that Crib Night around here the way I feel. You reckon there is?"

"I don't know Granpaw."

Granpaw laughed. The laugh turned into a cough. Granpaw pulled the screen door open and went inside. I went back reading my comic book. Superman was almost dead. Big drops of sweat were popping out all over his forehead.

Granny knocked the letters and all her sewing off on the floor. "Looky here, Orbie! It's a postcard from Ruby!"

———

I beat the rain barrel with a stick. Then I beat a place under the window. Pieces of paint flew off. I was mad. Mad at Momma. Mad at the postcard she sent. I went around the back of the house. Moses had scraped most of the old paint off there. I sat down on a rock and poked the ground with the pointy end of the stick. On the front of Momma's card had been a picture of a pink flamingo-bird. It was dated June 18th. That was Tuesday, almost a week ago. Now it was Monday.

The flamingo-bird stood single-legged on a long white beach. In back was the ocean. You could see people swimming in the ocean and boats. Granny said it was pretty. She thought Momma's handwriting was pretty. They were all doing just fine in Florida, the card said. Momma and Missy and Victor all had gone on a speedboat ride. Missy got sunburned. Momma did too. They still had a lot to take care of down there. Victor did. It might take another week. Maybe two. They would be back though. Maybe not as soon as I'd like, but soon. They all loved me and wished I was there. I should give their love to Granny and Granpaw, the card said. I should mind Granny and Granpaw and go to bed when they told me to.

A hand suddenly lay heavy on my shoulder. I jumped away from the weight of it, dropping my stick. Moses stood across from me, his long blue-black hair coming down out of his cowboy hat. Willis stood next to him.

"Thing seem bad. Den GOOD COME!" Moses said, his voice going up from down like a seesaw.

Willis picked up my stick and handed it back to me, smiling his mouth full of teeth.

"Tree mash my roof," Moses said. "Dat bad thing. Uh huh. BAD THING, sho 'nuff. but you know WHAT?"

I remembered the tree. The roof. The chimney that'd been knocked sideways.

"Wouldn't have learned 'bout no trees and rooftops hadn't it been to happen is WHAT!" Moses hooked his thumbs over his belt and frowned. "I about to learn to set a roof right too! Soon as old Foley finish Grinestaff's." Foley was a carpenter-man that lived in Circle Stump. "You knows what to look for, you ALWAYS find da good." He winked at Willis. "Ain't dat right boy?"

Willis smiled at Moses but shook his head 'no'.

"WHAT? You supposed to back me up on dat, RASCAL!" Moses quick reached down, grabbed Willis up in his arms and twirled him over his head. I was surprised at how fast he moved. Willis kicked out his potato foot and laughed. Moses laughed too—a big friendly laugh—his black face shining. I thought of Daddy, when he used to play like that with me.

Moses set Willis down and looked at me, egg white eyes, black diamonds in the middle. "I know 'bout yo Daddy, don't think I don't. I know he DEAD. Dat a bad thing too, SHO is,

134

but jus you WAIT. Dey be somepin good come bye and bye!"
He put his hand on Willis's head. "Dis boy mammy die. He
got dat bad foot too. Dat sad, SHO 'nuff. But LOOK HERE
now! Dis boy. He sang like da angels. Uh huh. Nobody sang
like he DO, not even up Kingdom way. Dey plenty folk SANG
good up Kingdom way too!" Moses patted Willis on the head.
"Nobody DRAW like he do NEITHER. Gone send DIS boy
Louisville. Gone be a AH-tist! Gone BE! somebody."

Willis smiled.

"See now! You gots to WATCH out fo da good!" Moses
said. I looked at Willis's foot. I thought about how good his
singing was the other day in the chicken house, how strange
and peaceful it had made me feel. Maybe good things did
come from the bad.

I couldn't see anything good coming out of Daddy's death
though. And what about Old Man Harlan and Reverend
Pennycall? They hated Moses. Where was the good in that?
There was a ladder lying on the ground. Moses picked it
up and set it against the house. He climbed up and started
scraping off what remained of the old paint.

Willis smiled a wide, wide smile.

I whipped the stick through the air in front of him and
went the other way.

———

Next morning, I was out on the porch drawing, and
there was Willis again. This time he was sitting with his
back against the Jesus Tree. He had a pad of paper and was
drawing too. How long he'd been sitting there I didn't know.

I tried to go back with what I was doing, drawing a sailing
ship on a rough ocean with big waves and whales, but I
couldn't think of where I had left off.

Willis pulled himself up on his walking stick, and came
over to where I was. "Dis fo-fo-fo you," he said in a quiet
little voice. He slid his pad of paper down next to me on
the porch.

What was there was a picture of me, sitting on Granny and Granpaw's porch with a drawing pad in my hands. It was drawn only with a pencil, but it looked real. The boy in Willis's picture looked just like me. The house looked just like the house. The porch did too.

"You want to look at my comic books?" I pushed the pile over to him. "You can look at my comic books if you want."

He bent his head sideways and smiled.

"There's Superman and Flash Gordon," I said.

"Who-who dey?"

"Don't you know Superman? He's on TV. You know. Faster than a speeding bullet?"

"Marshall barber shop got TV," Willis said. "In town. Can't go dare doh."

"How come?" I asked.

"White folk."

"White folks won't let you?"

"Uh huh," Willis said. He picked up one of my comic books. Superman was on the front.

"That's him," I said. "Superman." I looked at the drawing Willis made. "This is good Willis. You draw good."

Willis sat down on the edge of the porch. He smiled. Then he looked at the comic book. Sideways.

14
FRIENDS

Willis and me got to be friends. All the rest of that week and on into the next, we played. We had a corncob fight in the barn. It wasn't fair though, because of Willis's potato foot. He couldn't throw fast. I hit him in the eye. Granny made us quit. Then we played like there was a murderer in the barn. I told Willis I thought the barn looked like a skull.

"There could be a murderer in there," I said. "For real!"

"Uh huh," Willis said. "Dey could be."

We went like detectives then and tried to find him out. We played good that way.

———

Granny's calendar said June 29. It was Saturday. We had just finished breakfast and were out on the back porch. Elvis and Johnny came up to the back porch steps and made their heads go cockeyed, trying to look where I was. "I've been feeding them," I said. "They might be in a beauty contest. That's Elvis. And that's Johnny. See how Elvis has long hair? Johnny's hair is short."

Willis looked at me like I was crazy.

"Sometimes they follow me," I said. "You want to see something?" I went into the kitchen and got me a piece of loaf-bread. When I came back out, Granny was standing at the bottom of the steps with a basket of clothes under her arm.

Elvis and Johnny had jumped up on the porch.

"Them chickens better not shit on my canning jars," Granny said.

"They won't," I said. "Watch. Watch how they do!" I tore off two pieces of loaf-bread and put them on the railing. Elvis and Johnny, right away, jumped up there and pecked up the bread. They bent their heads cockeyed, waiting, trying to see if I had any more bread and what I was going to do with it.

"I never seen the like," Granny said.

I tore off two more pieces of the bread and put the rest in my shirt pocket. I held the pieces up in the air, one in each hand. "Flap your wings!"

Elvis and Johnny flapped their wings. They did it, both of them, at the same time. I fed them the bread.

"Lord God," Granny said.

"They do it by themselves, Granny. I just hold out the bread."

Willis nodded his head like he seen it all before. Like he knew all about it.

The railing ran along the length of the porch even with my shoulders. "Watch this." I went up to where the chickens stood and turned around. I broke off two more pieces of bread and held them up, one over each shoulder. The chickens hopped onto my shoulders then and I fed them the bread. I made myself stiff so they wouldn't fall. "All you have to do is feed them."

Willis smiled with all his teeth.

I turned around then to face the railing. "Fly!" The chickens jumped out over the railing into the yard, flapping their wings.

"The Lord as my witness." Granny laughed. "They'll shore win that beauty contest now!"

138

———

A couple days later Willis came over. He wanted me to go with him down to the creek. I told him I didn't know how to swim—plus I said I wasn't about to get on any mule.

"Aw now," Granny said from the porch. "Chester there's gentle as a pup." Chester looked at me with his big sad eyes.

He was a giant with a giant curved back and a giant rump with a rough black tail that kept swishing at the flies that were buzzing all around.

"He might buck me," I said.

Granny laughed. "Willis won't let him do that. Willis been riding mules ever since he was old enough to stand." Granny went and grabbed a chair off the porch. She set it down next to Chester. "Come on Willis. Show Orbie." Willis got up on the chair and grabbed hold of Chester's neck hairs. He pulled himself up and over and onto Chester's back easy as pie. He sat up tall and straight, his coveralls puffed out around him. "See?" Granny said. "You can do that much, can't you? Forget about that creek. Just go for a ride."

"I don't know," I said.

"I won't let you fall," Granny said. She helped me climb up on the chair. Willis put his arm down for me. I took hold of it and pulled myself up. All of a sudden Chester stepped away and I slipped. "Hold on there!" Granny yelled. I held on and jumped and kicked my leg over—Willis laughing and pulling at me—until all at once I was up.

"That wasn't so bad now, was it?" Granny said. "Hold on to Willis!"

I was already pressed right up against him. *Skinny black arms. Black monkey arms.*

Granny was grinning from ear to ear. "How do you feel up there?"

"Good!" I almost shouted. I was way tall, way taller than Granny and almost as tall as the Jesus Tree.

"I told you didn't I?" She handed me up a jug of water. "Take this out to Granpaw. He'll be wanting something cold."

Chester turned toward the road. He smelled like hot pee and shoe leather. His back—warm from being in the hot sun—bulged big as a barrel between my legs. I had to grab around Willis's waist with one hand and hold the jar with the other. Willis laughed. Chester's feet pounded and scraped over rocks and weeds, past the well, out to the road. The big bones of his rump lifted and sank. I sat up tall like Willis, stretched my head over Willis's shoulder and rubbernecked the road. I felt like a giant with big giant mule legs, stomping over the world.

We rode out to where Granpaw was hoeing out tobacco. Tobacco leaves brushed over our legs. Granpaw came up the row, limping like a whiskery old pirate, a white rag tied over his head. I handed down the water jug. Granpaw unscrewed the lid and turned the jug up to drink. Water curled over his chin down the front of his shirt. When he was done, he set the jug on the ground. "Where you boys off to?"

"Nowheres," Willis said.

Granpaw cocked his head to one side and looked up at Willis. "Nowheres? Reckon it's any cooler there than it is here? I'd like to go there if it is!"

Willis grinned.

"I bet it is, ain't it? That nowheres place." Granpaw grabbed a hankie out from his back pocket and wiped his mouth. "Phew, it's hot." He put the hankie back in his pocket and brought out his tobacco pouch. Tobacco leaves waved in the sunlight all the way out to the road. Granpaw bit off a piece of chewing tobacco and handed the pouch up to me. "Get you some in there boy. Make a man out of you."

"I don't want any, Granpaw!" I said too loud.

"You seen air'y black snake since you been down here?"

"No, and I don't want to!"

Granpaw threw his head back, hee-hawing, but that soon turned into coughing. Tobacco juice and blood spewed out of his mouth.

Willis looked around at me.

"You got blood Granpaw," I said.

Granpaw ran his hand over his chin and looked. "Why that ain't nothin'," he said, "You coming to the Fourth Willis?" He pushed his open hand along the thigh of his pant leg, leaving a reddish-brown stain.

"Yessah."

"Moses coming?"

"Don't know. He gone."

"Gone?" Granpaw said.

"Two day. Don't know where."

"He'll do that, won't he?" Granpaw stared out across the field toward Moses Mashbone's place. It was like his eyes were going out to meet something up the hill. He did that a while; then he hawked up another gob and spat. "Why ain't you boys out to the swimming hole? I was you and had time, that's right where I'd be."

"I don't know how to swim, Granpaw," I said.

"You can wade," Granpaw said. "It ain't deep enough to swim in no way. Been too dry. There's still snake up around there though. Have to get ya'll some rocks first. Scare them old water snakes away."

"Uh huh." Willis smiled. "I knows how."

I stared at the back of Willis' head. He might could sing chickens out of their eggs, but I doubted he could scare snakes away. Anybody skinny as he was would be more like to run off from something like a snake.

Granpaw turned and ditch-walked himself back down the row, growling over his shoulder. "Mind how you turn that mule around in here!"

————

We sat next to the swimming hole, drying off in the sun. There hadn't been any snakes, but we'd thrown a few rocks in anyway. Big tree branches drooped over the water. There was a tire on a rope over the water Willis and me earlier had taken turns jumping from. I sat in my underwear. Willis was naked. He leaned back on his hands with his legs stretched out in front of him. His thing peaked out between his legs—a little black tadpole I tried not to stare at. I looked at his potato foot instead. "How did you get that?"

"Ba-Bawn with it," Willis said. "Mammy die right after."

"After you were born?"

"Pappy run off."

"I thought Moses was your Daddy."

"Mo look after me. Sa-Sometime he take me in da wood. Sh-show me things. Snake. Flower."

"Flowers?"

"Uh huh. All kind. I sangs to'em. Snake too."

"That's the stupidest thing I ever heard of," I said.

Willis smiled sideways.

After while I said, "It'd be awful if my own Momma was to die."

———

We rode Chester back up Kingdom Creek toward the road. "What did Granpaw mean back there Willis? About the Fourth?"

"Fourth of July," Willis said. "Thursday. Gone be mmmeeting at da Kingdom Church."

"Moses bring his snakes?"

"Might."

There were bushes full of red and green berries growing on the other side of the creek. Skinny white trees—poplar trees, Willis called them—went up the hill behind the bushes.

"Gooseberry," Willis said, pointing at the bushes.

"Them are sour," I said. "Granpaw said they were the sorriest fruit he ever ate. You ever hear of Old Gooseberry?"

"He da Devil," Willis said. "Look dare."

"What?"

Willis made Chester stop. "On da other sa-side dare!" He was pointing toward the ground at something on the other side of the creek.

142

At first, I couldn't see anything but the gooseberry bushes. Then a breeze rattled the poplars and I saw a spooky shadow disappearing along the ground. It came into view again further up—disappearing and reappearing with the shifting light, with the breeze. "There's a path Willis. I can see a path."

"Mo place up dat way. In dem wood. Talk to da rain up dare." Willis smacked Chester with the rope and we went on.

I wondered how a person could talk to the rain, or to any thing that didn't have a mouth and couldn't talk back. "Moses talk to trees too?"

"Say he do."

"Don't you know? Haven't you never seen him?"

"I seen him talk to da sa-sky."

"How's he do it?"

"Smoke. And a broom."

"A broom?"

"Uh huh. He smoke da sky. Den sa-sa-sweep it. Make da rain be good."

I wondered what might happen if Moses and Victor were to get in a fight. Victor had those Superman muscles, but Moses had magic. At least, it seemed like he did. I bet he was strong too. He looked strong. Maybe he could beat Victor. "Let's go up there Willis. Let's go see Moses!"

"See him at da house. He painting."

"I know, but he ain't never there when I look. He's always sneaking up. Like you. Then he goes." It was true. Granny and Granpaw's house was getting painted, but, except for that one time, I'd never seen Moses do any work. "Let's go up there Willis."

"Na uh," Willis said. "Not 'less Mo say."

We went down a hill and up another. Then we found a path through the woods and turned off.

"This ain't the way home," I said.

"Ain't goin' home," Willis said.

In a while we came onto a field of yellow grass that went over a low hill with a church house near the top. It was

143

a white cinder block rectangle with yellow stained glass windows along the sides and a silver cross, sticking out bent-wise from the roof over the main doors. A dirt road curved down from the church and went off in the woods on the other side.

"Dat Kingdom Church. Fourth of July be dare," Willis said. "Ra-Road go Kingdom Town." He reached around with the rope and smacked Chester's rump. We went up the hill right up to the church house doors. There was a porch there with a little roof and a sign above the doors that read, KINGDOM CHURCH / WELCOME TO GOD'S HOUSE.

Willis slid off Chester first, then me. I followed Willis around the side of the church to where there was a junk car sitting up in the weeds, nudged up against the cinder block wall of the church house—a rusty old Buick—faded milky blue with flat white-wall tires and no glass in the windows at all.

Willis tied Chester to the door handle and gave me his walking stick. Then he grabbed himself up the front of the car, dragging his potato foot over the hood and up onto the roof to a place just under one of the windows. I could see someone had left the window open a crack. As Willis raised himself to a standing position, the roof of the car made a bunch of loud banging noises.

I reached the walking stick up. "Somebody sees you, we'll both be in trouble."

Willis pushed the window up with his stick and crawled in. A breeze whooshed through the trees behind me, bringing the sound of voices. "Goddamn it, Willis!" I whispered.

Willis stuck his head out. "What ya'll be waitin' on boy?"

"There's somebody out here," I whispered. "Out there in the woods!"

"Ain't nnnobody."

"Is too! Willis? Willis!" Willis had ducked back inside. I looked around again at the woods. Another breeze whooshed in through the trees. "Shit," I said, and climbed up onto the roof of the car. I tried to move careful but the roof made

144

another bunch of loud banging noises. Through the window I could see Willis, standing on a little stage next to a preacher's stand. Down the front was draped a silk flag—purple with flowing gold letters that read: *They Shall Take Up Serpents.*

"What you 'fraid of, boy?" Willis said.

"Don't be calling me that, Willis." I pulled myself inside and around and down on the floor next to a row of benches, plain long planks nailed together with high plank backs.

"Dis here Kingdom Church," Willis said.

"You already said that."

"Mo preach here. Bring da snakes."

It was pitiful—the hall of the church house was—more worn out and crack-walled than our store front church in Detroit, used up, plain as bones, strewn with tattered red songbooks and cast off bibles. Kerosene lamps, ugly with oily green dust, gawked pot bellied from the windowsills. Some stood guard on little tables off to the sides.

"We fixing to get in a whole heap of trouble," I said.

Willis walked himself to the front part of the little stage, looked at me and smiled. Then he looked up at the ceiling; his eyes all big and smiley like they were seeing something good. And then he closed his eyes. And then he started to sing—just like he did with the chickens—real high and pretty like a girl.

Amazing grace how sweet the sound
That saved a wretch like me!

I sat back on one of the benches and felt my own eyes close. Suddenly I was on top of a hill, looking out over an ocean of white clouds, nothing but blue peaceful spaces and the sun overhead. The sound of Willis's singing was everywhere, peaceful, filling up the sky, filling up me.

I once was lost but now I'm found
Was blind but now I see.

I wasn't mad any more. Nor was I afraid. I couldn't even remember how I got to be afraid in the first place. Or why I'd become mad. The whole world had gone to some deep quiet place. I opened my eyes and saw Willis at the preacher's stand, looking way off somewhere, I thought, with his eyes closed. We could've stayed that way a long time, but then came the sound of somebody laughing.

"Willis!" I whispered. "There's somebody out there!"

Willis came down from the stage, went over and unlocked one of the windows. He pushed it up a crack.

"They'll see somebody's here Willis. They'll see Chester."

"He on da otha side." Willis looked out the window. I went over and looked too. There were six or seven white boys out there, laughing, playing around, pushing at each other. A couple of them looked our age, the others older. Bigger. The littlest boy was without a shirt. He had a thick piece of rope in his hand; holding it away from him and shaking it, making it wiggle. "Lordy, Lordy, don't let this here snake bite me! Please Jesus! Don't let it!" The other boys laughed. I laughed too.

"Shhh!" Willis said.

Another boy started talking funny, shaking himself all spastic like. "Blah! Blah blah! Blah! Glah glah! Glah glah blah!" He got down on the ground and started rolling around, all the other boys laughing.

One boy stood away from the rest. A fat boy—so fat his cheeks made little bellies under his eyes. He had a gray ball cap with a winged horse on the front.

"That boy's wearing my hat!" I said.

"Shh," Willis said. "Dem Circle Stump boys."

Right then a rock smashed through one of the windows.

Glass splashed all over the floor with one of the kerosene lamps.

"Holy rollers!" one of the boys shouted.

"Niggers! Jungle Monkeys!"

Another rock splashed through the window.

"Goddamn," I said.

"Be still," Willis whispered.

I looked out again. The boys were all running off up the road now; laughing and yelling. The fat boy was last. He had one hand on top his head; trying to keep the ball cap from falling off.

146

Willis walked himself over to where the glass was and started picking it up—sharp splinters of yellow glass.

"They'll know somebody's been in here, if you do that," I said. He went on picking up the glass anyway. He picked up the kerosene lamp and set it on a bench. Its top was cracked, half the kerosene spilled. I found a cardboard box and a broom. Together we cleaned up the rest of the mess. In the window two ugly holes looked out on the day.

"What if it rains?" I said.

"It never rain." Willis looked sad. All the quiet from his song gone now. I put the cardboard box with the glass on the bench next to the lamp. Willis walked himself over to the window where we'd come in.

"What about them boys?" I said.

"Dey gone," Willis said.

"They might've heard you singing."

Willis shook his head, turned and climbed out the window. I followed after. On the way home I tried to talk. I tried to talk about his song, about my hat and the fat boy. Willis stayed quiet. When we came to Granny and Granpaw's, I got down. Willis rode off without even saying goodbye.

15
NeW CReaTUReS

Granny and Granpaw walked in front. Granny carried a lantern: Granpaw, a Bible. From the back Granpaw looked like a gorilla, a gorilla with a Bible and a hat and one arm swung out like a bow. The sun was going down. I had me a tree limb, busting up dandelion puffballs by the side of the road.

"What's he mad about?" Granpaw said.

"Got another card from Ruby today," Granny said. "No telling when they'll be back."

"Hell fire! How long's it take to see about a job?"

"Hush now; he'll hear you." Granny's hips worked under her dress.

"Quit swinging that and come on," Granpaw said to me.

I was tiptoeing over the gravels, trying not to hurt my feet.

Granpaw stopped. "Where's your shoes at?"

"Left them," I said.

"Left them?"

"Uh huh. Back the house."

"How come?"

"He's trying to do like Willis," Granny said. "Trying to make them calluses."

"You'll think calluses them feet start to bleed," Granpaw said.

Granny reached down in her bag and brought out my tennis shoes. "Yes, I brought them. We won't never get to church you picking along that a way."

"Look how red his feet is," Granpaw said. "He's pert near a hillbilly already. Better hurry up you want to see them fireworks. This here's Eisenhower's birthday!"

"It ain't got nothing to do with Eisenhower," Granny said.

———

All kind of colored people stood around inside Kingdom Church. Except for times at the Detroit Zoo, it was more colored people than I'd ever seen in one place. Nigger shadows jumping over each other. Shaking hands. Mixing in. Jigaboos. Negroes. The whole church house was full of them.

As we'd walked up to the church house, I'd seen firecrackers exploding and orange sparks skittering over the ground. I'd seen a United States flag on a pole next to the front porch. People eating corn on the cob. Black-eyed peas. Ham and sweet potatoes. Colored boys were running around, waving sparklers over their heads. Granny tried to get me to join in, but I was afraid. After while we went inside.

The kerosene lamps stood like before—in the windowsills and off to the sides—only now they were all lit up. The little stage was there too with its preacher's stand and the purple flag with its *They Shall Take Up Serpents* written in flowing gold letters across the front.

I stayed close to Granny.

"Howdy Miss Alma," Granny said. "You lookin' mighty fine this Fourth of July."

Miss Alma walked up to us; her dress ballooned out big as a tent, orange with white flowers and a shiny black belt.

150

"Good as can be!" she laughed. When she saw me, she put on a frown. "Your Granmammy done told on you. You know what she say?" Blobs of fat hung off her arms. "She say you 'bout the sweetest thing she evah lay eyes on. Sweet as shuga she say. I bet you is too! Hmmm hmmm. I bet you is." She laughed again, a big deep belly laugh like a man's.

"I won't never tell you another thing Miss Alma," Granny said. "Come on Orbie. Let's go find us a place to sit. I'll tend to you later, girl."

Miss Alma laughed.

Granny took me to one of the benches in back. "You and Willis can sit back here. Will you be all right?"

I wasn't sure if I would be or not. "Where's Granpaw?"

"Up front a praying. Stand up there, where you can see."

I climbed up on the bench and stood, leaning against the plank back. Up front I could see a bunch of coloreds kneeling around the altar. I couldn't see Granpaw anywhere.

"They's all preachers up there," Granny said. "Congregation will join in later."

"Moses coming?" I asked.

"Won't know till he's here in the flesh," Granny said.

Right then I felt a hard thump between my shoulder blades. "I want you to stop poking people with that stick Bird," Granny said.

Bird stood behind us, cane extended. She was looking right at me, hat-net bent up over her head. Purple smoke. "Spirit's trapped, ain't it?" She cackled so loud you could hear her all over the church house.

"What you talking about?" Granny said.

"Her! In 'at box!" Bird looked at me again. "You best be on the lookout boy."

What she said didn't make any sense; the way she said it did.

"Look out for what Bird?" Granny said.

Bird hit the floor with her cane. "What I'm saying is what! You kind a ignorant, ain't you?"

"I reckon I'm smart enough for the likes of you," Granny said.

Bird hit the floor again, cackling. "Now I got her mad! Yes I did! Ah! Ha!"

Granny frowned.

"You mind what I'm a saying boy," Bird said. She turned herself around and hobbled off toward the front. We watched her find a seat up there and sit down.

"Nobody will sit near her," Granny said. "Walked all the way over here by herself. Nealy will throw him a fit and blame us. I wouldn't lose no sleep over what she says." Granny pointed back toward the church house doors. "Look over yonder Orbie. Look what's arrived." There stood Willis, smiling like usual. He walked himself over and climbed up the bench next to me.

"Moses here?" Granny said.

"Yessum. He outside."

Granny looked at me. "You'll get to see something tonight."

I got one of those feelings like I was way up high somewhere about to fall.

"Willis, you stay here with Orbie," Granny said. "I'll be right up front."

———

Nobody dressed up much at Kingdom Church—not that I could see. Gray pants, coveralls, work shirts, suspenders and no neckties. Some people wore jeans. One man came in with dry mud splattered up his pant leg. There were a few church-i-fied, pretty smelling people too—some were white. Colored boys and colored girls came in, all smileyeyed, and some mean looking—hateful. One tall boy—black as a blackboard and wearing an orange hat like an upside down bowl—stood by the door with his arms crossed. He kept rubbernecking over the crowd of people like he was counting heads or seeing in his own mind who and who wasn't there. Willis pointed to the windows the white boys had busted out. Somebody had already covered them with pieces of cardboard.

"Think they'll find out who done that?" I said.

"Already know," Willis said. "Always know."

Right then a quiet went over the church house. It started by the door and hushed its way all the way up to the front. The boy in the orange hat hurried out the door.

There was a whistle and a heavy down-clomp of boots out on the porch. Then, through the door came Moses, carrying a flat white box by a handle fixed to the top. It was about the size and shape of a soda pop crate. 'In Jesus Name' was printed on the side. Moses held the box out in front of him and walked up the aisle to the preacher's stand. The boy in the orange hat came in carrying two more boxes, one with a screen over the end. Something inside buzzed and thumped fiercely against the screen.

"Rattlesnake," Willis said. "Coppahead too."

When the boy got up to the preacher's stand, all the people went in around him and Moses. They all kneeled down around the altar there and started praying out loud, all of them at the same time, filling the hall of the little church with a sound like bees—hundreds and thousands of bees humming around a hive—humming, humming, humming. Miss Alma got up in the middle of it all, raised one outstretched hand toward the ceiling and hollered, "Lawd has done make a new creature out of me! Thank you Jesus!" A man shouted, "Amen, sister! Amen!" Granny got up then and wiped her eyes. Other people got up. Some people laughed. Some cried.

A colored boy held up a drum-thing with jingles fixed around it. He went on the stage with another man who had a guitar and a gold tooth. A little skinny woman was there too, holding up a big bass fiddle, bigger than she was. She started thumping the strings and everybody got quiet. The thumping went fast and had a beat you could dance to, like Elvis Presley only better, and then the boy with the drum jingles joined in and the guitar man too and everybody got to swinging back and clapping their hands, singing.

I'm a soldier in the army of the Lord!
I'm a soldier in the army!

Oh I believe I died in the army of the Lord!
Oh I believe I died in the army!

Willis grinned and clapped his hands to the music. People danced and turned themselves around in little circles.

Moses was up on the stage in back of the music players. He picked up one of the boxes. He held it out to the people while they were all singing.

I'm a soldier in the army of the Lord!
I'm a soldier in the army!

When the singing stopped, a white boy jumped up in the middle of everybody. "I'm just fifteen but I believe in God's signs, praise the Lord! I believe in God's word! I believe in God!"

"Amen! Hallelujah!" the people shouted.

"Praise his holy name!" The white boy jumped up on the stage. "I believe in taking up serpents. I believe in drinking poison. I believe in whatever God puts on me to do! I believe in God! Say hallelujah!"

"Hallelujah! Praise his holy name!"

The white boy doubled over and frowned like he suddenly got a pain in his stomach. "And these signs shall foller them that believe in my name. You cain't get around the name of Jesus! Let me hear Amen!"

"Amen!"

"I said let me hear Amen!" he shouted.

"Amen!"

"Praise God!" The white boy held his Bible open so everybody could see. "It says right here that there came a sound from heaven as of a mighty wind, and it filled up all the house. And there appeared cloven tongues like as of fire! And it sat upon them. And they were filled with the Holy Ghost! And they began a speaking in tongues!"

Another preacher, a colored man, raised his eyes to the ceiling, "It don't matter who you is or where you come from if you loves the Laud! Thank you Jesus!"

"Thank you Jesus, that's right," said the white boy and everybody laughed and clapped their hands and the boy went over to the side and a big man in coveralls stepped in and started to preach like the boy had. It went on like that for a long time, one preacher after another, all colored except for that boy, going on about healing and snakes and what all. One began to holler around about hell, fire and brimstone, how people that weren't saved would be thrown in a lake of fire.

"What about Daddy? He was saved. How come he got thrown in the lake?

"Wha-what you crying about?" Willis said.

"I ain't crying," I said.

"Yes you is."

"I'm scared Willis."

Willis right away climbed down off the bench and went up to the front where Granny was standing. He took her by the hand and she looked down at him and then up where I was on the bench. Then she came back and sat down next to me. Willis stayed up front. Happy tears sparkled in the corners of her eyes. She wasn't mad or anything. She put her arm around me. "What's the matter sweetheart?"

"I'm scared Granny."

"Of what? These people?"

"Uh huh."

"Oh now, they won't hurt you none."

Granny's arm around me made me feel better, even with all her veins. "Moses will be bringing them snakes out in a minute. You want me to take you home?"

I looked off to the front of the church house. Some of the people had cleared away. There was Moses, standing in front of the stage now. One of the boxes sat on the altar. I could see the words 'In Jesus Name' printed on the side.

"I'll stay," I said.

Somebody shouted again. Then another and another till there were a whole bunch of people, doing it all over again, crying and praising the name of Jesus.

"You'll stay with me?" I said.

"I'm right here," Granny said.

And she stayed too, all through Moses walking down the isle, taking snakes out and offering them around. Some people took, some didn't.

The snakes turned their brown gold heads ever which a way, charging them around at the people. Their slick white bellies came up orange in the lamplight.

I hugged in closer to Granny.

A little black man with silver eyeglasses too big for his head stood with a copperhead draped over his hands. "Let a Baptist see one deze and he'll sho back off. Sho 'nuff. He be all right it come to baptizing and praying, but when it come to dis, he be partial. Ya'll can't be partial when it come to da Word." He held the snake out like he wanted to give it to everybody there. "Dis here da Word!"

Right then I saw Willis up front. A big golden rattlesnake stood up from his hand—like a giant letter 'S'—bigger around than his arm.

"That boy's something now ain't he?" Granny was facing toward the front but with her eyes closed. Her eyeballs moved underneath her eyelids. "Uh huh. He shore got the gift."

Moses came on down the aisle. The tall boy in the orange hat followed him with one of the boxes. Moses plucked snakes from the box, holding them up whilst they twisted and turned and slicked their tongues out.

"He offers you one, you just shake your head 'no'," Granny said. She stood up. I stood up with her.

Underneath Moses' black coat, I could see where the sweat had soaked through his shirt. He was holding two little snakes in one hand and a great big snake with brown and gold beads all over its body in the other. He offered that one to Granny but she just smiled and shook her head 'no' and then, without even looking at me, he turned and went over to the other side of the aisle where there were some other people he tried to give the snakes to. They didn't want any either.

That's when he looked back at me. That's when he walked

156

over. Granny tried to shake her head—I think to tell Moses not to bother—but he wasn't looking at her.

The big snake raised its beady head to look at me, and when it did, the two little ones in Moses' other hand swung around to look at me too, pea-colored eyes, black slits up the middle. I could see their bellies, their tongues slicking in and out. I stared into the pea-colored eyes, unable to move.

The church house got quiet. I could feel all the people, looking at us. Then it was like all at once all the people went away, and then there was just Moses and me, standing off somewhere by ourselves, looking at each other.

Then Daddy's face came on top of Moses' face. Daddy's voice, not out loud, but quiet came inside my head, spooky words I'd never heard before.

If you take this up son, you'll have to live with it. All you got to do is reach out.

Daddy jerked his chin and Moses' face came again. There was the church house again too and all the people. I could move now. I could run away if I wanted. I could shake my head for Moses to take away the snakes if I wanted. I looked around at all the people, at Miss Alma and Granpaw, at the fiddle-woman and at Bird. Granny stood beside me with her eyes closed like before. Without even looking at me, she raised her hand and put it on my shoulder.

That's when I reached out.

16
WHITE BOY

Going the old wagon road from Kingdom Church to Kingdom Town, Miss Alma's was the first house you came to. Kingdom Town was just clapboard houses—wet-wood shacks mostly—scattered over a hill of pine trees in front of the old railroad tracks. Miss Alma's sat back from the road, nice, not junky, not like some of the other houses. It was painted yellow with white trim and had boxes in the windows full of pink and white flowers that seemed to nod and bob about even when there wasn't any breeze.

Whenever Miss Alma laughed her teeth shocked out at you like a clean white plate. I liked her, and I think she liked me too because she was always kidding—not like Granpaw, not teasing or anything—just to get a smile across my face. "Boy I thought you's gonna kiss dat old snake! I shorely did! I thought old Moses gone marry you to it. Here dey come, I thought. Mister Orbie and old Missus Coppahead! Sho 'nuff!"

She was busy all the time. Everywhere you looked there her big self would be, hanging out clothes, chopping wood or sweeping the floors. She had two little boys me and Willis

159

played with. Fable and Vern. There were other kids too—all colored—Dewey and Daryl and Daryl's little sister, Jewel Anne. Jewel Anne had white eyes and braids going ever which a way over the top of her head.

They all seemed to like me. They liked me so much I forgot to be afraid. I think it was because of the grownups they liked me. And the grownups liked me because of how I held onto that snake. What with that and me being a white boy down from Detroit and all, I reckon they thought I was special.

———

Miss Alma put up with most anything we wanted to do as long as it didn't hurt nobody. She let us use her chairs to make a jail. I'd make us up a story to play, you know, like Mighty Joe Young or Elvis Presley and Jailhouse Rock, or some other kind of show with gangsters and guns, and Superman or Dick Tracy to be the good guy. There were always stories you needed a jail for.

Fable made up stories too. He said his stories were for real even when we all knew it was a lie. He was a little bigger than the rest of us, had a round face with big eyes that would go wide open all of a sudden like in a surprise. Sometimes he stared and walked at you, zombie like, with his arms straight down to his sides. It was hard to tell if he was being for real or just pretending. One time we found him sitting on a tree stump, boohooing like he was hurt real bad. We all came up real quiet and stood around him there. Vern reached out and put his hand on Fable's shoulder like to see if he was okay or not.

"Fooled ya'll!" Fable hollered, jumping up, sniggering and laughing, pointing his finger at everybody. "Ya'll just a bunch of fools!"

"Boy, what you do dat fo?" Vern said. "We thought you hurt." Vern's hair was like black fuzz. It stuck straight up off his head. He had a snotty nose flat as a spoon, and was all the time doing things with his hands. Like putting one hand up to shade his eyes, pretending to be like a scout. One time he stuck his arms straight out to the sides and hung his head down, pretending like he was Jesus. Jesus on the cross with fuzzed up hair. It was stupid. When we played our shows he was always the one that went to the electric chair. That was because of his hair. It already looked electrocuted.

Fable and Vern's pappy was Ezra. He had to be on a chain gang. Fable bragged it was because he robbed a bank and killed nine people. Miss Alma said Reverend Pennycall was the reason. "Dat Reverend. He gone beat dis po colored boy fa stealin' molasses. Matt Willy's boy. Yessah. Gone beat him wid a shovel! Would have killed him too, Ezra not stop his hand comin' down! All dat Circle Stump bunch jump in on him den. Uh huh. Brothas Of The Watch. Claim he hit Reverend Pennycall! Horseshit! Bullshit too! What I think."

It was the only time I ever heard Miss Alma cuss.

———

We played this game where you had to put your thumb in your mouth and blow till you passed out. Then you had dreams. I dreamed I couldn't move cause I was tied up on a railroad track with a train coming. The sky was pitch black and I was terrified, fighting, trying to get loose. The train got bigger and bigger till I could see sparks and smoke, boiling out from underneath. When the wheels cut into me, I let out a scream and came full awake.

Fable and Vern stood over me, laughing, which made me mad.

"What're you laughing at?"

"You," Vern said. "Twitching down there, look like a worm."

"How long was I gone?"

"Time it take a fly to jump," Fable said.

"No time," Vern said.

That's how it would go. You would think you were gone for a long time but really it was only a second or two—the time it took your breath to come back.

Fable said he dreamed two giant witches had him turned upside down by the legs. Said they were going to make a wish and then tear him apart like you would a wishbone. "But den I blowed dey heads off wit ma gun!"

Nobody believed him.

———

After about a week of playing together, we were all going down the road when Fable pushed into me and I yelled, "Nigger get away from me!"

Fable just laughed. The other boys laughed too, Willis and Vern and Dewey and Daryl, even Daryl's little sister Jewel Ann. They all laughed at me.

It made me get ashamed.

Then Fable yelled, "Les beat whitey's ass!" and they all jumped in on me. I ducked and waited for their hands to hit. *Black hands—gorilla hands—pink monkey-nails digging in.*

Instead, they started in tickling me.

I laughed so hard I almost peed myself. Then they started in tickling each other and it turned into that. I tickled Jewel Ann and she tickled me. I liked Jewel Ann. I liked her braids. I liked the way her eyes looked at me too, shiny black eyes—white cream all around.

Then Fable pointed to the railroad tracks. "Las' one get up dare a piece of po white trash!"

We all ran over there then, laughing and screaming except for Willis who couldn't run.

"Po white trash! Po white trash!" we all screamed at him. Willis's eyes slid off the side of his head, grinning.

———

Whenever I heard a car I'd look up the hill to see if it was the black Ford. Two weeks had passed since the Fourth of July, and still there was no sign of Momma or Victor.

162

Seemed like every time you turned around it was time for church. There were regular church services on Sunday morning with Sunday school, singings in the afternoon sometimes with dinner on the ground, Bible study, Sunday night service and Wednesday prayer meetings. That wasn't enough you could go to Saturday night meetings too.

The preachers hollered and jumped and slapped their Bibles and blew spit ever which a way, carried on about hell and the Devil and how God was going to throw people in a lake of fire. Then all of a sudden they'd go all quiet, start in soft talking the sinners, trying to get them to come down and shake hands with Jesus.

Only Jesus I seen was in a picture they had back of the preacher's stand of Him hanging on the cross like usual, all hang jawed and helpless. Didn't look to me like he could shake anybody's hand. I had the thought maybe they kept the real Jesus out back somewhere. Maybe it was only the saved people that got to go back there to shake his hand. You wouldn't catch me shaking hands with no dead person.

———

Moses hadn't been back to church since the time of the snakes. He'd about finished painting Granny and Granpaw's house, though I never saw him do any of it. "Moses has a way of slipping around you won't know he's there most of the time," Granny said. "Unless you looking right at him, of course."

Church was different without Moses. During the time of the snakes, it seemed like the air and all the people were shocked through with some kind of special electricity. People still got excited, even without Moses, but it was just the usual kind of excitement—not the kind that left you wondering at the nighttime sky, not the kind that left you happy and thankful to be alive. Willis and me would sit in the back and throw spit balls at Vern and Fable. We would laugh and cut up till Granny or one of the colored ladies had to come back and make us be quiet. When church was over, we would ride off on Chester.

One time we came across those white boys, the ones broke out the church house window. They were all walking down the road on the other side of a barbed wire fence. It was after church on a Sunday and Willis and me were in a field, going the same direction, only faster because of being on Chester.

The boys were dressed up in Sunday-go-to-meeting clothes. Nice shirts. Clean blue jeans. That littlest boy was there, the one who'd gone all spastic, pretending the rope was a snake. He cocked his head back, grinning at us with a Bible under one arm and a piece of straw, sticking out of his mouth. The fat boy was with them too; wearing the gray ball cap, the one that looked like mine, with the red winged horse sown on the front. He stood apart from the others.

A rock hit the ground in front of us. Willis pulled Chester's rope, and we started off in another direction. Another rock sizzled over Chester's head. Chester stopped and danced backward. Willis had to pull the rope to keep him from running off.

I looked back to see the boys, standing there, staring like nothing at all had happened. The little boy with the Bible continued to grin.

"Nigger lover!" somebody shouted.

I wanted to yell back, but Willis kicked Chester into a run and we went bouncing up and down over the field away from the fence.

———

"Chick, chick, chick, chick." Granny threw handfuls of feed from a big white pan. "Uh huh, and how would you know they's the one's broke out the church house window? Here, get you some of this." She reached the pan down to me.

I grabbed out a handful. "Me and Willis was over there and seen it." I didn't tell her we went inside.

"Ya'll stay away from there when they ain't no church on."

"Okay." I threw feed out over the ground and watched the chickens go after it.

"Sounds like them Circle Stump Boys to me," she said. "They're like you Orbie. They think they better than colored folks."

"I don't think that Granny."

"You did when you first come down here. It was *nigger* this and *nigger* that." She reached the pan down to me again.

"I changed my mind though."

"You just think you have. Chick, chick, chick!" Pieces of crushed corn sprayed out over the chicken's backs. "Them white boys is like them friends of yours up in Detroit. You don't see nothing wrong with the way *they* do."

"Yes, I do."

"No, you don't. You don't see because you a white boy. You think you're better."

"You're white!" I almost shouted.

"I been around long enough to see a few things too!"

"I don't think I'm better Granny. I like Willis. I like them Kingdom Boys. I like niggers, Granny—I mean, coloreds."

Granny gave me a hard look. "You think because you handled a snake and made a few friends you different than you was before?"

"I am Granny. You don't know."

Granny gave me another look.

Elvis and Johnny were out there with all the other chickens—Elvis in the middle and Johnny by the fence. Two white chickens in with all the coloreds.

"Them folks over to Circle Stump is good people I reckon. Good Baptists. Like you are. Like your Momma." Granny turned the pan over, dumped out the rest of the feed. The chickens went wild. She handed the pan down to me.

"I'm not no Baptist Granny. I don't even like Jesus."

"You better not say that."

"I don't care. He ain't never around to hear me anyway."

Granny started off toward the house. "Bring that pan and come on." She opened the gate for me. "You'll make Jesus sad talking that way."

I hit the pan against the gate-post. "Jesus punishes people, don't he Granny?"

"People punish people," Granny said. "People punish they own selves."

"God punishes people," I said.

"God?"

"Uh huh. He made me come down here. Momma said it was God's will."

Granny was halfway up the back porch steps. "You think being down here's a punishment?"

"No. Sometimes I do. Maybe. I don't know." I went up the stairs behind Granny. The pan banged loudly against the steps.

"Set that down a minute and come inside," Granny said.

We both went in and sat down at the table. I could see the calendar on the wall next to the door. July 17th. Wednesday.

Granny put one veined hand on top the other and looked at me. "Circle Stump folks used to come by all the time. Younguns too, when your Momma was a girl. They don't no more though, not since me and Strode started over to Kingdom. Do you know why?"

"Uh huh. Circle Stump people don't like coloreds. They don't like nobody who likes coloreds. They don't like you and Granpaw. Momma told me. But Granny, they don't like me either. I'm not one of them."

Granny raised her eyebrows. "You know, you just about the smartest little boy I ever laid eyes on. Folks is funny down here, Orbie. They say they love the Lord, but then again they won't abide His people. You know what I'm talking about?"

"Uh huh," I said. "Like Momma. She says she loves Jesus too, but she won't let Missy marry no coloreds."

"Lord!" Granny laughed. "How did you get to be so smart?"

"She says coloreds are nasty, Granny. She says they have blubbery lips."

Granny slapped the table. "See, now that there's what I'm a talking about! You been with Willis! You been over there to Kingdom Town with Fable and Vern and them other boys! And to that church too!"

166

"I know it."

"All right then! Would you say they was all nasty and blubbery-lipped over there?"

"What are you hollering at me for Granny? I didn't say they were!" I almost cried.

Granny laughed and patted me on the hand. "I'm not yelling at you hon. All this old stuff gets Granny's blood up is all." She got up and went over to the cabinet behind me, took out some dishes and brought them around to the table.

I watched her set them out. "Victor says Momma says one thing and does another. They fight about it."

Granny set one of the plates down in front of me.

"Victor give Momma a black eye," I said.

Granny made a little whistling sound.

"He hits me and Missy," I said. "But it's right what he said about Momma isn't it?"

Granny stopped what she was doing and sat down again. "Well maybe it is, a little bit. They's a lot more to your Momma than that though. For one thing, she's good hearted as they come. Too good, if you was to ask me."

"Momma's ignorant isn't she Granny?"

Granny laughed. "She might be, a little. But you are too. We all are a little bit ain't we?"

"She's going to die, isn't she?"

"Someday. We all going to die someday. How come you worried about that?"

"I don't know. I just am."

17
EVEN IN DREAMS

They were trying to get me to play the 'pass out' game, but I was afraid. "That train might come again. You don't know."

Fable made his eyes go wide. "Do too. Ain't no two dream alike."

"Some people dream the same," I said.

"Yo turn boy," Vern said.

"He don't ha-has to," Willis piped in.

Vern all of a sudden made his elbows go like wings and pretended to fly. "Caw! Caw! Caw!" We all laughed while he flew around to the back of me and stopped. "I hold you. Go head."

"Chicken shit," Fable said.

"He don't ha-has to," Willis said.

"It's okay Willis," I said. "I'll kill you Vern, you drop me." Vern wrapped his arms around me. I put my thumb in my mouth and started to blow. Granny's table with all her canning jars floated up in the air. Then it went all snowy like a snowy picture on a TV screen. I went down, or down went up, I couldn't tell which, but then it didn't matter because the world had turned black.

———

I'm looking up into gazillions of stars. I feel the ground under me but when I look there's nothing but more stars— gazillions of them I see on the other side of the invisible ground in front of me—and there's a round moon too, bright glowing but not enough to block out the stars. Then I see it's not a moon at all but a bright white tunnel that goes down in the invisible ground, with a silver ladder up one side. Way, way down inside the tunnel there's a speck or a dot of something that gets bigger and bigger until I see it's a man in a yellow helmet and coveralls climbing up the silver ladder. He climbs up and out and stands in front of me and he looks at me and his face is a crow's face with a black beak and sharp black eyes and one of his hands is not really a hand at all but a bird's claw—Daddy's bird claw hand—and I think the man must be Daddy or a half-crow-half-man-Daddy and I want to go up to him and I want to run away too but I'm so scared I don't do either.

Then lights come on and I see I'm standing on a cement floor. I see ladders and wires. I see pipes. Drums and big oily machines. More yellow helmets, moving in the lights above. Factory lights. Men climbing ladders, walking stairways, some laughing, talking, some sitting on catwalks with their legs hanging over the edges, eating floppy white sandwiches and drinking coffee.

Thunder noises start to pound up in the floor, making the air hot all around me. A furnace flashes full of fire. Daddy or that Crow Man or whatever he is throws a cardboard box in front of the furnace's open mouth. The box stays a second then explodes into flames.

"Remember this place son?" It's Daddy's voice. The man standing in front of me is Daddy, his face back like it used to be, the crow's face gone. A happy feeling swells up inside me. Daddy smiles. I run over to where he is and hug hold of him. Daddy laughs and hugs me back. I feel his claw hand go through the short hairs on my head. "Whatever you put your mind to, you can do," he says.

We start to float up in the air together. We float up to a ledge where a fan in a casing big as a garage door sits with three motionless dusty blades. We land on a metal catwalk next to the fan. Daddy grabs one of the fan blades. "You got to pay attention, son. Even in dreams." He gives the blades a spin. First they go slow, then faster, then faster than faster, blowing so powerfully Daddy and me sail off past ladders and machines and steel mill workers into a huge warehouse space of echoes and lights and black metal walls—a gigantic railroad station—where ingots are standing in long motionless lines on rail cars on tracks stretching far away. Daddy used to work on ingots. Tall triangular shapes with their tops lopped off. We sail down to one. Daddy takes up a push broom and begins sweeping the glassy slag off the top.

Above us a black ceiling of catwalks and factory lights shines down. Like before I see men in yellow helmets, walking, climbing up and down. I see a huge steel beam, moving along on tracks under the ceiling toward Daddy and me. Two arms hang from the beam; they are holding up a gigantic rust colored iron pot, black smoke boiling out the top. It floats along toward us—like the bow of a ship—so hugely quiet you wouldn't know it was there unless you looked right at it.

I'm tugging at Daddy's arm and shouting, "Look Daddy! Look!"

"Time you was going, son," Daddy says.

I feel my feet lift off the ingot. "Please, Daddy! Pay attention, you said! Look!"

"Take care of your Momma son," Daddy says. "She don't see things all the way through." He laughs and waves his bird claw hand. "I expect you know that already."

I float away from him and down onto the cement floor. The beam with the giant arms and the pot rolls over Daddy's head and stops. At one end of the beam is a cage with a white tiger inside. The tiger is pacing from one end of the cage to the other. It lets out a roar. The men in the yellow helmets turn into monkeys. The ladders, catwalks and machinery turn into jungle trees with long branches and vines. The white tiger roars again. The monkeys scream and run upward along the branches of the trees. A door opens at the bottom of the iron pot and a yellow liquid fire comes pouring. Daddy tries to jump out of the way. The fire knocks his helmet off, burns over his shoulder. He tries to struggle, to knock it away but the fire takes him down, crushing him against the top of the ingot. I'm screaming as loud as I can but no sound comes out of my mouth. I look again at the cage. I see a giant unlit cigar, slowly turning, pointing like a weather vane ornament—floating, floating, turning behind the bars.

———

I'm crying. I look up into a craggy black face, shiny like coal. Two black eyes stare back at me, diamond eyes that see right through me; that will not let me go. I can't stop crying.

Moses rubs my forehead with the flat part of his thumb. It's all sandpapery and stiff. "Rest you, little one. Rest you."

I can see Fable and Vern, sitting up on the back porch rail, sniggering and poking at each other, trying to make each other fall off. Willis stands next to Moses, a worried look on his face.

"It was Victor done it!" I cry. "Victor!"

Moses moves his thumb over my forehead. His words go like a seesaw, high and then low. "Shhhhhh. Rest you little ONE. Rest you."

I roll over on my belly. It is like the whole world is in a bad trouble and I can't stop crying. I cry for Daddy and I cry for Momma and I cry for Missy. I even cry for Victor.

"Good," says Moses. "Good."

I can feel his hand, rubbing between my shoulder blades. When I stop crying, it is quiet. Moses' hand is gone. I turn over and open my eyes.

Willis, Fable and Vern are standing over me.

"I cried a long time," I said.

"Shit," Fable said. "You wasn't gone but two seconds. You didn't cry."

I sat up and looked around. I looked at Fable. "But you and Vern were sitting right up there on that rail. You saw me! And Moses was here."

Fable looked at Vern. Vern looked at Fable. Then they both looked at me.

"Mo not here," Willis said.

"He was. He put his hand on my back."

Vern and Fable and Willis all looked at each other again. "You wasn't gone two seconds," Fable said. "Time it take a fly to jump."

PART SIX

18
BUTCHER KNIFE

I was looking for crawfish, turning rocks over with Granny's big butcher knife. It'd been over a month since Momma's first postcard. Thunder shook the ground.

da Doom! Doom! Doom!

It did that most afternoons. Thunder but no rain. No water. The creek bed was almost dry. You could see how wide it would be if it was full. Now it was mostly just rocks with crisscrossing little streams down the middle.

I dug a rock up from one of the streams. A crawfish squirted out. I tried to pinch it from behind like Willis showed me, but it squirted away.

I had me five—no, six. Six crawfish in a Maxwell House coffee can. They were all lying quiet down there on the bottom, gray pinchers like hands inside mittens, beady black eyes. I held the knife in front of me, it's point bent from where I'd worked it between the rocks.

Blue light flashed above the trees. More thunder. Then giggles, teensy weensy little midget giggles like in a cartoon. They were coming from way up where the creek made a bend—where water trickled through a wall of muddy logs. On the other side was the swimming hole. I'd left Willis there a while ago before I went looking for crawfish. Again I heard giggles. I thought it was the Kingdom Boys, maybe they'd come down to the swimming hole to play.

I picked up the can and started running along the creek bed. The rocks were sharp but my feet were already thick with calluses. I had the thought I might be like one of those crane birds on TV that could run or fly away fast when crocodiles come in the water. The ground in front of the log wall was just mud and sand. From the swimming hole came a ruckus of splashing water and swearwords.

"Nigger freak!" somebody shouted. "Cripple!"

The wall butted up against an old cottonwood tree. The tree had knots and hollowed out places you could grab onto, easy to climb. I set the can of crawfish down and, Granny's butcher knife in hand, scooted and climbed my way up to a place where the branches forked apart. I could see everything from up there, the branches of the tree and the tire we used as a swing. Water spilled over a miniature-sized rock ledge on the other side of the swimming hole. Willis was on the side closest to me, not far from the tree and on his hands and knees, naked, looking out over the swimming hole. He was crying and his coveralls were floating in the water. A bare-chested boy stood over him, his skin tanned dark orange with splotches of yellow. He wore blue jeans without any belt and a pair of brown work boots. The jeans had slipped down around his hips. He was scrawny looking with a sunken-in chest, but tall, way taller than me—or even Fable—a big mashed in skeleton with splotchy orange skin.

There were more boys scattered out around the swimming hole. Circle Stump Boys. None wore shirts. They stood around on the bank, laughing, sniggering, throwing rocks at each other and at the coveralls in the water.

The Skeleton Boy's hair was also orange colored, combed straight down around his head like an upside-down bowl. His upper lip looked like a night crawler somebody had cut in two and sown back together. Whenever he opened his mouth, it would give a little spasm and try to jerk itself apart. "Lose something, nigger-boy?"

That littlest boy, the one that had pretended the rope was a snake, stood on the other side of the swimming hole, throwing rocks at Willis's coveralls. A purple birthmark clung like a bent hand to the rib bones over his heart. "Throw him in too Raymond! We need us a better target."

"Yeah throw Sambo in!" another boy shouted.

A sheet of white light flashed over the trees.

"It's coming up a storm, you boys! We'd best be going!" It was the fat boy. He stood up a ways from the bank, shouting at the others, the gray ball cap planted so the bill stuck out sideways atop his head. The boy with the birthmark skipped a rock off the fat boy's arm. "I hope you get the shit shocked out of you, Neddy!" the fat boy shouted.

"You go to hell, Sow Face!" Neddy said. The other boys laughed. Neddy threw another rock; Sow Face jumped to one side, twisting away but the rock hit him in the back.

"Goddamn you Neddy!" Sow Face blew his cheeks up with air, made a little run at Neddy, stopped, stood with his fists balled. "I'll stomp you till your nose bleeds!"

"Come on then!" Neddy raised his little fists.

Sow Face was twice his size, but he didn't do anything, just stayed where he was, a fat boy statue with a gray sideways ball cap, his eyes all red and glaring.

"You jest a pussy," Neddy said.

The other boys he-hawed. Willis tried to get up. Raymond, the Skeleton Boy, pushed him right back down. "Whoa there, nigger-boy! Where ya'll off to?"

"Come on Raymond," Neddy yelled. "Throw his naked ass in!"

Willis tried to crawl away but Raymond grabbed him by his potato foot and pulled him back. More thunder dropped out of the sky.

da Doom! Doom! Boom!

"Do it, Raymond! Pitch him in!"

"Na uh!" Willis cried.

"Let's get away from here!" Sow Face hollered. "They's lightning!"

Raymond turned suddenly and kicked Willis in the stomach. Willis let out a rush of breath and curled up in a ball, his potato foot jerking as if trying to run off on its own.

Raymond pried up the foot with the toe of his work boot. "I want you just to look at this boys. That ain't a goddamn freak, I don't know what is."

Willis lay there, whimpering. I wanted to help him, but there were too many boys. More sheets of light flashed overhead—white, then blue, then white again. A gust of wind bent the tree-tops, hissing down through the leaves. Raymond grabbed Willis by his potato foot, pulled him screaming to the edge of the water and threw him in. I squeezed the handle on Granny's butcher knife, its blade dark like the sky.

Cut him Lawrence! Cut his dick off!

Stones whizzed through the air, split the water around Willis's head. He tried to swim away but one of the stones cut him over the top of the eye. He flipped over backwards, got a mouthful of water and tried to spit.

Sow Face threw his ball cap at Raymond. The red winged horse turned over and over and landed in the water; the hat floated there in front of Raymond upside down like a boat with a gray flapper-tail, sticking out behind.

"Uh huh," Raymond said. "You done it that time." The other boys laughed and started throwing at the hat.

"Come on boys," Sow Face begged. "Don't be doing that."

Willis flopped around in the water. Raymond picked up a rock so big he had to hold it with both hands.

"Smash his head in Raymond!" Neddy yelled.

Raymond stepped to the bank.

I thought of Jesus in the temple with all the money changers. Of David and Goliath. The US Army and the Alamo. Momma throwing her magazine at Victor. Daddy with his baseball bat. I thought of the copperhead snake. How it had reared back in my hand, slicking its tongue out at all

180

the colored people. How they all held back, looking at me, a scared little white boy that had come all the way down from Detroit just to hold a snake in the dark church of Kentucky.

Raymond raised the rock over his head, looking down at Willis.

I held up the knife. "Hold it right there! You skinny ass motherfucker!" It was the meanest thing I could think of to say. I pushed myself back and away and jumped down from the tree. Raymond looked even bigger from the ground—a giant skeleton with a sunken in chest and a rock—me standing there just by myself with Granny's old butcher knife. I pointed it at Raymond and tried to make my voice sound big. "You leave him alone!"

Raymond smiled. "You that *Detroit* boy, ain't ye?" He held the rock in both hands against his stomach. It looked like Granpaw's anvil, narrow on one end, thick on the other. Raymond made his voice go friendly, a friendly neighbor boy, passing the time of day. "Pappy told me about ya'll. Said ya'll was staying up there to Harlan's with old Mattie Wood and Strode." His lip tried to pull itself in two. "You Jessie's boy, ain't ye?"

Granny's knife blade trembled. "You just stay right where you are."

"I know all about you," Raymond said, his voice all of a sudden sad. "I heard about Jessie too. That was a shame, wasn't it? The way he died and all."

"You don't know anything about it," I said.

"You wrong there Honey Pie," Raymond smiled. "Everybody down here knows." The other boys giggled. I could see Willis moving now toward the little waterfall on the opposite side. Raymond went all friendly again. "Your Daddy's folks went to Circle Stump. You knowed that didn't ye?"

"Don't call me Honey Pie."

"Everybody knowed Jessie. They still talk about him too." Raymond made a half step closer. "That's a mean looking knife you got there. The point's bent though."

"Stand back!"

"You know that fire boiled your Daddy's eyes? I didn't know fire could do that, did you?" Raymond moved a little to one side. I kept the knife blade shaking between us. He was right about its point. Even if I managed to stab him, it wouldn't go in. His voice oozed with false sympathy. "His eyes was still in his head. All rubbery and white—like boiled eggs, they said—flesh burned black as pitch. Did you know they had to scoop all that up with a shovel?"

Something whizzed past my ear. A rock. It landed in the trees in back of me. I could see Willis out in the swimming hole—back peddling—trying to get to the other side.

Sow Face was down to the bank, trying to fish his hat out with a stick. "You better quit torturing them Kingdom Boys Raymond. Pappy'll hide you!"

I was surprised and proud too to be counted as one of the Kingdom Boys. Maybe Granny was wrong about me after all.

Raymond said to Sow Face, "How'd you like this here rock up your ass?"

"Go on! You thank you man enough!" Sow Face turned around; pushed his butt out at Raymond and farted.

Everybody laughed. Even I did, a little. Raymond didn't though. He tossed the rock off in the swimming hole on top the gray hat. A big splash of water went up all over Sow Face.

"Goddamn you to hell Raymond!"

Everybody laughed.

I stood there with the knife. All of a sudden Raymond turned and swiped at me with his empty hand, smiled that friendly neighbor boy's smile of his. Another rock cut through the leaves. Raymond picked up a dead tree limb. It was long and thick around as a baseball bat, rotten through and through. He swished it at me and the end broke off. "What's the matter Honey Pie? I bet you miss your Momma now, don't ye?"

I backed up a step, two steps; looking for a way out. I didn't feel like Jesus in the temple anymore. Raymond swung the tree limb again, almost knocked the knife out of my hand. Another rock buzzed my head, then another and another. One hit me square in the chest, sharp as a bullet. "Bastards!" I yelled. Then I saw Willis, trying to pull himself up by the waterfall. That little boy Neddy, his birthmark swollen into something like a purple fire, stood over Willis, throwing rocks at his bare back, one after another, cutting him, making welts.

"Orbie!" Willis screamed.

I didn't know what to do. I couldn't run away and I couldn't stay where I was. Sheets of blue light, a bunch of them, flashed overhead. A black gust of wind slashed through the trees.

"I told you," Sow Face said.

Before anybody could answer him, a thick bolt of white static crackled and spat; it hummed and arced like something out of a Frankenstein movie, electrical and snaping over the swimming hole. There was a smell of burnt hair and sulphur. One of the boys began waving his hands wildly, pointing at the cottonwood tree. "Jesus in hell boys! Look!"

A spooky blue line of glowing light had begun to draw itself up and around the branches of the tree. We were all of us rooted to the ground, watching the mysterious light trace itself up and down and around the trunk, around all the branches, every little leaf and twig, the tire and the rope. When it had finished, it stayed awhile—a neon sign glowing in the middle of the woods— then it just popped like a log in a fire and went out. The smell of rotten eggs and burning hair was everywhere.

I almost dropped the knife, its blade glowing with blue light. There came a roll of thunder. Then for some seconds I seemed to lose track of who and where I was—I seemed to go down, or down went up—like with the pass out game, and then something or someone took hold of me on the inside, someone that wasn't me at all but was me too, like Geronimo or Davy Crockett, way mightier than me but me at the same time, its voice, my voice, strong and true. "In thy blood!" it shouted, I shouted, the same words Moses used on Granpaw. It raised, I raised the knife, blue and burning toward the sky.

Raymond backed away.

"In thy blood, live!" boomed the voice.

Neddy dropped the stones he'd been throwing.

There was an explosion and a flash of light and a crack went up the side of the cottonwood tree. The branch with the tire swayed to one side, moaned and then crashed into the swimming hole. Raymond and all the other boys high-tailed it off through the woods.

Willis had pulled himself out of the water and had come around to where I was standing. He held in his hand the gray ball cap. It was heavy with water. He reached it out to me.

"What happened Willis?" I said.

"You standing right dare boy! You see dat tree branch fall!"

"I reckon I did," I said. "I don't know. I feel funny Willis. Are you all right?"

Willis nodded. He had a gash over his left eye where the rock had hit him, but it had stopped bleeding. "Dey say you a witch, Orbie. Dem boys."

I looked at the hat. It was a darker gray from being in the water. The red winged horse looked darker too. I turned it over and looked on the inside. There were the letters, just like before—'J C' stitched in blue.

19

WHEN A CLOUD CHANGES SHAPE

Granpaw yanked the steering wheel left, then right. "Good God A Mighty!"

I slammed up against the door. The station wagon fishtailed, then pulled straight.

"I never seen the like!" Granpaw yelled. "New gravel all up and down these roads! And for what?" He hawked up a gob and spit it out the window. Pink snot. "For somebody to get killed on I reckon."

"I thought it was fun Granpaw," I said.

"You'd think fun we was to slide off in that ditch by grabs!"

"I *would* think it was fun! What's 'by grabs' Granpaw? You're always saying that."

Granpaw looked at the road. "It's just something people say from time to time, like some folks will say 'by God'."

"'Grabs' ain't like 'God' Granpaw. You could be by 'God', but I don't see how you could be by 'grabs'. What's that mean?"

"Boy, you shore got you some questions!" Granpaw laughed. "I don't know. Grabs is grabs is all. It's just what it is." After while he said, "I bet this old Buick's got more rattles than that Ford of Victor's."

"It's Momma's Ford!" I almost shouted. "It doesn't belong to Victor!"

"All right, all right," Granpaw said. "How come you so contrary today?"

"I ain't contrary."

"Yes you are. Everything I've mentioned you've had to fuss about. You ain't mad at me are you?"

"No Granpaw."

Granpaw drove on down the road and up a hill. At the top was a barn, its big red doors almost on the road. We passed it and went down around a curve and then over a bridge. Below the bridge a skin-and-bones mule was drinking from a half dried out mud hole, the few hairs left in its tail flicking about like a wrecked broom. The smell was awful.

"That down there's Kingdom Creek," Granpaw said. "What they is of it, this far up."

The sun made a star in the chrome next to the window. It turned itself into a smoky blue ball. I closed my eyes and there it came again, a blue ball of smoky light floating behind my eyelids.

"You all right over there, Mr. Baseball Cap?"

"Yeah," I said.

Granpaw reached over and pulled the bill of my ball cap down. I laughed and pushed it back up. "That hat's bigger'n you are."

"Is not!"

"It is too," Granpaw laughed. "It's a wonder it stays on at all."

"Granny fixed it," I said. "She put a piece of quilt inside." I took it off and held it over for him to see. Pieces of red quilt showed out from the inside. So did the letters 'J C'.

"What's them letters stand for? Jesus?"

"Jim Conlin. He's the one give me this hat. He's a gas station man, Granpaw." I turned the hat to where he could see the red winged horse and the words that said, Mobilgas. The horse stood out like a champ.

186

Granpaw smiled. "That's a real one ain't it?"

"Uh huh." I popped it back on; proud that Granpaw liked it, even if it was too big. It was strange how I'd got it back, that fat boy throwing it in the water, the blue light and the lightning, that tree branch crashing down.

Granpaw took out his leather pouch, undid the string and skinned back the leather. A black twist of tobacco poked out. He bit off a piece, moved it around inside his mouth, and then let it go back to the back of his jaw.

I looked over the seat at the back of the station wagon. A stack of boards rattled back there with a can of white paint and some brushes. Next to all that leaned three big bags full of groceries.

"Can I open them Sugar Puffs, Granpaw?"

"You just had a hamburger. At Grinestaff's."

"Yeah, but I need me something sweet."

"No now. Mattie will pitch a fit."

"I don't like Grinestaff."

"How come?"

"He called me a City Slicker."

"Well you are, ain't you?" Granpaw laughed. "Would you rather he said you was a hillbilly?"

"No. I don't know. Maybe. What you gonna do with all them boards?"

"Make signs. Crosses, you know. Put them up and down the road. It's the Lord's work."

"If it's His work how come you have to do it?" I remembered signs in Indiana—on the way down from Detroit—signs on the side of the road. White crosses with Bible words. *John 3:16. Jesus Saves! Prepare to Meet GOD.*

"You can help me if you've a mind to," Granpaw said.

"I don't have one, Granpaw. I don't like Jesus anyway. I'm a witch. Witch's don't need Jesus."

Granpaw spit tobacco juice out the window and wiped his chin. "Where'd you hear that at?"

"Circle Stump Boys. I made a light come around a tree, Granpaw. I scared all'em Circle Stump Boys away. They said I was a witch."

"A light?"

"Yeah Granpaw, like lightning. It came around a tree. Lightning knocked a branch off. That's how I got my hat back. It was magic, Granpaw. Victor took my hat away and magic brought it back."

"Well," Granpaw said. "It don't matter what a person can or can't do. Who'd you think protected you when you handled that snake?"

"Moses. He's a witch too."

Granpaw spit more tobacco juice. "The Lord protected you. Not Moses."

"You believe in magic Granpaw?"

"Not like you do, I don't."

"I mean like when a magician cuts a woman in half and she's still alive? Or when she floats?"

"Floats?"

"Yeah, Granpaw! When she floats in the air and the magician shows you with his hoop!"

"That's just thinking something *is* when it ain't," Granpaw said. "They's a power inside things though. Like in that snake you handled. I believe in that. Remember how you felt?"

"I felt good," I said. "I felt tall." Right then a bug left a yellow splatter up the dirty windshield.

"I know you did. I could feel you feeling it. That's a natural thing. Like when the sun comes up of a morning. Or when a cloud changes shape."

"Or like lightning!" I said.

"The power of God, that was," Granpaw said. "Power of God's like a dream. You'll think it's real enough but then when you try to grab hold on it, won't be nothing to grab. It's there and not there at the same time."

"I had a dream, Granpaw. Moses came inside it." I told Granpaw about Daddy on the ingot with the fire coming down. About the tiger in the cage and the cigar I thought was Victor's.

Granpaw slowed the car a little. "You say it was Moses that come?"

188

"Uh huh. He came after. Black Jack didn't kill Daddy, Granpaw. Not in my dream. It was Victor."

"Lord God," Granpaw said. "What all will you come up with next?"

"Were you going to stab Victor that time?"

"Stab him?"

"With your knife that time. When you and him was arguin'? You hate Victor, don't you? I do."

Granpaw shook his head. "I don't hate Victor."

"You hate Mr. Harlan," I said.

"No I don't. I hate the way he does. There's a difference."

I couldn't see it. To me if a person did things you hated, you would have to hate them too. It didn't make any sense otherwise. We went past Moses' place and over the next hill. I could see the black skull of Granpaw's barn.

"Do you see what I see?" Granpaw said.

"No."

"Up to the house there. Looks to me like a car."

"I don't see it."

"By the well there. Look!"

My heart leaped up. "Momma's back!"

Granpaw laughed. "I knowed you was sharper-eyed than that!"

We came down to where the house was and turned in. The black Ford was parked next to the well. Right away, I got a scared feeling. I could see Missy's doll baby twisted up in the back window, naked, one of its arms missing. One glassy blue eye stared out zombie-like across the road. I pushed open the door and jumped out.

"Wait a minute here," Granpaw called, but I was already half way to the front porch.

I could hear blubbering sounds way back in the kitchen. I pushed through the screen door into the front room, ran part way across the crackly linoleum and stopped. There was a smell of perfume and cigarette smoke. From the kitchen I heard Granny say, "They Lord honey, that's awful."

Then I heard Momma. She sounded stuffy like somebody with a cold. "I know it is Mamaw, but that's how it was. I wouldn't have hesitated anymore than if it was a bug!"

"Aw now, Ruby," Granny said.

"I mean it Mamaw. The next time that son of a bitch will be dead!"

Granny let Momma cry; then she said, "I thought ya'll was goin' in on a house together."

"We was. Then he fell in with those men." Momma blew her nose.

"What men?"

"Ones to do with that Pink Flamingo. You know, that hotel? If you was to ask me, that bunch is up to hell and no good!" A sound like a kicked dog came out of Momma then. "They had women, Mamaw! Sorriest looking old Jezebels you ever seen!"

"Whores?"

"Waitresses, Victor said they was, worked in the bar there at the hotel."

"Whores then," Granny said. "Lord."

"Them men. They treated me like I didn't have sense enough to spit."

"You run off, didn't you?" Granny said. "They's plenty sense in that."

"They was lots of places down there," Momma said. "Too expensive, most of them. Ones we could afford was too far away. Then he up and buys one on his own, a ranch house on the beach. Like it wasn't none of my business. Armstrong give him the money."

"That lawyer?" Granny said.

It got quiet a while; then Momma cleared her throat. "Fords made Victor take a leave of absence."

"They Lord!" Granny said.

"They made a bunch of people take a leave. Victor said it was just a formality, a temporary thing he said, just to make everybody happy. A period at the end of a long, long sentence is how he put it. We fought over it. He started in bad

190

mouthing Jessie then. Said Armstrong had found out Jessie was some kind of stool pigeon. I never heard of such a thing. Talked like it was all Jessie's fault what happened!" Momma was full out crying now. "I tell you what's the truth, Mamaw. He so much as even touches me or my little girl again, I'll kill the son of a bitch!"

"Try not to think about it, Sweetness," Granny said. "You'll make it worse. Victor will get his due, as sure as I'm sitting here he will."

I stepped into the kitchen and saw Momma bent forward in Granpaw's chair at the end of the table. Granny's calendar flashed a big number 27. It was Saturday. Momma was making blubbering-drippy sounds in a hankie she held over her nose, her hair piled on top, still combed nice but with some loose strands hanging down. Her left arm rose up slim and pretty as a movie star's. She wore black slacks with a wrinkled yellow shirt pulled out at the waist. Granny sat with her arm around Momma's shoulder. With her eyes still closed Momma took both her hands together with the hankie and blew her nose.

"Momma?" I said. "Momma, it's me."

Momma opened her eyes. The whole left side of her face was swollen half again its normal size—a puffy purple bruise with a two-inch-long scabbed over gash bleeding around her eye. The other side was still pretty, but her eyeliner stuff had run down, streaking her cheek with milky gray tears. She looked like a beat up clown, ugly and bulging on one side, sad but still pretty on the other.

"Oh, Momma!" I yelled and jumped in between her arms. I hugged her so hard my hat fell off.

"I missed *you!*" Momma said, letting that you-word stretch out. We stayed like that awhile, hugging each other by the kitchen table. "Victor throwed that thing away," Momma said. She was looking down at the cap that now lay right-side-up on the kitchen floor. "Out the window, he did. I could have killed him."

I bent over and picked it up. "A boy found it. I got it back from him Momma. It was magic."

"If that don't beat all," Momma said. "Magic. I could use a little magic right about now. We all could I guess. You ain't been in no trouble, have you?"

"No," I lied. "Momma, what happened? Where's Missy?"

"In there in the bedroom," Granny said. "Poor thing." Right then Granpaw came walking up on the back porch with an arm full of boards and the paint he had bought in town. He put it all down out there on a table by the door and came in. The second he saw Momma he grabbed his hat off and whacked it against his pant leg. "What did that *jackass-fool* do now?"

"Strode," Granny said.

Granpaw gave Granny a look but didn't say anything. He stood over Momma, waiting, his hat resting against his pant leg.

Finally Momma said, "I don't know Papaw. He went crazy I reckon." She looked at me real quick, then back at Granpaw. "We tried to set up house down there but it didn't take." She started to cry again. Another string of hair fell over her face.

Granny passed Momma another hankie.

"Sum bitch." Granpaw looked around the room as if he thought Victor might be hiding somewhere, behind the stove maybe, or maybe behind the refrigerator. "Where's he at?"

"Florida, I reckon," Momma said.

"Floridy?"

"He can rot down there for all I care."

"She run off, Strode," Granny said. "Had to."

Granpaw looked around the room again, mad, lost, that one hawk eyebrow like a hook. Then he reared back like a horse and I saw the gray of his eyeball disappear upward inside his head. He started to cough. He coughed and coughed till he had to go out on the back porch. Out there he kept on coughing. Granny and Momma both had to go out there with him. I went too. He coughed up blood and knocked over the table with the wood and the paint cans. He fell down on the porch trying to get his breath.

"Strode! Strode!" Granny yelled. "Lord, he's having a fit!"

"Papaw!" Momma said.

Granpaw's mouth was going like a fish when you take it out of water, opening and closing and opening again. Pink foam bubbled over his bottom lip.

Momma got down on the floor, lifted Granpaw's head and put it in her lap.

"I'll run get Nealy!" Granny stomped down the porch steps and out across the yard, her big boney hips swinging side to side like a bell. "Don't let him swaller his tongue!"

Granny had already got back and was standing over Momma and Granpaw when Old Man Harlan came up in the yard. Bird came up behind him, both arms moving like a bug in a glass of water. Granny wrung her hands, rocking one foot to the other.

Old Man Harlan pointed to a place on the door where the screen had come loose. "Thought ya'll was gonna mend that."

"We ain't had time Nealy," Granny said.

"Humph. It was my farm I'd make time."

"It *is* your farm, Nealy," Granny said.

Granpaw groaned, "Ohhh, ohhh." He lay face up in Momma's lap. The knot on the side of his head glowed fiery red. Momma bent over him; trying to wipe his face with a washrag, her own face lopsided and splashed with tears. I was sitting on a bucket next to the door. I looked at the screen, at the paint cans that were scattered over the porch.

Bird's lips went tight. She frowned and shook her head and looked at Old Man Harlan. Then she looked at Granny. "Bad time for such as this. What with the crops and all."

"That's right, Mattie," Old Man Harlan said. "I can't offer you no more credit."

"Well, I ain't asking for none!" Granny said. "You gonna help us or just stand there complaining?"

Granpaw was breathing fast now, moving his head this way and that.

Old Man Harlan put his beak nose forward. "Strode?"

"He can't hear you!" Granny hollered. "We got to get him up from here!"

Right then, Moses and Willis came round the corner. Moses with a stepladder. It was the first time I'd seen him since I took a hold of that snake.

Old Man Harlan's face soured over.

"Moses! Thank God," Granny said. "Strode's about gone!"

Moses dropped the ladder and went up on the porch. He put one hand on Granpaw's forehead and with the other took out from his pocket something looked like a little skull, bone white with eye sockets and fangs. A swishing, hissing sound came from inside. Moses kept his hand on Granpaw's head. He shook the little skull, making the swishing sound all up and down Granpaw's body. Nobody said a word. Momma's eyes followed the movements of Moses' hand, the movements of the swishing white skull. After what seemed a long while Granpaw's breathing started to calm down.

"Thank you Jesus," Granny said.

"Lord A Mighty!" Old Man Harlan whispered.

Bird had lost interest. "Dark meat," she said, touching Willis's arm. "I will like me some of that."

Willis backed away.

———

It took them all four to get Granpaw up, get him to the station wagon. Granny and Momma carried him by his arms. Moses and Old Man Harlan carried him by his feet. I carried his hat.

They got Granpaw in the back seat and Granny got in with him. She got Granpaw's head in her lap. Old Man Harlan spied the groceries in the back seat and told Granny.

"They'll keep," Granny yelled. "Drive this thing! Drive it fast!"

A hateful look came up in Old Man Harlan's eyes. "Been driving pert near all my life, Mattie. Don't need no dirt farmer's wife telling me how!" He started for the driver's side door but Moses beat him to it. Willis crawled in on the passenger side.

Moses started the station wagon, slammed it backwards and out into the road. Granny hollered out the window. "They's biscuits and ham-gravy in the refrigerator Ruby!" Before Momma could answer, Moses changed gears and the station wagon roared off, dust and gravel blowing out the back end.

"Old Gooseberry!" Bird cackled.

"You got that right," said Old Man Harlan. "In the flesh."

20
GO THROUGH THE WORLD

Willis and me were out on the porch steps at his house, eating 'maters and baloney on white bread Miss Alma had made.

"Yo s-step pappy do dat to yo mammy?" Willis said.

I nodded that he did. "He got in with some men. In Florida. Bad men, Willis. Crooks. He broke Missy's arm. Momma caught him rubbing on her."

Willis brushed a fly off the end of his sandwich. "What you talking 'bout?"

"You know. There," I said, pointing between Willis's legs. "Her privates."

Willis opened his eyes wide. "Yo mammy tell you dat?"

"No, but I heard her talking to Granny. He was supposed to be giving her a bath. But Momma walked in."

Missy hadn't said a word since her and Momma came back, just laid on the couch, thumb inside her mouth, staring at nothing in particular. She wore a cast with a sling down the front like a sail. Four little purple fingers and a thumb curled out the end.

"Victor said he wasn't doing anything. Momma didn't believe him. She tried to pull Missy away, and that's how her arm got broke. Victor beat Momma with his fists."

"Call da police?"

"Don't know. It was bad though. Like what happened to Granpaw."

Granpaw'd been in the hospital three days. Me and Granny and Momma and Missy all went to see him there, all the way up to Glascow. The room they had him in smelled like pee.

"Granny got Miss Alma to help out around the house," I said.

"I know," Willis said.

"She had to get somebody to take care of the tobacco too."

"'L' brothas," Willis said. "From church. MMMiss Alma. She tell me." He took another bite off his sandwich. Granny had hired the 'L' brothers—Lester, Luke and Lionel—tall colored boys with muscles and scarves and long handled hoes and jugs of water. She was going to pay them from her and Granpaw's crop money. She figured out she could pay off Old Man Harlan and still have enough they could make it through the winter even with Granpaw being sick. She was sure of it. People from Kingdom Town would help.

Old Man Harlan didn't like the idea. "Ya'll can't run a farm this way. Why don't ya'll move into town and let me handle things? I'll loan you the money."

"Yeah and what about the tobacco crop?" Granny said.

"I'll take care of that. Give you your share when I get mine."

"You crazier'n you look, you think I'd do that," Granny said. Old Man Harlan's face soured over. "Bad enough you going t'at nigger church. You got to hire out the congregation too?"

"That don't concern you," Granny said.

A red grin opened one corner of Old Man Harlan's mouth. "Reckon they's niggers in heaven, Mattie?"

"I don't have to listen to this." Granny turned to go back in the house.

"Or you reckon niggers got they own heaven?"

A mangy brown dog laid out next to the porch where we were eating. I threw it a piece of sandwich. "Let's go see Moses."

"Mo not say," Willis said. "He got to sssay first."

"He isn't ever going to say. I been down here all this time he hasn't."

Willis took another bite off his sandwich. "Ca-cain't go dare 'less he say. Dey mmmagic in dem wood. Snake."

"I ain't scared of no magic," I said.

"Make you crazy, boy. Dem wood will."

"Don't call me 'boy'," I said. "We can run away, can't we? If we get in trouble we can."

"Na uh," Willis said.

"Moses might could help me, Willis. I had a dream about Moses." I told Willis the dream I had when we were playing the 'pass out' game, about the fire pouring on Daddy, about Moses. I threw another piece of sandwich to the dog. "I think he did it Willis. I think Victor killed Daddy."

Willis looked at the ground.

After while I said, "You reckon if Moses was to fight Victor he'd win? I bet he could knock Victor's block off!"

Willis took another bite off his sandwich. He closed his eyes and chewed. Then he looked at me. "We go, you ca-cain't tell Miss Mattie. Yo Mammy neither."

"I won't," I said. "Cross my heart."

"Cross my heart don't mean shit," Willis said.

———

I was cocky then. Now, with the wind blowing through the poplars and the sun playing peek-a-boo, I wasn't so sure. I kept looking on the ground all around Chester, checking to see if there were any snakes under the gooseberry bushes. Granny's butcher knife blade was fixed inside my belt. I had wrapped it in newspaper and put it in an old sock. Every now and then I'd feel of the handle to make sure it was there.

Chester stopped short of a big tree root. One of his ears went around to the front. The other stayed.

"Come up dare, Chestah!" Willis yelled. Chester backed off instead. "Come up! Come up!" Willis yelled. Chester went ahead, stopped, then stepped over the tree root and out onto an old roadbed that was partially hidden under wild bluegrass and dandelions and white dandelion-puffballs.

"Use be da train run here," Willis said.

I could see what was left of the railroad tracks under the grass. They ran in both directions over the bulge of the hill. On the other side of the tracks dark green trees—Christmas trees, they looked like—crowded against one another, making a wall that ended at the side of a giant fist of rock. The rock shot straight up out of the ground and was covered in thick vines. The hill we'd been climbing continued up behind it, hidden under a bumpy green carpet of Christmas trees. White pine, Willis said they were, bald cypress and cedar too.

Willis pointed to the wall of trees. "Mo in dare. Pa-Place I told you 'bout."

I slid off Chester. Willis got his walking stick from the rope tied around Chester's neck and slid off too. I walked across the tracks and up to the trees. They made a solid wall so thick you couldn't see through to the other side.

"You goes in dare!" Willis called. "Behind dem trees!"

"There's no way!" I got down on my hands and knees and tried to look under, but the branches were too close to the ground. I stepped back away from the trees and looked upward, up the hill. It was all green forest under a clear blue sky. "There ain't no way," I said.

That's when I heard something big—a bull maybe or a bear—snapping limbs, crashing down through the trees. Suddenly the tree-wall bulged and spat out the man I knew to be Moses except he was all strange and smoky looking, not like I'd ever seen before. He had the same long blue-black hair and it was under the same dusty black cowboy hat, but his face was like a piece of burned wood, all smoky and gray around the edges.

Chester started back on his hind legs.

Moses looked at me, his voice going like a seesaw. "you

COME! Boy!"

I pressed my hand against the sock with the butcher knife. Moses nodded. "BRING it!"

Chester went all wall-eyed and danced backwards.

"Whoa Chester! Whoa!" Willis yelled.

Moses was over there in a second. He got the rope from Willis, reached up and grabbed the strap around Chester's mouth. Chester went even more wall-eyed. He pulled Moses back into the poplar trees, kicked and snorted and showed his teeth. Moses put his hand flat between Chester's eyes. Then he rose up and whispered something in his ear. Something good it must have been because Chester quieted right down, just like that, stood nice and peaceful like there'd never been anything to worry about.

Moses led Chester out from the trees and gave the rope back to Willis. He walked back over to my side of the tracks, gestured for me to follow and slid back inside the wall of trees. What he did with Chester, the way he moved, so quick and springy like a cat, had spooked me.

"It okay now," Willis called. "Go on."

I looked again at the wall of trees. "I can't see how!"

"It easy," Willis said. "Go!"

"You do it, if it's so easy," I said.

"Na uh," Willis said. "I gots to stay."

A dandelion puffball twirled on the wind in front of me. I closed my eyes, pushed hard against the wall of trees and slid slick as butter, falling almost, right through to the other side. A field of long white boulders leaned together there, stone fingers, all pointing upward along the slope of the hill. The woods continued up there, and there was Moses standing bow-legged and balanced atop one of the boulders. I couldn't tell if he was watching me or looking off through the trees.

I was wearing only my Davy Crockett tee shirt and red shorts but no shoes, nothing to protect against the hard grainy stones. I had to pick my way, crawling, stepping, sometimes jumping one stone finger to another. When I came to the end of the field, I saw there was a path through the trees and that Moses had gone up it a ways. He motioned for me to follow and stepped off the path into the woods.

"Moses! Wait!" I ran up to where I thought he'd gone in. A giant pine sailed up there taller than all the others. One of its huge bottom limbs was growing right out of the ground on the side the path was on. I heard thunder and looked up to see rain clouds moving in where a minute ago it had been clear. The trees were so still I could almost see the quiet. It was hot too, hot as a room in ninety-degree weather with all the windows closed. I stood listening to the quiet. A drop of sweat made a crooked path from under my eye down along the side of my nose.

A tree branch cracked in the distance and I saw a shadow or the flicker of something, disappearing over a rise. "Moses!" I yelled and ran after the shadow, slipping and sliding in my bare feet on the prickly pine needles. I climbed down a place where the hill had washed out, jumped a stream at the bottom and started head first up the other side. A giant crab creature rose up in front of me. I yelled and tried to duck away but slipped on the pine needles face down. Then I saw the crab creature was just the mess of a dead tree, black bonylegged branches poking up from the ground. I got to my feet and looked up the hill. Nothing there, just more trees, the sky now full of dark purple rain clouds.

A whistle jumped through the quiet. It came from in back of me—sharp—like a jungle bird I heard once under the big glass dome at the zoo. "Moses!" I shouted. "That you? Moses!" The trees sucked away the sound of my voice. Thunder tumbled overhead. *Why won't you wait for me?* I went back the way I came; back down the ditch, over the stream and up the other side toward the whistle. I walked fast. I walked straight along the hill, till I got back to the giant pine. The huge bottom limb was there just like before, but the path was gone. I looked for the field of finger shaped boulders but saw only the slope of the hill and endless trees.

Trick you boy. Make you crazy.

The whistle sounded again—this time from down the hill.

Then it commenced to rain. One drop. Two. Then a bunch. I half walked, half ran down the hill toward where I thought I had heard the whistle. A gray hump of rocks began to rise over the trees, small at first, then big, then bigger than big. My Davy Crockett tee shirt was soaked through with rain. I came to a place steep enough I had to dig my heels in sideways to go down. I picked my way over rocks and little ledges, all the way to the bottom of the hill. The hump went up in front of me, so big now it blocked out half the sky. It seemed to bulge and shrink back behind the sheets of rain, a great breathing creature—a dragon asleep on the ground. And that's exactly what it looked like. On one side a long tail trailed off into the woods; on the other sat a head, big as a house at the end of a long neck. It even had horns, two dead trees bowing to each other atop the head—the head red with gooseberry bushes. The rain died to a sprinkle, but the sky was still dark, full of flashing lights and thunder.

"Moses!" I yelled.

My voice echoed back. *MOSES! Moses! moses!*

"Don't do me this a way! Moses!"

WAY! Way! way! MOSES! Moses! moses!

Again it started to rain. Smoking sheets of it blew from one end of the dragon to the other. I saw a place where the dragon's belly had given way; a low gap big enough a person might be able to walk through. Thunder boomed overhead. I wanted to run for the gap but I was scared it might be the home of some bear or a lion. Then out of the dark of the gap stepped Moses. "Come boy!" he shouted and went back in.

"Goddamn it, Moses! Wait up!" I ran across the wet rocky ground to the opening, cold rainwater splashing up my legs. Beards of cobweb hung in white shreds from the entranceway ceiling. A log laid split and rotting on the stone floor. I walked in a ways. Dripping sounds echoed in a pitch-black space that loomed to my left, a space I imagined to be huge, though I had no way of judging it. To my right was a wall of moss and sweating rock that seemed to go down along a stone passageway toward a greenish light, glowing dimly in the distance.

"Moses!" I yelled and began to feel along the wall—the dark airy space looming behind me, the greenish light growing little by little as I went—until I came to a green-lit room, a cave-room that was round with a rounded hulled-out ceiling, everything stone solid and sweating with the damp. On the other side of the room two bumpy openings, like portholes, looked out on the rain. Through them I could see white-blue flashes of lightning, hear the sound of thunder.

In the middle of the room in front of a little pool of water sat Moses, smoking a long stemmed corncob pipe. The water was lit green. The smoke from Moses' pipe was green. "Come boy. Sit you DOWN!"

"Why'd you run off from me?" I said. "I got lost."

"First go through the world! Then CHANGE come." His voice reminded me of Mr. Slabodnik's accordion back home, wheezing up loud, then dragging bottom. "COME BOY! Sit."

"I ain't no puppy dog Moses!" I kicked a rock. The rock rolled a little bit in front of me and stopped.

Moses took a puff off his pipe and looked into the pool. He started to sing. It was the same sweet song Willis had sung to the chickens. With Moses though it came out like a cat, yowling on a backyard fence. He stretched his mouth every crazy way.

just a cLOWLser walk with thee
GRAN-it JEsus is ma plEEee
DAAAYly wowlking clOWse to thee
let it be, dear LOWrd, let it beeeEEEEEE!

At the end his mouth was stretched out so crazy I had to laugh. Moses watched me from under his hat and grinned. "YOU! think dis be FUNNY?" The way he said this made me laugh even more. Moses laughed too. "Come boy. Sit you down!" He reached around in back of him and brought up a dingy gray towel. "Dry you off BOY! Keep you warm!"

I wasn't cold, but I took the towel anyway and wiped myself off. I sat down and looked at the pool, a shiny green pool if you looked at it one way, a clear pool, not deep, with little pebbles on the bottom if you looked at it another. The

204

green smoke was all over the place. It smelled like matches. I could hear rain slapping against the rocks outside the two bumpy portholes. Moses reached down to where I had the knife and tapped it with his fingers. Looking at me, he said, "put it IN BOY!" He motioned toward the pool of water.

"It's Granny's knife," I said. "It doesn't belong to me."

"Put it in! See!"

"See what?"

"Go through the world! SEE!"

Going through the world made no sense to me, but I got hold of the knife handle anyway and pulled it out. The blade looked gray in the shadowy cave light, its end still bent from where I'd used it to dig for crawfish. Lightning flashed outside the portholes. It made a shadow-picture of me with the knife and Moses against the opposite wall. There was another sound of thunder. The bottom of the blade started to glow. My hand began to shake.

"Good," Moses said.

I watched the glow climb up to the top of the blade. Blue neon, like at the swimming hole.

"Good," Moses said. "NOW! Put it in."

I looked at the pool of water. It was clear now, not deep at all. I could see the pebbles on the bottom, pink and blue and gray. I put my hand in with the knife just under the surface and let go. The water was ice cold.

The blade fanned this way and that till it reached the stony bottom. The whole thing glowed now, even the handle part. Then it was like the glow streamed out and away from the knife, mixing in with the green glow of the water, turned over and out like a fan or a flower until all the water was glowing, not green anymore but silvery blue. Moses swirled it with a stick. Little pearls of silver light splashed out onto the floor where they stayed a while—like beads of mercury— before slithering back in. "Look!" Moses said and took away the stick. Right away the water went like a mirror.

In it I saw myself—a wet, tired, scrawny boy. I saw Moses too, smoky black eye sockets and no eyebrows under a cowboy hat. Behind us though were things that weren't there before. Beams ran under the dome ceiling of the cave-room. Dried plants and thick knuckled roots hung from the beams along with rusted lantern bottoms, loops of rope and bunches of chicken claws tied together with string. I looked away from the mirror up at the real ceiling. There were the beams and things just like in the mirror. "Where'd all that come from Moses?" I asked, but got no answer.

More lightning flashed. Again I could see our shadows on the wall. There was something else too, next to the wall, a table and chairs, boxes stacked up next to the table. Flat boxes like the ones Moses used to carry his snakes in, screens over the ends, something bumping, hissing inside. I looked at Moses. He jerked his chin back toward the room. When I looked, the table, the chairs, the boxes, the beams, everything that had been there a second ago was gone.

"Not always what you think. Now, isn't it boy?" Moses jerked his chin again, this time toward the pool.

What happened when I looked at the pool confused me way more than anything else. It was like the pool or the light of the pool had somehow sucked me inside itself, surrounding me in silvery blue light. I tried to yell but no sound would come out of my mouth. I was lost in the middle of a silvery blue nowhere. Then, a little way in front of me, the light began to darken and blend, to turn into a something—the figure of a boy, a dirty uncombed little boy, lying on his belly in a kitchen, elbows underneath, writing out something on a piece of paper. He wore thick black eyeglasses too big for his head, one of the corners broken and held together with orange electrical tape. He had no shoes. The heels of his socks had worn through.

"Hey!" I hollered, this time finding my voice. "Who are you?"
He didn't answer.

I bent down next to his ear. "Little boy! Don't you ever take a bath?" I tried to touch his head, but my hand went right through. Three men and a woman sat at a table in the kitchen. One of the men pounded the table with his fist.

206

Everybody laughed. Next to the table was a sink piled with dirty dishes—above it, a darkened window. I walked up to the people at the table. Nobody noticed. Bottles of beer and ashtrays sat everywhere. There was a big, square shouldered whiskey bottle too. It was half empty.

The men looked like factory workers. They were big muscled and wore gray pants and long-sleeved shirts. White long john underwear showed out the necks of their shirts, the ends of their sleeves. They smoked and drank beer, took turns taking little sips from the whiskey bottle.

One man clinked his glass with another man's. "Here's to the cat's meow!" he said.

"Pussy, pussy, pussy!" the other man said.

All three looked at the woman and laughed.

The woman laughed too, her face long and smiling. She was smoking a cigar. She was pretty, but kind of horse-faced with dull black hair, red powdered cheeks and wide flaring nostrils. Eyelids painted green. She sat with her feet propped up on the leg of the man next to her, her knees in the air, her dress pushed back you could see the hemline of a pair of red panties.

She took a puff off the cigar and grinned, letting the smoke leak out small slits between her teeth. She talked like a Yankee; her words jagged-edged, deep and rough sounding like a man. "So now, who wants it first? Michael? You? Don't be shy. You boys." She punched the shoulder of the man next to her. "Come on now. It's not nice to keep Momma waiting."

One of the men grabbed up the whiskey bottle, took a long pull, and then passed it to another man who did the same. The third man, the one next to the woman, put it back down on the table. All three sat with their eyes lolled out, grinning at each other and at the woman. The man next to the woman grinned and ran his hand up her leg, right up to the red panties.

The woman pressed her feet harder into the man's leg. "Oh baby, I know what you want."

The man slid his fingers inside the panties but the woman laughed and slapped it away. All the other men laughed too.

"Ma! No!" The little boy was on his knees now, looking at the people around the table.

The three men looked at the boy and at each other.

The woman's hair wrapped itself around her head like a towel, one loose end hung over the back of her chair. "Get your ass downstairs! I told you."

"It's my house too!"

The men sat at the table with their heads down, waiting. "What did we say? Huh? Tell me. Didn't we say to stay downstairs?"

"Yes."

"Well?"

"It's cold down there!"

"Go by the furnace like we said."

"You go by the furnace! There's no light down there!"

The woman picked up one of the ashtrays and threw it across the room, cigarette butts and all. It landed upside down on the floor next to the boy. "I'll send you back to goddamn Salina Street! To that son of a bitch calls himself your father!"

"Do it then! See if I care!"

The woman turned back to the three men. "Christ Jesus Michael, give me a drink."

The boy started to cry.

It made me feel sad, that woman with the factory men, smoking cigars and laughing, talking now, not paying any attention at all to the little boy. I wanted to give the woman a piece of my mind. I wanted to tell her that a Momma shouldn't act that way. I tried to remember how my own Momma acted but that only made me sadder. I could smell the woman's perfume, the stink of the cigar, the beer and the whiskey.

I went over to the boy who was now lying on his belly with his head down, ashes and cigarette butts scattered all around. The paper he'd been writing on was dirty with cigarette ashes. Across the top it said, Room 5A. Dearborn Elementary. Mrs. Reed. On the line underneath was the little boy's name. *Victor Denalsky.*

Moses' accordion voice wheezed from above. "LOOK at the KNIFE!" it said. The kitchen and the little boy quickly vanished. In their place was the pool again with Granny's big butcher knife at the bottom. It lay down there on the pebbles, a blue flame. I reached in and pulled it out of the water; held it, glowing, in front of me. *If you take this up son, you'll have to live with it.* I had no idea what to do with the knife or why I was holding it—why it was supposed to be held. Seeing Victor's name on the little boy's paper had confused me, had turned everything I thought to be mine inside out and into somebody else's. I liked the little boy; I felt sorry for him, but I couldn't bring myself to feel the same for Victor. Victor, I hated. *Wasn't I supposed to hate him? Didn't he kill Daddy? Isn't that what the dream said?* My arm began to tremble with the knife, with my shoulder, the whole front part of my body.

"Good! Good!" Moses said. The light from the knife blade shined in his eyes. He nodded and opened his mouth at me, a black jack-o-lantern head, the mouth cut in a way you couldn't tell if it was smiling at you friendly or laughing at you mean.

Some son of a bitch, a Negro, poured hot steel on Jessie. That's what happened. Burned him up alive!

"Good, good," Moses whispered.

"What you whispering for, Moses?" I said, but it was like the words belonged to somebody else.

I could see the green flicker of the water, the pebbles on the bottom. Then a picture came to me of Moses, hanging upside down in a tree, naked, his hair so long it almost touched the ground. Blood curled around his wrists, dripped off the ends of his fingers.

"What you mean, Moses? What's good?"

Before I could get the answer, my head hit the water.

———

I woke up dazed and sitting with my back against a rock wall. I was at the high end of a long ridge that looked like an

209

empty swimming pool with the floor tilting up from the deep end. A forested hill rose up in front of me, taller than the ridge. Wind howled, but the sky was clear, and the sun was still high. Granny's knife was tucked in my belt, wrapped in its sock like before. I got up and leaned against the wall, waiting for my head to clear. Under my bare feet stretched a smooth rock floor. I pulled a hard bulge of something out of my pocket—a bone white skull with eye sockets and fangs—the skull Moses used on Granpaw. Something inside made a swishing sound like sand or maybe seeds. I pushed it back inside my pocket and looked out over the ridge. I saw then that I was on top of the hump, atop the dragon's back. In one direction it tapered and curled down into the woods. In the other it also tapered but to a place above the trees, a place thick with gooseberry bushes. Two black pine trees bent toward one another there— the dragon horns I'd seen from below.

My shirt was still damp from the rain, but the day now was bone dry and hot. No puddles. No sign of rain anywhere. Wind howled over the hump. Half a white dandelion-puffball twirled in front of me and twirled away. I looked out along the neck of the Dragon. Beyond the head, waving in the light, I could see the shiny tops of a few poplar trees. I started along the spine of the neck, picking my way toward the head where the two dead trees bowed, waded through gooseberry bushes out to where the dragon's head ended—out to the very end of its nose—and looked down. There I saw the grassy roadbed and the railroad tracks. I saw Willis and Chester, waiting under the poplars. I was on top of the fist of rock I'd seen when we'd first rode up. Vines and little bushes grew all down the front.

"Ah Willis!" I shouted.

Willis looked up to where I was and smiled. "Ca-Come down, boy! Dey a path!" He pointed to a place above where the vines started. A narrow ledge went down from there, down the face of the rock and disappeared behind the vines.

"Ain't wide enough!" I yelled.

"Ya'll gots a hold on dem grape vine!" Willis shouted.

"Come down dat way! It easy!"

"It don't look easy!" I shouted. "Shit Willis!"

Willis picked up a rock and threw it halfway up. "Right in dare! It get wide!"

"I don't know Willis," I said, but I started down the ledge anyway, my back to the rock. I tried not to look down. I grabbed for the vines, knocked off a bunch of grapes and heard them smack against the rocks down below. I grabbed out again, got a hold of the vines and started down. The ledge was broken and not much wider than a six-inch plank but the vines, they steadied me. I held on, working my way down until the ledge finally widened and the going got easier. When I got all the way down, I ran over to Willis. I had a bunch of grapes in my hand.

"Dem grape mmmake you sick," Willis said.

"I don't care." I put one in my mouth but it was so bad sour I had to spit it out.

Willis laughed. "You a sight! Pine needle all ova you!"

I looked back at the fist of rock. From this side you couldn't tell it was the front part of a dragon. You couldn't even see the horns.

"There's a cave Willis."

"Cave?"

"Uh huh. In that ridge. There's a cave-room down in there." I looked at Willis. "I was gone a long time."

Willis shook his head. "Fifteen minute. Maybe twenty."

"Liar," I said. "Didn't you get wet?"

"Na-uh."

"The rain! Didn't you see the rain?"

"It didn't rain," Willis said.

"It did! Look at my shirt!" I pulled my tee shirt away from my body so Willis could feel of it, but it was already dry.

21
THe Rain SKULL

They brought Granpaw back from the hospital on a Friday, the second day of August. His right eye stared straight ahead. The left stared off to the side. He sat in his wheelchair all day—day after day—out on the front porch or in the front room. Sometimes he hollered out words. "Tribulations!" he would yell, or "Goddamn!" Sometimes he called Momma, 'Mattie' and Granny, 'Ruby'.

He called me 'Jessie' once. I was trying to tell him about Moses and the cave. I even showed him the rattlesnake skull. "You see it, don't you, Granpaw?"

"Jessie," he said. "What you doing with that gun?"

———

I was holding up the pan of water. Granny scraped the beard off Granpaw's neck with a straight razor she held up like a wing. Every now and then she'd splash the pan-water with the blade. Silvery soapy water now, water mixed with old beard.

All of a sudden, Granpaw got up out of the wheelchair and started grumbling about his hat. No drooling. No retard sounds. Just crabby old Granpaw-words, like before.

I was glad.

"You'll fall, Strode," Granny said.

"I had it on just this morning!" Granpaw said.

"You ain't had nothin' on that head except what little hairs you got. Hat's where it usually is, on that nail by the door."

Granpaw put his hawk eye on me. He put it on my chickens, Elvis and Johnny, both half asleep on the front porch steps. He put it on Willis, who sat with his back against a post drawing on a pad. Granny had tied a towel around his neck. Foamy white shaving cream hung off the end of his chin. It was spread like cake icing up one side of his jaw.

Granny gave him a hard look. "Strode? You back?"

"I'm tired of sitting around here." Granpaw ditch-walked over to Willis and put his hand out. "What you doing there, boy? Let me see."

"Praise God, he *is* back," Granny said.

Willis smiled and handed his paper up to Granpaw.

Granpaw wiped off his chin with the towel and looked at the paper. "Sumbitch."

"Don't be saying that," Granny said.

"This here's good as one a them camry pictures, Mattie! Just you look!" Granpaw turned with the picture and showed it to Granny and me. It was a picture of Granny shaving Granpaw—of me standing next to her with the pan of water. Granpaw had a dumb look on his face, mouth half open.

"We always knowed Willis could draw," Granny said. "You best sit down now."

"Time I was gettin' back to the fields," Granpaw said.

"Not while I'm alive," Granny said.

Granpaw put his hand up to the back of his neck. "I feel like I been asleep a long time. I had a bad dream Mattie. I dreamed we was about to lose our place and they wasn't nothing I could do about it. Have I been?"

"Have you been what?"

"Sleepin', by grabs!"

"You can see where you've been. Look at that picture Willis made."

Granpaw looked again at the picture then let it go down by his side. "I remember Ruby. I remember her face. It was all beat up."

"You had a stroke," Granny said.

"A stroke? Hell!"

"Don't be saying that. You was up Glascow the better part of a week." Granny took the water pan from me and dumped it in the yard. She wiped the razor on her dress. "That Glasgow Doctor said you'd never talk normal again."

"Get me my hat, Orbie," Granpaw said. "I got to go see about my crops."

"No now," Granny said. "If you was to have another stroke, that'd be it. 'Sides, the farm's took care of, for now anyway."

"Hell it is," Granpaw said.

———

Granny put her foot down when it came to working in the tobacco. You couldn't keep Granpaw in his wheelchair though. He always had to be off doing something. Always somebody had to watch him too. Momma, Granny, Miss Alma. Sometimes Willis and me. Sometimes just me by myself. Granpaw didn't seem to mind or even to notice very much—just went along being his crabby old self, doing small things here and there around the house.

Sometimes he'd get started on something, forget what he was doing, then remember again. Sometimes he'd go like before, all zombie-eyed and still. The day after he got up from his wheelchair, I saw him in the middle of the pigs with a slop bucket; just standing there, looking off at the hills back of the barn. The pigs were humping and shoving themselves around the bucket, waiting to be fed. I yelled from the yard, "Granpaw! What you doin'?" He just stood there, frozen. Granny and Miss Alma had to go bring him in.

215

While they were walking him back to his wheelchair, he came back to himself. "What you two hussies doing with an old man like me?"

"Lawd, Lawd, Brotha Wood!" Miss Alma laughed. "You the devil, sho 'nuff!"

"I'm serious," Granpaw said. "Ya'll was takin' advantage of me, wasn't you? Helpless as I am."

"You the sorriest excuse for a preacher I ever seen," Granny said. Her and Miss Alma helped him to sit down in the wheelchair.

Granpaw looked up at Granny. "If you all wanted to be loved on, you could have asked."

"Hush that sorry talk," Granny said.

Granpaw got loud. "Well, you could have! I would have give you some!" His eyes went over to Miss Alma. "Would have give you some too, girl! White sugar on brown!"

Miss Alma laughed so hard her titties shook.

Granny looked disgusted. "And you call yourself a man of God."

"I never said no sich a thing," Granpaw said.

Granpaw sat on a stool beside the cow. He got hold of one of its teats. "Come here boy. Feel this. Grab 'at other stool there."

I pulled the other stool over and sat down.

"Take a hold of her, right there," Granpaw said.

I reached under where Granpaw's hand was and got a hold on the teat. I was surprised how warm it was—warm and squishy like a sponge.

"Now squeeze her," Granpaw said.

I squeezed but no milk came out.

"Let me show you." Granpaw got a hold of the teat and squeezed in a way to make the milk whistle in the bucket. "See? Squeeze and pull. Pretend that little hand of yours is a calf's mouth. Suck it right out of there."

I tried again, got a little bit to come, then nothing.

"It's a wonder any milk comes at all, it's been so dry," Granpaw said. "Ain't had a drop of rain in weeks."

Granpaw was right. All we had were thunderheads in the afternoons that would flash and boom a while—then blow away. We hadn't had a real rain since I chased after Moses in the woods. That was almost two weeks ago.

"Can it rain on one side of a hill and not on the other?" I asked.

"I reckon it could," Granpaw said. "Don't rain everywhere all at once. It ain't likely though."

"It did when I was following Moses," I said. "It rained. It rained hard. But when I got back on the other side of the dragon, it was dry."

"Dragon?"

"A hill Granpaw. It looked like a dragon on one side. I was inside its belly. Inside a pool of water. Green water that went all silvery like a mirror."

Granpaw looked at me flat on. "You was with Moses then?"

"Willis took me," I said before I could catch myself.

"Willis did?"

"Yeah Granpaw," I said. "I wasn't supposed to tell you that, but he did. Don't tell Granny."

Granpaw shook his head.

"I was scared, Granpaw. I thought Moses might could help me. I dreamed Victor poured fire on Daddy. Remember I told you?"

Granpaw shook his head. "A dream's one thing. What's real is another." He got up from the stool with the milk bucket. I got up too. He set the bucket on a shelf, and then undid the rope holding the cow. The cow walked out to the middle of the open barn door and stood.

"Get out now!" Granpaw yelled. But the cow lifted its tail and pooped a big pile of soupy green poop right there on the barn's dirt floor. Granpaw got mad and bounced a corncob off the cow's rear end. The cow knocked against a milk can and leaped out the door.

217

"Razor-backed bitch!" Granpaw shouted. He ditch-walked himself back to his stool, sat down and motioned me to sit down on mine. He gave me that flat-on look. "Now. Tell Granpaw. What all happened out there with Moses?"

I sat down and told him everything I could remember. How the beams appeared and disappeared. How the little boy who was Victor tried to get his Momma to stop what she was doing. How the men around the table laughed. About the sight I had of Moses, hanging upside down in a tree. How the blood dripped from his fingers. I reached in my pocket and pulled out the rattlesnake skull. "He gave me this, Granpaw."

Granpaw took it between his first finger and thumb, raised it up to the level of his eyes.

"He used it on you, Granpaw. He made you better with it."

Granpaw turned the little skull around, looking at it every which way. "Moses wouldn't give this away unless they was good reason to. This is his Rain Skull. You know what a Rain Skull is?"

"No Granpaw."

Granpaw shook the skull, making that swishy hissing sound. "Them's herbs and things Moses put in there. Walked all over these hills gathering them. I know. I helped him do it. A Rain Skull is power, son. Contrary power. You'll think it's going one way but then it'll end up going another. Then it's too late."

"Too late for what, Granpaw?"

He gave me another flat-on look. "To save what you was wanting to destroy, by grabs."

I thought about that a minute. "But that doesn't make any sense."

"No," Granpaw said. "And I don't reckon it ever will. That's how it works though."

"Like magic," I said.

"Not magic. Contrary power. Moses is a medicine man, son. Takes a good long while to get what a medicine man is saying. It'll seem unnatural." Granpaw nodded his head at me real slow like. "You'll see though. In time."

I was glad I would see. Still I wanted to know about the little boy, about Victor. I wanted to know what he was doing there with his momma in that kitchen with all those men.

"Victor's the enemy, that's what you think," Granpaw said. "To feel sorry for the enemy runs agin the blood. An eye for an eye is what the blood says. Vengeance is mine, sayeth the Lord."

"But what if the enemy was going to kill your family, Granpaw?" I said. "Like in a war. Like, if somebody was going to drop a bomb on your house. What would you do then?"

Granpaw laughed. "Well, I reckon I'd have to kill the sumbitch!" He reached up around his neck, took hold of the leather draw-string his tobacco pouch was tied on and pulled it over his head. "You got to keep that in a good place. You got to keep it protected." Granpaw emptied the pouch of chewing tobacco and pushed the rattlesnake skull inside. "I can't chew no more no how. Here. Put this around your neck."

I'll skin it back for you, if you want me to. You can put its skull on a string for a necklace.

"How's that feel?" Granpaw said.

"All right I guess." I ran my finger along the draw-string. "Granpaw? If you wanted to destroy something, why would you want to save it too?" I looked up for the answer, but Granpaw had gone all zombie-eyed again.

———

It was the 7th of August. Granny was sitting in her rocking chair on the front porch. Granpaw was in his wheelchair, staring at something across the road. I was throwing little stones at the picture of Jesus in the Jesus Tree.

"Orbie, cut that out," Granny said. "You'll put a hole in Jesus."

"Yes. Stop that," Momma said. She was sitting on the edge of the porch with Missy in her lap. Her face had healed some, more yellow now than purple. Missy still wasn't talking.

"Aw shit," I said.

219

"I'll wear you out boy," Momma said.

"Them kids ought not be missing their school," Granny said.

"I ain't leaving Harlan's Crossroads Mamaw. Not till you and Granpaw get more situated."

"Lord hon, that might be a while," Granny said. "Won't see any crop money till the fall."

I sat down next to Momma. "I could go with Willis, Momma. They got school in the Kingdom. Missy could go too."

Missy laid her head against Momma's chest, staring, the white sail of the sling falling across the front of her. All she did anymore was suck her thumb and stare—or else whine around like a little lost puppy dog.

"Missy won't be going there," Momma said.

Granny cracked her gum. "You afraid she might turn colored?"

"She can't go to her own school let alone someone else's," Momma said. "Look at her."

"I could go," I said. "Willis is my friend."

The other day I'd brought Willis in to meet Momma. I think it surprised her, him being colored and crippled and all. He told Momma he was sorry about her face, about Granpaw and Missy getting hurt. After he left, Momma went on about how sweet he was, how well behaved. She didn't use the 'nigger' word even one time.

"He's a nice boy, Willis is," Momma said. "We'll see about school when the time comes. Victor will have something to say about that."

"You mean to take him back then?" Granny said.

"No. I don't know, Mamaw," Momma said. "I never was one to stay mad."

Granny spit her gum in a tin can she held up to her mouth. "I'd learn to stay mad if I was you. He might get to feeling bad someday and decide to kill somebody."

Missy tried to hug herself closer to Momma.

"They something not right," Granny said. "All that business in Floridy. Him on a leave of absence."

"It worries me too," Momma said.

I wanted to tell them about my dream of Victor killing Daddy, of how Moses had come, of how I met with Moses in the cave and what all I seen when Victor was a little boy. I almost did, but then I remembered my promise to Willis.

"He's like a bucket got a hole in its bottom," Granny said. "More you put in, more goes out."

"We all got holes," Momma said.

"Don't it bother you none him takin' that feller Armstrong's side against Jessie?"

"'Course it does. He was just mad though. At all that business with the Union." She looked away over the yard over the crossroads toward the cemetery. "Jessie's gone, Mamaw. Won't nothing bring him back."

The other day me, Missy, Granny and Momma had all gone over to the cemetery. Momma had stood over Daddy's grave, arms wrapped about her body, shivering in the hot sun.

"I need Victor," Momma said. "Even with all he's done, I still think of him."

"That little patch between your legs is talking now," Granny said. "That's old pussy talk!"

I couldn't keep from laughing out loud.

Momma sent mad eyes to me, then back to Granny. "You sorrier than Granpaw is, I swear."

"I wasn't born yesterday, daughter."

"What about forgiveness Mamaw? Ain't they no room for forgiveness?"

"Well, cut my ears off and feed 'em to the hogs!" Granny almost hollered. "Victor ain't been around to ask for no forgiveness, and here you are a giving it away already. I wouldn't be so quick to forgive a sorry son of a bitch! Excuse my French, Orbie."

"Revelations!" Granpaw hollered from his wheelchair.

PART SEVEN

22

A WALL AGAINST VICTOR

Willis and me were lying out on an old blanket by the well. It rained a few little sprinkles after supper, and we had spread the blanket over some grass sacks to keep it dry. I was reading my comic books. Willis sat, drawing a picture of Granny in her rocking chair. She was up on the front porch, fixing holes in Granpaw's socks.

A car grumbled down Bounty from Circle Stump followed by another. When it got to Granny and Granpaw's, it pulled up in the yard and backed out again, turning so its nose pointed back the way it had come, back toward Circle Stump. It was Reverend Pennycall's white police car, the gold 'SHERIFF' star on the side speckled with orange mud.

The other car was a flashy blue Cadillac, shiny new with long smooth tail fins, double chrome headlights and whitewall tires. It waited for Reverend Pennycall's police car to turn around, then pulled in the yard along side Momma's Ford. The driver turned the motor off and got out. He walked around the front of the car, put his hands in his pockets and smiled at the yard.

He wore sunglasses and a red sport coat over a pink shirt, a skinny white tie down the middle. He looked like a movie star, like Dean Martin maybe or Matt Dillon on Gun Smoke but without the hat. The way his hair was combed was more like Dean Martin's, long and black and waved up over the top of his head.

He walked closer and smiled a movie star smile at Willis and me. Then he looked the well up and down and smiled at it, like he was thinking it might look good someplace else, that he might could buy it with his movie star money and take it off to be wherever that was. He ran the palm of one of his hands, his left hand, along the side of his head like to smooth the hair flatter there. On the back of the hand I saw the heart shaped tattoo.

"Victor!" I whispered to Willis but Willis had already stopped drawing on his picture and was staring at the man. I could feel my own heart doing somersaults inside my chest. I wanted to get up, but my legs wouldn't go. "That's him," I said. "Victor."

Victor stepped toward the Jesus Tree. He looked the picture of Jesus up and down. I could see Granny, watching him from the porch. If he saw her, he never let on. He reached inside his coat to bring out a gold cigarette case. I could see a bunch of cigarettes with gold filters, all in a line. He tapped the case to get one out, shut it with a little click and slipped it back inside his coat. He put the cigarette between his teeth, looking at the Jesus Tree while he did. The way he cocked his head, the way he smiled at the Jesus Tree was like with the well, like he was figuring where a better place for the Jesus Tree might be and how much money it would cost to move it there.

I found my legs and got up. "That tree ain't for sale!"

The unlit cigarette was planted in the middle of Victor's movie star smile. He scissored it between his fingers and took it away. *"Isn't. Isn't* for sale, is what you mean, son." He smiled at Willis then and nodded. Willis pulled himself up on his walking stick. Victor came a step or two closer and

226

stopped. "It's been a while, hasn't it? You look good boy! Kentucky's toughened you." He nodded toward my feet. "You've got calluses." I looked down at the hard half-moon slices that'd grown around my big toes. Victor gestured toward Willis. "Who's your little friend?"

"Willis," I said. "His name's Willis."

Willis tried to smile but it wouldn't go.

Victor had always dressed nice, but today he flashed out like a page in a magazine. You wouldn't think he was from Detroit at all, but some other place fine and rich and pink. Someplace with palm trees maybe, with blue skies and sandy beaches. The buttons on his red coat matched the gold of his watch. Sharp creases sliced down the front of his creamy white slacks. A pair of shiny brown alligator shoes waited like real alligators, all smiley-mouthed and staring against the dirt. He gave the bill of my ball cap a friendly tap. "Never thought I'd see that thing again," he said, his voice all-smooth-sounding like a radio announcer's. "Pegasus. The winged horse."

He took off his sunglasses, nothing nasty in his eyes now, no worms cutting themselves and getting mean. He dropped the sunglasses in the slit of his pocket, his voice smooth as cream. "I've behaved badly son. Not just about the hat but about a lot of things. I hope you'll forgive me. I hope you can."

I thought of the little boy in the cave; how confused I'd been, seeing his name written at the top of that page.

"Ah. But that was then, wasn't it?" Victor said. "Back then all I could think of was Florida and The Pink Flamingo. Got so caught up I forgot the reason for my going down in the first place." He looked at me as though I could fill in the blank for his reason.

So you could steel my Momma away, you sneaky-ass son of a bitch!

"To be with you and Missy and your Momma," Victor said. "As a family, Orbie. That's all that matters." He stood to the side so I could see the shape of his big new Cadillac. It looked like a boat or maybe a whale or a blue shiny rocket ship on white rubber wheels. Beside it Momma's Ford looked pitiful as some old tractor engine rusting in a field.

"It's a wonderful place, Florida," Victor smiled.

"I'm not going to Florida," I said.

Victor shook his head to say 'no' but in slow motion. "I understand how you feel. Really I do. We all need time. We all need to take time. To consider things, I mean." He put the cigarette back in his mouth, more like Dean Martin now than Clark Kent. He had that glow still—the thing that flashed out at you like a friend. "We've got plenty of time. We can take it slow. Can't we son?"

Only thing I wanted to take was a swipe at his head. Out the corner of my eye I could see Willis wall-eyeing him with a stone face. It was the first time I'd seen anybody meet Victor and not smile. Victor turned and walked back down to Reverend Pennycall and his police car.

"Orbie!" Granny called from her place on the porch. "You boys! Come away from there!"

Right then, Momma came out on the porch with Missy. "Mind what Granny says."

"We got all our stuff out here," I said.

"Leave it!" Momma said.

Willis and me went up and sat on the edge of the porch. "It's Victor, Momma. He's back."

"I know. Be still."

"I want you just to look," Granny said.

Victor stood out by the police car, talking to Reverend Pennycall. Reverend Pennycall pushed up his straw hat and smiled at Victor, a pink smile in the middle of a pink face. He passed a fruit jar out the window to Victor. Victor held it to his mouth a second and passed it back.

"I never seen the like," Granny said. "In broad daylight now."

Momma said nothing. Missy sucked her thumb.

Victor said something to Reverend Pennycall and they both laughed. Then Reverend Pennycall put the police car in gear and drove away. Victor stood, looking back at the house, figuring what it would take to buy and move someplace else.

Granpaw and Miss Alma came around the corner. Miss Alma had a hold of Granpaw's arm. "I'm all right. Shit," Granpaw said but then he caught sight of Victor. "Sumbitch."

Miss Alma smiled. "Dat the purdiest white man I ever see."

"He's purdy all right," Granpaw said.

Victor came up in the yard and stopped next to the Jesus Tree. The ground was still wet from the rain. The toes of his alligator shoes were splattered with mud. "I got turned around," he said in a loud voice. "Sheriff was good enough to show me the way."

He smiled his movie star smile and spread his arms out wide. He stood like that a second, like he was waiting for us all to come down and give him a big hug, welcome him back. "Here I am! Your one and only!"

Momma sat still.

Granny reached down and picked out another sock from her sock basket.

Miss Alma shook her head, smiling, and went back around the house.

"One and only what?" Granpaw said.

"Quiet, Strode," Granny said.

"What's the matter with him?" Victor said.

Nobody answered.

"Well?" Victor said.

"Well what?" Momma set Missy down. "Go on inside, honey." Missy ran over to the screen door, opened it and went inside. She stood behind the screen and stared out at Victor.

Victor looked at Willis and me. "What do you make of all this, you boys?"

"Leave them out of it," Momma said. "You got something to say, you say it to me."

"Oh come on, Ruby, baby. You're not still mad, are you?"

Momma looked daggers at Victor. The side of her face still faintly yellowed. The gash around her eye, a curved scar.

Granpaw hawked up a gob and spat.

Victor looked at Granny. Then at Granpaw. Then at Granny again. A worry came in his eyes. Then he looked at

Momma. "Of course you're still mad. I know that. You're probably thinking I've got some nerve. Coming here like this, I mean."

Momma stayed quiet.

Victor wagged his head side to side, shaking it to say 'no' but in slow motion, like before. "I'd be upset too. I mean, if I were you." Victor looked at Momma straight on. "What I did to you was terrible. I know that, Ruby. I lost my head."

"You lost more than that." Momma got up from her chair, stepped to the edge of the porch and crossed her arms. "Look at you, dressed up slick as a car salesman. Expecting me to take you back 'cause you sorry. It don't work around that easy Victor!"

"I know," Victor said. "I know it doesn't."

Momma looked out toward the blue Cadillac. "I reckon Armstrong give you that. Like he did the house."

"It's just a loaner, baby. Temporary, you know."

"You look different. Your hair's different. You're not wearing your glasses."

"Armstrong thought I looked better without them."

"Armstrong did?"

"Yeah." Victor put the cigarette between his teeth and smiled. "He thinks I look more professional this way."

"Professional wife beater," Granpaw said.

Victor went on like he didn't hear. "He's sort of taken me under his wing. Armstrong has. He wants me to be happy. He wants you to be happy."

"He can kiss my hillbilly ass!" Momma said.

Willis covered his mouth.

Granny looked up. "Lord, Ruby!"

"That's how I feel, Mamaw. That's the sorriest bunch you'd ever want to see, and I don't want my kids around it!"

"They won't have to be," Victor said. "Armstrong knows. I mean he understands how you feel."

"I ain't married to Armstrong!"

"I know. I explained it to him though, and he understands. That's what I'm trying to tell you. Armstrong will stay out of the picture from now on, as far as our family life is concerned." Victor turned toward Granny then. "You don't know me from Adam, Mrs. Wood, but I'm not a bad man. I can change. I've always been able to change."

"I never heard such a load of bullshit in all my life!" Granpaw growled.

Granny gave Victor a nod, green eyes flashing from a face of red leather. "It ain't up to me to tell you, you can come back, and it ain't up to me to tell you, you can't. Ruby's a mind of her own." She looked at Momma, then back at Victor. "I tell you what's the truth though, if you was a husband of mine and done what you done? Why, I'd tell you to hit the road Mister! I wouldn't even have to think about it!"

"It's a long way back to St. Petersburg!" Momma said.

Both her and Granny stared at Victor, Momma leaning against the post with her arms crossed, Granny sitting straight up in her rocking chair, her hand stretched out, touching Granpaw's arm. They were like a wall against Victor.

I looked at Willis and grinned.

"All right, okay. If that's how you all feel about it." Victor put the cigarette back in his mouth. He took out a silver lighter, lit the cigarette and sucked till the end of it glowed. He forced two streams of white smoke from his nostrils. "Think about what I said though. No trouble this time, Ruby. None."

———

It wasn't two days Cecil the mailman brought Momma chocolates from Victor. Then it was roses, red roses. Then a card with a note said how much he loved her. How much he cared about Missy and me. That he wanted us all to be happy together, in a nice house on the beach in Florida. It made me want to throw up. It made me want to use cuss words and spit.

After that we started to see the blue Cadillac around. One day it was parked at Old Man Harlan's store next to Reverend Pennycall's police car. Another day it was at the cemetery gate—then up the road from Granny and Granpaw's—just the Cadillac, no Victor. It was kind of spooky.

Momma got mad about it. "Who does he think he is? And what business does he have at Nealy Harlan's anyhow?"

"I reckon even Victor got to buy things," Granny said.

"He don't need to be coming all the way out here!" Momma nearly yelled. She turned to me then, a sharp wrinkle knifing up between her eyes. "You see that car anywhere about, you stay away!"

Two days later the Cadillac was parked up the road again, a little ways up from Granny and Granpaw's. This time Victor was with it, leaning against the front-end in his shirtsleeves. He had his sunglasses on, smoking a cigarette. He saw me standing in the yard and waved. When I looked later, he was gone.

———

Momma let Victor see her again—finally. Two or three times she did. Mostly they argued about Florida, about Armstrong and his men, about Daddy or Fords or the investigation that was still going on. Every now and then, they would forget to argue though. Victor would get all gooey-eyed, and Momma all soft and smiley. I worried the wall was starting to crumble, but then Granny would butt in with some of her two cents and put an end to it. "Ya'll remember where you at now, you two!" she might holler. "We don't need none of that kissy stuff! Not around here we don't. That slobberin' around on each other spreads germs!" Such would fluster Momma and make Victor's face turn red. It was all I could do not to laugh.

One other time, again in the living room, Granpaw came out of his spell long enough to tell Victor what he thought of a man that would beat up a woman and take advantage of a little girl. Victor told him to mind his own business. Said Nealy Harlan owned his property and from what he understood, him and Granpaw weren't on good speaking terms. He warned Granpaw he might lose what little he had if he didn't watch his mouth.

We all waited for Granpaw to say something back but he

had gone all zombie-eyed again. Stood next to the picture of the Lord's Supper with his arms down to his sides, staring at Victor like he was a wall.

"Get out, Victor!" Momma yelled. "Leave us be!"

"I was just trying to straighten him out a little," Victor said.

"I'll straighten you out is what I'll do, straight out that door!" Momma grabbed up a stove poker and threw it at him.

Victor knocked over a table getting out of the way. "It takes two to do the goddamn tango, Ruby!" He got in his Cadillac and like a mad man gunned it, thundering dust all over the road.

————

I crawled to a place, not under the kitchen, but to another place I guessed was just under the living room floor.

Willis crawled in after me. "Dey spider web and all kina ole shit unda here. Wha-What you gone do boy?"

"Shh," I whispered. "They can hear you."

We sat with our heads almost touching the underside of the plank floor. There were some tobacco sticks in a pile, two cans of rusty nails and a posthole digger. I sat on the handles of the posthole digger. Willis sat on the sticks.

"Can't see nothin'," Willis said.

"It'll get to where you can." The gap between the house and the ground let in the daylight. Still, it was so dim I could hardly see Willis's face. "I wish Granny was here." Granny and Miss Alma had taken Granpaw and Missy to Circle Stump to see the doctor. Not two minutes had gone by before Victor pulled up in his Cadillac. He walked right by me and Willis, not saying a word, went in the house and started up a talk with Momma. That's when I got scared and crawled under the house to listen.

Little streams of dirt sifted down from the planks. We could hear Victor talking on the other side, his radio announcer's voice all calm and smooth. "I understand how you feel baby. I do. If I'd known they were going to behave like that, I'd have said something beforehand. I would have said, this is my wife, gentleman. My pride and joy." Momma said nothing. "I should have said something later on too. I know I should have. I was nervous, Ruby. You know how I get."

Momma said, "I reckon it was nerves made you do what you did to Missy. I reckon it was nerves put your hand up that woman's ass—me not two feet away."

"I was drunk, baby."

"Your hand wandered up some strange woman's dress because you was drunk? How come she let you keep it there?" Momma's words were coming out full of steam. "You think I'm a fool, don't you? You think I don't know any better?" There was a loud crash of something across the floor. "Answer me!"

"Goddamn it Ruby!" Victor shouted. "No! I don't think that! I don't think that at all!"

"That hillbilly's so ignorant, she can't see shit for stepping in it. That's what you think."

"Now baby, I never said that."

"I see a lot more than you imagine. I see what the Pink Flamingo's about. I see better than you! All that gambling and them men with guns. Guns, Victor!"

"Oh, come on. They were security personnel. Armstrong's people," Victor said. "I explained all that. I thought you understood."

"What's he need a bunch of men with guns to watch a hotel for?"

"They're not watching the hotel. They're watching him," Victor said. "Armstrong's an important man. They're his bodyguards."

"Bodyguards, playing cards."

"That's right. I told you. Security."

"It ain't Christian," Momma said.

"Who said it was? It's not church we're talking about here. It's an organization. They own the hotel. I explained all this." Victor was trying hard not to lose his temper.

"The Lord's not pleased with it," Momma said.

"You've got a handle on that do you?"

"I know when something is not right."

"Maybe you do," Victor said, his voice going all soft suddenly. "We can talk about it another time, can't we baby? Maybe you can enlighten me."

It got quiet a minute, and then Momma said, "I don't know what to believe. I can't tell what's real anymore."

"The whole thing is real baby. I'm real. I'm standing right here."

"I see you," Momma said.

"I feel like a teenager asking a girl out on a date for the first time," Victor said, all soft and gentle-like.

"Wha-What he say?" Willis whispered.

"He's being good looking for Momma, Willis. Trying to get her to like him again."

"You ain't a teenager," Momma said.

"Well I feel like one," Victor said. "In a man's skin. Afraid you'll say 'no', but here nonetheless. Asking. Asking for another chance to make things right. For you. For the kids."

"Oh," Momma breathed.

No sound came for awhile.

"What dey do?" Willis whispered.

"Kissy stuff. He's doing it again. Making her be like him."

Don't do it, Momma! Don't like him again!

"Victor, no," Momma said.

Victor was all out of breath. "It's been so long, baby."

"Not here. Not now," Momma said. "Let go."

"The Lord is in me now," Victor breathed. "I know he is."

"I know he is too. I feel him inside you," Momma said, like it was true, like the Lord really was inside Victor. "What am I going to do with you?"

I could feel the wall against Victor begin to crumble.

"You vulgar bastard!" Momma shouted. "Let go of me!"

There was a stomping sound, a sound of things being dragged across the floor, knocked over, a table maybe or Granpaw's rocking chair. I could see dirt raining down from a bunch of places under the floor. The sounds dragged back toward Granny and Granpaw's bedroom. I crawled after them. Willis followed. A door slammed.

"Git off me!" Momma yelled.

Take care of Momma son. She don't see things all the way through.

I got hold of a tobacco stick. "Momma's in trouble, Willis." I would have crawled out except then I heard Momma's voice, all whispery sounding and out of breath.

"Oh, Victor, Victor," breathed Momma. "Not here, hon! Not now."

Victor's words also came between gasps of breath. "Yes *now*, baby. Relax. We both need this. You know it, I know it." More dirt rained down from the floor. A fear squeezed around my heart then. A hand I couldn't see.

"You filthy vulgar dog!" Momma said, but she was laughing again.

23
SMILES AND SMOOTH WORDS

That night Victor slept with Momma in the trailer. When I came down to breakfast the next morning he was at the table. He was wearing his pink shirt but no tie, his hair combed over like Dean Martin. Momma had fixed him some eggs and he was sitting there in what used to be Granpaw's chair. When he saw me, he smiled.

"Sit down sweetheart," Momma said.

"Where's Granny?" I asked.

"Out on the front porch, feeding Granpaw. He had another one of his spells." Something in Momma's voice made me jump, something high-pitched and chirpy like a bird's. She hopped around the kitchen like a bird. She wore her black skirt and the blouse with the roses, the one you could see the soft part of her titties in. Her hair was piled on top, fixed together up there with a green tortoise shell comb.

"What's wrong, Momma?"

"Nothing's wrong. Sit down."

"Where's Missy?"

"In the front room, still asleep."

Victor held up his cup. "More coffee, Momma."

Momma smiled, brought the pot over and filled his cup.

"Thank you Momma." Victor took a sip from the cup and set it down.

Granny's calendar said August 19th. I sat down across from Victor. Momma placed a glass of milk in front of me. "I want coffee."

"Coffee?"

"Yeah. With biscuit mixed in. Sugar too."

"You're too little for coffee, son," Victor said.

I looked at Momma. Yesterday she was ready to throw Victor out, now she was chirping like a bird—hopping around everywhere he pointed.

"Did you hear what I said?" Victor said.

"I ain't your son," I said.

"Orbie," Momma said. "Be nice." She hopped to the refrigerator, took out a plate of ham from last night's supper, and set it on the table. "You want me to warm this Victor? It'll be good with them eggs."

"No thank you Momma. Maybe Orbie will have some." He smiled at me and sipped his coffee. He was cleaned up, clean shaved with that smelly stuff, the sleeves of his shirt turned back.

"I said I want coffee and biscuit! I want soak! Granny lets me have it."

"Watch your tone, son," Victor said.

"I reckon a little coffee won't hurt him none." Momma got a cup and set it down in front of me. Her hand trembled. She filled the cup halfway with coffee.

The mole next to Victor's nose glowed like a little slicked over hill. He pushed himself away from the table and got up. Momma kissed him on the lips. I felt like throwing coffee at the both of them. Victor grabbed Momma's butt and squeezed her to him. "You shouldn't let the boy talk to you that way baby."

"I know. We'll talk about it later."

"I love you Momma." He squeezed her butt again and

kissed her on the lips. Then he went out the door.

Momma sat down in Victor's chair, smiling to herself. She reached and got one of the biscuits and cut it in half. Then she reached for the blackberry jam. She scooped the jam out with a spoon onto half of the biscuit, put the other half on top and bit off a piece. Her hands trembled. "These is the best blackberries I ever eat," she said as she chewed. "You and Granny get these?"

I got a biscuit and crumbled it in my coffee, pushed it down in there with a tablespoon. I mixed in two big tablespoons of sugar.

"Have a little coffee with your sugar," Momma said.

I dug out a spoonful of the soak and put it in my mouth.

"I know what you're thinking," Momma said. "People can change though. Victor can change."

We sat there a little bit, Momma with her biscuit, me with my soak. I got another tablespoon of sugar. I watched it fall out of the spoon a little bit at a time into my cup.

Momma said, "You can see how he's changed can't you?"

I kept watching the sugar. "You're the one always changing Momma. Victor's always the same."

Momma almost dropped her biscuit. "I'll wear you out boy! Talking to me like that!" Momma grabbed the spoon away. Sugar went everywhere all over the table. She grabbed the cup away too. "You know better than to act this way! Look here now." She put the spoon in the cup and set it down on the table next to her. "Yes, it's true. We're going to try again; Victor and me are. He's made mistakes but he's changed now. You can't just give up on people Orbie." She took hold of my hand and looked me direct in the eye. "We got to be good to one another from now on."

"I hate him Momma! I wish he was dead!" I jerked my hand loose. "I hate you too! You're just stupid is all! Stupid! Stupid! Stupid!" I jumped down out of my chair, slammed through the screen door, ran out down the steps and under the house—into the crawl space underneath. I sat, crying and kicking at the dirt, staring at the shadows, at the old cans and rocks and tobacco sticks that were scattered all about.

I had me a shoebox there in a hole under a board. I slid the board away, got out the box and opened it. It was lined with some of Granny's store bought cotton. Granpaw's tobacco pouch lay in there with the Rain Skull inside. There was Granny's butcher knife too, its point bent to one side. Still crying, I took it up from the box and looked at its long gray blade. I remembered how it had glowed with the blue light. I remembered the voice, the lightning, the tree branch cracking down with the tire in the swimming hole. The Circle Stump Boys running away.

I laid the point of the butcher knife on a piece of orange brick and pounded it flat with another. I got Granpaw's pouch with the Rain Skull and put it around my neck. I held the knife blade up in front of my face, the point now straight and sharp. I could hear Momma above, boohooing at the kitchen table.

"In thy blood," I whispered. "In thy blood, live!"

———

Momma went on like usual, talking about the Lord and how He'd made everything all right, how He changed Victor, made him into a good person again—a better person.

Victor brought all his stuff from the motel he was staying at in Glasgow—his tan suitcase and green file box—and moved into the trailer with Momma. Soon as Momma was ready, he said, we'd all go back to Detroit, take care of our business there, sell the house and move down to Florida—where the sun always shines and the fishing is always good.

"Oh I know he won't never be good as Jessie," Momma would say to Granny. "You can't have everything perfect though."

Granny would just crack her gum. "You both growed up people. I reckon ya'll can handle your own business." Usually she had a lot more to say than that, no matter whose business it was. I figured she was just too busy what with Granpaw and there being a million things to do around the farm and all. The 'L' brothers helped with the fields. Miss Alma brought over pies

240

and occasionally did things around the house. Said there wasn't as much housework at Moses' place anymore. "He gone. He do dat way. Mmmm. Go off, not tell a soul."

I hadn't seen Moses since the time in the cave. He'd finished painting Granny and Granpaw's house except for one little triangle-shaped patch under the roof above the attic window. Willis and me would look up there from time to time just to see if he had come to finish it.

Granny got Willis to stay with us while Moses was gone. I was glad about that. We slept in Granny's big feather bed together. Sometimes we'd laugh and talk so much that Granny'd have to holler up the ladder hole just to quiet us down.

———

Granpaw's wall was still up against Victor. Granny told him it wasn't none of his business—or hers—what decisions Victor and Momma made together. "It would just confuse things if we was to interfere," Granny said. "I think he's trying, Victor is. I really do."

"Trying my patience is what he's doing," Granpaw said.

Victor was all smiles and smooth words, trying to get along with everybody, even with Granpaw. One time I was standing next to the rain barrel at the side of the house, watching Granpaw use his jackknife to cut yellow callus away from his thumb. Victor came around the front of the house, this time a fat new unlit cigar stuck out the corner of his mouth. When he saw Granpaw, he got a big smile on his face. "Another miserable day in paradise, hey Mr. Wood? Glad to see you up and around!"

"Uh huh." Granpaw sliced a thin piece of callus away from his thumb.

"Is it always like this?" Victor asked. "Muggy and rainless, I mean?"

Granpaw slipped the knifepoint in around his thumbnail. "No. T'ain't."

Victor raised the hand with the snake tattoo and took the cigar away. "I thought you were some sort of meteorologist."

Granpaw cocked an eyebrow at Victor. "A what?"

"A meteorologist. You know, a weatherman. A meteorologist loves to talk about the weather."

Granpaw went back, working on his thumb. "Well I ain't one of them."

"That's not what I hear, but all right. Anyway, I'm glad to see you up and about." Victor's eyes warmed over with friendliness. "Orbie here thinks the world of you. Don't you son?"

I kept quiet.

"His Momma says he does," Victor said.

"He don't have to repeat it then, does he?" Granpaw said, still working on his thumb.

"I know that. That's not what I meant." A cloud passed over Victor's face, but then he caught himself and smiled. "You be careful with that knife now, Mr. Wood! With skin that tough, you might dull the blade!" He reassigned the cigar to the corner of his mouth and walked off toward the trailer.

"Dumb ass City Slicker," Granpaw said under his breath, but then he looked at me. "I ought not have said that. Ought I?"

———

Once, when Granpaw was in one of his spells, Victor out of the blue offered to take care of him. Granny wouldn't let him. "This is woman's work. Man's got more important things to do." Something in the way she said it made me think she wouldn't let Victor take care of Granpaw even if it *was* a man's work.

He did help out with things though, Victor did, like when he went into Circle Stump to buy groceries. Sometimes he brought back soda pop and potato chips for us kids. Willis and me would each get a bottle and take the chips out on the front porch.

Missy wouldn't have any.

She stayed close to Momma. Only time she said anything was when Momma asked her questions, simple questions like, "You want to eat now hon?" or "You got to pee?" Missy would answer "No Momma," or "Yes Momma," but in a whiny little voice made you want to slap her direct in the face, not to be mean or anything, just to wake her up from her spell. If Victor got too close, she would let out a scream that would soar up to the ceiling so loud Momma would have to take her off in another room. Granny would get a look on her face and shake her head.

Victor stayed sober. Him and Momma went to church in the fancy blue Cadillac. Circle Stump Church. People there liked Victor.

"He got a natural way with folks," Momma said. "When he wants to have, he does. Reverend Pennycall was plumb beside himself, introducing him around. I never seen the like." She liked to be proud of Victor—of the way he looked, of the way he dressed—so fine, so important. I think his being important made her feel important too.

Still they fought. I would hear them yelling at each other in the trailer. I heard things thump against the wall. One time Momma screamed. I saw Victor push out the door and go cussing all the way up the little wagon road toward the barn.

Another time I saw him up at Old Man Harlan's store, standing out on the porch there with Old Man Harlan. Reverend Pennycall was there too. Victor laughed with them and smoked his cigarettes. Reverend Pennycall put his hand on Victor's shoulder. Victor let it stay.

"You can't never tell how things will work around," Momma said to Granpaw one day. "Why, the Lord might be working through Victor to make things right between you and Nealy."

"Hell He is," Granpaw said.

"I don't care much for Nealy's ways myself, you know I don't. He attends church though," Momma said. "I saw him over to Circle Stump."

"The Devil attends church, Sweetness," Granpaw said.

"I'd rather Victor was talking to somebody just the same," Momma said. "Rather than him moping around here everyday."

That was one thing about Momma I couldn't understand. How she fit things together sometimes. Like Old Man Harlan and Victor. To me they fit together all right but more like a gun and a holster than friends.

He spent a lot of time in the trailer, Victor did, with the door and all the windows open. When he wasn't there, he kept the doors locked. Momma got the key from Granny. Momma said it was because he was writing letters in there. Letters to Armstrong and to Fords. Private important business he didn't want anybody else to mess with.

"He's still trying to get things straightened around, I reckon," Momma said to Granny. "About all what happened up there, you know, with Jessie and all. 'Investigation's still going on."

"I thought that was done with," Granny said.

"It is. There's just some loose ends, you know."

"You'd have thought they'd have been tied by now," Granny said.

———

It was getting toward the end of August. Victor started to talk more about Detroit, about us going back to Detroit, what he would do to set things right when we got there. He talked about the move to Florida and the manager job at The Pink Flamingo. It was his big chance to get ahead. Not to take it made about as much sense as flushing money down the toilet. I heard him talking to Momma in the trailer. "You've got to strike while the striking's good, baby! I admire your parents. I care about them. I do. Mr. Wood seems quite capable when he's up and about. And your mother *certainly* is."

"I know, but I can't just up and leave," Momma said. "Not till they're better situated."

"The kids will have to begin school soon."

"I know. I'll figure something out."

"Well, figure it out now!" Victor said. "I'm tired of all this nonsense! I've got important matters to see to."

"Go on to Detroit then, if that's what you want!"

"Leave you and the kids?"

"We'll come as soon as we can," Momma said. "I told you."

"Jesus, you're stubborn."

"Look who's talking," Momma answered. "Mr. Easy-To-Get-Along-With, himself!"

Victor agreed that he would go on to Detroit by himself but he never did. Seemed like there was always something else he had to do. Another letter to write. Another letter to wait for. A talk with Old Man Harlan or Reverend Pennycall. A drive into Circle Stump to use the pay phone at Grinestaff's. The important thing is that we stay together as a family, he kept on saying.

Momma would pretty herself up, put a bunch of makeup over what was left of the bruises on her face and smile for Victor. She helped Granny cook and clean, took care of Granpaw, slopped hogs and fed the chickens. I showed her some of the tricks Elvis and Johnny could do, and I told her about the beauty contest coming up at the fair.

"I'm so proud of you, Orbie. You know that don't you?" Momma ran her hand over the top of my head, her bright blue eyes all sparkly and full of smiles. "You look so much better. I mean it. You look happy. Your Daddy would be proud."

I didn't feel so happy though—not with Victor and all his business taking up Momma's time. The Dark Thing was everywhere—in Victor's letter writing, his Dean Martin haircut and fancy cigarettes. It was in Momma not knowing what to do, in her trying to be a married person, a mother and a daughter all at the same time.

"You and them chickens are a regular circus act," Momma said. "We probably won't be around for that fair though. You know that, don't you?"

"Yeah," I said sadly. "Granny will take them."

"I'm so proud of you sweetheart." Her eyes went away from me then, looking a way off toward the trailer and Victor. Sometimes they'd be in there with the door and all the windows closed—even in the middle of the day—even with it being so hot a person would sweat buckets just standing in the shade. "Real proud," she whispered. But I could feel her slipping away.

———

That's how it went, all through the end of August and on into September. Victor and Momma shutting themselves up in the trailer every chance they got. Momma worrying over what direction to take. Granny's eyes flashing with something she knew but wouldn't tell. Victor, Reverend Pennycall, and Old Man Harlan talking on the porch in front of the store. Missy sucking her thumb one minute, screaming the next. Granpaw spitting cuss words all over the yard, then laughing about it, shaking his head like he just heard the best joke. Me under the house with Granny's knife, standing my army men in a line, or else down to the swimming hole with Willis and the Kingdom Boys, the days so hot you could fry eggs on the rocks, ugly black thunderheads reaching out over the afternoon sun, sometimes pissing out a little rain, most times not.

24

SIGNS

Granpaw opened the back of the station wagon and got out one of the signs he made, a white cross with crooked black letters wrote across the arms. 'love tHine eneMy', it said. With the sign in one hand and a hammer in the other, he ditch-walked up the road where there was a red clay bank and a field behind a barbed wire fence. Willis and me followed after him. The fence posts stuck out every which a way, some rotten and falling apart, tilted toward the road like frozen pieces of black fire. Some of the barbed wire made thorny loops along the ground.

Granpaw stopped in front of one of the posts. He lifted his hat off his head and set it back down. A nail stuck out between his lips. He tilted his head the way the post was tilted; then he stepped up and nailed the cross to it. He nailed it tilted like the post, like a hitchhiker, sticking a thumb out for a ride.

He stepped back to look at his handiwork. "That ought to grab somebody's attention. Don't you think?"

"Yessah, Mista Wood," Willis smiled. "Dat do fa-fine."

Granpaw smiled, then looked over where I was standing.

"Go get them others I laid up next to the car there."

"You ain't supposed to be out here, Granpaw," I said. "You ain't supposed to be driving."

"Who said I wasn't?"

"Granny. You might have a spell and run off the road."

"Maybe I will, maybe I won't. Why didn't you say something before?"

"Cause of what you said. What you said about clouds."

"We ain't come to that yet." Granpaw looked up toward the station wagon and back at us. "A body can't just give up, just because of a little sickness."

Willis fitted his walking stick snug under his arm. "Ya'll ba-bad sick dough."

"Yeah," I said. "What if you were to go in a spell?"

"What if a pig was to shit roses?" Granpaw said. "Who's side you boys on?"

"Yours," I said. "Willis is right though."

Willis grinned a mouth full of teeth.

Granpaw frowned. "Go fetch 'em signs like I told you to. Won't be no more driving after this."

I went and got the signs. Some of the letters were capitols, some weren't. And most were crooked. One said, 'in my Name shall tHey cast ouT devils'. The other said, 'These signS shall fOller them what beLieve'. I reached them up to Granpaw. "Who's side are *you* on, Granpaw?"

"The Lord's, if I'm able." Granpaw took the signs, then reached in his pocket and got out more nails. He put the nails in his mouth like before and got the signs and nailed them to other fence posts. When he was done, he motioned us to come walk with him to a place out on the road.

"Now. Look there." He pointed toward the signs. He'd nailed them so they were far apart from each other, so when somebody passed by on the road, they could read one after the other, first 'love tHine eneMy', then 'in my Name shall tHey cast ouT devils' then 'These signS shall fOller them what beLieve'.

"Circa Stump folk be ma-mad!" Willis said. "Dat church land."

"Road don't belong to them."

"Fence do," Willis said.

Granpaw spat. "They don't take care of it, if it does."

All three signs leaned toward the road. Hitchhikers, waving down cars, each with a little message wrote across the front.

"Love thine enemy," I said. "What about Germans Granpaw? What about Japs?"

"What about them?" Granpaw said.

"You can't love somebody wants to kill you," I said.

Granpaw grabbed out a hankie from his back pocket. He wiped it down the side of his face and patted his forehead.

"They'll kill you Granpaw. The enemy will."

Granpaw stuffed the hankie back in his back pocket. He looked up at the sky, at the clouds, shading his eyes with the bent part of his wrist. Then he walked back to the station wagon with Willis and me. He put the hammer away and got out a frying pan he'd brought from the house and something that looked like a witch's broom without a handle. The frying pan was full of white gray coals he'd got from Granny's wood stove in the kitchen. He gave the witch's broom to Willis, then looked at me. "You bring that skull like I told you?"

I pulled the pouch with the skull from my pocket and loosened the drawstring. There was the smooth bone of the rattlesnake skull, its eye sockets and fangs.

"You seen that before, haven't you?" Granpaw said to Willis.

"Uh huh. Mo's. MMMake da rain be good."

"That's right." Granpaw took a pinch of something from his shirt pocket and sprinkled it over the coals in the frying pan. Thick white smoke boiled up. He held the pan down to me. "Now, run that in there. Through that smoke."

I held the skull between my thumb and first finger and put it through the smoke. "Like that?"

"More!" Granpaw hollered. "Do it a bunch a times!"

I did like he said.

"Hold to it now." Granpaw closed his eyes and began to mumble under his breath. Hocus pocus nonsense it sounded like to me. He did that a while, then made a little half turn and stepped up the bank. He stepped through a place where the barbed wire lay on the ground, stepped over it and into the field. He had either gone completely crazy or into another of his spells.

"We better go back now!" I called. "Granny'll be mad!"

He kept on walking. Willis and me had to go after him. It was just an empty field; dried out mostly; with weeds and some grass growing here and there. Granpaw got to the top of a low hill and stopped. He turned around and around, looking up in the sky at the clouds. "Hot. Hot weather this is, for September." He set the frying pan on a rock and sprinkled more stuff from his shirt pocket. Smoke boiled up. "Fan that a little," he said to Willis.

Willis started to wave the witch's broom at the smoke. "Towards the sky there," Granpaw said. "Fan towards the sky." Willis made a motion with the broom like to lift the smoke toward the sky. "Keep on that a way," Granpaw said. "Sang 'at song. Sang *Amazing Grace How Sweet The Sound!*"

Willis started to sing the song. The sound of it lifted up with the smoke to the sky. It was lonesome and strange like the time me and him snuck in Kingdom Church, Willis singing Amazing Grace in that pretty girl voice of his, me thinking I was on a hill somewhere wide open, looking off at clouds in a blue sky.

"Now, Orbie," Granpaw said, "I want you to pick one of them clouds out. I want you to stare at it, you know, like it was the only one up there. Hold that skull like this." Granpaw made a fist and put it in the middle of his chest. The sky was clear except for a few little cottony-white clouds. I held the rattlesnake skull like Granpaw said, the fangs of it poking me in the chest. I chose one of the little clouds. Willis kept on with the song.

We've no less days to sing God's praise...

"Look at it," Granpaw said. "Like you loved it more than anything. Like it was the only thing in the world. That cloud."

I tried to stare at the cloud like Granpaw said. Like I loved it. I stared and stared. I stared until the cloud started to go all shifty like. Fuzzy. Different shades of gray and blue.

"Think about all the people you love. That love you," Granpaw said.

I thought of Momma and Granny. I thought of Missy. The cloud jumped around and changed color. "It isn't working Granpaw. It's not melting."

"Don't force it. Here, let me show you." Granpaw took the rattlesnake skull, put it in the middle of his chest and looked at the cloud. I looked too.

...ten thousand years, bright shining as the sun!...

Right away the cloud started to break apart. It broke into smaller pieces; wisps of steam that stayed a few seconds then melted away.

Granpaw handed the skull back to me. "These signs shall foller them what believe!"

I picked out another cloud. It went all fuzzy like the first one, changing shape and color so fast I began to get dizzy. I felt Granpaw tap the back of my head. Suddenly I was up there in the sky, right next to the cloud—I mean I was almost touching it—and there inside the cloud was Daddy, smiling, waving his bird claw hand, dressed in steel mill clothes.

You have to pay attention, son. Even in dreams.

A great happiness welled up inside me then. I felt something warm and flowing, giving out as if from where the skull's fangs touched my chest. It flooded me and gave outward toward Daddy until there we were, together, one person skyward, not separate at all. Then just as suddenly I was back on the ground. The cloud had broken into two pieces, one small and one big.

"I never thought I'd see the like." Granpaw looked over at Willis and laughed. "He's a good one, ain't he?"

Willis nodded that I was.

"What?" I said. "It didn't melt."

"Took me most a year to do that much," Grandpaw said.

———

Granpaw drove up Bounty toward Harlan's Crossroads. Hot air rushed in through the window over my face. It felt like spider webs.

"You don't have a Rain Skull?" I asked Willis.

"Na uh."

"How come Moses never give you one?"

"He don't need one," Granpaw said. "He's been showed."

Up ahead a bunch of cows had wandered onto the road. Granpaw slowed the station wagon and blew the horn.

I felt good. Happy and excited. "I seen Daddy, Granpaw. In that cloud. Heat came inside me from that skull. It went out to Daddy."

"You the smartest little boy I ever seed next to Willis here. But you wrong, if you think heat came from that skull." Granpaw pulled at the brim of his hat. "Bone. That's all that is."

"You said it was power."

"Power's in you." Granpaw blew the horn again at the cows. They made way, running off both sides of the road. Granpaw went slow. He had to yell over the sound of the engine. "By itself t'ain't nothin'! Bone with a bunch of seeds rattling around inside!"

We came to the little bridge that went over Kingdom Creek. On the other side there were two cars parked nose to nose along the side of the road. The car facing us I could see was Victor's blue Cadillac. The other was smaller and red colored. I couldn't tell what kind it was right off because it was turned the other way. Something like a towel maybe or maybe a flag hung from the antenna.

Victor stood in front of the Cadillac, leaning against the front end. He was talking to some little man that sat crosslegged on the hood of the red car. As we came across the bridge, the little man passed a jar over to Victor. Victor set it down behind him and out of sight.

"Well, I'll be." Granpaw slowed the station wagon to a crawl and stopped. He leaned over from where he sat at the steering wheel, over Willis and me, and hollered out the passenger side window. "Hot day to be sittin' at the side of the road!"

252

The branches of a dead cottonwood tree hung over the Cadillac. Victor pointed to them and grinned. "What do you mean, Mr. Wood? There's plenty of shade!" A joke nobody thought was funny. "Should you be out here driving?"

Granpaw didn't answer.

The red car was a Mercury, and the thing hanging from the antenna was a coon's tail. The little man wore a dark gray hat and a vest over a white shirt rolled to the elbows. He was bony-looking and had a jagged pockmarked face with a broken, Dick Tracy type nose. He squinted from under his hat and grinned. I'd seen him before.

"These gentlemen came all the way from Florida." Victor motioned toward the man on the hood. "They're on their way to Detroit."

"That right?" Granpaw said in his most deadpan voice.

"That's right, Mr. Wood. They're with Armstrong." Victor smiled. "The one who's helping me and Ruby."

"I know who Armstrong is," Granpaw said.

Something wasn't right. Victor sounded way too friendly for one thing. For another he was talking about more than one man.

Granpaw saw it too, still leaning over Willis and me, he said, "Where's the other at?"

"Other what?" Victor said.

"Other man or men." Granpaw nodded toward the little man on the hood. "All I see is the one."

"Oh," Victor said. "In the car there. Resting."

Slouched behind the wheel of the Mercury was another man, huge—it was a wonder we hadn't seen him—his arms crossed in front of him, asleep. He wore sunglasses with white frames, and there was sweat streaming down one side of his face. I'd seen him before.

The boney little man leaned back and with the ball of his fist, pounded against the windshield. "Zeek! Look sharp! Company!"

Zeek jerked up and pushed the back of his hand against his mouth. Something or somebody had caved in one side of his face. He yawned at the back of his hand.

"This is Jimmy The Diamond," Victor said, jerking his chin toward the man on the hood. "Jimmy, meet Mr. Wood."

"Strode," Granpaw said. "Name's Strode."

Jimmy The Diamond smirked. "Oh, yeah, the dirt-farmer." He sat up on the hood of the Mercury like that's where he belonged, like he was controlling things from there. "The man with the knife."

"That's right," Granpaw said. "The man with the knife."

Jimmy The Diamond grinned at Granpaw.

Cut him, Granpaw! He can't talk to you that way!

Victor nodded toward Willis and me. "That's my son, Orbie. I forget the darkie's name."

Jimmy The Diamond and Zeek both laughed at the word 'darkie'. Willis bowed his head.

"Willis!" I yelled. "His name's Willis! I ain't your *son* neither!" I felt Granpaw's hand on my shoulder.

Zeek laughed even louder. He hit the steering wheel with the palm of his hand. Jimmy The Diamond grinned. Victor stayed quiet.

When that settled, Jimmy put his eyes on Granpaw. "We're discussing a little business here, Gramps. We'd like to finish and be on our way. If you don't mind, that is." It sounded final; like there wasn't anything else a person could do but go away.

"No," Granpaw said, "I don't mind." He sat up straight behind the wheel and started to put the station wagon in gear. Then he got another idea and leaned once again over Willis and me. "Quicker you all are gone the better, far as it matters to me!" He straightened again, put the station wagon in gear and spun away.

I was excited. "I know those men, Granpaw! They talked to Daddy. They were from the Union."

"Say what?" Granpaw said.

"Inspectors, Granpaw. Daddy told me. It was a long time ago!"

"What they want with Jessie?"

"I don't know. Help them I reckon. Daddy told them 'no'."

Willis looked at me wide eyed.

"You shore it was them?" Granpaw said.

"No, but they look like it. And they got a coon tail too."

"Coon tail?"

"On the antenna."

"I seen it," Willis said.

"I never!" Granpaw growled. "God A Mighty!"

We went on down the road. After a little while we drove past Moses' house and over the hill to Harlan's Crossroads.

"Can the power kill people Granpaw?" I asked.

"Kill people?"

"Yeah. You know. That contrary power. Can it kill people?" Granpaw turned up into the yard. "It don't work around that easy, son."

————

Next day Cecil came up in the yard, skinny arms fighting to keep the handlebars straight. His letter bag bulged with letters and magazines. Willis and me were standing out by the Jesus Tree, watching Elvis and Johnny catch pieces of loaf bread before they hit the ground.

Cecil fought the handle-bars by us and out to the trailer. Victor was there, smoking one of his cigarettes. He frowned at Cecil, his hair all stuck up in back. He looked like he'd been sleeping in his clothes. The Cadillac was gone. Jimmy The Diamond and Zeek had taken it up to Detroit with them after dropping Victor off in front of the house before supper last night. Victor tried to let on like it didn't bother him, but you could tell it did.

"Armstrong needed it back, that's all," Victor said. "Hell. It was just a loaner anyway."

Cecil gave Victor a letter he had to sign for, hopped back on the bicycle and waggled off. Victor ripped open the envelope, slid the letter out and began to read. His face fell in around his eyes as he did. When he finished he looked around at the trailer, then out at the barn, then where Willis and me stood. He looked up at Old Man Harlan's place. He folded the letter, stuffed it in his pocket and threw his lit cigarette over the fence. He walked past me and Willis as though we were invisible, crossed the road and went up to Old Man Harlan's store. He tried the door, but it wouldn't open. He cupped his hands and looked through the window. He rapped on the RC cola sign so loud it made me and Willis both jump.

Most times the store would be locked, even in the daytime. Daddy and me used to go up to the house to get Old Man Harlan or Bird one to come down and open. I was thinking Victor would have to do the same when Old Man Harlan's scarecrow face jumped up in the window, veined beak nose, eye sockets thrown open like in a surprise. When he saw Victor, he smiled his sad crooked smile and opened the door.

———

Later that afternoon, me, Willis, Vern and Fable went down to the swimming hole. Fable and me and Vern sat on the tree branch that got struck by lightning. Vern and me sat on the good side of the break, closer to the main part of the tree. Fable had edged way out on the bad side, his feet dangling off in the water.

Granny's butcher knife stuck out my belt, inside the sock lined with paper. The pouch with the Rain Skull hung around my neck. We had been out in the field next to Kingdom Church trying to melt clouds. We had taken turns with the Rain Skull. I tried to do like Granpaw said. I tried to love the clouds. I tried to send warm rays up to the clouds, to think of the people I loved, but it didn't work. It didn't work for Vern. It didn't work for Fable. It didn't even work for Willis. We'd come down to the swimming hole to cool off.

Willis sat on the creek bank, telling the story again about me and the knife and the blue light, what all happened that day with the white boys. "Dat knife ga-ga-glow just like da tree," Willis said. "And dem boys, dey all run away. Say Orbie a witch."

"You done tole dat fib a thousand time boy," Fable said.

"He's telling the truth." I picked off a twig from the tree

branch and threw it in the water. "Can I tell Fable and Vern about Moses, Willis?"

"Don't care," Willis said.

"You won't get in no trouble?"

"Na uh. Don't tell Miss Alma dough. She be mad."

"Ya'll keep a secret?" I said to Fable and Vern.

Vern looked at Willis and crossed his heart. "I won't tell nobody Willis."

"I won't neither," Fable said.

"I don't care," Willis said. "Ain't no secret, no way. Not like da one I got on ya'll."

"What?" Fable said.

"Miss Alma's jam."

"That wasn't us," Vern said.

"I seen ya'll take it."

"Nobody's going to tell on nobody," I said. "Ya'll want to hear this or not?"

They all nodded their heads that they did.

I started by telling them about the dream. I told them how I wasn't sure Victor killed Daddy, and how I had to find out, and that was why I went up to see Moses. Then I told them all about the pool, about the woman and the little boy.

"You say dat little boy, Victa?" Fable asked.

"Yeah, Fable. I thought Moses was going to help me. I thought he could see things. Like Superman."

"Supaman?" Fable said.

"Yeah, you know, like in comic books and on TV. You know about Superman, don't you?"

"I does," Willis grinned. "In dem comic book. He see through things."

"What you talkin' 'bout?" Fable said.

"X-rays," I said. "That's how he sees through things. Like walls. That's how he knows things."

"Jesus know things," Vern said.

"Jesus don't know shit." I broke off another twig and threw it in the water. "Armstrong's men took Victor's Cadillac away."

Willis nodded.

"I seen 'em before," I said. "In Detroit. They said they were from the Union. They lied."

"Why dey lie?" Fable said.

"I don't know. It was something about money. They wanted Daddy to keep his eye on it." I grabbed out a wrinkled envelope from my butt-pocket and showed it around. I was excited again but I wasn't sure why. "I found this, this morning, after Victor went up to Old Man Harlan's. Look in the corner there." Over the address in pale pink squiggly letters it said, *The Pink Flamingo Hotel*, and under that, *St. Petersburg's Best*. "Victor's letter was in this enevelope. I bet you anything it was from Armstrong!"

Vern and Fable looked at me like I was crazy.

"I think Victor's mixed up in something. I think he's in trouble."

"You in trouble, you ask me," Fable said.

"Maybe," I said. "But if I knew for sure Victor was the one, I might could do something."

"Stab him," Vern said. "I would."

25
DARKNESS GOING DARKER

Thinking we might try to melt more clouds after supper, I put the shoe box with the Rain Skull and Granny's butcher knife in a bucket by the well. Victor had come back from Old Man Harlan's. He'd been drinking. We all saw that he had been. He was trying to be nice about everything, rubbing Momma's shoulders, smiling, talking to Momma and Granny.

Supper was almost ready. The afternoon thunderheads had already come and gone. There was a smell of baked ham, taters and sweet corn all through the house. Willis sat with his back against the wall in the front room, drawing a picture he didn't want anybody to see. Vern and Fable were over on the couch, thumb-wrestling. I tried to look at Willis's picture but he jerked it away.

Fable pinned Vern's thumb under his. "Dat make three time."

"Damn you!" Vern said.

Fable punched Vern hard three times on the arm.

"Damn you!"

"Ah, you boys in there!" Granny called from the kitchen. "Don't be cussing around that a way!"

Fable and Vern looked at each other and sniggered.

I was trying to read the Body Snatcher book. Body Snatchers from outer space were snatching away people's bodies, making copies and walking around like zombies. Victor had snatched away Daddy's body. Now he was trying to snatch away Momma's. I could see him standing in the doorway to the kitchen.

He'd put on a fresh shirt since coming back from Old Man Harlan's, long sleeved with the cuffs rolled back. He'd also put on his glasses—the first time I saw them since he came back from Florida. He looked good—part Clark Kent, part Dean Martin. Still you could tell he had been drinking. He stood with his hand raised over his head against the doorframe, looking in at the kitchen. Stuck between the fingers of his raised right hand was a cigar, not like his others but long and skinny with a red band around one end. Smoke curled up from it—golden doll hair curls—carried to the ceiling with the rising heat.

I could hear Momma and Granny walking around in the kitchen, putting things on the table, dishes, forks, knives clinking together. Granpaw was in there too, in his wheelchair. Yesterday, after we got back from putting up signs and melting clouds, he'd limped off to bed without saying a word. This morning he'd got up in another one of his spells.

"Mr. Harlan's a good man," Victor said. "He's got spirit." He took a pull off the cigar and blew a bomb of smoke toward the ceiling. "Yes indeed, a man to reckon with. Reverend Pennycall too."

Nobody said anything.

"I like the way Mr. Harlan thinks," Victor said. "He's got a number of good ideas."

"Shoot!" Granny said. "That man wouldn't know a good idee it was to jump up and bite him on the ass!"

"Mamaw now," Momma said.

"He's got ideas all right but they ain't none of them good. Not to my way of thinking. The kind of idees likely to keep a feller down."

"Mamaw."

"Don't hush me, I know what I'm talking about."

"A working class sentiment if ever I heard one," Victor laughed.

"Humph!" Granny said.

There was another little quiet time when nobody said anything.

"Take this cigar, for example. It's a Panatela." Victor held it out for Granny to see. "Mr. Harlan has a cedar humidor full of these, wrapped in red velvet. Do you know what a humidor is Mrs. Wood?"

"What makes you think I'd want to know?"

"It's a special box for cigars, keeps them fresh. Mr. Harlan gives these Panatelas out from time to time. It's like his signature. His way of acknowledging special occasions."

"Humph," Granny said. "I don't see nothing special 'bout no occasions around here. What with Strode sick and the Devil to pay. Orbie, Willis, all you boys! Come on to the table now! Supper's on!"

"Okay Granny," I said.

We all stopped what we were doing and went in the kitchen. A moonshine smell floated in the air around Victor. He looked at me first, then at Willis. Then at Vern and Fable. "You boys wash your hands. We always wash our hands before we eat around here."

"Go on and wash up. Orbie, you too," Momma said. "There's a pan of warm water and a bar of soap out there on the porch."

Victor moved out of the way. He held the cigar over the place where we would have to walk through to get out to the porch. A piece of ash fell off onto the floor. "Looks like some little Jigaboo's going to get burned."

Granny slammed a bowl of peas on the table.

"Victor!" Momma said.

Victor raised the cigar to his mouth and grinned. "Go on boys. Go wash up."

———

"You seen him," Fable said to Vern. "What more you want boy?"

"Don't prove nothin'.'"

"Do." Fable looked up from the pallet to the featherbed where Willis and me lay.

"Maybe," I said. "I don't know."

"It liked to," Willis said.

"Maybe Momma was right. Anybody would get mad."

Fable laughed. "You see how he look? Hot damn! I thought he gone shit hisself!"

Vern started laughing too.

Granny yelled up from the bottom of the ladder hole. "Put out that light, you boys! Go to sleep!"

Vern went over to the little table next to the dresser and blew out the lamp. After while all the lights went out downstairs.

What had happened after supper seemed like proof my dream was right, like Fable said, or almost proof. The sun had gone down, and we had all moved to the front yard except for Victor who went to the trailer, he said, to get another cigar.

Granny had spread a blanket out next to the Jesus Tree. She brought out two kerosene lamps and a dinner plate. She set the dinner plate in the middle of the blanket as a platform for one of the lamps. The other lamp she kept with her and Granpaw on the front porch where Momma sat with Missy in her lap.

Willis had brought his drawing pad out, and I had my comic books. Me and Vern and Fable laid out on the blanket, looking at the comic books. Willis sat, leaning against the Jesus Tree. Overhead bloody Jesus flickered in and out of the lamplight. After while Victor appeared, standing out by the rain barrel with his arms spread wide, looking up at the nighttime sky. "The soul looks out!" he said in a loud voice. "Breathes in the starry wonder of its own war and gratefully dies!" He staggered to the porch, arms still spread. The light from Granny's lamp set his face off in yellow shadows. "Giving up the ghost as high as old office buildings! A new mown lawn sparkles off with a machine to be married with!"

Fable and Vern sniggered.

"Hush Victor!" Momma said. "You had too much to drink." Victor looked at her and in a softer voice said, "But I

262

can't sleep with you anymore, she says."

"You're making a fool of yourself," Momma said.

But Victor shouted, "The body aches out of disuse! Like a mind resting! Like a silvery saucer of light around darkness going darker!" He staggered sideways, fixed his eyes again on Momma and in another softer voice said, "There is no love anywhere, anymore, she says."

"Lord God," Granny whispered.

Victor tripped backward over the Jesus Tree, fell toward Willis but was able to grab onto one of the branches. Jesus rattled in the limbs. Willis dropped his drawing pad and scrambled out of the way as Victor crashed to the ground; lay there, rubbing his forehead with the back of his hand. "My, my, my. Oh my."

Fable looked at Vern. Vern looked at Fable.

Victor tried to get up but fell backward onto his elbows. The ugly shrapnel scar gleamed at the base of his neck. Momma leaned forward, Missy clinging to her like a little white monkey. "Victor, you all right?"

"I'm a long way from all right, Ruby baby." Victor turned his head then and looked at me, then at Fable and Vern. His eyeglasses had slipped to the front of his nose.

Fable and Vern sniggered.

Victor sat up next to Willis's drawing pad. "What the hell is *this?*" He picked up the pad. Everything about his face was lit in yellow light except his eyes. Crickets chirped by the well. "Orbie, what in *hell* have you been up to?"

"What?" I said.

"This! This is what!" Victor tossed the drawing pad my way. It was a picture of Daddy. A good one too. And of another man. A giant. The giant was pouring fire from a black pot on top of Daddy. The giant was drawn to look like Victor—complete with grin and cigar and the mole by his nose. Victor lurched forward but as he got to his feet the blanket gathered about his shoe. In a fit of sudden rage he kicked it away. Comic books went flying. The kerosene lamp turned over. Fire whooshed over the blanket. I jumped away.

Victor began stomping at the fire. Vern and Fable had run up onto the porch. Willis stood on one leg with his walking stick drawn back.

I got Granny's butcher knife from the shoebox by the well. The fire went out. Victor stood bow armed and smoking, staring around at the yard. I held the knife but couldn't think what to do. Victor grabbed it away. "Now. You tell me! What's this about?"

Granny jumped down off the porch and stepped in between us. "Put that knife away Victor! This is still my house!"

"It is for the moment, old woman," Victor said. "Get out of the way!"

"Over my dead body!" Granny stood up to him. She was big but not nearly as big as he was.

"Victor!" Momma yelled. "Put that knife away!" She was standing up with Missy now.

I could feel my heart beating almost up in my neck. The light from the porch, from the other kerosene lamp and from the light bulb in the front room cast a strange glow over the yard. Victor frowned, tried to smile, and then frowned again. He held the knife pointed toward Granny, its blade dimly catching up the light.

Granny stayed put.

"Are you crazy!" Momma yelled from the porch. "Put it away! Put it away before somebody gets hurt!"

Granny made a fist.

Missy hugged herself tighter around Momma's neck.

"Whoremongers!" Granpaw yelled from his wheelchair. "Pharisees!"

"This isn't over, old woman," Victor finally said. "Not by any stretch of the imagination. Least of all that boy's." Then, knife still in hand, he stormed off around the house toward the trailer.

The whole yard smelled of kerosene. Kerosene and burned blanket. Lightning bugs blinked in the crown of the Jesus Tree. Crickets chirped by the well. Momma sat back in the rocking chair with Missy, her face half in shadow. "I'm sorry you had to see that, Mamaw. He gets that way when he's upset."

"When he's drunk you mean," Granny said. "What was he going on about anyway?"

I picked up the drawing pad and handed it to Granny. "This is what." Granny looked at the picture, then walked it over to Momma. I told them all about the dream I had. "He killed Daddy, Momma! He poured fire on him!"

"Reckon there's anything to this?" Granny asked.

"No," Momma said. "Anybody would be upset. I mean if they was accused of something like that. You ought to be ashamed Orbie."

"Maybe they would be upset," Granny said.

"Not if they didn't do it," I said.

"It ain't right to go around accusing people," Momma said. "Just because you had a dream. Just because you don't get along with Victor."

"You sure you all right Ruby?" Granny said. "You sound a thousand miles away."

"I'm all right. I got to get ready for bed Mamaw. We all have to." Without saying another word, Momma got up with Missy and went inside the house.

"I never seen the like," Granny said. She looked at Willis and me. "Clean all this up now, you boys. Fable. You and Vern too. It's time for bed."

———

Willis lay in bed next to me, sleeping. Moonlight flooded in through the window, making with the crosshairs of the frame a black cross that stretched over the floor. I still had my Rain Skull, but I was absent the knife. How was I going to help Momma now? Keep her body from being snatched away? It worried me that she didn't believe me. And I wondered if Granny did.

I had lain in bed a long time, thinking about everything, when suddenly I heard the screen door in the kitchen yawn open. I got down from the featherbed and tiptoed over to the window. There in the distance was the barn, a black shape against a black hill. And there was the trailer, a light still on inside. Somebody was walking out there in the moonlight, a ghost in a bathrobe walking toward the trailer. Momma.

PART EIGHT

26
COMPLAINTS

"What I got here Ma'am, is paypahs from the court. It ordahs you to desist using hired help to work yo land. Until futhah notice, that is." Reverend Pennycall held the papers up for Granny to see. The way he talked sounded like somebody reading out a book. "Complaint is issued on behalf a one Nealy Hawlan of Hawlan's Crossroads."

Granny had been hanging out towels and washrags on the back porch line. Now she stood, glaring at Reverend Pennycall. "Complaint? What you talking about, complaint?"

"Says here ya'll usin' hired help, Mrs. Wood."

"T'ain't nobody's business if I am," Granny said.

Willis and me were sitting on stools, breaking up string beans for supper. The sun was so hot, not even bugs wanted to fly. Elvis and Johnny were out in the chicken yard, the only chickens out there, bobbing their heads up and down at the water trough.

Reverend Pennycall pulled out a white hankie and wiped his forehead. "It is somebawdy's business Ma'am, if ya'll agreed not to."

"I never agreed to such a thing Reverend."

"Well, begging yo pawdon Ma'am, but you have. See here, cawdin' to Mista Hawlan, ya'll agreed not to bring in no help less it was okayed by him. When ya'll rented the place."

"Okayed? By Nealy Harlan?"

"Yes Ma'am." He held out the papers for her to see. "It's right here on this paper ya'll signed."

Granny came down the steps half way and squinted at the papers. "Where's it say that? Show me."

"Right there Ma'am." Reverend Pennycall pointed and gave the papers over to Granny.

Granny glared at the papers. "He's going to hold us to this?"

"Well, yes Ma'am, I reckon he is." Reverend Pennycall ran his thumb behind the police badge on the strap of his suspenders. It wobbled sunlight back to us.

Granny looked off across the road to Old Man Harlan's. Without looking back at the Reverend she said, "I got me a sick man laid up in the house. Did you know that?"

"Well, yes I do Ma'am." The Reverend took off his hat, wiped the inside band with his hankie.

Granny looked away off over the fields. "When it rains it pours don't it?"

"That's what they say Ma'am." Reverend Pennycall looked at Willis and put his hat back on. Then he looked at Granny. "That's a court ordah Ma'am."

"I can't have them boys working for me because they're colored?"

"Cawdin' to Mista Hawlan, ain't got nothing to do with colored."

"Hell it don't," Granny said. "Excuse my French, Reverend Pennycall, but I don't need this sorry-assed business."

"No Ma'am, I don't reckon you do. Ya'll have to talk to the judge anyhow. See, right there." He pointed a stubby finger to a place on one of the papers. "Day aftah tomorrah. Up Circle Stump way."

"If this don't beat all." Granny stood looking over the papers.

"I don't reckon ya'll would have a cold drink a watah? I'm a might thirsty Ma'am," Reverend Pennycall said.

"Orbie, go get the Reverend a drink of water," Granny said. I went inside and got a dipper full of water, brought it out and handed to Reverend Pennycall.

"Much obliged son." Reverend Pennycall got the dipper in his hands and turned it up over his nose. Some of the water circled around his mouth to the fat part of his chin. From there it dribbled to the ground. When he was done, he handed the dipper back to me. "Nothin' like cold spring watah on a hot day is they?" His fat cheeked eyes smiled on Willis. "You Moses Mashbone's boy, ain't you?"

Willis nodded that he was.

"Ya'll seen him recently?"

"No. We ain't," Granny said. "None of us has."

Reverend Pennycall looked at the house, up over the porch where Moses had painted. "I thought he was working over here."

"He was," Granny said. "What's this about Reverend?"

The question caused him to pause. He seemed to take stock of things a minute. He looked at Willis and a sadness came in his eyes. "I'm sorry to have to tell you this son, but they hung one a yo kind t'othah day. Up to Mudlick. Bunch a that renegade Klan. Hung him from a sycamore. He had that long hair too. Like yo Moses."

Something heavy sat down inside me when he said that. I remembered the vision I'd had in the cave, of Moses hanging upside down from a tree, his long hair almost touching the ground, the blood around his wrists.

The smile fell off Willis's face.

"They Lord!" Granny said in a loud voice. "I thought I heard just about every lie there was till now!"

Reverend Pennycall's face soured over. "I ain't in the habit of telling lies Ma'am." He walked out to the police car and grabbed something off the front seat. He walked back. He held out a dusty old black hat with a snakeskin band. "You evah see this befowah?"

Willis stood up from the stool, got his walking stick and put it under his arm. "Dat Mo hat."

"Mmmmm. I thought it might be," Reverend Pennycall said.

"Where'd you get that at?" Granny said.

"Them renegades burned a cross up Kingdom Church last night and left this on a stake. I'm reckoning they sending a message. I'm reckoning this here hat belonged to that niggah they hung."

"I'm reckoning you done forgot your manners Reverend!" Granny was almost shouting at Reverend Pennycall. "I'm reckoning you done wore your welcome plumb out!"

"I'm sorry Ma'am, if I have. I'm just tryin' to do ma job."

"Why don't you do it then? Why don't you put that renegade bunch in jail? You know who they are!"

"I can't just go around arresting folks Ma'am. Ya'll know that."

"Humph!" Granny said and looked at Willis.

"I'm sorry Ma'am. I'm sorry son," Reverend Pennycall said. "I reckon I best be on ma way."

"I reckon you best," Granny said.

Reverend Pennycall looked up again at Moses' paint job. "I see he's missed a patch up there." He took a step backward as if to study the place over the attic window.

Nobody said anything.

"Well, ya'll let me know if he shows up." He turned then and started walking away, his white hankie hopping up and down in his butt pocket.

"Walks like a fat ass duck, don't he?" I said.

Willis wouldn't even look.

When Reverend Pennycall got out to the police car he opened the door and looked back. "Ya'll can't work'em boys now Mrs. Wood, not till ya'll talk to the judge." He squeezed his belly in behind the wheel of the police car.

"He don't know nothin'," Granny said. "Bunch of rumors and old horseshit is all he knows."

Without looking at Granny or me, Willis walked himself down the steps of the porch and disappeared around the corner.

———

The day after Victor threw his fit he stayed in the trailer. Momma had to take his food out there. That was Tuesday. Granny's calendar had said September with a big number 8, the same day Reverend Pennycall had come. The next day, Wednesday, Victor showed up to breakfast on a hangover.

He frowned at the coffee Momma set before him. He picked up a slice of bacon and smelled of it. He looked at me and put the bacon all in his mouth, all at the same time, chewing it with his eyes on me. Wormy bloodshot eyes.

I tried to eat my oatmeal. Some dripped on the table.

"You're making a mess," Victor said.

Momma reached over with a rag and wiped it up. "Orbie honey, be careful."

"Coffee Momma," Victor said. "And bring me the aspirin. This head's killing me."

Momma brought him his coffee and aspirin. She sniffled around like somebody with a cold, her hair rolled in big pink curlers. She was wearing her bathrobe, pink with white swans on the pockets. One of the pockets was all bulged out with Kleenex. She set the coffee and four white aspirins on the table next to Victor. That's when I saw the shadows under her makeup, new bruises on both sides of her neck.

Victor watched me while he chewed his bacon. "What are you looking at?"

I wanted to ask him the same question. I looked at my oatmeal. A pad of butter floated on top. I poked it with my spoon.

Victor popped all four aspirin in his mouth, washed them down with coffee. "You managed to put one over on me, didn't you? The other night. You and your little colored friends." He leaned back, unbuckled his belt and slipped it off. He wrapped it around and around and set it coiled on the table next to his plate.

I pushed the pad of butter underneath the oatmeal, dug it back out again.

Victor grabbed hold of my wrist. "Look at me when I'm talking to you!" His breath was heavy with coffee and bacon.

"Let go of me!"

Something crashed behind me. I turned to see Momma trying to set the coffee pot straight. Coffee dripped through the cracks in the stovetop, sizzling down into the flames underneath.

Victor jerked me back around. "I said look at me!"

"Don't do this a way," Momma said, her voice empty of spirit, not telling Victor but asking. She stood with her back to the stove, a rag full of coffee grounds wadded in her hand. "It wasn't him, hon."

"The hell it wasn't!" Victor pulled me off the chair. I tried to break loose.

"You'd like to hurt me wouldn't you? Your old stepfather." He picked up the belt with his right hand and let it uncoil to the floor. Then he gathered it into a loop and brushed the end of it along my cheek. "By the way, I'm going to keep that knife of yours. Yeah. I know what you've been up to. I know how important it is."

"Victor, leave him alone hon," Momma said, her voice trailing away. I felt like I was falling down a black hole with nobody to help me. No Daddy, no Moses, no Momma, no knife.

"This is going to hurt you way more than it's going to hurt me," Victor said. "I can guarantee you that."

"Hey ya'll! Somebody in there! Come get this door!" It was Granny. She was yelling from the front door. "We finished shaving out here!"

"Just in time, as usual," Victor said. "Go on. Go let your grandmother in. We'll finish this later." He let go of my arm. The place where he'd grabbed me burned like fever.

"Do like he says, sweetheart," Momma said.

I went around his chair and into the front room. Missy was in there sleeping—even with all the noise she was. Granny and Granpaw filled up the whole front door almost, one lumpy shadow with the morning light a glare behind them. "Come hold this door for us old people," Granny said. "You get old, you'll wish you was young."

I went over and held the door open. Granny pushed Granpaw in the wheelchair over the bump into the front room. She looked at me. "What was all that ruckus about?"

"Nothing," I said.

"Didn't sound like nothing to me. Come on." Granny pushed the wheelchair across the living room, through the kitchen door and up to the table. "Somebody in here mention a knife?" I squeezed around behind her and went off down to the end of the table away from Victor. Granny looked at me. "I thought I heard somebody mention a knife."

"Victor did," I said.

Granny looked at Victor. He was busy again, eating his eggs. He shoveled up a fork full and put it in his mouth. The belt was still on the table. "It was you walked off with my knife the other night," Granny said.

Victor looked at Granny then continued with his eating. "It's in safe keeping, Mrs. Wood."

"What you keeping it safe for?"

Victor gulped and swallowed and wiped his lips with his napkin. "It's safe, that's all."

Granny tied a rubber thing around the muscle of Granpaw's arm. "Knives belong in a kitchen."

"Tell that to the boy," Victor said.

Granny reached around in back of her to the top part of the cabinet. She brought down the little black case with Granpaw's medicines and the hypodermic needle she used to give him his shots. "I got plenty of knives. In my drawer yonder. Keeping one out won't make a bit of difference somebody wants to stick you with one."

"Mamaw now," Momma said.

Victor sipped his coffee.

Granny squirted some of the medicine out the end of the needle. She put her mouth close to Granpaw's ear. "Strode. Make a fist now, hon."

Granpaw blinked and made a fist.

"Hold that a minute now." Granny finished giving Granpaw his shot and untied the rubber-thing. Momma was still standing by the stove, arms crossed, the coffee-ground rag balled up in one hand like before. Granny put the black case and Granpaw's medicines back atop the cabinet. "Victor, you remember what you said to me t'other night? When you called me an 'old woman'? I said this house was mine and you said it was for the moment. You remember that? For the moment, you said."

Victor kept eating.

Granny tied a dishtowel around Granpaw's neck, straightened it down the front of his chest. "It was awful strange Reverend Pennycall showing up here like he did. Talking about court orders. All that old stuff about Moses and his hat. The cross they burned over to Kingdom Church. And now I got to go to Circle Stump to talk to that judge. I was just thinking Old Man Harlan wouldn't have had sense enough to do all that. Not by himself. He wouldn't know a court order from a chicken's ass, it staring him right in the face. You have anything to do with that Victor?"

Victor answered with a mouth full of food, "I don't know what I said the other night and I don't care. I don't know what you mean." He jabbed his empty fork toward where I was sitting. "What you *should* be concerned with is that boy. He needs a good straightening out."

"Now let's just all of us eat our breakfast why don't we," Momma said in a weak little voice. "There's been enough upset for one morning." Momma was wrong though, I could feel she was.

"Did you know he's been threatening people with that knife?" Victor said. "Not just me and not just the other night. He's been threatening some little boys down by the creek. Mr. Harlan told me."

"With that knife?" Granny said.

"Yes," Victor said.

"They were scaring me and Willis," I said. "They pushed Willis in the water and threw rocks at him."

"Willis wasn't even there," Victor said. "You went after those boys by yourself for no reason. Mr. Harlan told me."

"That's a lie!" I yelled. "Old Man Harlan's a goddamn chicken buzzard anyway!"

"Orbie!" Momma said.

"See what I mean?" Victor said. "The boy's out of control."

"That don't make it all right for you to be," Granny said. "Look at what you did t'other night. Kicking and stomping around at something silly as that little picture Willis drew. What you do that for?" The air around Granny was full of electricity. I thought any second a blue light might start drawing itself around her.

"Let's just everybody calm down," Momma said.

Victor threw his napkin on his plate. "That's just fine, isn't it? The boy insults me, threatens me with a knife and you sit there apparently bent on taking his side. Has it ever occurred to you that I'm the closest thing that boy has to a father? That he needs a father's hand?"

"You a long ways from a father, Victor," Granny said. "You might make a proper stepfather someday if you was to sober up."

Victor's voice suddenly became sad. It was like he'd become a poor innocent person everybody was making out to be bad. "You're right Mrs. Wood. I do need to sober up." He leaned back from Granny a little. "If you want to accuse me, go right ahead, but hear me out first. I didn't know anything about Reverend Pennycall coming over here. Mr. Harlan never spoke to me about any of this business. I'm sorry though. I really am. Having to deal with eviction at a time like this, well, that must be rough."

"It don't give me no easy feeling," Granny said.

"I'm sure it doesn't," Victor said. "Perhaps, well, if you would allow me to, perhaps I could help you. I'm not unfamiliar with such proceedings."

"I don't reckon it'll amount to much," Granny said. "Judge Beechum's a reasonable man."

Victor went on in his sad, be sorry for me, voice. "As for the other night, well, I overreacted, I know that. Not without cause, though." He bowed his head a little; still looking at Granny. "Seeing that drawing the other night was a slap in the face to me, Mrs. Wood—after having done so much for Jessie—after having gone so far out of my way to help.

277

With the investigation I mean. I've told everything I know to the authorities. I was sitting at my desk, doing payroll when it happened. The night janitor saw me there; and that's all there is to tell." He stopped to clear his throat. "I wish I'd been there to stop that man Jackson, but I wasn't. Blame me for that if you want to. I do. Every day." He bowed his head a minute then looked back up at Granny. There were tears in his eyes.

"Ruby, mash up some of them eggs, would you?" Granny said. "Granpaw can't eat them they ain't mashed."

Momma fixed Granpaw's eggs. She handed them to Granny and sat down in my old chair next to Victor, a sad little smile on her face. She looked at him and her eyes went soft. She reached out and touched him on the arm.

"Ruby, Sweetness, you look awful," Granny said.

Momma started to cry.

Granny said to Victor, "I appreciate what you said just now Victor. We all sad over losing Jessie."

Momma reached out again and touched Victor's arm. She slipped her hand in his.

The room turned quiet. I listened to all the quiet sounds. Granpaw slurping eggs from the spoon Granny held. A fly bouncing along the screen on the door behind Victor. The Dark Thing was going in places it'd never gone before. Granny took off Granpaw's dishtowel and wiped his mouth. "There's one thing I don't understand though."

Victor blew his nose in a hankie. "What's that Mrs. Wood?"

All of a sudden the room perked up. "Well, I never said anything about no eviction. Alls I said was a court order. Now, them papers Reverend Pennycall gave me, they did mention eviction, but I haven't said a word about that. Not to nobody. So... How did you know about it?"

Momma and Victor both looked at Granny. Victor let go of Momma's hand. "Ruby explained your problem to me. I just assumed eviction was part of the package."

"Because I was letting them colored fellers work my land?"

"No. But if you didn't abide by the order, you could be."

"And how would you know that?"

"I told you, I just assumed it. What is this anyway?"

"How'd you know Nealy Harlan was our landlord then? I don't recollect ever telling you."

Victor picked his coffee cup up and set it back down. "Of course I knew. Ruby's told me everything about your situation." He looked at Momma. "Haven't you Baby."

Momma sniffled and looked up. "What? Well, yes. I reckon I did. If you say so hon."

"Sure you told me."

"If you say so. I reckon that's right Mamaw."

Victor threw his eyes back on Granny. "I don't like where this is going. A minute ago you seemed sympathetic. I could've guessed your situation from the nature of the court order alone. I didn't need anybody to tell me. I could have..."

"You could have talked to Old Man Harlan!" Granny slapped the table with the palm of her hand, not hard, just enough you knew she was mad. I almost slapped the table myself.

"Wait a minute, wait a minute! Even if I had, so what?"

"You and Old Man Harlan could have got this up between the two of you is so what!" Granny was fuming now.

"That's ridiculous! What would I gain by doing such a thing?"

"I don't know. But there's something. I can feel there is."

Granny and Victor looked at each other over the table. If I closed my eyes I could see a black cloud, twirling over the table inside the room—full of wind and sparks. Granny stood up. "You been nothing but a burden since you been down here. A sight more on my daughter here and her younguns."

"There's no need in stirring things up again," Momma said.

"There is too!" Granny snapped. "I want you to stop this whatever you're doing and wake up girl! Can't you see what he's up to? Poor little Missy, why, she ain't said two words since she been down here, and all cause of this man here, or whatever you want to call him!"

"You're full of shit," Victor said, dry-eyed now.

"I'm not through yet!" Granny stretched herself taller over the table. Her flowered housedress caught some of the light from the window. "I'll tell you what's the truth, I

279

don't know whether you played a part in what happened to Jessie or not, I hope for your own soul's salvation you didn't have anything to do with that. If I were you though, I would humble myself. I would get down on my knees in front of that woman there." She pointed to Momma. "And I would ask her to forgive me what I done to her and to her kids."

Victor, red faced, stood up out of his chair.

Granny didn't flinch. "I want you out of my house, Victor, and the sooner the better! There's a bus on Saturday. Ruby can ride you to town. Or Reverend Pennycall can. I don't want to see you after that!"

"Oh Mamaw, no," Momma said.

"You think you're going to keep me from mine? You better think again, you old bitch!" Victor grabbed up his belt so fast from the table he flipped his plate over. He tried to catch hold of it but it fell to the floor and smashed into a gazillion pieces. "Sorry for the mess," he said. "Maybe you can get one of your *niggers* to clean it!" He looked at Momma one last time and threading the belt through a loop as he went, slammed the screen door.

27
CHICKENS

Victor staggered across the road from Old Man Harlan's, his hand like a claw over the lid of a canning jar. I ducked behind the well and watched him come up in the yard. He was talking out loud to himself, his words running together, still fighting with Granny over what she had said. "Yes. We'll see about that! Old woman!" He was all red in the face and glassy-eyed, shaking a finger at his thoughts. "We'll see who has to go!" He unscrewed the lid on the jar and took a drink, screwed it back and staggered on. I followed after.

He grabbed onto the rain barrel and swatted at the air with the canning jar. "Think I don't know what you're up to? Armstrong? All you people? I'll show *all of you!*" He pushed himself from the barrel; zigzagged across the yard out to the trailer, unlocked the door and went inside. He left the door standing open.

I waited a little while before creeping up to the door. I saw Victor on his knees in there by the sofa bed, praying. "Forgive me Father! I didn't know. I didn't! I didn't!" He sucked tears up his nose and wiped at his eyes. "If I could make things right. If only I could." He kept on like that, praying, mumbling about letters and what all some people had said, bits of stories, shreds of things that had happened I could make neither heads nor tails of, asking God over and over to forgive him without ever really saying what he'd done. Finally he crawled up on the bed and lay over on his back, crosswise with his feet on the floor. In a minute he was sound asleep.

I kicked my tennis shoes off and tiptoed barefoot up the steps. I stood just inside the door on the dirty gray carpet. The little egg shaped room of the trailer closed in around me, hot and stuffy, even with the door and all the windows open. I could feel grainy little pieces of dirt in the carpet under my feet. On a table next to the bed sat the coil of Victor's belt and a wind up alarm clock, white with black hands—the big hand on the twelve, the little on the two. Tomorrow would be Friday. Then Saturday, the day Victor was supposed to leave. I knew he wouldn't though, not without a fight. I had to find the knife.

He lay with his eyeglasses pushed up to the top of his head, snoring inside a cloud of moonshine smell and body odor. Past the bed on the other side of the room were shelves that went up the wall on one side of a little stainless steel sink. The sink had no faucet but was piled high with dishes Momma had brought over from the house. There was a jalousie window over the sink, its slats filled with smoky white sunlight. The sunlight threw a lumpy white square across the bed. The clock ticked in the corner. Victor took in a deep breath and slowly let it out; then he went on snoring.

I tiptoed to the sink and pulled at a drawer under the counter. It made a screeching sound. "Come to bed baby," Victor muttered. I waited, the blood building, pounding drumlike in my head. Again I tried the drawer, pulling it out a little at a time. Inside were pencils and pens and other odds and ends—two wrapped cigars, a tin of Band-Aids, a lidless half-used jar of Vaseline. Other things were arranged on the shelves beside the sink—Pamolive Aftershave Lotion, a tube of Pepsodent, combs and brushes, razor blades, a can of Barbasol. There were magazines too, Popular Mechanics,

Life Magazine and Reader's Digest, and nail polish remover and aspirin and Brylcream—all organized in straight rows and neat little piles.

On one of the upper shelves sat Victor's green file box and a slotted stand full of envelopes and manila file folders, some with papers inside. I pulled the counter drawer out a little further and ran my hand into the shadows at the back. I found a tablespoon there; two bent forks and a rusty can opener but no knife.

I got down on my hands and knees and looked under the bed. The mattress made a belly toward the floor. The carpet smelled like cigar ashes and spilled moonshine. There was a card table lying flat under there with a folding chair. Victor's tan suitcase was there too along with his smiling alligator shoes.

I stood up. The bed was now between me and the door. Victor's head lay directly in front of me—almost at the edge— his face red and shiny with heat. I could see the chicken yard fence through the door. Beyond it was the chicken house, weather-blackened and baking in the sun.

Victor moved his head. He placed a hand on his chest and yawned. The yawn turned into a groan. I pressed myself back against the wall. Victor closed his hands into fists and stretched them over his head. They were almost touching me. I felt beads of sweat pop out across my forehead. All at once Victor sat straight up on the bed.

"Christ Almighty, it's hot," he whispered to the open door.

All he had to do to see me was turn around. I looked along on the floor up to the little table where the clock sat. There underneath the table lay the knife. I held my breath.

Again, he made fists, stretching them this time toward the ceiling. I thought for sure he was going to turn around, but then it was like all the air went out of him and he dropped back on the bed. I waited for the longest time, not daring to move or hardly even to breathe until I again heard the sound of his snoring. The big hand on the clock had gone down to the three.

I edged along the wall to the little table, reached down under there and got the knife. When I got back to Victor, I stopped. His eyeglasses had fallen onto the floor.

I could kill him now if I wanted. I could stab him in the neck. Punch a hole in one of his big veins there.

I lifted the knife, the straightened-out-point pointing directly at Victor's head.

We wouldn't have to worry about him, ever again. We would be free.

The thought seemed simple enough, sensible even, but somehow I knew the truth of it wouldn't be. The truth would be bloody, the truth would be real—something I could never take back.

I let the knife go down by my side, trembling, remembering now the little boy of my vision, his horse-faced mother and the three sniggering factory workers, remembering the question I asked Granpaw about the Rain Skull and the contrary power—'Too late for what Granpaw?' I had asked—and his answer coming back strong and clear—'To save what you was wanting to destroy, by grabs.'

I wanted to destroy Victor, not the boy. How was that possible?

———

There came a loud banging noise from outside—loud enough I thought it might wake Victor. I raised the knife, holding it as before directly over his head. The noise came again, louder this time. Still, Victor went on sleeping. I carefully tiptoed around the bed and out the door; pulled on my tennis shoes and looked out across the chicken yard. A dust bomb exploded out the chicken house door, chickens flying every which a way, running, bumping into each other, squawking, cackling over the yard. I thought maybe a fox had gotten in there.

I hid the knife in some weeds by the fence and climbed over. Another noise came from inside the chicken house, wings flapping, the sound of something metal like a bucket banging across the floor. I found a good rock and ran toward the chicken house door, filled now with a bomb-cloud of smoky black dust. There was a smell of chicken poop and rotten feathers. A great big bird body flew out of the bomb-cloud, whooshing, flapping its wings, squawking over my head. It landed next to the water trough—Geronimo The Rooster—his green and black butt feathers shivered in the hot air.

"Come out of there you old fox!" I shouted.

Somebody inside the dust hollered back, "City boy? That you? You best get out away from here!" It was Old Man Harlan's bad-tempered voice.

I let the rock go down by my side. There were more squawks, more wings—another bucket-sound. Old Man Harlan hollered again. "I hope to God you two is worth the trouble! Thick as pitch in here!" He came in the doorway then, red eyed, almost no hair on his head at all. A black hankie covered his nose and mouth, making a little point below his chin like a bank robber's mask. He had a hold of Elvis and Johnny, holding them upside down by their legs, one in each of his long bony hands. He stepped sideways over a busted plank, reached up the hand that held Elvis and pulled the hankie from his mouth, fixing his red blistery eyes on me.

I wanted to say something but for the moment had lost my voice. Everything—my eyesight, the smell of chicken poop, the feel of the rock in my hand—became super sharp. I could even hear the dust settling in the doorway behind Old Man Harlan's feet.

"What are you doing with those chickens, Mr. Harlan?" I was finally able to say.

"That ain't none of your beeswax; now is it?" came Old Man Harlan's reply.

Johnny tried to reach up to peck Old Man Harlan but fell back, flapping her wings and squawking against his pant leg. Elvis hung quietly, her white wings open and still.

"Those are *my* chickens, Mr. Harlan."

Old Man Harlan's face seemed to gather up about his nose. "Who said they was?"

"I been taking care of them. For Granny. I been getting them ready for the beauty contest. At the fair. That one there's name is Johnny, and that one is Elvis."

"Beauty contest?" Old Man Harlan snorted. "We *eat* chickens down here son."

Johnny had stopped struggling, her wings fanning out now like Elvis's, open and still.

"Please don't hurt Johnny and Elvis, Mr. Harlan. I've been training them. They're my pets. You can eat those other chickens can't you?"

Old Man Harlan said nothing, stood there with a blank look pasted over his features.

I tried again. "I said you can eat those others can't you?"

"I can eat these," Old Man Harlan said.

All the air went out of me then. I didn't know what to do. I had the rock, which felt rough and dangerous, but I didn't dare throw it at Old Man Harlan.

He set the chickens down one at a time. They stayed right beside him, looking around at the yard. "Holding them upside down like that calms them," Old Man Harlan said.

I got an idea then and hauled off with the rock, throwing it over Old Man Harlan's head. It came down with a loud bang on top the tin roof of the chicken house.

"Run Johnny! Run Elvis!" I yelled, but they just stood there like fools. I stomped my feet at them. "Run, you stupid ass chickens!" Johnny turned her head sideways, trying to remember. The sunlight had changed her comb into a bright red saw-blade. "Run goddamn you!"

Old Man Harlan grinned. "You want to see'em run?"

Before I could find the breath to answer, he grabbed hold of Johnny and Elvis by their necks, both of them, jerking them up off the ground, their white wings flapping in a panic. He held them like that. "Watch here now," he said and then he just twirled them—like you would the ends of a jump rope around and around until their snow-white bodies leaped away from his hands. They hit the ground running. I thought at first they had gotten away and for that brief moment I was glad. But then I saw what had happened, that blood was spurting everywhere.

One bumped up against me and I tried to grab it, thinking crazily that if I could take hold of it, I could pet it, make it all better. It tore through my hands and made a wide looping dash neck first into the water trough. The other had run almost all the way out to the gate. It lay there on its side in a white bloody heap, one wing flapping.

"Looky here, boy." Old Man Harlan held out Elvis and Johnny's heads, the neck feathers wet with blood. "All she wrote for them buzzards." He tossed the heads over the fence.

He may as well have tossed me. Carrot colored puke exploded out my mouth all over my tennis shoes and onto the ground in front of me.

Old Man Harlan stood, wiping his hands down the front of his vest. "Hell now boy, you'll be all right. I told you to stay away. Didn't I tell you?" He went over to the trough and pulled out the chicken that had run there, bloody water dripping from the headless neck. "This one's good sized," Old Man Harlan muttered. He went over and picked up the other, carried them both upside down like before with their wings flopped open.

I ran after him, wiping my mouth and crying, "You Goddamn Chicken Buzzard, Old Man Harlan! I hope you rot in hell!"

"What's all the ruckus out here!" It was Victor, yelling from the doorway of the trailer, no shirt on now. No eyeglasses. "I'm trying to sleep in here!"

Old Man Harlan pushed open the gate. "It's this here boy a yorn! He's mad about these chickens. Said I couldn't kill these cause they was his. I never seen no little boy with as much sass. Like to hit me with a rock."

"Liar!" I cried.

Old Man Harlan looked up at Victor.

"Apologize to Mr. Harlan," Victor said.

"That rock would have hit me, it hadn't gone wild," Old Man Harlan said.

287

"Liar!"

Right then, Granny stepped out on the back porch. "What's all this about?"

"He's been throwing rocks at Mr. Harlan here," Victor said.

"Have not! He killed my chickens Granny!"

Granny spied Elvis and Johnny hanging from Old Man Harlan's hands. "They Lord!"

Old Man Harlan's face soured over. "These is my chickens. I reckon I can do what I want with them."

"He twirled their heads off Granny! He killed them!" I was crying so hard now I could hardly get my breath.

"They Lord, hon, I'm sorry you had to see that."

"For crying out loud." Victor ducked his head back inside the trailer.

Granny came down off the porch. "I was afraid something like this might happen. Come on hon." She gave Old Man Harlan a look. "I reckon if you threw a rock at old Nealy he shore enough deserved it."

"No wonder he's spoilt," Old Man Harlan said.

"He could use a little spoiling around the likes of you."

"Say what you want to, old girl. Your days is numbered."

"All our days are numbered Nealy."

"Humph!" Old Man Harlan stepped to one side of Granny and walked off with the dripping chickens. Dotted lines of blood followed him across the yard.

———

Everybody was eating supper except Victor, who was still passed out in the trailer. I wasn't hungry. I got me a coffee can and went out by the chicken yard. A breeze was coming in from back of Granpaw's tobacco patch, blowing up bits of straw and making the tin roof on the chicken house tick. Granny's knife was still where I left it by the fence. I stuck it in my belt and went looking for Elvis and Johnny's heads. I found them in one of the tracks of the wagon road covered with flies. Elvis's floppy comb had shrunk to about a third of

288

its size. Johnny's beak was frozen in mid squawk. I picked them each up by their bloody neck feathers and put them in the can, crying so hard now I could barely see.

I slipped past the house with the can and out across the road to the cemetery. I'd never been out there by myself, and never so late. The 'Harlan's Crossroads Cemetery' sign faced outward from its curve over the gate. The cottonwood limbs were rocking in the breeze. I pushed open the gate and crossed the weedy, picker-filled graveyard to the busted out place. The sun was going down and the umbrella of the weeping willow tree stood black in the haze.

I came across Granny and Granpaw Ray's graves, crumbling white slabs, darkened now, though I could still make out the worn letters of their names. And there was Daddy's grave too—the shiny gray stone—the words 'Loved By All' cut across the front.

I dumped Elvis and Johnny's heads out of the can and onto the grass. Taking up the butcher knife, I made a hole at the foot of Daddy's grave. I put the heads in there and covered them with the dirt. I sat listening to the breeze. It was true, what the words on Daddy's grave said. *Loved By All.* Everybody loved Daddy. Missy and me loved him. Momma loved him. Granny and Granpaw did. The church people did. People he worked with too. Why would anybody want to kill Daddy? Why would Victor?

A voice cracked behind me. "What you burying chicken heads in my graveyard for?" I whirled around with the knife. Hunched over like a gray bug, standing just inside the busted out place, was Bird Pruitt. "Chickens ain't peoples." She had that same purple dress she always had on, the purple hat with the purple net. "Answer me, Ruby's boy! I said what you burying chicken heads in my graveyard for?"

I couldn't believe it—first Victor, then Old Man Harlan, now this. I scrambled to my feet. "This graveyard doesn't belong to you Bird!"

Bird ran a tongue over her lips, grinning. "You just like your Momma was. Course now her spirit's robbed away. Ain't it? In 'at box! And here you are all by your lonesome agin that man. Eee! Eee! Eee! Poor thang." Half her teeth were gone, her face watery with watery gray eyes and a mouth like a brown hole of black gumline and yellowed bits of bone. The perfect cousin for Old Man Harlan, I thought. She shuffled up under her hump and started toward the weeping willow.

"What box?" I said.

I could see just one side of her face as she paused, one watery eye looking up in the sky. "You know they's a storm coming don't you? A big un too. Look up there." She pointed to the sky. The sun had gone down but it was still light out. Up where Bird pointed was a round moon, floating in the dark sky, around it a hazy white ring, one diamond star inside. "Storms a coming, shore 'nuff." Bird wagged her head and shambled off into the black shape of the weeping willow tree.

"What storm?" I called.

28
BODY SNATCHERS

Friday morning Granpaw woke up from his spell. Granny told him what all Reverend Pennycall had said and about Victor too. "I got to go talk to that judge."

"Judge Beechum?" Granpaw said.

"Yeah, Judge Beechum! I got to go talk to him."

"You mean *we*, don't you?" Granpaw said. "I'll tell you what's the truth; Nealy and the Reverend can both kiss my ass! Victor too. Ought to've run him off long ago."

"You don't have to get all worked up about it," Granny said.

"I ain't worked up!" Granpaw growled. "I'm mad!" He waited for that to sink in; then said, "Reckon what Reverend Pennycall said is true? Reckon they hung ole Moses?"

"I don't know," Granny said. "I didn't believe it at first, but now they all talking about it."

"I'd trust the Devil for I would the Reverend."

"Strode," Granny said.

"Well I would, by grabs."

After breakfast they both got in the station wagon and drove off.

———

All the rest of the morning and on into the afternoon it was so sweaty hot outside you could hardly get your breath. Victor wouldn't eat breakfast. He wouldn't eat lunch. Both times Momma took food out to the trailer, and both times she had to bring it back.

I went around the side of the house and looked out across Nub Road. A huge cloud was swelling up over Granpaw's tobacco patch; the top so bright it was hard to look at, the underside all charcoal gray and bulging with dark green bubble shapes.

Willis sat Chester in the middle of the road—the first I'd seen of him since Reverend Pennycall's visit. "What ya'll doing?" he said.

"Watching that cloud. What you?"

"Nothing. Too hot." Willis slid off Chester. He looked at the cloud. "Rain ca-comin'."

I remembered what Bird said. I remembered the circle around the moon and the diamond star. "It'll blow over."

"Might," Willis said.

"Where you been?"

He didn't answer, but I could see he had been crying.

"He ain't dead," I said. "Can't be."

"Can be too."

"Granny don't think so."

"Miss Alma do."

We watched the cloud a while, and then we went around to the front porch. I had my comic books and drawing papers and all my colors out there. Momma was sitting at the end of the porch in the rocking chair with Missy. Willis drew a picture of them. Then he started coloring it in. The colors looked good. Momma with black slacks and a blue blouse, little white flowers stitched across the front. Missy in a pair of black pedal pushers and a pink tee shirt. I sat back against the wall and read about body snatchers, about this man who

292

was trying to warn people about the invasion of the body snatchers but nobody would listen.

Momma took up a little brown make-up case and looked at herself in the mirror. She took out the powder-puff and rubbed powder around the bruises on her neck. Willis worked on his picture. A blue dragonfly zoomed down next to his arm, flickered in the sunlight and zoomed away. Momma put the powder-puff back in the case. She dropped the case in a makeup bag by her chair. She took up a fan with a picture of Jesus on the back and began fanning herself and Missy.

I put away the Body Snatcher book and looked up in the sky. The cloud had moved up closer to the house and had mushroomed big as an A-bomb, twice the size it was before. The sky underneath was almost green with black-green curlycues and cave holes going through it. I had on my red shorts and Davy Crockett tee shirt. Flies kept tickling me, landing in places I couldn't reach. I was smothering in the heat.

Something, a suitcase, Victor's tan colored suitcase, ka-thumped down on the end of the porch right next to Momma, causing her suddenly to sit straight as a board. Victor kathumped his green file box on the porch too. He stood there a minute, looking around at the yard, all fidgety-like and nervous. "Momma," he said. "I've decided. I've got to get out of here honey, and I want you and the kids to go with me."

He broke down then and started to cry. Tears streamed down around his nose. He was wearing his silvery gray pants and that pink shirt with the cuffs rolled back to his elbows. Two pens and the end of a fat cigar stuck out the breast pocket. "I want you to come right now Momma. I've worked everything out. You don't even have to think about it. We'll just get in the car right now." He took out a hankie from his back pocket and wiped his eyes. "Get the hell away from here."

Momma sat up even straighter. "I can't do that hon, what with Granpaw in the shape he's in—and all this other business going on." Missy began to whimper.

Willis looked up from his picture. He looked at me. He looked at Victor.

"I know," Victor said. "But your mother and father, they're going to be all right. I mean, listen. They could move to town. People will help them." The color was gone from his face. "I've got it all figured out, Momma. Forget Florida. Forget the house, for now anyway. We can go anywhere we want. I've heard Texas is a good place. We could go to Dallas or Houston. Or how about Arizona?" When he said Arizona his eyes went wide. "Tucson? Yes! It's hot there, but the winters are mild. We can go there! Sell the house later. I've got money. A little. And you'll have Jessie's insurance. I love you Momma! I don't know what I would do without you and the kids!"

You could tell he'd been drinking. His forehead gleamed whitely in the sunlight. I could see the worms in his eyes— even from where I was sitting—cutting themselves on the glass behind his tears. Thunder rumbled across the sky. "Say you'll come with me Momma. We don't have much time."

No Momma! Don't believe him! Don't say you'll go Momma!

"Time?" Momma said, "Victor honey, what do you mean?"

Victor frowned. "I mean if we don't hurry, your parents will be back. And then we'll have to explain everything. You know how stubborn they can be. Your mother will start asking a lot of questions. Confuse things. I can't have any confusion right now Momma. You can understand that, can't you? Sure you can."

Momma hugged Missy tighter, her voice weak and trembling. "Oh hon, now. Try to calm yourself. Mamaw. She just wants what's best for the kids and me. She don't mean any harm."

Victor blew his nose in the hankie. "Uh huh. Then, what about me?" His voice had turned suddenly unpleasant. "What is it she wants for me I would like to know?"

"Well. She wants the best for you too. I think she does anyway. I don't know. I don't think she understands you good Victor. Sometimes. Sometimes I don't know if I do." She leaned a little away from Victor. "I mean like now. You wanting me to leave without even saying goodbye."

294

Victor's face went like a rock. "Write her a note."

"I can't do that hon."

"I can't do that hon," Victor said, his voice mocking and hateful.

I got to my feet.

"It wouldn't be right," Momma said. "Please hon; don't do this a way!"

Victor made his face go like Momma's. "Please hon; don't do this a way!"

I looked around for something to use against him. I remembered the knife but it was in the box with the Rain Skull under the house. Granpaw's wheelchair sat empty. Maybe I could turn it around somehow and push it at Victor. There was an old iron Granny used as a doorstop; it was sitting upright on the floor behind the wheelchair. I reached down and grabbed it up by the handle.

Momma said, "It would break Mamaw's heart I was to leave without telling her goodbye."

Victor grabbed Momma by the wrist, jerking her toward him. "Break it then!"

Missy started to cry. "Victor, you're hurting me!"

"Victor, you're hurting me!" Victor answered. "Better think of your kids Momma. You want what's best for them don't you? You want them to be safe?"

"Course I do!" Momma said.

"Course I do! Course I do!"

Take care of your Momma son. She don't see things all the way through.

I tried to lift the iron over my head, but it was too heavy. I thought maybe, if I ran at Victor with it and let it go, it would hit him in the ribs, maybe knock the breath out of him. To do it though, I would have to run in front of Granpaw's wheelchair, past Momma to the edge of the porch.

Willis grabbed me by the ankle. "What you gone do boy?"

"Let go of me Willis!"

"Well, well, what have we here?" Victor was looking right at me now. He still had a hold of Momma's wrist.

"We ain't going with you!" I said, trying to hold up the iron.

"So! Momma's little hero," Victor said.

"Let him alone," Momma said. "Orbie put that down."

Missy was crying full out now, screaming almost. There came the sound of a truck lumbering up the road, gears grinding hard. Missy got quiet. I thought it would pass but when it got to Granny and Granpaw's, it turned up in the yard—Moses' old pick-up truck—with Miss Alma behind the wheel. Vern and Fable were standing up in the truckbed, holding onto the cab.

Victor said, "Son of a Goddamn Bitch!" He let go of Momma's wrist, grabbed up his suitcase and stormed away. The green file box stayed on the porch. A cool breeze rushed over the yard. Bunches of clouds were moving overhead now. They made an upside down floor over the crossroads all the way almost up to the house. Black green bubbly clouds they were, big bruised titties hanging down. A white bolt of lightning streaked to the ground followed by a roll of thunder.

Miss Alma had climbed down out of the truck and was huffing and puffing her way up to the porch—she was huge—a gigantic huge black woman in a sweat stained housedress. Wrapped around her head was a black, green polka dotted hankie with two little rabbit ears sticking out the sides. She came up, sucking air and blowing wind, but when her eyes fell on Momma all her everything just stopped. "Lawd Ruby! What happen?"

Momma put on a friendly face. "Why nothing, Miss Alma."

"You a ghost, girl." Miss Alma said. "What happen here?"

Momma forced a smile. "Nothing Miss Alma. I'm fine. What are you in such a hurry about?"

Miss Alma looked at Momma still with a question in her eyes, still trying to get her breath. "Radio say dey twistas! North a Circle Stump!"

"Oh, but this will blow over," Momma said. "It always does."

"Dis house is what gone blow over, girl!" Miss Alma shouted. "Everythang gone blow! Ya'll bes come on now, down to Moses'! Wait dis out!"

Without warning, a wall of cold wind bent the Jesus Tree.

It took Miss Alma's dress between her legs and caused Willis to have to hold on to his papers. Thunder shook the house. Momma got up with Missy, looked around at the trailer and then at the angry clouds. "Can you take the boys? I got to shut down the stove and warn Victor."

Miss Alma frowned. "Ya'll bes hurry girl!"

"I ain't going nowhere," I said.

"Leave dem windows open," Miss Alma said. "House blow, you don't!"

Momma headed for the door, serious now. "Put them comic books away and go on! You and Willis. Don't argue with me now! Go on with Miss Alma!" Momma hurried around me with Missy in her arms and went inside the house. I got my comic books and papers and Willis's picture of Momma and piled them all in a stack with my colors on the top. I picked it all up and carried it in the house in the front room and put it on the couch. I could hear Momma, messing with the stove in the kitchen. I quick got my ball cap and went back out on the front porch. Miss Alma had already turned the truck around. Chester was tied to the back end. Willis sat up in the cab with Miss Alma. Vern and Fable stood in the truck bed, signaling me to hurry.

———

It took us only about a minute to get to Moses' house.

Willis got out and untied Chester. Me and Vern and Fable followed Miss Alma up to the house, her two giant butt halves battling each other all the way.

"I thought we were going in the storm cellar Miss Alma," I said.

She huffed and puffed herself up to Moses' front door and stopped to look in the sky. "Let see what da radio say. Fable. Vern. Ya'll go on now. Get dat cellah ready. Dey a broom down there. Some rag in a bucket."

Vern made a face.

"Go on now! Fable, you too. We be down soon! Willis, you and Orbie come with me. Ain't no time be horsein' round."

"Momma will be along soon, won't she?" I said.

"Uh huh. Soon," Miss Alma said.

Moses' house was maybe about half the size of Granny and Granpaw's, the outside walls covered in brown sandy shingles. The tree that had fallen on the roof was gone. Still there was a place inside where the ceiling had bellied down.

"Tree almost break through," Miss Alma said. "Mo gone fix it 'fo he up and vanish."

Just then, it was something grabbed me around by the neck. I tried to twist loose, but whatever had me wouldn't let go. I turned around to face the thing and there sat Bird, outfitted like usual, hunched forward in a rocking chair. She'd hooked me around by the neck with her cane. "That is you, ain't it? Ruby's boy! I knowed it was. Come closer to me!" She opened the brown hole of her mouth and a world of garlicky dead breath washed over my face.

"Unloose dat chile," Miss Alma said.

Bird unhooked her cane from around my neck. "He thanks I'm crazy but I showed him the moon. Didn't I, Ruby's boy?" She spied Willis then, standing in back of me. "Zat that brokeleg boy? Tiz ain't it?"

"Let dem boys be," Miss Alma said.

Bird poked the floor with her cane and a grin gashed her face. The front room was small, the ceiling so low the rabbit ears on Miss Alma's hankie almost touched it. Off from the room was a kitchen. A radio was playing scratchy hillbilly music out there. Bird worked her rubbery mouth around in a circle. "Radio say a funnel cloud touched ground. Up Glasgow way. Mudlick too. Two drowned up there! Flash floods!"

"Lawd!" Miss Alma said.

Willis and me looked at each other.

"I hope to God that cellar's clean!" Bird said. "Last time it was so nasty, I couldn't find no place to sit!" Miss Alma's eyebrows hitched together. Bird got up and spider-walked herself toward the kitchen.

Miss Alma looked out the window. "Sun gone now. Lawd Lawd." Right then a white sheet of light flashed all around

298

Miss Alma, all around the house, in through the windows in the kitchen. There was another sound of something like boulders hitting the ground. The radio went dead. Miss Alma turned away from the window. White whiskery hairs—little pieces of silvery green fire—stood out on her chin. It started to rain—a million hands, slapping against the house, against the window in the front room, against the windows in the kitchen. Miss Alma hollered over the roar. "Bird! It time!"

Bird shambled back into the front room, carrying a basket now with a red-and-white-checkered dishtowel over the top.

"Dis rain let up, we go!" Miss Alma hollered.

"What about Momma?" I said. "What about Missy?"

Miss Alma smiled. "We'll keep dat cellah door open till dey come."

"Not if they's a twister we won't," Bird said. "They's a twister that door will be shet!" Miss Alma hitched her eyebrows together. Willis touched me on the arm.

Bird held up the basket. A warm good smell flowed out from the dishtowel. She spider-walked herself to the front door and pulled it open. The rain had already started to let up, the air cool as the inside of a well. Bird went out, then me and Willis—then Miss Alma. Bubbly purple and green clouds circled overhead. The storm cellar was a stone's throw away from the house, a bulge of red clay with a rusted slantwise door that was now open and lying off to one side. I could see the dark box of the cellar's opening and Vern's fuzzy head sticking out.

As we walked toward the cellar, I turned and looked up Bounty, halfway expecting Momma and the black Ford to come barreling over the hill. What I saw instead was a little river of red muddy water, boiling down the side of the road. A new pond had formed at the bottom of the hill, covering the road there and spreading out over Moses' front yard.

"I be fit to tie!" Miss Alma said, but she was looking in the other direction, toward Circle Stump. From there came Reverend Pennycall's white police car, rushing toward us with its red bubble light madly circling on top. It slid around

299

into Moses' driveway; slinging orange muddy water and spinning its wheels before coming to a stop. Old Man Harlan got out the car on the passenger side. Reverend Pennycall on the driver's. The rain was just a sprinkle now, but cold and steady. Both hurried up to the red hill of the cellar, Old Man Harlan holding the lapels of a black coat around his chin, Reverend Pennycall with his hand pressed flat against the top of his dingy straw hat.

Old Man Harlan's eyes were bloodshot. Beads of rain slid off the end of his veiny nose. "Cold son?" he said to me.

I stood next to Willis just in my shorts and tee shirt. I was cold, but I wasn't going to talk about it with Old Man Harlan.

"Not cold as his grandparents is going to be," Reverend Pennycall said. Both stood in the rain, grinning and nodding their heads like the truth was a secret nobody knew but them.

A loud cracking sound wandered across the sky—like an earthquake I heard on TV once, like the ground cracking apart. A fist of wind knocked Reverend Pennycall's hat away. He went chasing after it, his hair thin and light brown, circling a bald spot on top his head. Old Man Harlan laughed. White popcorn shapes began hopping across the ground.

"Hail!" Miss Alma shouted. I looked up to see a white curtain of hailstones clacking over the hill toward us.

Reverend Pennycall trapped his hat against a fence post, got it on his head and pushed by Willis and me. "Let's go Nealy! Hell fire!" Him and Old Man Harlan both hurried themselves down the cellar stairs. The rest of us just stood there, dumbfounded, watching the curtain advance down the hill.

"Go on!" Miss Alma finally shouted. Willis and me ran for the cellar. Even with just one good leg Willis could go fast. He walked himself lickety-split to the cellar door and did a quick hobble down. Some of the hailstones were big as marbles. Some rock-sized. They popped off the bill of my ball cap and stung the back of my legs. I turned to look up the road one last time and almost knocked into Bird, her eyes filled with miseries and water.

300

"I don't thank she's going to make it, do you?" she said. "I'm a feared she's in some bad awful trouble."

29
COMES A STORM

"Twister took half a Grinestaff's store," said Old Man Harlan. Bird set the basket with the checkered dishtowel on a little bench in the middle of the cellar. "Radio said them funnel clouds was north. Not *in* Circle Stump!"

"I don't care what the radio said!" Old Man Harlan squawked. "I'm tellin' you what I seen! What the Reverend here seen!"

Reverend Pennycall nodded. Him and Old Man Harlan had parked themselves in the only two chairs in the cellar. Willis and me sat on a pile of grass sacks. Vern and Fable squatted against the wall. Bird eased herself down on the little bench next to the basket, facing Willis and me. The cellar door was open, and a green light lay like a ghost across the stairs.

"What's 'at ole pancake nigger doing up there anyhow?" Old Man Harlan said. "Don't she know they's a storm on?"

Willis stayed quiet. Vern and Fable looked at the floor. "You shouldn't call her that, Mr. Harlan," I said.

"Who says I shouldn't?"

"Miss Alma is Vern and Fable's momma. She's waiting up there for my Momma. My sister too. She's keeping a watch out for them."

"Well, why ain't they showed up yet?"

"Momma had to get the house ready. Cause of the storm. She had to warn Victor. She said they'd be down in a little while."

"She did, did she?" Old Man Harlan caught Reverend Pennycall's eye. "You say she aimed to warn Victor?"

"Uh huh. Then they'll come."

Old Man Harlan and Reverend Pennycall looked at each other and laughed. "Sounds easy, don't it," Old Man Harlan said. "Like they never had no disagreements."

"He'll straighten her out," Reverend Pennycall said. White light flashed across the cellar stairs followed by another boom of thunder. "Thank Gawd court ended when it did."

"Amen on that," Old Man Harlan said. "We just did make it."

"We did," Reverend Pennycall nodded.

I wondered how Granny and Granpaw made out, whether the judge had agreed with them or Old Man Harlan. Damned if I'd ask Old Man Harlan about it though. I wondered if Granny and Granpaw were driving back now; trying to get home in the storm. A fuzzy light bulb dangled from a wire in the middle of the ceiling just over Bird's head. There were some plank shelves on the other side. Dingy glass jars, moldy looking, full of pear halves and apples. Dark tomatoes. Gray corn.

Bird grinned her rotten-toothed grin and uncovered the basket. "Ya'll want a bite of this?" A good warm smell overpowered the musty smell of the cellar.

"Give that here." Old Man Harlan took a hold of the basket and set it on his lap. Him and the Reverend both took out a napkin with something wrapped inside.

"They's tators and corn too," Old Man Harlan said. "We'll have that later." He reached the basket back to Bird. "Get you a piece in there Bird." He looked at Vern and Fable, then at me and Willis. "You negroes will have to wait." Reverend Pennycall laughed. Willis, Vern and Fable looked on hungrily. I hadn't eaten anything myself since breakfast. My mouth began to water.

Bird took out a crusty piece of something and bit in—like some old spider jawing on a bug. "Chicken smells good fried, don't it Reverend? Eats good too."

The Reverend held his piece in the napkin in front of his mouth, grease shining all around his lips. "It do, don't it?"

Old Man Harlan held up a golden brown drumstick and pointed it toward me. "These is them chicken-friends of that boy there. I believe this leg belonged to Elvis. That right Reverend?" Reverend Pennycall winked at me and went on feeding his face.

"You know that boy loves chickens," Old Man Harlan said. "Pitched him a fit t'other day cause I killed me two. Pets he said they was! His pets." White meat turned over in Reverend Pennycall's half open mouth.

Bird looked up from the piece she was gnawing on. "Buried they heads in 'at graveyard a mine."

I watched as they ate my snowbirds, as they looked for fresh places to bite in. The good smell of the dinner spread all throughout the cellar. I tried to swallow the water in my mouth and almost gagged. I thought of Momma, the bruises around her neck, Victor's hands like Old Man Harlan's around the chicken's necks.

Bird pushed the good smelling basket into my thoughts. "Get you a piece in there, Ruby's boy!"

I swatted it away. "Do that again and I'll knock the rest of your goddamn teeth out!" Bird's mouth dropped open. What I said, how I said it, like a grown-up person, surprised even me.

"Keep on that a way and I'll whip you myself," Old Man Harlan said.

I jumped off the sacks. "You can go straight to hell! You and Bird both!" Old Man Harlan got up from his chair, but I dodged him and ran up the steps.

Miss Alma was standing outside in the rain, the umbrella raised over her head. She grabbed hold of my arm. "Hold on, boy! Where ya'll off to?"

"Momma's in trouble Miss Alma! I just know she is!"

Old Man Harlan was at the bottom of the steps. "That boy's meaner'n a snake! Send him back down here!"

"He's the mean one, Miss Alma!" I yelled. "They're eating my chickens down there! Momma's in trouble! I know she is!"

"Laud, Laud! Ya'll don't know dat. Cain't go running off in dis no how!" Miss Alma gestured with the umbrella toward the sky. Black clouds in a spooky green soup were chasing after one another up there, circling around and around like water going down a drain.

"I said to send him back down here!" Old Man Harlan yelled, bald head hanging off his crooked neck.

Miss Alma rose up big as a mountain. "Hush yo mouth, Nealy! We ain't down to no crossroad now!"

Reverend Pennycall appeared next to Old Man Harlan. "I wouldn't go so faw with that tone a voice, Miss Alma. That tone a voice might upset folks. Ya'll wouldn't want that now."

"Alway somebody get upset!" Miss Alma answered. "Ain't nothin' new on me." I tried to jerk away. Miss Alma held on. "How you know she in trouble?"

"I just do. I had a dream Miss Alma. Daddy told me I had to take care of her."

Miss Alma frowned. She looked off over the little rise toward Granny and Granpaw's. Then she let go of me and yelled down the cellar. "Fable! Vern! Willis! You boys, come on now! We gone find Ruby!"

"You ain't long for this world then!" Old Man Harlan said. Fable and Vern came running up the steps. Then came Willis. Miss Alma said, "We be back fo' long." She turned away then and walked off toward Moses' truck—us boys trailed after.

Old Man Harlan yelled from the cellar. "You cain't talk to me that way! Come back here!"

Miss Alma walked on. "See all dat?" she said, sweeping her hand over the ground. "Dat hail. I neva see no hailstone pile up dat way befo'." The hailstones were piled thick as snow. They crunched under our shoes. "I hope we find yo mammy soon. Out here in all dis."

We got out to the truck and Miss Alma opened the door. I crawled in behind the steering wheel and over to the passenger side. Willis crawled in with his walking stick, then Fable and Vern. Vern sat up in Fable's lap.

Miss Alma positioned herself behind the steering wheel

and started the truck. She backed out and went up the road toward Granny and Granpaw's, went into the pond of water at the bottom of the hill. The truck went a little ways in, slid sideways and stopped. "Lawd! Wata three feet deep if it a inch!" Miss Alma shouted. She stomped the gas pedal. Water shot out the back end. The whole truck tilted sideways. Our side went lower than Miss Alma's. "We *sho* stuck now."

"We can walk Miss Alma," I said. "It ain't that far."

Miss Alma looked out the windshield up in the sky. A spooky green light surrounded everything. "Dem cloud like to cut loose any minute. Bad 'nuff be ridin' in dis truck. Dey some board back da house. Ya'll wait here." Before we could say anything, she was out the door, holding up her housedress, sloshing her way through the water back to the house. We waited and waited but she never came back. I doubted she'd be able to get the truck out anyway. I turned the handle of the door and pushed but it wouldn't budge.

"Storm tear you up boy," Fable said. "It like one dem comic book monster. I know. I seen it befo'. Tear you up."

"That jus a lie," Vern said. "He don't know."

I pushed again against the door. It made a sucking sound and gave way. Muddy red water rushed in over the floorboard. It stretched away and out over Moses' yard.

"We all gone get a whippin' now," Fable said.

I splashed in up to my knees. The water was ice cold.

"What you gone do, boy?" Fable said.

"I'm going," I said. "It'll be too late."

"You nutty as a fruit cake," Vern said, his fuzzed up hair tinted with green light.

Willis said, "Twista blow you away, boy."

"Don't call me that, Willis. Come with me. Vern, you and Fable too."

They all three just stared at me; three black ducks hunkered there on the front seat. I turned and sloshed my way around the door toward the hill, got to where the road started up and ran to the top. There was a bad smell. A dog lay dead up there, covered with hailstones that were already melting. Dead birds were scattered everywhere, killed by the storm.

From the hilltop, I could see down to Harlan's Crossroads, how Bounty Road went down and up again to a bigger hill on the other side. I could see the graveyard and part of Old Man Haran's store. Across from it, Granny and Granpaw's house, Momma's car, the trailer and the chicken yard.

A twang began over the hills, like a row of piano keys played all at once, low and sustained, then in seconds rising up until it was blaring louder than a steel mill, making it almost impossible to move or think or do anything but listen. I could see black funnel clouds, coiling and uncoiling above Granny and Granpaw's barn, monster snakes, three of them, slithering downward out of the upside down floor of clouds, black and whirling, circling, passing each other like partners at a dance. One reached, curling toward the barn, making itself long and shrinking back. The barn stood like always, a black skull laughing at the day. The snake reached again, this time touching the barn, sucking the roof away—whirling the walls around and over the field, busting them to smithereens. The snake shrunk back and disappeared. The other snakes disappeared too. The thundering twang went with them.

"Ole Gooseberry!" Willis shouted. He was standing a little ways in back of me, walking stick tucked under his arm—potato foot, a glob of mud. "Blow dat barn, kingdom come!"

I was so glad it was him I almost laughed out loud. "God A Mighty, Willis, come on! Momma and Missy's down there." I turned and started running, slogging and splashing my way down the hill, down the middle of the road, to the house. Willis did a fast hobble with his stick, not far behind. If I could go around under the house to my secret place, I could get the knife and the skull. I could save Momma from Victor and the storm.

I stopped at the crossroads. The rain was starting up again. Mud had splashed up along my legs and onto my shorts. "Go there behind the well, Willis. Don't let anybody see you!"

"Wha-What you gone do?" Willis said.

"I don't know yet. Go behind the well. Wait for me."

I ran up Nub Road a ways and climbed the bank. Fat cold drops of rain smacked against my legs. I ran around to the back of the house to the porch, crawled under there next to the steps and over to the board that went over the hole where I kept the shoebox. I took out the knife, Grandpaw's pouch and the Rain Skull. I looped the leather cord of the pouch around my neck, gripped the knife and crawled out. Granny's washtub lay upside down on some boards by the steps. Raindrops thumping across the bottom. I looked up the path toward where the barn had been. The trailer had blown sideways—had mashed through the fence into the pig yard. Black planks and splinters of wood were scattered everywhere all over the chicken yard. I ran around to the front of the house. Momma's Ford sat near the fence with its trunk raised. Momma was there too, inside the car on the passenger side, eyes closed, her head thrown back against the seat. "Momma!" I yelled, running up to the car. Her hands were tied together with clothesline. Missy sat holding onto Momma's arm, eyes wide open, trembling like a bird.

"Momma! Wake up Momma!"

"No Victor, don't," Momma said, her eyes still closed.

"Momma? It's me Momma."

Momma's eyes fluttered open. She looked at me. "Oh no. No. Orbie, sweetheart," she whispered, her voice raspy as sandpaper. "Orbie, you got to get away from here. Victor. He's... What you said about him. Honey..." She closed her eyes then and went back to sleep.

The rain was coming almost straight down now. My tee shirt had soaked tight to my skin. I looked around the yard. There was the Jesus Tree, the picture of Jesus, hanging with his belly against the cross. There was the well with its round roof full of flowers tilted back in the rain. Willis peeked out from behind it. I hurried over. "Victor's got Momma tied up in the car, Willis." I looked up the road. "Where's Miss Alma?" Up on the porch I could see Victor's green file box had turned over, its papers scattered and stuck to the wet floor.

...spirit's robbed away! Ain't it? In 'at box!

All at once, the screen door opened and out stepped Victor with Momma's blue suitcase. He set it down on the porch and went back inside. In a minute the screen door opened again. I ducked back behind the well. "Stay down, Willis." Victor stepped out with my army tank and Missy's baby doll under his arm. He stopped and picked up Momma's suitcase. The whole front of his shirt was soaked dark pink with rain. His hair was soaked too. One black curl fell like a hook down the middle of his forehead.

He stepped down off the porch; talking out loud to himself now. Crazy talk like before. "It's the only thing. Yes. I know it is. No! Don't say that! Just get everything in the car. Then we'll see. Then we'll be on our way. Florida? Forget Florida. We can go anywhere Momma. Tucson. Yes! That's right Momma! No, goddamn it! Just do what I tell you to do!" He walked to the car, put the suitcase, Missy's doll and my tank in the trunk. He took up a jar and started back toward the house. He stopped next to the Jesus Tree and unscrewed the lid. Green black clouds circled overhead. He drank from the jar and looked up in the sky. In a big booming voice he yelled, "The falcon cannot hear the falconer! Things fall apart!" He tried to stand straight, staggered backward and yelled, "The centre cannot hold!"

I put my hand over Granpaw's pouch and squeezed. If Victor were a cloud I might could melt him away. I'd have to do it with love though, and nothing seemed more unlikely than that.

Granpaw's station wagon, with Granny driving, suddenly sloshed up into the yard behind the Ford and stopped. In the back seat sat Vern and Fable. In the front, on the passenger side, sat Granpaw. He stared out the window zombie-eyed. Granny got out and slammed her door, opened a black umbrella over her head. "What *is* all this? Victor? What you think you doing?" Victor didn't even turn around—went on to the porch and inside. The screen door slammed behind him.

Granny walked around to the side of the Ford and saw Momma. "What in this world!" She opened the car door. I could just see her, trying to untie Momma's hands.

Willis and me ran over to the station wagon, to the other side where Victor couldn't see. I tried to get Granpaw's attention, but he just sat there frozen.

"Where Miss Alma?" Willis asked Vern.

"In dat Reverend car," Vern said.

"Had 'nuff a her ole mouth," Fable said. "Dey gone electricute her now."

"No they ain't," Vern said.

Victor came back out of the house with another armful of our things—comic books, drawing papers, Missy's plastic make up kit. He walked past Granny around to the trunk and dumped it all in there. Willis and me went around the back of the station wagon where we could see.

Granny stepped away from the car. "I said what do you think you a doing here, *Mister?*"

Victor walked up to Granny, stood a couple feet away from her. Granny had to look up to meet his eyes. He made like to straighted out the pens in his shirt pocket. Then he just hauled off and backhanded Granny across the mouth, knocking her sideways to the ground. Her umbrella went upside down in the mud.

"This is *my* family!" Victor yelled.

Granny tried to get up, but Victor, with the muddy toe of his allegator shoe, kicked her hard in the stomach. She let out a cry and fell back in the mud. Victor kicked her again.

I was so scared I peed my pants. Lucky the rain had soaked them through. I looked back up the road. No sign of Miss Alma, only the graveyard and the hill. I held up the knife, trembling, remembering how it had once glowed.

Take care of your Momma son.

Willis pointed suddenly up to the house, shaking his finger at the place over the attic window. It had been painted. "Mo back!"

I don't know what but something came up inside me then, something good and strong. With the knife raised, I jumped out from behind the station wagon.

Victor turned my way, unconcerned now, in charge of things. "Well now, look at the little waif."

"Get away from Granny!" I shouted but my voice was almost gone.

"You've strayed so far away. Haven't you? Little waif. So far, far away." Victor's words made me feel all sad and undone. He was right. I was far, far away, down here in Kentucky inside a storm with a butcher knife dressed in shorts that smelled like pee.

Victor stepped toward me and stopped.

"Stand back!" I said. "Get away from Granny!"

"Shhh, hush now son. You think I don't love you, but you're wrong. I've got plans for you and Missy—for Momma too." He looked away into the stormy light. Rain dripped from his hair—from the hook-shaped curl. I could see Granny in back of him, struggling to get up. His chin began to tremble; then he was crying again—like so many times before—big crocodile tears streaming down his face.

He continued to look into the light, weeping, talking to no one in particular. "Of course, there was that letter. But they'll never pin that on me. Circumstantial. All of it. Still, I didn't mean for her to see it. Not until I could explain. That was too bad, wasn't it? Unfortunate. Well, no matter. None of it matters now anyway." He looked at me. "Does it son? We'll be so happy, won't we? All of us together?"

What letter? What didn't matter?

"You tied Momma up," I said. "You kicked Granny!"

A shadow passed over his face. "They were interfering, son. I can't have that. People interfering." In the rain, crying and talking crazy like he was, he seemed dangerous and pitiful at the same time—more even than I imagined myself to be. I hated him. I hated him for making me see him this way. For confusing me. I hated him for what he had done to Missy, to Momma—what he had done to himself—for what he was doing now.

I raised the knife; hoping that the blue light would come, make Victor go away, make things to be good and normal again—like when Daddy was alive. The knife stayed dull.

A low rumble of thunder crawled overhead. The rain came harder. Victor stood, arms down, hands open, a question in his eyes, waiting. His eyeglasses sat crooked across the bridge of his nose. In my mind's eye I saw the boy in the cave again, his eyeglasses, the frame held together with electrical tape.

Victor pushed his hand through his hair, frowning at the knife. "Come on. Don't be stupid now." I could see the worms in his eyes, sad worms, crazy.

Granny lay still in the mud.

I was holding onto the knife so tight I thought the bones in my wrist might break and I was sure I had peed myself again. I felt of Granpaw's pouch, the Rain Skull inside there tied around my neck, its power contrary and useless. Red puddles had formed in the yard, all of them trembling in the falling rain.

There was nothing I could do to bring Daddy back. Killing Victor wouldn't do it. Melting clouds wouldn't. The Rain Skull wouldn't. I wanted Victor out of my life—that was for sure—but killing him, even if I could manage such a thing, would be killing the little boy too, and that, I realized, I was unwilling to do.

Inhaling one deep rain-misted breath of air, I stepped forward and placed Granny's butcher knife on the muddy ground in front of Victor.

Stepping back I said, "In thy blood live, Victor."

Victor shook his head. He seemed confused. He looked again into the stormy light. The rain was coming down in thin slapping sheets. There was a rush of splattering wind and the gassy smells of animals killed by the storm. He bent over and picked up the knife. "Is this what they're teaching you down here? To point knives and utter mumbo jumbo at your elders?"

"You don't have to do this," I said. "God will forgive you."

Victor smirked. "What do you know about forgiveness? Shoot-em-up in the backseat with your army men. Blood and guts and bombs away! What do you know about God?"

Right then, I saw another light. Not blue but shiny red, flashing off Granny and Granpaw's windows.

"Answer me goddamn it!" Victor grabbed up a handful of my tee shirt along with Granpaw's pouch.

"That's my Rain Skull," I said.

Victor jerked it from around my neck and back fisted me across my face. I tasted blood; I saw lights—factory lights in the black ceiling of the steel mill—an old jalopy dropped from a claw, thundering into a metal bin; the bones of my skeleton falling like junk onto the wet rocky ground.

"I told you not to interfere!" Victor yelled. "Didn't I tell you not to interfere!" He tossed the pouch away.

I brought myself around onto both hands and got to my feet. My lip cut and bleeding. I stood, holding myself with both arms, trembling. "You can't do this. I won't let you do this."

Victor back fisted me again even harder. There were more lights, explosions of fire and more blood. Again the old jalopy dropped into the metal bin. A white piece of bone with a bloody root lay in the mud before my eyes.

"Stay down now!" Victor yelled. "I'll kill you!"

Look at it like you loved it more than anything. Like it was the only thing in the world. That cloud.

I wanted to do as he said, just to lie there, not to interfere anymore. Drift off. Go to sleep. "People punish people," I sobbed. "God don't." I got to my feet.

He grabbed me again but the bright threat in his eyes had vanished. He drew back to strike, but I could see his heart wasn't in it, that there was fear, that there was shame. Something had gotten through. I had gotten through. I shook my head, not at Victor but at Willis who was about to swing his walking stick. Victor caught it in mid air, shoved the stick with Willis at the other end backward to the ground.

Somebody laughed. "Little Jimmy Crow to the rescue!" It was Old Man Harlan. He was standing with Reverend Pennycall up from the police car. The police car was parked on the side of the road, its red bubble-light going around and around. Miss Alma sat in the back seat.

A hairy thick-knuckled fist with coils of muscle bulging around the wrist came out of nowhere—out of the sky as if. Like a rock it hit Victor up side the head. He let go of me and staggered sideways. Granpaw stepped around me and hit Victor again, this time square between the eyes. His eyeglasses cart wheeled off his face. He fell backwards in the mud, the bridge of his nose cracked and bleeding. Granpaw spat. "Been wanting to do that ever since you come back."

Reverend Pennycall pulled out his gun. "Hold on there now, Mista Wood."

"You hold on Reverend!" Granpaw shouted. "Last I recalled this is still my house! This man assaulted my wife and was about to kill this boy. He got my daughter tied up in that car over yonder. Don't tell me to hold on!"

Reverend Pennycall pointed the gun at Granpaw. Old Man Harlan stepped up next to him. "Only assault I seen is you, hittin' this man here. That right Reverend?"

"That's right," Reverend Pennycall said. "That's how I seen it." Victor tried to get up but slipped and fell back on his knees.

The knife was still in his hand. Blood mixed with tears ran from both his eyes. He began to crawl like a blind man, feeling around in the mud for his eyeglasses. When he found them, he sat back on his knees and put them on. They were bent cockeyed, one corner up, one corner down. I thought again of the little boy in the cave.

Granpaw stepped forward to hit Victor again, but I grabbed hold of his arm. "No Granpaw, don't. It's enough."

Victor sat back on his knees, crying, blubbering to himself now, barely holding onto the knife. "Don't hit me anymore, Daddy. I'll be good. I'll mind."

Granpaw spat.

Reverend Pennycall looked at Old Man Harlan and shook his head. He put the gun back in his holster.

A roar started up in the sky, like before, only this time like a hundred railroad trains, all at the same time, all running down from the whirling clouds.

I saw Bird, standing up next to the well with the Rain Skull held out over her head. The blue light had swallowed her hand, surrounded the skull and the whole length of her arm. She screeched inside the roar. "And when I passed by thee, and saw thee, wallowing in thy blood! I said unto thee! In thy blood live!"

Victor jumped up with the knife and ran at Granpaw. "Watch out, Granpaw!" I yelled, but the roar slammed my voice away. On the other side of the fence, inside the pig yard, a giant black funnel whirled in a coiling length, stretching and shrinking, fifty feet or more across, chewing up everything, tearing out big chunks of ground.

It was one a them racers I think. And it come at me so quick!

Fence posts, trees, the pig trough, what was left of the trailer, all flew up and around in a whirl. Victor raised the knife. The funnel jumped over the fence and whirled above the yard. Old Man Harlan and Reverend Pennycall ran for the police car.

I looked up through a gigantic green-glowing tunnel-hole—its walls solid, then vanishing, then solid again—like mist but deadly powerful—wind driven, whirling, spiraling up in the sky, threads of lightning zapping, rising, arcing upward across a heaving gap. I saw Victor and Granpaw struggling in a haze. Victor stabbed Granpaw through the heart with the knife.

I grabbed hold of a place in the middle of my chest, my fist wrapped in blue, shining like a blazing heart. "In thy blood!" I cried, trying to remind myself, trying to remind Victor.

Victor turned but the knife was gone. The blue light spread over my chest and down my arms. I was bigger than Victor now, taller, looking down on him, the worms in his eyes twisting to get away. He tried to run but one of his alligator shoes sucked off in the mud. Still, I didn't want to hurt him. I wanted to help. I wanted to tell him that everything would be all right—only he had to stop. But then it was like the whorl had grabbed him by the nap of the neck and he was pulled backwards toward the well, arms flailing—surprised now, afraid, not strong, not like Superman anymore, not like Clark Kent—and while the whole world seemed to rise with the wind, the well broke and the posts and the well's roof, all the flowers up there and the circle of rocks, everything around it, with Victor in the middle dove into the ground.

————

I'm in Granny's featherbed. It's nighttime, and it's raining outside. I can hear it on the tin roof, a light rain. By the bed a kerosene lamp burns. It makes yellow light on the beams overhead. I feel the soft blanket against my skin. It feels warm and good. There's a leftover smell of ham and pinto beans in the air. I try to snuggle down in the featherbed. I wonder how I got here, how long it has been.

The rain gets louder. A gust of wind presses against the tin, makes the beams tick. The lamp goes out. I'm looking up into the dark. Rain pours like a waterfall, millions of raindrops all at the same time, pounding against the tin roof. There's thunder and lightning. More wind.

I feel a chill. I pull the blanket over my head to keep warm. There's something wet and warm, spreading out from the middle of my back. It spreads all around me and then it turns cold. I've peed the bed. Granny will be mad. Granpaw will laugh.

But Granpaw's dead! Stabbed through the heart with a knife!

I start to cry. Tears stream down my face.

Sharp things are picking into my back. I can't move out of the wet. The blanket presses down on top of me, hard but soft too, like a wall with a carpet. A musty carpet. It's pitch black dark. I smell cigars and moonshine. I hear a voice. I can't tell whose. It's muffled and far away.

"Orbie! Ah Orbie!" it says.

I beat against the carpet. "I'm here! Here I am!" I try to yell, but my voice falls flat against the carpeted wall thing. I hear huge splashes of water, somebody, a giant outside Granny's house, crashing through huge puddles of mud. The carpeted wall thing shifts. Light comes in. I think it's the

317

sun. I think it's morning and the sun has come up and it's shining in the attic window, but still it rains.

Then the carpeted wall thing and all the covers, the pitch black dark, the beams and the tin roof, the whole house is lifted off and away. Cold rain splatters my eyes, my face. I choke. I spit. Somebody stands over me. A man. I can't see who it is. He's giant sized, old and wild-eyed with wet crazy gray hair, his chin covered with blood. I wipe the rain out of my eyes and see the gray pant legs of Granpaw's coveralls. Granpaw holds up the darkness with both hands.

And with both hands he pushes it away.

———

Granpaw pulled me to my feet. I saw a destroyed yard, trailer parts scattered everywhere, broken glass, sheets and towels, the dinner plates Momma had left in the trailer, the roof over the front porch of the house sagging almost to the ground at one end. A dead pig, its belly split open, lay bloody across the hood of Momma's Ford.

"Ruby and Missy's in the house, safe and sound with Granny," Granpaw said. "Willis and them friends of yours is in there too. It's a wonder any of us is alive." A section of the trailer lay in front of me, the carpeted floor and part of the wall—the shelves still attached.

"I had to lift that off you," Granpaw said.

"I thought I was in bed."

"You was in bed all right!" Granpaw laughed. "Laying down there in all that mud. Look at you!"

Mud was all down the back of my legs, my arms.

The wind was gone now. The rain had let up. Across the road I could see Reverend Pennycall's police car had been turned upside down. Three of its wheels were missing.

"Miss Alma's all right," Granpaw said. "Nealy broke a leg. I ain't seen the Reverend nowhere. Bird neither." Behind us stood the Jesus Tree. Granny's butcher knife was stuck in Jesus' back.

318

"I thought you was dead Granpaw!"

"I seen you thought I was," Granpaw said. "I'm an old tom cat Orbie. I got nine lives."

Where the well had been, there was nothing but rocks and splinters of wood. Tin cans of flowers were scattered everywhere.

"I didn't want him to die." I said.

"I know you didn't." Granpaw patted me on the back. "That's the good part."

"Did Jesus save you Granpaw?"

"He did that a long time ago son."

"I mean, he saved you today didn't he?"

Granpaw turned around with me then and we both looked at the knife. "You could say that. But that ain't what you seen, was it?"

"No Granpaw. I saw Victor stab you in the heart. I didn't see Jesus. What happened?"

"Well, you seen me get stabbed, so I reckon I was stabbed. But now you see the knife up there in Jesus. So that must be so too. I reckon you could say Granpaw's dead and not dead at the same time."

What Granpaw said didn't make any sense. I thought what really happened was I got mixed up, that Victor somehow must have stabbed Jesus instead of Granpaw. But why would he do that? How could that have happened? Behind the hill where the barn used to be, there was a half-arc of rainbow and a fan of sunlight beaming down. Granpaw looked at me and in a voice that sounded like Moses said, "Not always what you think. Now, isn't it boy?"

PART NINE

30
Home

We were on the other side of Toledo on our way to Flat Rock. After that we'd be in Detroit. For a while I watched the telephone poles go by; then I went back on the floorboard, playing with my army men and wondering about school. It was already the middle part of March and getting on toward spring. We'd stayed in Kentucky until Granny and Granpaw were back on their feet. The storm had flattened pretty much everything except for the house.

I got to go to Kingdom school with Willis and the colored boys. The schoolhouse there was just one big room with tables and chairs and a pot-bellied stove, so cold in the wintertime you had to wear your coat during lessons. Momma wouldn't let Missy go to school there. Said when we got back to Detroit, she'd explain everything to the teachers, get somebody special to help us with our schoolwork. We'd be moving back to Kentucky anyway, she said, when the house got sold.

We'd left Granny and Granpaw's this morning before the sun came up. We'd gone only a little ways down the road before Momma had to slam on the brakes. There, in the light of our headlights—in the middle of the road—stood Moses, puffing on a cigarette.

Momma hollered at the windshield. "Moses! I swear to God!"

He had an old coat pulled around his shoulders and was taking his time, looking up at the stars, like being there wasn't anything unusual. Finally he stepped on the cigarette and came around to the passenger side window.

"Roll the window down for Moses, Orbie," Momma said.

I rolled it down and Moses looked in. In that wheezing, up and down voice of his, he said to me, "CLOUD boy! MIND you."

"We thought you was dead!" Momma hollered. "We thought they'd hung you!"

Moses' face was just black shadow, dim lit eyes between two long curtains of hair under a black hat. It was the first I'd seen of him since the cave. He reached his hand in the window and dropped a bundle in my lap. It was bone chilly cold outside and his breath came in frosty-white puffs. "mind you, BOY!"

"They been looking all over for you," Momma said.

I was so tongue-tied I couldn't even open my mouth. I wanted to tell Moses what all had happened. About Victor and Granpaw. About Bird disappearing. How the storm had broke every bone in Reverend Pennycall's body. But then, like smoke, Moses slipped away and into the shadows at the side of the road. In my lap lay Granpaw's old tobacco pouch, the Rain Skull tucked inside.

I was feeling of it around my neck as I sat on the hump in the middle of the floorboard. I had my army men lined up on the seat in front of me. Good guys against the bad.

"That's stupid," Missy said. She was leaning over the front seat with her baby doll. Her cast was gone. I pretended to blast away at the bad guys. "It's stupid to do that way," Missy said.

"I know it is. Hush now." I was too happy to be mad at her though, happy she was talking again.

"If you know it's stupid, why you doin' it then?" Missy said. I kept on blasting at the bad guys. "I don't have to tell you every little thing."

324

"Yes you do," Missy said, but when I looked up to answer, she'd already slid down the front. Since the storm blew Victor away, she hadn't screamed or whined around one single time.

All the pictures Willis and me drew were piled up under the window in the back. I reached up and pulled them down, spread them out on the seat in front of me on top my army men. It was easy to tell which ones were Willis's and which ones were mine. Mine were all messy with smudged airplanes and fire and sailing ships sinking down. Willis's were good and clean. Real pictures, his were. Of me on the porch with my drawing pad. Of Granny shaving Granpaw. Of Victor, pouring fire on Daddy. Momma and Missy in the rocking chair at the end of Granny and Granpaw's porch.

She was going to have a baby, Momma was. You could see her belly sticking out. I wondered if the baby would look like her or if it would look like Victor. I wondered about Victor—about Armstrong and his men and The Pink Flamingo. A week after the storm Cecil had come with a package for Momma. It was postmarked from Detroit but it didn't have any return address. In it was a Kellogg's Cornflakes box with a Detroit newspaper folded up inside.

In the paper was a story that Momma didn't want me to know about; but then she went ahead and read it to me anyway. A story there about Reverend Bill Jackson, 'Black Jack' Jackson, and how they thought he was the one got drunk and poured hot steel on Daddy. How they found out it wasn't him after all because investigators received new information from secret people nobody would talk about. How the fingerprints and things they found pointed to Victor Denalsky because, for one thing, the night janitor lied about what he had seen. And also Victor was in with the Mob. And the Mob was afraid Daddy would do something they didn't like, but they couldn't say what that was. Something had to do about the Union, but it was confusing.

"Double crossed by Armstrong and that bunch," Momma said. She sat next to me on the back porch steps, looking all teary-eyed and out of place. Between her fingers a cigarette trembled. "He done it, Orbie. Victor. You was right all along." She stood up sadly and went inside the house. I thought I'd be happy, being right, but I wasn't. It was like Victor had stabbed Daddy in the back and now the Mob had stabbed Victor, even after he was already dead. Me being right about things didn't seem to matter very much. I heard Momma in the kitchen, boohooing, talking to Granny and Granpaw. "I just cain't hardly believe what all's come to pass. I feel so ashamed."

"They ain't nothin' you done anybody else wouldn't have. Not with what you had to face," Granpaw said.

"That drawing Willis made drove him crazy, Granpaw. He almost choked me to death. Said Orbie and little Missy would be minus a mother if I didn't toe the line." Momma boohooed a while, then said, "I should have seen what was coming. My own little boy had more sense than I did."

"Your own little boy had help." Granny looked through the screen door to where I was sitting out on the back porch. "Ain't that right Orbie?"

I tried to make myself small.

Granny smacked her lips. "You can't keep nothing secret from old Big Ears out there."

"I didn't want to believe it," Momma said. "I didn't believe it—till I came across those papers."

"From that box," Granpaw said.

"I come across that letter from Armstrong said the investigation had turned against Victor, I knowed they was something bad wrong," Momma said. "I should have got away from there then. I should have run."

"You looked so pitiful tied up like you was," Granny said.

"He violated me, Mamaw. In front of Missy."

"Shhh," Granny said. "Orbie's still out there."

Momma let out a big sob. "I could have spared my kids! I could have spared you and Granpaw!"

"Shhh," Granny said. "Don't be so hard on yourself."

Momma blew her nose. "At least Nealy had a change of heart."

"Hell he did," Granpaw said. "I threatened to tell Judge Beechum about his moonshine. That changed him."

"I'm so ashamed I don't know what to do," Momma said.

"Blind love," Granpaw said. "It's the Devil's Confusion."

Momma boohooed even more then, making deep gulping sounds and blowing her nose.

"Powerful blind," Granpaw said.

———

When we got to Flat Rock, it was getting dark and had begun to snow. There was the 'ding ding' sound the hose makes when you run over it at a gas station. Momma stopped the car and somebody knocked at the back window. I looked up at a man with orange hair and freckles, wearing a hat like mine with a winged horse. I rolled down the window.

"Never thought I'd see you again," he said, smiling a big happy smile. The snow fell straight down in the lights of the gas station behind him. "Let's see... Your name is...?"

"Orbie!" I almost shouted. "And you're J C!"

"That's right. Good memory, son. I see you're still wearing the hat."

Momma looked back from the front seat. "Who you got there, Orbie?"

"That man, Momma! It's J C!"

J C looked in through the back window. "Evening Ma'am."

"Ruby," I said. "Her name is Ruby. She's my Momma." Missy stood up on the front seat.

"And who's this pretty little girl?" J C smiled.

Missy put her fingers in her mouth and backed away.

"It's all right hon," Momma said. "Say hidy."

"Her name is Missy," I said.

"How do you do Miss Missy?" J C said.

Missy kept her fingers in her mouth and said nothing.

"How can I help you Ma'am?" J C said.

"Fill it up with reg'lar," Momma said. "And check the oil please."

"Right away Ma'am," J C said.

"He's nice, ain't he Momma?" I said after he had gone to do the work. I showed her the inside of my hat again, the letters J C stitched in blue. "He was good to me. He was gonna show me how to pump gas, but Victor wouldn't let him." A shadow passed over Momma's face. J C finished with the gas and came around to the window on Momma's side.

"Oil was fine Ma'am," he said. "Three dollars for the gas."

"You take checks?" Momma said.

J C nodded. "You can make it out to Sunshine Mobil."

Momma wrote the check and handed it to J C along with her driver's license.

J C smiled. All his freckles smiled too. "Says here you're from Detroit Ma'am. Going up there pretty soon myself. I understand there's work up there."

"There is," I said. "My Daddy worked in the factory." Momma gave me a look, but smiled anyway. "He worked in the steel mill at the Ford Rouge."

"Is that right?"

"I don't mean to be nosy," Momma said. "But how come you looking for work up there? Don't this place belong to you?"

"No Ma'am," J C said. "I'm just a manager. Work on cars occasionally. I've been looking for something with a little more pay."

"We're moving to Kentucky," I said.

"Is that right?"

"Uh huh. To Harlan's Crossroads! I'm ten going on eleven now."

"He don't need to hear about all that Orbie," Momma said.

"That's all right Ma'am." J C handed Momma back her driver's license.

"He gets excited," Momma said.

"No I don't," I said.

I thought J C would walk off then, but he didn't. He took off his hat, ran his hand through his hair and put it back on. "I was wondering Ma'am. I was wondering if you might know of anybody up there that I might talk to? About a job, I mean. Or maybe your husband would be the one to ask."

"My husband's dead," Momma said.

J C rested his hand on the door above Momma, waiting for the answer to a question nobody had asked. Leaning a little forward he said, "I'm sorry to hear that Ma'am. Really, I am."

Momma drew back a little. "Ain't no call to be," she said, her voice going all deadpan. "We all have to go sometime."

"Yes, I suppose that's so," J C said. "It's just. Well. It must be difficult for you I mean. I see you're in a family-way."

"I am," Momma said. "But that's no concern of yours."

"No Ma'am. I didn't mean to say it was."

There were no other cars at the gas station and almost no traffic on the road. The kindness in J C's voice matched the kindness in his eyes. It seemed to be settling softly over everything like the snow was. I listened to the snow ticking against the front window, wondering why Momma was being so mean.

"I better get back to work," J C said. "I'm sorry for your trouble, Ma'am." A big truck wheezed by the gas station, slow grinding its gears up the road. J C made a move to walk away.

"Hold on a minute," Momma said. She got out a piece of paper from her purse, wrote something on it and gave it to J C. "I cain't promise you nothing but here's the name and number of one of Jessie's friends. He works at the mill."

"I appreciate this Ma'am."

"Tell him I sent you," Momma said. "Ruby Denalsky. The name is on the check."

"Thank you Ma'am." J C looked in through the window at Missy, then at me. "You kids take care of your Momma now. Nice seeing you again, son."

Momma started the car and pulled away. J C smiled and tipped his hat at her, but I could see in the rear-view mirror that Momma wasn't smiling back. When we got out of Flat Rock, the snow came thick in the headlights. Momma's face was in the mirror, inside the orange glow of her cigarette, her eyes frozen to the road, lips unpainted and stretched. I had the thought she might be like that a long time.

I looked out the front window, listening to the back and forth noise of the windshield wipers. The snowflakes zoomed into the headlights, making swift white lines right for the car. They glowed like the blue light had glowed, only white. I thought of the power Granpaw said was inside me. *Power to dissolve clouds. Contrary Power.* I couldn't wait to get back to Kentucky. I felt again of the pouch around my neck. Up front the snow lay white across the road. Past that it was all dark.

THE END

ABOUT THE AUTHOR

North-South Structures
Composite Personae

My parents moved from Kentucky to Detroit soon after I was born. Detroit was where I grew up. As a kid I visited relatives in Kentucky, once for a six-week period, which included a stay with my grandparents. In the novel's acknowledgements I did assert the usual disclaimers regarding the book's fictional complexion, i.e., it is a made-up story whose characters and situations are fictional in nature (and used fictionally) no matter how reminiscent of characters and situations in real life. That's a matter for legal departments, however, and has little to do with subterranean processes giving kaleidoscopic-like rise to hints and semblances from memory's storehouse, some of which I selected and disguised for fiction. That is to say, yes, certain aspects of my history did manifest knowingly at times, at times spontaneously and distantly, as ghostly north-south structures, as composite personae, as moles and stains and tears and glistening rain and dark bottles of beer, rooms of cigarette smoke, hay lofts and pigs.

I read the usual assigned stuff growing up, short stories by Poe, *The Secret Life of Walter Mitty*, *The Scarlet Letter*, *The Cherry Orchard*, *Hedda Gabler*, a little of Hemingway, etc. I also read a lot of Super Hero comic books (also Archie and Dennis the Menace) and Mad Magazine was a favorite too. I was also in love with my beautiful third grade teacher and to impress her pretended to read *Gulliver's Travels* for which I received many delicious and longed-for hugs.

It wasn't until much later that I read *Huckleberry Finn*. I did read *To Kill A Mockingbird* too. I read *Bastard Out of Carolina* and *The Secret Life of Bees*. I saw the stage play of *Hamlet* and read *The Story of Edgar Sawtelle* too. However, thematic similarities to these works occurred to me only after I was already well into the writing of the novel. Cormac McCarthy, Pete Dexter, Carson McCullers, Raymond Carver, Flannery O'Conner and Joyce Carol Oates, to name but a few, are among my literary heroes and heroines. Tone and style of these writers have influenced me in ways I'd be hard pressed to name, though I think the discerning reader might feel such influences as I make one word follow another and attempt to "stab the heart with...force" (a la Isaac Babel) by placing my periods (hopefully, sometimes desperately) ' . . . just at the right place'.

Freddie Owens (aka Fredrick Owen Wegela)
www.freddieowens.com